Richard Wilson is 66, married with two grown up sons and lives in Huddersfield. He and his wife, Karen, have worked abroad for the last eighteen years or so, but now he is retired. He is still working on a full length fantasy novel.

SHORT STORIES
for LONG JOURNEYS

Richard Wilson

SHORT STORIES
for LONG JOURNEYS

Vanguard Press

A CIP catalogue record for this title is
available from the British Library.

ISBN 978 184386 359 5

*Vanguard Press is an imprint of
Pegasus Elliot MacKenzie Publishers Ltd.*
www.pegasuspublishers.com

First Published in 2007

**Vanguard Press
Sheraton House Castle Park
Cambridge England**

Printed & Bound in Great Britain

Dedication

This book is dedicated with love to my family
and friends both near and far.

Contents

A matter of time

'Right class three, no time to waste, pay attention. You're here to work, you are not on holiday!'

Mr. James had to raise his voice because the class was making too much noise. Not much noise, but too much noise for Mr. James, he liked silence in his class.

'I won't tell you again!' He fiddled with the edge of his almost red beard. 'The next one to utter a sound will do the cross-country run TWICE!' He glared at the class over his glasses like he always did.

'That is not a threat that is a promise.' Mr. James let the ensuing silence wrap round him like a heavy winter coat.

'Thank you. Now tonight's homework. Be quiet.' His eyes swept round the class. Not a sound was made. He pushed his reading glasses into position.

'Tonight's homework is from page thirty-nine to forty-nine inclusive. The reign of Henry the eighth. I want a three page essay, a thousand words minimum on.' He paused a moment and looked up at the ceiling. 'Em, yes. A day in my life with Henry the eighth, for the girls. And for the boys, I want a day in my life with any one of his wives. Yes I think three full pages will do!'

He heard one of the class say, 'boring' and then another one say, 'I'm with you'. His finger pointed at the two pupils sitting at adjacent desks in the far left hand corner of the classroom.

'You two.' He gestured with his hand for the two to come to his desk. There was a scraping of chairs and futile 'but sirs' from them both as the two made their way to the front of the class.

'Don't waste your breath, you'll need it.' He turned to the others. 'The rest of you get out what you need and get down to the sports hall.'

'Do we need our history book now Sir?' Graham asked. Mr. James sighed, took his glasses off and slowly shook his head.

'How old are you lad, sixteen in August? And you want to know if you need your history book. Of course you don't, Forbes, you need your geography book, you ninny.'

'But Sir.'

'Of course you need your history book, book two, the one you have in your hand. You're not coming back here are you? Come on, get a move on!'

Mr. James waved both hands towards the door as if he was shooing hens. Patience wasn't one of his strong points. He was in his late forties and attitudes to teaching and discipline had fallen dramatically over the last decade, and in his opinion for the worst. His ideas on discipline hadn't changed one iota. Not even a part of one iota. The rest of the class piled out.

'Now you two, let's see if you are as good at running as you are at groaning. Go on, get down there. I'll see you at the finish.'

He was sitting next to Mr. France the games teacher on a bench by the fountain in Farrow Park as Morgan D and Parson S, who were well behind the rest of the class ran past the tennis courts. Mr. James waved them on. The pair hadn't expected him to be waiting half way round the course. Dawn, with a face the same colour as a just under ripe tomato acknowledged him with the grimmest of smiles. Simon, a similar colour and breathing hard pretended he hadn't seen him. Mr. James watched them as they set off up the hill for the first time.

As soon as they were on the back road to Bolsworth and out of sight they stopped for a breather.

'It's well off-side this rubbish, Dawn!' gasped Simon in between breaths. He was sitting bent forwards on a low wall rubbing the backs of his legs. Dawn was sitting on the grass bank at the side of the road trying to sort her hair out and trying to get a piece of gravel out of her trainer at the same time.

'I bet it's four or five K's. He's a real no, no. We hardly made a sound!'

'He's not that bad, at least he knows what he's on about. Most of the other teachers don't, or they aren't bothered. Come on, we might as well get on with it.'

Dawn got up and her hair fell down. 'Looking well!' she griped. She had another go at tying it up. It was a waste of time. She'd forgotten all about the cross-country run and she'd forgotten to bring her bobbles. It fell in straggles halfway down her back.

'Leave it; it looks pretty cool like that. You look like that woman on the telly who's being chased through the African jungle by a tiger.'

'I doubt it; there aren't any tigers in Africa. It's a lioness and it doesn't have any stripes!'

'Whatever.' said Simon who couldn't have cared less. 'It's going to be bad news for tonight. My legs are killing me!'

'Why what's happening tonight?'

'It's disco night round at Cooper's place. Don't say you've forgotten! You said you were coming!' Simon's face fell. He thought they were an item.

'Don't spit your dummy out, I was kidding.'

'Very funny, I don't think.'

'Come on.' Dawn trotted off down the road. Simon watched her hair swinging in time with her bum for a second then he dragged himself off the wall and followed her. He caught up with her as she passed the gateway to the old windmill. They jogged side by side at a slow walking pace.

'How's your mum?' asked Dawn who was still trying to do something with her hair. The wind had just wafted it across her face and into her mouth. 'Looking well!' she spat, pulling the strands out of her mouth.

'She's ok. She came home yesterday night.'

'What's she like?'

'Same. Looks tired though.'

'Dork, I was asking about your baby sister.'

'I know you were! She's brilliant. She looks like a squashed toad. Every baby I've ever seen does! They were all round ours last night saying she's lovely and she's got your eyes. She's got Dad's nose. Dad's still got his nose and I couldn't see her eyes, they were all screwed up.'

Dawn shook her head. 'Grandma Doreen says she's beautiful. She must have been looking at a picture of me when I was a baby!'

Simon flung his arms out and did a daft pose. 'You wish!'

She laughed, squinted her eyes, flopped her tongue out like a dork and put a spurt on. He went after her.

Then he heard a car coming. 'Get to the side, a car's coming! Get up the banking.' It sounded to Simon like it was coming fast and it was a narrow road. Dawn scrabbled up the banking. Simon did the same. A car came roaring round the bend. It was an old open-top sports car and it wasn't half moving. The driver, a young man wearing a straw hat, was having a hard time keeping the thing on the road.

'Throttle's jammed on!' he shouted as he shot past. 'Sorry! Very sorry!' he cried out at the top of his voice.

'You crack-head!' screamed Dawn as she was showered in bits of gravel.

'Moron!' yelled Simon as a piece hit him in the face. Then the car disappeared round the bend but as it did so an envelope flew out of the car and went over the wall into the field.

'Did you see that Dawn?'

'What, the car? Course I saw it. Look at me, I'm covered in grit. Looking well, it's all in my hair.' She tried to shake it out.

'No not the car, something flew out of it and went over the wall down there.'

'You're bleeding. You've cut your forehead!'

'Where?' Simon put his hand to his head.

'There.' Dawn took his finger and touched it to the small cut. 'It's only a scratch, Simon. It's a good job it didn't get you in your eye! Spit on your finger and wipe it off.' Simon used his tee-shirt.

'Wow, when did you have your belly-button pierced? It looks sexy!'

'Wednesday,' answered Simon doing his best to look cool. He nearly managed it.

She laughed. She liked him a lot. 'Come on, or we'll be in more trouble. And no, I didn't see something fly out of the car. I'd shut my eyes.'

'I'm going to see what flew over the wall before I go anywhere.'

He ran off down the road. She chased after him shouting we can come back later. Simon was leaning over the wall where he thought the thing went over.

'Can't see it.' Dawn leaned over the wall next to him and spent half a second looking in the long grass.

'I can't see anything.'

'I can, it's over there.' He pointed to it. 'I'll get it. No point both of us risking the nettles!' He jumped over the wall and treading carefully through the big patch of nettles he went to get the envelope.

He got it. 'Ow,' one's got me.'

'Watch what you're doing or some more will.'

'Ouch, another's got me!'

'That's only a thistle. Come on hurry up, you're out of them now.'

'Mr. James is going to throw a wobbler if we don't get a move on. When we've finished we've to go round again remember.'

Simon wasn't listening. He was reading what it said on the envelope. When he'd read it he ran to the wall and climbed back over. 'Here, read what it says.' He gave the big white envelope to Dawn.

'It's not sticky then?'

'It is a bit. Don't bother about that, read it. It says:

To whom it may concern. If by some chance you find this envelope please return it as fast as you can, if not faster, to the address on the other side. You will be handsomely rewarded for your trouble. Yours truly. Mr. Nigel Oswald Body.

I've never heard of a place called Tickentock Grange, have you?'

'No, wish I had. Bit of a bummer, I could have done with some spare cash. We could ask about the place later if you want. Dad might have heard of it. He was born round here. Wait, I've just realized something. I didn't see the car go up the hill. Did you?'

'No, but I had my eyes shut, remember.'

'I didn't, have mine shut and I didn't see it so it must have turned off somewhere between here and Sedgehill Heights.'

Simon's eyes lit up. 'Come on girl, I know a shortcut to the park. We'll look on both sides of the road for a turn off. If there is one we'll take the shortcut back here and try to find Tickentock Grange.'

Simon stuck the envelope under his tee-shirt and tucked it back into his tracky-bottoms then set off down the road like a rocket. 'Come on Dawn, let's kick ass. It's only a K this way! You look on that side; I'll look on this side.'

There wasn't a turn off before the bottom of the hill. Reluctantly, Simon turned off towards the cricket field. Dawn followed him through a gap in the hedge and through the allotments. She followed him over a wall at the back of the church and into the park via the far side of the old cemetery. This time Mr. James was at the finish. So was the rest of the class and they weren't impressed. They'd had to wait at the top of Park Hill for Dawn and Simon. The pair got to the top and they got some grief from their classmates.

'Only twice more up this hill Parson, Morgan. Hurry along.'

'There's such a thing as Child Line, now Sir!' Simon managed to gasp as he set off down the hill.

'Well you certainly act like one at times Parson. Remind me to give you the telephone number in the morning!' His classmates thought that was hilarious.

'Right the rest of you, get back, get showered and get off home. Hard day tomorrow, double algebra if my memory serves me well.' It wasn't algebra double or single it was Saturday. But he had to wait a fair time before one of the brighter ones realized it and passed it round. Mr. James went home. He knew they would follow his instructions. Not to the letter, he didn't expect that, in fact he hoped they were bright enough to work out a dodge or two. It was what the rest of the class thought that mattered to Mr. James.

Dawn found an entrance this time round. It was hardly big enough for a car to get through but Simon insisted they should see where it went.

'It could lead to anywhere, come on.' He pushed his way through the tangle of undergrowth that partially blocked their way.

'It could lead to nowhere just as easy,' said Dawn as she pulled a couple of dead twigs out of her trainers.

The entrance led to a wide path that ran perfectly straight, through the wood. On both sides of the path and at equal distances apart were Rhododendron bushes. All were in full bloom and they went red, purple, white. Red purple white. Red purple white, till in the distance the colours melted into one.

'Wow Simon, they look terrific.'

Simon nodded. 'Yes, they don't look bad. They've been planted!'

'Never!'

'They have, it's obvious,' Dawn laughed.

Simon realized what he'd said without thinking. 'Ok, ok. You knew what I meant, girl. It's a good job you're smaller than I am or I'd throw you over one of 'em. That one there if you don't leave off.'

Dawn smiled and followed Simon's finger. The bush was enormous. The one on the other side of the path was its twin. And as they hurried along they saw that this pattern continued all the way along the path.

'Every seventh bush is a giant compared to the others,' said Dawn. Simon nodded and pointed at the end of the path.

'Yes I counted them as well and guess what, look, there's the car on the other side of that gate. I've no idea how it could have got there, but that's the car. And it didn't come on here. There's no tyre marks. Look.'

Dawn looked down at the path and behind her she could see their footprints in the soft, mossy soil. But no tyre marks.

'It's no big thing.' She shivered. 'What's it matter? 'It must have gone up Sedgehill Heights. There must be another road down the other side.'

'It's freezing cold in here.' Simon shivered. 'Let's deliver the envelope and get our reward. Don't forget the disco starts at seven. Come on let's get back into the sunshine!' Simon was positive the car hadn't gone up the hill!

They had to climb over the gate. Not only was it locked with a big old rusty padlock, the hinges were rusted solid.

'It came through here then? I don't think,' said Simon, looking at the state of the hinges and lock on the gate. 'Look at the state of these.' Then he walked over to the car, which was facing away from the gate. There was no number plate at the back or on the front and the whole car was in ratty condition.

'This thing's a shed; there must be two of these,' said Simon looking round the car. The one I saw looked terrific. That's why there aren't any tyre marks here either! Hey, I hope it's the right place. What time is it? We won't have time to look for somewhere else.'

'I don't know, my watch has stopped,' answered Dawn shaking her wrist. 'I only got a new battery for it last Tuesday. Rubbish thing!'

They both saw the house at the same time. It looked like something from a horror film. There were spires and towers, crenulations and flying buttresses.

'It's a dump!' said Simon.

After leaving the car, they'd followed another path halfway round a small lake till they'd come to a break in the trees. They'd both looked to their left. More than a hundred metres away and right at the end of a badly neglected ornamental garden stood the house.

'Come on Dawn let's hope they've loads more money than they've got gardeners!' He grabbed her hand and squeezed it. She went all soppy. They ran up to the house.

'They're coming mother.'

'Are they like you said they were? Will they like to stroke my fur?'

'They are exactly like I said they were and stop those silly rhymes. You don't have fur.'

'Are they healthy; are they strong, have they brought some friends along?'

'They are exactly as I said. But if you don't stop with those stupid rhymes I'll send them away and stuff you in a dark cupboard and lock the door! So stop it!'

'Ha, ha, ha and tee he he, my little boy is cruel to me.'

'MOTHER! For goodness sake. Are you trying to drive me sane?' His mad laugh started at his toes and spread up his body like flames drawn up a chimney. They only stopped when he heard a knock at the door and a tug at the bell pull.

'Behave Mother!'

'Shut up, I'm getting into the right mood.'

'So am I so for Beelzebub's sake put your fanged teeth in.'

The strange looking man went to answer the door. The mother opened a little silver box on her lap, took out a big spider and ate it. Then she told the box she'd have an earwig for pudding. The box began to wriggle then it stopped – there was a scurrying sound then a popping sound. The sounds were really small sounds but the ugly old woman could hear them perfectly well. The earwig was a lot sweeter than the spider. She told the box she wanted seconds. The box ignored her. She threw it against the far wall. It staggered back on its little bent legs and did her seconds.

Simon knocked on the door. Dawn pulled the bell pull. The bell rang.

'Welcome and well go to Tickentock Grange,' smiled the odd-looking man in the dirty old coat and the ragged trousers. Stuck on his head, but to one side, was a dirty yellow wig. It looked ridiculous.

'Come in, do come in. Come in and close the door. It looks like rain. It definitely looks like rain!'

Dawn looked up at the sky not looking directly at the sun; it would have burned her eyes out.

'As Uncle Max always said, "Well, be quick. It's starting. Do be quick, quick, quick, quick!"' urged the odd looking man. And he was right. No sooner had Simon and Dawn stepped inside, than the sun cleared off, the skies went black and the heavens opened. Great splashes of rain bounced off the front steps. The man slammed the door. It was freezing cold inside the house and both teenagers shivered. He told them to rub their hands together and follow him. Simon had already decided he'd wasted his time coming here. He wanted to get on with it and get off home. This place was creepy. Dawn wasn't that keen either. She wasn't scared. Well not much. She was more stunned by the strange dusty furniture and the paintings of weird looking people. She wanted to look round the house, but when she heard the creaking and moaning sounds from somewhere below the floor she decided she didn't. She thought it might be better to wait outside. But she decided she wouldn't.

They both followed the man into a long room with a high ceiling. There was dirt and clutter everywhere and the room smelled like rotten cheese. There was an ugly old woman eating what looked like sweets from a silver box. She was watching the rain race down the windows.

'Mother, the children are here.' Simon wasn't a child, neither was Dawn but they were so stunned by what they saw in the corner, they couldn't speak a word.

'That's Father – he's dead.' The man giggled.

Dawn was beginning to get scared now. Simon could see it in her eyes. He hoped she couldn't see what was in his eyes.

'Don't worry about Father. He can't get free. Have you got the envelope for me?'

Simon, whose face had paled, could only nod.

'Put it on the table please! The odd man's eyes went as big as tennis balls and a green worm wriggled out of his nose. Simon, who thought he would puke up any second turned to Dawn for some sort of support. Dawn looked at Simon but never took her eyes off the worm in case it came near her. She edged closer to Simon. When a yellow one wriggled out of his other nostril, fell to the floor and burst open, yellow stuff splattered all over her trainers. She screamed and ran for the door. Simon didn't scream as his mouth was too dry but he was right behind her. The odd-looking man went to poke the fire. The old woman sang a song about 'Incey, Wincey Spider, climbing up your snout, when down came a bogey, and knocked the spider out.'

The door wouldn't budge. Simon tugged at the handle but it was rock solid. He kicked at the door as hard as he could. He wanted out of here. They could stuff the reward. The pain that shot up his leg did make him yell out.

'Don't be frightened children come over here.' The odd man wagged his finger. It was an incredibly long finger. 'Put the envelope on the table and dooooo come and sit down,' continued the odd-looking man who looked to have aged twenty years in as many seconds. 'You don't have to sit with Father. You can sit by me if you like. Would you like a jellied baby Miss? There are lots of them in the cellar. Perhaps I have one or two in my pocket.' He fished about in his coat pocket and brought out a dead rat then another.

'Oh Dear, that's a rat, and oh Dear so is that.'

'Give me one. I'm starving to death,' hissed the ugly old woman.

The odd-looking man threw her both rats at once. She snatched them from the air with her long bony fingers and crammed them right in her mouth. Dawn's hand shot to her mouth to stifle a scream.

'I might take you down the cellar young Miss for a jellied baby if the young master doesn't soon put the envelope on the table and be pretty ugly quickly about it.'

Dawn, terrified, edged over to Simon and said out of the corner of her mouth, 'For God's sake, put the envelope on the table. I know I've gone mad. I know I have.'

'No you haven't, it's some sort of trick. I bet it's You've Been Framed, or another one like it,' he hoped.

'No it isn't a show don't you know. Yes do; yes do; before my nose turns blue. Do put the envelope on the table or round your neck I'll chew,' hissed the ugly old woman with the dreadful teeth and with the rats' tails hanging out of her mouth.

'MOTHER! Shut up. Father, tell her to shut up. The weird man ran over to the skeleton tied in the chair. Tell her to stop making rhymes, Father. She's beginning to make me cross. You know I don't know what I'm doing when I get cross. I might wring her neck. I MIGHT!' he screamed.

'He can't hear you, you loony! He hasn't any ears.' The old hag's laughter was hellish.

Dawn pressed her hands to her ears. It was when the weird-looking man shook his Father and the skeleton fell to bits that Dawn fainted. It could have been the dust and the sound of brittle bones snapping and cracking that did it. Or was it because the skull wouldn't stop rolling round and round the chair? Simon couldn't ask her. He'd grabbed her as she'd fallen backwards and he'd gone down with her. He'd whacked his head on the door handle and the impact had knocked him out.

'You bad, bad boy,' cackled the old hag. 'Look what you've done to Daddy-phoo, and we haven't any super glue,' she began to laugh.

'Don't bother Sel, they can't hear you, their brains have temporarily shut down. We'll have to try some other method.'

'It was your idea, Val, to scare them rigid.'

'You agreed it seemed a good idea at the time Sel, and talking of time, how many minutes have we got left?'

'Twenty-one-and-a-quarter!'

'We'll have to re-adjust the time warp sequential and try another way. We haven't much time. We've only one time-change token left but we'll have to use it. No seeing the pyramids now.'

'You should have snatched it off him as soon as you got the chance.'

'I didn't get a chance; he has it under his top. And even if I had got a chance I couldn't risk touching him. He could be covered in all sorts of bacteria. No thanks, it's not worth the risk.'

'You could take swabs from them now. They've both got their mouths open.'

'That's just as risky. No, we'll have to try a different way!'

'Before you do Val, make sure you've got the exact time you opened the door and exactly how long they've been here.'

'I set the sequencer as the bell rang Sel. We can re-set it from then.' The odd-looking man took out an even odder-looking pocket watch from his waistcoat pocket. It was decagon shaped. Each of the ten faces showed the time. They were all different. Val read one of the faces and the one directly underneath it. He then made a few mental calculations. 'Six and nineteen seconds and five jiffies.' He pressed a tiny red button. There was a click and a whir. 'That's near enough, Sel!'

'It had better be dead on Val, or we'll be in serious trouble. Father said we hadn't to do this again!'

Val gave Sel a very strange sign of agreement. Then after saying don't I know it, he counted, 'Three two one!' There was a tiny bleeping noise. He slotted a tiny white disk into a slot in the watch and pressed a tiny blue button. Suddenly, there was a high-pitched buzz from the watch. Then at the speed of light a lot of strange and impossible things happened.

Simon knocked on the door and Dawn pulled the bell pull. The bell rang. The door was opened by a young man who was wearing blue jeans and a red sweat-shirt. Behind him stood a young woman wearing a smart red dress and holding a Pekinese puppy in her arms.

'Hello,' said the handsome young man.

'Hello,' said the beautiful young woman. 'Say hello to the nice youngsters Pipit.' The puppy yapped and snuffled.

'What can we do for you?'

'We found an envelope that flew out of your car. It's a great car.'

The young man smiled. 'It's parked round the corner there in front of the garage. We came up the drive from Bolsworth Road. The gates were open but it did say Meadow Grange on the gate so we brought it here. The address is on the back. Is this the right place?'

'It is young man, and there is a reward mentioned somewhere I think.'

'That's written there as well,' answered Dawn.

Simon took out the envelope and offered it to the smart young man. 'It's a bit sticky.'

'Is it?' the young man replied. He didn't take the envelope. Instead he said, 'Come in and pop the envelope on the hall table. We'll go and prepare your reward.' Dawn and Simon stepped into the hall. They were both puzzled by his actions.

'I thought it was important.'

'So did I,' replied Dawn.

Dawn glanced through the inner door. The place was magnificent. It must have been a barn at sometime but it had been beautifully converted. Everything was perfect. 'Wow, this place is brilliant!'

Simon popped his head round the inner door. 'Pretty neat.' Simon wasn't into superlatives much. Dawn got a lip on. Simon put the envelope down on the hall table and turned to look out at the immaculate gardens. The sun shone on an array of flowers the likes of which Simon had never seen before.

'Must have a load of gardeners here. Look at that lot round that little building over there.'

'It's a Pergola, Simon', said Dawn coming to stand beside him.

'It's not half bad, whatever it is.'

'Ah, there you are. I see you're admiring my garden.'

'It's some garden!' replied Simon. The young woman smiled and the puppy yapped. The young woman didn't put it down. She looked at her watch. They'd only five minutes left before time warp meld.

'Are you bringing the reward, David?' she called sweetly and patted the puppy's head. She was getting stressed, but she mustn't let the visitors see. 'David! Hurry up, please. These youngsters haven't got all day!' Again she looked at her watch. Simon turned and looked at the table. The envelope had gone.

Val was mixing chemicals. He was frantic. He'd put enough test-adhesive on the envelope and he'd got enough of the youngsters D.N.A. from it. That's all they needed to be on their way. He'd been extremely careful when he took it. He'd used the remote transference system to get their D.N.A. He felt sure he'd got enough. But if the children's D.N.A couldn't be reproduced in the next three minutes and blended with their own, he wouldn't be able to give them their reward. And he and Sel would be stuck here in a time warp until Jupiter knows when.

'Coming Celia, I won't be a jiffy. Last one,' he muttered. He took a tiny glass capsule and snapped off the pointed end where the white line was. He put five drops into a small test tube and shook it hard. Now he had to wait. Would it work? He bit his lip but he didn't feel a thing. Would it work? Come on, come on. It emulsified.

'Perfect!' he cried out loud. 'Bring them through Celia, it's ready.'

'Come on you two; let's see what you think to of your reward.' Sel looked at her watch. Two minutes left. Two minutes to go and they'll have their reward. She hurried Dawn and Simon into the kitchen.

'There, drink that as fast as you can then you can count out your reward.' Val offered them what looked like orange juice. The kitchen table was stacked with bundles of fivers. They took the glasses. Neither of the teenagers gave the request a second thought.

Simon's went down his throat without touching the sides. Dawn was slightly more ladylike with hers but it too was gone in a split second. They both dashed to the table to count their reward. Sel looked at her watch.

'Twenty seconds David.'

'How many piles of hundreds are there on the table?' asked David.

Why not count them and see?' said Celia sweetly.

'We will count with you,' they said in unison. 'One-two-three-four-five-six-seven-eight-nine-ten.'

Dawn and Simon were ready for bouncing round the room with delight. There was a fortune on the table, but when they reached ten, there was a huge hiss. Then a sort of wobble hit them and the whole kitchen melted.

Then somebody said in a klicky-squeaky voice,

'The money wasn't your reward.' Dawn thought it was one of the silver things who said it. The one standing by the window.

'Your reward is much better than money. But you can have the money as well if you want. We don't use money ourselves. Dawn wondered where the garden had gone and why she couldn't scream. Simon knew it was the one by the window who was speaking. He was watching his lips moving but he couldn't see his nose.

'This is your reward!' The silver man pointed to a four dimensional screen positioned centrally in a control panel. The panel was a mass of dials and a thousand other buttons, displays and levers. They were where the kitchen walls should have been. But now they were crammed into the car but it wasn't like a car at all. The silver man plucked one of the spinning planets from the screen and spun it on his finger. It reminded Dawn of what a performing seal does with a beach ball.

'Yes you are both going on holiday with us to Pluto. That's your reward for helping us so magnificently. Without your help we would have been stuck on Earth till who knows when and father would have gone mad with us. We thank you!' The silver man and woman bowed their heads. Neither Dawn nor Simon could thank the silver people because they couldn't move a muscle. Dawn wondered if Mr. James would go mad with them. Simon wondered how many extra times they'd have to do the cross-country run when they got back!

'No he won't,' clicked the silver woman, answering Dawn's thought.

'None Simon,' clicked the silver man. 'I'm' sure I did the sequence exactly as our teacher said we must do it! We'll be off to Pluto and back in no time at all.' The silver youngsters laughed ever so sweetly. 'No time at all.'

Simon knocked on the door and Dawn pulled the bell pull. The bell rang.........!

Richard Lee Wilson. 2005.

A shop with
something for everybody

'Good morning Sir, how may I help you?' The shopkeeper smiled. He spoke very softly and the syllables seemed to float in the air.

'I'm looking for a good, reliable second-hand hunting rifle with an infallible anti-jam system,' boomed the big man with the red face. 'I would prefer the "Makepiece" if you have one?'

'Indeed I do Sir. Deadly accurate up to a distance of one-thousand yards. It's a true warrior who hunts big game at such close proximity.'

The big man who had never hunted before frowned and wondered if the funny-looking rash on the shopkeeper's face was contagious; he also felt that the shopkeeper was being facetious.

'They would be in that room there.' The old man turned his back on the customer.

'That room?'

'Yes Sir, that room! But be careful, it's very dark in there.' The old man turned, scratched his chin and pointed to a dark doorway at the back of the shop.

'That's a rather bizarre legend over the door isn't it? "Dare you carve your name in the dragon's heart?"'

The customer having read it out once, read it again.

'I don't think so; they've always been there Sir. The shop would hardly be the same without them! For some reason there's one over every door.' The man's almost skeletal hand wafted to each of the many doors in turn.

'It's a lot bigger in here than it looks from the outside,' said the customer with a puzzled look.

'Is it? Do you wish to go through then?' The old man snapped impatiently. 'I do have other customers waiting.'

The old man in the brown smock sat down behind the cluttered counter. There appeared, at least to the big man with the moustache, to be nobody else in the shop.

'Of course, of course.' The big man puffed and pulled at the corner of his moustache. He looked somewhat embarrassed but he hurried across the shop and through the doorway. He wasn't in there very long.

'I was given this by a foreign-looking midget. Scared the life out of me. I could hardly see him. He said it was the best one in there! Thought for a minute the damned walls were talking.'

'He knows best Sir. Ex-big game hunter himself. But that was before he lost his sight. He was mauled by a leopard.'

'Oh I'm sorry to hear that and between you me and the gatepost, I'm in a bit of a funk. A lot of a funk if the truth be known and for the same reason. Terrified of my rifle jamming. Terrified of wild animals. Said I'd go. Don't know why. Can't back out now. Must have had one too many. Happened to a friend of mine; lost his right arm and half his face. Gun jammed. Tried to fight the creature off. He hadn't a hope in Hades! But in his case it was a lion. He looks terrible. Doesn't leave the house now.'

'Is that so? Now Sir. That will be fifty pounds for the month.'

'I don't want to rent the damned thing, I want to buy it!' the man guffawed loudly.

'Purchase it Sir? Quite out of the question. I only hire my goods. There is a top class gun shop further down the street but a hunting rifle like that with its patented anti-jamming feature will cost well over three-thousand guineas. I think it would be far better to rent that one Sir. You may find after your first safari that you no longer wish to be a big game hunter.'

'Nonsense! Why on earth would I wish that?' The old man didn't reply but the merest of smiles touched his thin bloodless lips. The big man in the houndstooth waistcoat looked longingly at the rifle for a moment.

'Well if that's the best you can do, I'll take it.'

'Thank you Sir. You will return it on the tenth of July before three o'clock. There's your receipt. Good day Sir.'

'Just a minute, I'll need some damned ammunition won't I,' blustered the big man.

'I don't sell ammunition Sir,' said the old man quietly and again his voice seemed to waft round the shop. 'Damned or otherwise. I wouldn't want to be party to slaughter.'

'Did you say slaughter?'

'No. You misheard,' snapped the old man putting his hands in his smock pockets. 'I said I would be preparing a party for my daughter. The gun shop down the road should have all you need! Good day Sir,' and the red-faced man, muttering loudly, left the shop.

'Good morning Madam. How may I help you?'

'I would like a silver cutlery service if you have such a thing.'

'I do indeed Madam. You want that room over there. I think you will find exactly what you're looking for in there. Is it for a close family dinner party?'

'What?' snapped the woman. 'What it's for need not concern you,' pouted the well-dressed middle-aged woman with the heavily made-up face and very tired eyes.

'I didn't enquire solely to satisfy my curiosity Madam,' snapped the shopkeeper in reply. 'I only asked to enable me to confirm that the room I indicated is the correct room for your needs!'

The woman sniffed, tried to smile but failed miserably, then with a sigh and following the shopkeeper's pointing finger, she entered through the darkened doorway to the left of the gun room. She read the same sign in red-on-white hanging starkly above the door and shivered. She didn't tarry long in the darkened room.

'You should tell your assistant not to lurk about in the shadows. He startled me!'

'Did he give you his complete aid in your selection?'

'He gave me no other option. It's much too dark in there to see anything! He thrust this into my hands and said that's the one Dear! Dear indeed. It will have to do!'

'It is a rather impressive set Madam, that you must admit! It will impress the most fastidious guest. I might go so far as to say it would impress even the most dragon-like of mother-in-laws'

'It will do I said. And what do you know about my mother-in-law,' sniffed the woman.

'Nothing Madam but I too had a mother-in-law of whom I was terrified. So if it will suffice, I can hope for nothing more. That will be thirty pounds for the week, Madam!'

'For the week? I don't want it for a week. I want to buy it!'

'Purchase it Madam? I'm very sorry but to acquire a solid silver hand-crafted cutlery set such as that would cost well over a thousand guineas. It's a Gibson set. You do see the coat of arms and the gold relief work, don't you? Cutlers to Her Majesty. Doesn't it glow and Madam, it does bear your initials!

'How do you…'

'I think a week at thirty pounds is a very fair offer,' interrupted the old man ill-manneredly. 'If you disagree Madam or think you may need something permanently?' He peered again at the woman. 'There is a rather grand cutlery shop not two-hundred yards further along the street. I do know they stock Gibson cutlery!' He continued peering at her patiently over his spectacles. She felt unnerved.

'I'll take it.'

'Thank you very much Madam. Return it by three o'clock a week today. There is your receipt. Good day Madam.'

The woman gave a couple of furtive glances up and down the street before leaving, and then hurried out of the shop. From the gloom of the shop the old man in his comfortable big fat slippers watched her go.

'Good morning Sir. How may I help you?'

'Have you any good quality second hand potholing gear Chum?'

The old man curled his toes in his comfy slippers at being addressed as chum but he offered a tiny smile just the same.

'I have some of the finest ropes, the strongest fixings and the brightest lamps available young man. They would be in that room over there.' The old man's eyes gleamed as he directed the young man with the bushy beard and the nervous twitch to a darkened doorway. 'The third door on the right young man. Everything you could wish for is in there.'

'It looks darker than a pothole from here!' laughed the young man nervously.

'It is indeed,' said the old man quietly. 'Are you frightened of the dark or at the thought of potholing young man?'

'No I'm not frightened I'm terrified. I'm claustrophobic. I always have been but Sharon wants me to go and I fancy Sharon and want to marry her so I'm going.'

'I see, and how brave of you. I know the terrors of claustrophobia-being claustrophobic myself. Brings out the sweat on the brow just thinking of all those tight, narrow passages one has to squeeze through. Now hurry along, I close for lunch quite soon.' The grim-faced young man read the strange legend above the door. He took a deep breath and went through the dark narrow doorway. The old man with the crinkled shirt collar opened the top right hand drawer of his desk under the counter.

The young man came hurrying out within seconds carrying a big green canvas bag.

'I don't know if your assistant in there is a garden gnome but he gave me this lot!'

'Ah, I see he's given you the Dreadnought. That's the only model that has the flush-fit lamp switch. It can not be turned off by accident and leave you stumbling about in the dark.'

'You ought to give him a miner's lamp – it's pitch black in there.'

'A lamp would be of no use to my son. He was crushed and lost his sight in a rock fall while caving in Yorkshire! That is why he is of short stature. He won't step into a lift now.' Tears filled the old man's eyes.' Sweat stood out on the young man's forehead. He moistened his lips and swallowed.

'That will be thirty pounds for the ten days.'

'I don't want to rent the gear and I'm sorry for what I said about your son.'

'Thank you but I sell nothing in this shop young man. I only hire my goods. You may decide after you get down there in the endless darkness and with the walls seeming to close in on all sides, that you don't ever want to go potholing again. Silly to throw such equipment in the corner of the garage.'

'I'll be going again if Sharon goes.'

'Maybe so young man but if you leave this shop and turn left, not fifty yards along the road you will find a well-known shop that sells everything for outdoor pursuits. But to purchase equipment of that quality! Even the most slender of the ropes has a breaking strain of two tons. And the clips are tool steel. What more could you want?' He wagged his finger. 'I fear you will get no change from five-hundred guineas. The choice is yours my adventurous young man.' The young man wasn't sure what a guinea was.

The old man took off his spectacles and polished them vigorously. He replaced them on the end of his nose and proceeded to open a small tin box he'd taken from his desk. He glanced at his pocket watch and stood up. 'Lunch time. Have you reached a decision or would you like to go away and think about it?' Scratching his cheek and with silent footsteps the old man walked slowly towards the shop door.

'No I'll take them now. Thanks Chum.' He handed the old man the money from a moist palm.

Without returning to the counter the old man said, 'You must return the equipment before three o'clock ten days from today! There is your receipt. Good day young man.' He followed his customer to the shop door and locked it behind him. He returned slowly and with difficulty to the counter and his lunchbox and his first piping-hot meal of the day.

'Quite a lucrative morning children.'

'Yes Father,' sang a chorus of crisp clear voices from somewhere within the many darkened rooms.

Business in the afternoon was even better. The old man hired out a twin-skinned unsinkable and self-inflating dingy. Designed for the roughest

31

of whitewatering. A hang glider with a wing span of thirty five feet, with ten hours of high octane fuel in the tank and a self opening parachute. An all inclusive weekend in a five star hotel in Baghdad. A scuba diver's outfit in sea blue and with the Van Strom triple circulatory safety valve. And the last customer of the day hired a magician's kit. Including the infamous 'catch the bullet in the teeth' trick. Every customer remarked about the strange legend hanging above the doors. The old man acted as though nothing had been said and then, with the slightly-stained tie, closed early. He was very tired and his feet hurt.

'We must see what tomorrow brings children. Goodnight.'

A tuneful chorus of goodnights echoed round the shop.

Robert Hales had never been on safari in his life. But he was determined to make them eat their bloody words. The Makepiece felt extremely comfortable in his hands. He'd bag a lion if he'd to run after it and batter it to death with his rifle butt. Bloody arrogant swine, the lot of 'em. Laughing at his gear like that. He couldn't think why he'd ever got involved. It had taken most of his savings to keep up with them. Carol wasn't happy about it. In fact she was damned unhappy. He cursed the day he'd met them. Now he was paying a small fortune to keep up with them here, in this hell hole. What with the sun beating down, the insects going at him as if he was a walking meal ticket and food cooked over a damned open fire; food that tasted like that muck he used to get from the kebab shop after the local disco when he was half wrecked. The nights were no better. The din was unbelievable. What with the screeches, the howls, the never-ending buzzing, whirring insects and the heart-stopping snarls and roars. He wished from the bottom of his heart that he'd stayed at home with Carol. At least one gets a bloody night's sleep at home.

'Are you all right Bob old chap? You look pretty hot and bothered if you don't mind me saying so.' He did mind the chinless-wonder saying so. He minded a great deal.

'I'm fine Malcolm. Not quite acclimatised yet but I'm getting there. It certainly mirrors its name. It is as hot as a dragon's den.' He smiled as best he could. Why did they have to talk as if their mouths were full of hot potato?

'Try to keep up then old chap, the trackers have called us forward! We're at the tail-end of the dragon now and a pride has been spotted around here.'

'No problem old boy.' I'm younger then he is, the ponce. Hell fire, he snarled to himself almost speaking his thoughts.

It was a magnificent creature. It stood proud and majestic, head held high and very still. Only its tail moved. It swished left to right like a supple, gold pendulum. It was almost hypnotic and it was only twenty-five yards away. Unfortunately, neither the trackers nor the party saw the three females or their cubs crouched low and near invisible in the undergrowth. Robert had the male in his sights. His finger was on the trigger. The trackers looked at him. They pointed at the lion and jabbered to each other. The lion roared.

'Shoot please, shoot,' begged the head tracker whose eyes were as big as dinner plates. Suddenly, one of the cubs came prancing down the track. Robert had never seen anything as cute in his life. He froze momentarily as he watched it skip about trying to catch its tail. It rolled about in the dust like a kitten. He couldn't pull the trigger. The male roared again and pawed the ground. Its teeth were enormous.

'I'll be damned if I'll shoot such a beautiful creature,' bellowed Robert at the sky. Then as though moving in pantomimed slow motion and with their spears pointing like lances in the direction of the lion, the three trackers backed away. Malcolm and Ambrose raised their rifles.

Robert knocked them out of the way and bellowing, 'Yagh yagh, yagh, yagh,' he slammed the Makepeace into the trunk of the nearest tree. He ran fast but awkwardly towards the big male waving the battered rifle over his head and shouting even louder. Suddenly, there was a hellish commotion from the undergrowth behind him and on his left. Dust spurted, undergrowth parted and a dreadful snarling filled the air. The females leaped into view. They tore through the clearing past Robert, who by this time had thrown caution to the wind and was staring in awe and without fear at the magnificent animal. The females tore the ground with their massive claws as they ran towards the male. Robert now stopped in his tracks. The squealing cubs tumbled and tripped, trying to keep up with the females. The big male roared, turned away and disappeared from view. The pride followed him in a cloud of swirling red dust. The trackers had dropped their weapons and screaming and scrabbling in terror they'd disregarded the lethal thorns tearing at their bodies and clambered as high as possible into the surrounding trees.

Lord Masket was furious. 'You mad man! You absolute madman!' He stormed down the track as though he would attack Robert. You could have had us killed! These are wild animals! You're not visiting the local zoo! Damn you! We could have been torn to pieces man!'

'And no great loss in my opinion! I can't think why I ever got involved with men like you!' raved Robert. 'And you're bloody damned right!' Robert looked as if he was going to explode. Spittle flew everywhere. 'I am mad. Raving mad even to think of slaughtering beautiful animals like that!' He dragged his forearm across his face to wipe the sweat from his eyes. 'I should have bit the bullet long ago. But I've bitten it now. I'm finished with the lot of you. If you were real men instead of cowards you would hunt the animals and fight them on their own terms! Goodbye and good riddance!' He left the both of them there spluttering incoherently. 'You up there! Get my gear and be damned quick about it!'

Robert hurled the Makepiece into the undergrowth and stormed off. The rest of the party stared open mouthed at each other in stunned silence. The head tracker was down the tree in seconds and away into the bush for the rifle. One of the other trackers grabbed Robert's gear and ran after him to one of the Land Rovers. In three hours he was back at the hotel and settling his bill. He caught the first available flight back, as he told himself – to England and sanity. He'd have to pay for the rifle but he'd get the cash from somewhere. How much had the old man said? Was it three-thousand guineas or two? Damn everything to hell.

He couldn't raise the money, so he tried every one of his so called good friends. He dreaded facing the shopkeeper. As he walked along the road and turned into the shop, he thought to himself that perhaps he could pay over a period of time. The old man was sitting behind the counter with a smile on his face. He greeted Robert warmly.

'Your time's not up until a week yesterday. I don't do refunds. What makes you return the Makepiece early?'

Robert didn't know where or how to start. 'Look I don't know how to say this but I haven't got the damned thing. Everything turned sour. I couldn't bring myself to use it. Beautiful animals like that. It's nothing but slaughter. I've never been hunting before. The things haven't a chance. I'm extremely sorry but I'm afraid I lost my temper and smashed the rifle against a tree. Then I threw it away. Never want to see another. Look, I'd lost my temper. Should never have gone in the first place.' Robert swallowed hard and he looked deathly uncomfortable. 'The truth of it is I can't pay you immediately for the Makepiece. I'm terribly sorry but I can't. Would you allow me to pay for it over a period of time – say three years?'

Throughout the one-sided conversation the smile had never left the old man's face.

'Forget about the rifle, there are plenty more where that came from. Do you have the receipt?' The old man held out his thin-skinned hand.

'But, but,' stammered Robert, 'what do you mean forget about it? How, but…'

'Please my good Sir, think nothing of it and relax. The rifle wouldn't have worked anyway. In your hurry to leave the shop you left the safety release lever on the counter. I'm very relieved to see that you are still in one piece. Now Sir, do you have the receipt?' Robert's head was spinning but he managed after fumbling through his pockets to find the receipt and hand it over.

The frail hand of the old man picked up a big rubber stamp and slammed it hard down on the receipt.

'There you are Sir.' He pushed the receipt across the counter. 'Account settled.' The old man beamed happily. 'And please accept this as a thank you for your custom and your safe return.'

'What is it?'

'Why not read it when you get home I do have customers waiting Sir.'

'Well good enough and many thanks. Don't know what else to say,' blustered Robert. 'By the way, I'm not terrified of wild animals anymore. Ran at the beautiful thing to scare it away! I think if any of the others had shot it I'm sure I would have shot them.'

Whether the old man heard him was debateable. He showed no sign that he had but he was smiling as he slowly made his way over to one of the darkened doors. It was only in the taxi that Robert realised he'd fired the rifle at least half-a-dozen times to zero the sights of the damned thing.

'Was you talking to me mate?'

'No, no, just thinking out loud.'

Robert opened the little parcel. In it was a small plaque which read "You carved your name on the Dragon's heart". 'What on earth's all that about?' he mumbled. He'd ask Carol over their evening meal. By gad he thought, it's good to be home.

'Were you talking to me mate?'

'No and keep your eyes on the road if you wouldn't mind.' The taxi driver's eyebrows nearly disappeared under his cap; he thought, who does the pompous bugger think he is?

The dinner table was laid and everything was immaculate. The cutlery gleamed bright as Venus on a perfectly clear night. The flames of the elegant, mauve candles reflected in the knife blades like so many golden "Will O' the Wisps". The long stalked roses had chosen exactly the right time to display the fullness and glory of their blood-red petals. Their scent hung in the air like a soothing balm. Gloria, feeling near screaming pitch picked up an Edwardian lead crystal wine glass. She held it lovingly by its delicate stem with the thumb and forefinger of her right hand she pinched the lip.

It was still ringing when Bertrand called, 'Should we come through darling?'

She dimmed the lights a little more and called back, 'Yes, everything's ready.' The caterers had done a super job. God this is going to be a disaster.

She straightened her back. 'Come through!' she called as calmly as possible.

She fiddled with one of the hand woven linen napkins and tried hard to stop biting at her bottom lip. She stepped back from the table as Bertrand led in his mother and father. She smiled at them and gestured to them to sit down. His father was a big-hearted love. Gloria adored him but she couldn't let it show. He waited to be shown his seat. His mother was a heartless fiend and Gloria hated everything about her but she couldn't let that show either as she watched her take Bertrand's favourite chair at the head of the table. Gloria took a deep breath and took the chair facing her father-in-law. Bertrand took the chair facing his mother. She smiled at him and he smiled back. Gloria wanted to stick a full slice of toast into her mother-in-law's sneering mask and swore she'd go insane if the witch started nit-picking tonight of all nights. She'd dreaded this moment with every fibre in her body and had wanted to go away for the weekend, just the two of them to celebrate their silver wedding in blissful happiness. Instead she sat there like a tightly coiled spring.

The caterer brought more pâté, and more toast.

'I think we've all had enough of that. I found it a bit sickly and we want to leave room for the rest.'

'I would like some more. What about you two?

'I'm fine,' replied Bertrand a little too quickly.

'No more for me thanks,' smiled her father-in-law.

'There's just me then,' smiled Gloria. If the stuff had been oozing from her ears she would have had more and she didn't rush her food! The Gorgon sniffed disdainfully and remarked about the food shortages around the world. Bertrand suggested half a slice of toast and an extra morsel of pâté wouldn't help much.

'But, if you multiply it by a trillion Bertrand, it certainly would.' She wasn't looking at Bertrand when she said it, she was looking at Gloria. Keep it up thought Gloria, do keep it up you witch.

They were half way through the second course when the Medusa, having already said the lamb was too fatty and the mint frightfully bitter and the sauce lumpy, smirked and said, 'Was it too much trouble to get a matching set of cutlery, Gloria?' She made the name Gloria sound like 'slut'.

'Mine is E P N S; the pattern's different and the fork is bent!' Gloria froze. The forkful of food hovered between plate and mouth as if someone offstage had shouted CUT!

Then something strange happened to Gloria's whole demeanour. It was as if a current of high voltage electricity had passed through her body. The dread of her mother-in-law was suddenly a thing of the past and Gloria couldn't understand why she'd put up with it for so long or why she could ever have been terrified of the pitiful wretch sitting there like a lice-ridden old crow waiting for scraps.

'Well you'd better have mine,' screeched Gloria and threw her fork at her. It bounced off the table then her plate like a deranged ground to air missile and landed in her lap. The food from the fork and a decent amount from the Gorgon's plate splattered all over her pale-cream dress and the lower half of her face. Then Gloria followed up with the knife, the spoon, the serviette ring and the remains of her meal. Leaping to her feet and with her arms waving as if being attacked by a swarm of bees, the Gorgon tried unsuccessfully to ward them off. Gloria picked up her wine glass to throw that as well but realised just in time that it was an heirloom. She put it to her lips slowly and deliberately and took a small controlled sip. She then stood, pointed at the witch and said with perfect control, 'Get you're coat and get out of my home. You are not welcome here and you never have been! For twenty-five years you have made my life hell. Nothing I have ever done has been good enough for you and that includes me. Not everyone born on a housing estate is a mindless no-good. So kindly leave this house.'

Her mother-in-law leaned like a drunkard against the dining room wall. She was ashen-faced and shaking with anger – and her arms were held out as if the splattered food on her clothing was sulphuric acid. Her father-in-law was trying desperately not to burst out laughing. Bertrand stared at his wife with stunned, open-mouthed admiration. He was in a delightful dreamy shock but he desperately wanted to believe what had just happened. He'd only had two glasses of wine and they were only three-quarters full.

'Surely I can't be drunk,' was all he could say. And he kept on saying it till Gloria asked him to be quiet.

'You are not drunk Bertrand, you are perfectly sober. Now would you please get your mother a taxi, say goodnight to her and show her to the door! She is going and your father, who I think is a gentleman and an angel, is staying. He's going to finish his meal and I wish to explain my behaviour to him. Bring another main course through would you. I spilled mine!' called Gloria to the caterers.

Henry could hold it back no longer. He roared with laughter. He'd always thought the world of Gloria. Mira stormed out of the room then Bertrand followed her out after giving Gloria the thumbs up. Gloria sat down.

'May I call you dad?' she asked with a cheeky grin as she picked up her glass. He nodded. Gloria said, 'Cheers Dad!' The explanation went on as long as the party.

The following morning she walked into the old man's shop.

'I would like return these,' she said without preamble. 'It's not a matching set but it doesn't matter one bit. It took the fire out of the dragon perfectly,' she smiled. He noticed she wasn't wearing makeup.

'I don't do refunds of any sort!' intoned the old man in his gentle, wafting voice but there was a gleam in his eyes.

'I don't want a refund I want to return them.'

'I'd better make sure they are in order. You said it is not a matching set. It was when it left here Madam.'

'I also said it didn't matter!'

'It could well matter to the next customer who requires them!' he replied crossly.

He inspected the contents. 'You are correct. They don't match! You might as well take them with you.' There was a fountain of giggles from deep within the darkened rooms. Gloria turned in surprise.

'Did you hear that?' He ignored her.

'There's no point leaving them here.' He closed the lid and pushed them dismissively across the counter.

'I'd rather not waste money on luxuries.'

'Take them there is no charge. I can't hire an unmatched set and I have dozens more in the back. Take that with you as a thank you for making me aware of the mismatch.'

'What is it?'

'Open it when you get home. I'm closing for lunch.'

'It's only eleven o'clock,' laughed a very relaxed Gloria.

'I close early on Mondays.'

'It's Wednesday!'

'And Wednesdays!' the old man said crossly. He stood up and shuffled towards the door. Gloria picked up the little parcel and the cutlery and beat the old man to the door. 'Thank you for everything,' she called back. But the old man was nowhere to be seen.

'Look what that funny old man has given me Bertrand.' She passed him the cutlery set. 'He said it was no good to him because it isn't a matched set.' Bertrand opened the box and looked at the source of their happiness.

'Which one doesn't match? They're all exactly the same! Look!'

'That's really weird,' said Gloria. 'I don't understand! They didn't match last night!'

'What's this? It says. "You carved your name on the dragon's heart."'

'I've no idea. The funny old man gave it to me as a thank you.'

Bertrand said, 'Hem,' and put it in a drawer. 'I think we should be thanking him. Mother rang this morning. She was not herself. I wasn't sure it was mother! She actually apologised for her terrible attitude towards you and asked me to ask you to please forgive her.'

'I'll think about it!' said Gloria and squeezed Bertrand's hand.

Sharon and Paul changed into their gear whilst Tom and Geraldine got changed round the other side of a small hillock. The cave entrance was about forty feet away at the head of a rock-strewn cutting no more than two feet wide. To Paul it looked no bigger than a rabbit hole. He put on a brave face and smiling said, 'I hope this suit is waterproof. I don't fancy crawling on my belly in there. The water's freezing.'

'Come on you softie. I'll go in first. Everybody check your lamps.' They all worked perfectly.

'Carry your rope like that Paul,' said Sharon slinging the rope across Paul's head and over his shoulder. That way you can get them off it if things get a bit hairy.'

'Woman, man, woman, man,' suggested Geraldine.

'Yep fine by me.' 'Whatever,' said Tom.

'Who's leading?' asked Geraldine setting her lamp at the centre of her helmet.'

'I will,' offered Sharon.

'But you're the slimmest,' Geraldine replied. She sure is thought Paul having just seen her naked for the first time.

'Well why don't you lead, Tom, you're the biggest.'

'Man, woman, man, woman then.' Tom walked into the trickle of a stream. Geraldine followed. Paul followed Geraldine. Sharon brought up the rear. The rocks were covered in moss and they had to watch their step.

'Bad underfoot,' warned Tom. Paul walked like a ballet dancer in leather slippers. Sharon laughed.

Paul turned round and said, 'It's slippy here. I don't want to finish up on my arse.' He laughed with her. 'And there'd better be some diamonds in there or I'm not coming again.'

They all joined in. 'Do you know what this cave's called? It's called "The Twisted Orme".' Nobody said they knew. 'And did you know Orme is Viking for worm?'

'Is it?' they all said in turn.

'And did you know worm is the Viking word for dragon?'

'That's all very boring Tom, but I'm sure we'll all remember.' Geraldine pretended to yawn. Paul's palms were beginning to sweat. He was dreading this.

Tom dropped to the ground and wriggled through the hole. The small pond of water at the cave entrance didn't seem to bother him one bit. Paul saw it was bigger than a rabbit hole but to him, only just. Geraldine followed Tom. It was Paul's turn. He was so terrified he nearly refused to go in. Then he pictured Sharon's naked body. He had to go in. He took a deep breath and gingerly, lowering himself into the water, he wriggled in.

God almighty, he'd forgot to switch his lamp on. He hadn't – he'd caught the switch on a protruding rock. He could see past Geraldine to where Tom was and the tunnel was turning into a keyhole. He'd never get through there. He nearly fainted when his head began to spin. Don't pass out, he urged himself silently. Please don't let me pass out. He fumbled for the switch on his belt and it took some finding.

'It's on the other side,' said Sharon. 'Turn on your side. There's lots of room.'

Paul knew there wasn't lots of room. There was no bloody room! Any minute now the roof was going to collapse and crush his guts out. He took a few good deep breaths and rolled onto his side. He was nearly sick when his elbow caught the roof and a few bits of gravel fell on him.

'Is it safe in here?' he said and somehow managed to keep the panic out of his voice.

'Last person to be killed in here was over thirty years ago. Heavy rain flooded all the main chambers. The poor sod drowned. He'd no tanks with him.'

'We haven't any tanks have we?'

'No it hasn't rained for weeks. It's as dry as a witch's toe in here!'

Oh that's good news thought Paul. That's bloody terrific news. He'd seen the weather forecast and it had warned of thunderstorms in the North. He had to get out. They all had to get out. He'd have to tell them.

'We have to get out! It's going to pour down!' The three of them burst out laughing.

'Come on,' laughed Tom. 'There's nothing to fear! We've been through here a dozen times. Wait till it gets narrow mate!' There was only just enough room for him to nod his head. They pushed on. Paul felt sick.

'Main chamber coming up,' called Tom. 'We'll shelter in there from the rain.' More laughter.

Paul nearly bit through his lip. 'Ten yards or so.' He did his sums in his head. 'That's thirty feet and the passage is narrowing.'

'Give me a push Gerry. It narrows quite a lot here,' said Tom as though he'd said I'll have a pound of apples please. There was a scrapping and a puffing and blowing from up front and Tom called out, 'I'm through. Give me your hands Gerry and I'll reel you in.'

Paul's voice had gone. He couldn't even croak. Had it not gone he would have screamed at the top of his voice and never stopped. But his mouth, his throat and his lungs, were dry as powder and his palms and the soles of his feet were wet-through with sweat. Sharon suddenly gave him a push from behind and Geraldine pulled him by his arm. His other arm was trapped against his side and the cave wall. He was stuck. If he could have moved his legs he would have had an almighty tantrum.

'I've got you Paul,' said Tom and pulled him out of the narrow tunnel like a cork from a wine bottle. Paul sank to his hands and knees as though he'd been kicked in the stomach by a shire horse. He didn't cry, he giggled. He couldn't stop. Sharon dropped beside him and threw her arms round him.

'What is it Paul? What's the matter?' He still giggled.

Tom slapped him in the face. He stopped giggling, got to his feet and would have knocked Tom's head off if Sharon hadn't got between them.

'Sorry Paul,' said Tom. 'But you'd lost it. You had Paul. You frightened me to death.'

41

'Frightened you to death. You haven't a clue what it means Sharon. Frightened you to death! I've already died three times in that rat hole. How am I going to get out? I can't go on and I can't go back. I was absolutely terrified. I'm not so bad now I can stand up in here but I'm claustrophobic! For God's sake. I love you Sharon but I can't go any further. I can't. I don't care what you think I am, but I can't go any further.' Paul's whole body shook like mad. I only came in because I wanted to be with you and I didn't want you to think I was a wimp!'

'Why did you come? I can't believe you've done it.'

'I've told you why. I love you. One of you help me out. Tie a rope to me or something but you've got to get me out of here and pretty quick.'

'We'll all go out together Paul. Don't worry. It's easier going out because the protrusions go the other way. You don't have to struggle round them.'

'Are you going first Tom?' asked Geraldine looking worried. She thought she'd heard thunder.

'We'll go out man, man, woman, woman. Give me your rope Paul.'

Paul shuffled it off his shoulder, catching his belt switch and turning his lamp off again. He didn't panic. He waited till Sharon switched it back on. But he swore he'd tie it round the old man's neck when he took the rubbishy thing back.

Tom took control. 'Fasten that under your arms and round your chest.'

Paul fumbled with the rope. 'Leave it! Let me do it.' Tom did a "figure-of-eight" knot and tugged on the rope. That's sound. He fastened the other end round his own waist and showed Paul what he'd done. He didn't want him to have a panic attack in the tunnel. There was a small seam of shale half way through and Tom knew it wasn't all that stable. But they all had collapsible shovels. It wouldn't take long to dig through if there was a bit of a fall.

'If you're ok let's do it.' Paul didn't reply.

Tom climbed into the tunnel and pulled Paul's rope with him. He kept it taut. Paul couldn't speak. He just climbed like a rigid automaton into the narrow tunnel. His breath came in gulps. His head throbbed, his heart was pounding like mad and he focused only on the tunnel floor. He couldn't force himself to look forward. He crawled two or three inches at a time.

'Get a move on Tom! Water's started dripping through a fissure just above my head.'

Tom muttered something under his breath and speeded up. Paul tried to do the same but his elbows were creasing him.

'Come on Paul,' urged Tom. 'We're nearly there.' Sharon pushed from behind. Tom was out.

It was pouring with rain. Paul followed and nearly broke down. Sharon squirmed out. Geraldine wriggled out like a performing seal; her suit was wet through and covered in mud.

'It's bad in there you lot. I think we got out just in time.' She took a deep breath and took her helmet off, shook her hair and put the helmet back on.

'A bit iffy in there Tom.'

'I think you're right Gerry.

Paul sank onto the rubble at the side of the stream and tried to unfasten the rope. He didn't sob, but he felt sobbing would release the knot of terror in his stomach. He coughed and swallowed as lightening flashed up on the moor and a deafening crash of thunder followed almost instantly.

The trickle from the cave became a stream. The stream a river and suddenly a wall of water spewed out of the cave. Paul scrambled backwards up the steep banking because the water was backing up where the little valley narrowed downstream.

They heard and felt beneath their feet a rumbling shudder from well back in the cave and the gushing water almost stopped.

'Get up onto higher ground. There's been a fall by the sound of that lot. Come on. Leave the rope fastened Paul,' Tom shouted at the top of his voice as he scrambled up the banking. 'We'll get it off you later! It's damming up inside the cave!'

Sharon and Geraldine were scrambling onto the ridge as Paul suddenly snapped out of it. He almost ran after Tom. Tom stumbled over the rope but managed to keep his balance.

Just as they climbed onto the ridge and with a deafening roar, the mouth of the cave exploded. Boulders as big as footballs and a great slurry of soil, loose stone and shale was thrown twenty feet in the air then pushed downstream at an unbelievable speed by the force of the flood water. The four of them watched stony-faced as it dawned on them what would have happened but for Paul's terrifying phobia.

'It's a bigger hole now,' said Paul, grim-faced. 'There is a God in heaven. He granted my wish!' They tried to laugh it off but they couldn't. It had been a very close call. Paul didn't even try to laugh. He meant every word he said!'

Sharon burst into tears and threw her arms round him and trying to stop crying said, 'You went through all that for me? You'd no need you

43

silly fool. I loved you when I first saw you. I loved you!' She stood back, wiped her eyes and looked into his eyes. 'I can't believe you did all that for me Paul.' She kissed him as hard as she could.

'Come on Gerry, what about me?' said Tom throwing his helmet to the ground and pursing his lips. Do I get a kiss like that?'

'No you don't, you got one yesterday!' They all laughed.

'What about we get changed and get to the nearest pub? No more caving for me! I'm going to have a go at fell racing. I could do with losing a bit of weight. Come on. I'll be having nightmares after this!'

Paul took his equipment back the following morning. He went into the darkened shop. The old man was polishing a trombone. Paul dropped the bag on the floor in front of the counter. It was darker in the shop than the pothole.

'I'm returning the caving gear. I won't need it anymore. Sharon and I are getting married and she's had enough of caving. We were nearly killed!'

'Were you?' The old man in the trilby hat didn't seem bothered in the least.

'And the switch for the light is faulty!'

The old man continued to polish the trombone.

'I don't give refunds if you're expecting some of your money back!' The old man put down the trombone. Something made a shuffling noise at the back of the shop. Paul looked round but there was nobody there.

'I don't want money and I don't need that.' Paul gave the bag a little kick.'

'It is no good to me if the switch is faulty.' The old man turned and peered at Paul over his glasses. 'You might as well throw it in the corner of your garage! That is the best place for it!'

'I don't have a garage.'

'Then throw it in the dustbin.' He picked up the trombone.

'I am not an electrician you know. And you can't get tradesman for love or money these days. Take it away before a customer trips over it. It's dark in here.' There was a tinkle of laughter from deep within the many rooms.

'What's that?'

'Probably my son bumping into a wall. I'm closing for stocktaking now. Take the bag and take this as a thank you for letting me know the switch is faulty.'

'What is it?'

'It is a gift. You can open it when you get home. I'm closing now – we are moving to new premises.'

There was more laughter from deep within the darkened rooms. Paul didn't ask what it was as he wanted to be out of there. He shuddered and he took the small parcel from the counter and the bag from the floor.

'Well thanks chum,' he turned and called in to the darkness.'And thanks whoever you are? See you later.' Paul left the shop.

The sun was shining and the street was busy with traffic. He felt glad to be outside. He saw a skip further up the street; he strolled up to it, threw the bag in and went to meet Sharon. The old man locked the door and shuffled off into the darkness. Something came out of one of the rooms and took his hand. Whatever it was it had a big long nose and a long swishing tail.

'Let me have a look at your son. Because Tony didn't fulfil his task. He remains claustrophobic.'

'But Father, he did his absolute best.'

'Let me see your chest. As I thought he forgot to cross the T.'

Richard Lee Wilson 2006.

A Tale of two Kitties

It's well known in medical circles, the laundrette on Muck Road and the Nag's Head on Betterhalf Street, that every so often even the most sober-minded people have moments of temporary insanity. These temporary moments can vary in length from a couple of heart beats; wash time to spin time; from opening time to closing time or the time it takes to lever your kids out of bed on a cold and fro-osty morning. There are abundant examples that spring to mind.

Have you heard of those who, with a long forgotten apache war cry, hurl themselves off suspension bridges, footballers' wallets, and cloud piercing towers with very little more than plaited knicker elastic tied to their feet. I've heard of people with their faces the colour of bleached ash hitting the ground so hard they get a quick glimpse of Australia, say a speedy hello to Bruce and Sheila, twang off over the Post Office Tower and back......and again and back...... and again and back! My friend Sam was only five-feet-six when he did his first bungee jump. Now his legs are that length and his head's a Frisbee! Two good things did come out of this daring leap. The first was it got rid of his haemorrhoids! The second was, he got a part in Star Wars XXI. When he's not doing anything else he doubles as a coffee table. They will all come down to earth one day.

In days gone by there were others who, without a by your leave, put aside all other duties, including seeing to their husband's every need. And instead of ploughing the top and bottom meadows and bringing in the sheaves, they sat down to make a tapestry out of yards of mucky old bandages and then colour it in with a sooty stick and some sort of mediaeval lipstick. Totally foreign to someone with the capacity for clear thinking. One can only say. 'C'est la vie.'

Whatever that means!

I've heard there are some chaps and chapettes who get togged up in thermal carpet slippers and fleece-lined baby-grows, then they set off for the North Pole or the South Pole if their map's Australian. I'm told they travel with a couple of dozen tins of corned beef and a sack full of muesli. Do they expect to get there on a dinner tray towed by a couple of Pekinese dogs and a brace of wild rabbits! Is it possible? Who knows! I think their Northern Lights must have gone out.

Somebody told me (but I found it hard to believe) that there are those who are dying and have died, to bomb half the world because they don't want to raise the price of oily stuff in their own great and good land; the dipsticks! It's only fifty pence a gallon off that nice chap at the boot sale, and it's a nicer colour. And you get a free DVD with every purchase. And they're in super little boxes with lift up lids. They're exactly like the ones you have to sell your body-parts for if you want enough cash to buy them from the shops.

Can anybody believe there are people with secure employment, steady incomes and crippling mortgages, who suddenly get a stubborn urge to move to the countryside? When there, they finally acquire a smallholding with huge scope for development. Agent speak. In truth it's a derelict barn and some lengths of worm-ridden floorboard abandoned under a rhubarb tree. Then when they settle in, they plant a load of ornamental trees, convert what's left of a hen run into a bijou dwelling, complete with pool, fountain and small zoo and make their own clothes out of sisal twine, dog hairs and kitchen foil. They must have fallen out of their apartment block!

Tell me Doctor, can the people who, with the aid of a couple of soup ladles, a chamber pot for bailing, and a Jolly Roger just in case, row round the world in a hip-bath like our one? Is it possible? Can they be right in the head; maybe they have water on the brain! I do sink tho!

What about those who, pedal off into the Sahara Desert with only a pocket full of tuna and salad cream on brown, five bob, a packet of mints, and dressed in their Lawrence of Arabia nightgown. Have they not had a temporary aberration? Is their sand running out? And will no amount of pills or electric shock treatment stop rich people paying a golden hand-shake to be blasted over the rainbow in a billion pound firework!?

Would clear-thinking men buy a star in exchange for wads of pound notes and name them after their girl friends? I think not. I bought my star for seven-shillings-and-six-pence including choir and bells and she had a name already. Just think how long it would take to make sure alien squatters hadn't moved in. You can see the stars but I bet they're a lot further away than the nearest post office. Then again, maybe not!

Have you seen the trendsetters that have so much body-piercing, the weight of it makes them sag at the knees and their secret bits ding and dong like happiness bells? They look as if they've fallen into the cruel hands of my Dear wife's mother's coven! You won't believe it but some people have them in their bellybuttons, nostrils and other nose-like parts. Must be dreadful trying to use your hooter, and your nose for that matter! But what about the rings and things through the lips and tongue? Just imagine a passionate kiss, a sudden tangle of silverware, mouths inseparable, tongues interlocked. Quick girl, phone for the fire brigade! How?

Just imagine it. Ring, ring. 'Which service do you require caller?'

'Furbrigurf! Ourmuthsaththucktogethu!' Hoax-calls carry a hefty fine and could inconvenience the budding arsonists and the genuine hoax callers among us.

The list of occasional confusion is endless! And then there's Bert up the road, happily married for twenty-five years; now he's called Mary, and Gloria, his wife is called Stanley! What's all that about?

My many moments of temporary insanity suddenly assailed me when I was about sixty-years-old and had caught the downhill bus. The first sign I had was when I suddenly discovered I'd lost my voice and had become invisible all at the same time. I only found out I wasn't invisible when I was waxing the dining room floor and spotted my reflection in its gleaming surface. I only realised I hadn't lost my voice when I realised other sixty-year-olds could hear me speak.

Another thing I wanted to do when I was Napoleon, was to wear trainers like the hooligans next door wear. Trainers that can breathe without lungs or gills and have soles designed to let you climb up wet plate glass windows. Bouncy trainers in which you can run round the world and back with an anvil under each arm without any discomfort! Trainers that shine in the dark and have a built-in alarm that alerts you if you get within five yards of a bag of crisps.

Mine play 'Bat out of Hell' and the 'Mikado' both at the same time. They're only three-hundred quid a pair, you should get some! You do get a free Beckham Alice-Band and linguistic course with every pair this week, so that's something for the guys!

Another urge I got one day while sitting in Ikea on some bath sponges nailed to some coloured planks in the settee department and watching the third repeat of 'Changing rooms', was to wear my Dear wife's mother's Halloween wig. And my Dear wife's father's chenille blouse. The blouse was two sizes too big but it didn't seem to matter. Everyone on the ward said how splendid it looked. It sported contrasting shades of brown and purple across the pageboy cuffs and up the rather extravagant bouffant sleeves. The sweet little curls of the ruff collar were in alternate colours of green, lilac and burnt peach. It really was a delight to wear while creosoting our ferret's hut. The occasional blackish splatters blended in most adorably. I've sent my portfolio of flourished full-frontal photographs and my right index finger to the producer of Big Brother. I'm keeping my remaining fingers crossed!

Later, and not wanting to be left out, I just had to have those jeans. Well, everybody is wearing them! They make one's backside look like a split-pea. That is until you take them off and it flops back to the shape of a bag of wet flour. You know the jeans I mean? Those with special hand-beaten copper rivets. Each one forged and formed over an open fire near a glorious blue lake with a delicate swathe of silver weeping willows and a glorious golden sunset in the background. I know that's where they make 'em 'cos I've seen it on the television. One can wash-n-wear them by lying prostrate in a stream or on a pebble beach near Hawaii. It doesn't work if one lies for hours in the canal behind our house. I tried it and it didn't get the oil off where my bicycle chain catches my leg. These are the same jeans that one can slip off in the laundrette and have one's shreddies admired by all the ladies. Unfortunately what usually happens is, some smarty-pants shouts, 'You need some sun on them legs mate.' Or because of all the ladies screaming one gets dragged off to the local nick to look closely at some garden hose for being a perve!

I had a sudden urge to wear fleeces in glaring colours and with big writing on them. Writing that said things like, 'Schools are for kids. Nurseries are for flowers. Batteries are for hens.' Colours that dazzled a butterfly at thirty-paces. I wanted to have three pockets up each sleeve, two on each shoulder and a secret pocket behind the label for loose change! If they didn't have a four-way zip, crocodile-shaped toggles and a big inside pocket for my baseball cap, I wouldn't wear the inferior things.

I took to using after-shave that could stun sewage-workers at twenty paces and could stain stainless steel. Why not? It only cost two weeks wages for that rather smart black, green and red bottle. You know the one! It's shaped like three interlocking pyramids. One day I'll get the twelve-year-old who lives across the road to show me how to open it!

Then one night, and without a change of medication, I headed off in another direction. I wanted to sell all our worldly possessions and with the two-hundred-quid I got, I wanted to wear old clothes, never shave again and convert an old ambulance into a motor home then drive round St. Trop in it looking for celebs. Well, why not? It was none of my probation officer's business. And it had nothing to do with my social service worker or his assistant or the lay-persons' social advisory committee quorum!

But what should have had me safely encapsulated in a long-sleeved jacket that fastens round the back was my wish to purchase at ridiculous expense two Persian cats! I won't tell you their names in case they read this later and take revenge. On second thoughts, I might as well because they're sitting on my shoulders cleaning their nether parts and watching me type this out. But please, don't fear for my safety, I'm wearing my chain mail hairnet, a cut down plastic dustbin and my cricket pads. The big one sitting on my right shoulder with her tail in my eye is called Armageddon, or Whiningfatgreedybitch, for short. And the small one sitting on my left shoulder with her tail in my cup of coffee is called Apocalypse now, or Rag-arse.

My darling wife and I raised two sons up to the time when they started going out with what could be girls. Do girls wear donkey jackets and Steely-Dan boots? Do nice girls wear axes in their belts and spit on the floor? There was one thing we did like about two of their girl friends, Charlene and Westham, that is once I'd realised one of them wasn't a cockatoo. The one thing was, they went to church every Sunday, which we thought was a super thing to do. Then we caught them with a barrow load of lead, the offertory tray and its contents. I told them the wheelbarrow would be confiscated and that the money the tray and the lead must be returned.

I have a clear picture in my mind of me leaning forwards to take hold of the wheelbarrow, and croaking, 'Bloody-well let go of it Charlene and Westham take your hands off my throat. Now give it to me!'

Then I remember being struck by lightning and seeing a close up of the Milky Way. Then, in a haze of clouds I vaguely remember hearing a giggling nurse say, 'This might hurt a lot.' Then in a sort of mist I remember seeing a group of either young children or junior doctors of both sexes watching on, smirking and taking notes. Then I remember a wheelbarrow handle being removed from a mostly hidden part of my body and finally I remembered being helped into a bed on a corridor with some more pensioners. Don't worry, we were "top-to-toe" so there was adequate room for the six of us. The rest of my stay in the hospital corridor is just too dreadful to relate, and anyway they made me sign a disclaimer with a plastic spoon dipped in gravy when I was deeply sedated. I still go to church but I don't chop firewood anymore.

But even the task of bringing our sons up, proper like, you know what I mean like, difficult as it was at times like, was a mere stroll down a leafy lane on a golden September evening compared with the never-ending slavery of catering for the unrelenting needs of these two felines. The following are but some of our hourly, daily or weekly tasks.

GROOMING & DELOUSING! They will allow one to comb or brush them if one uses a rubber-toothed comb or a pastry brush with bristles made of thistledown. If, and even with the greatest of care one causes the slightest discomfort, they will in the time it takes to buy a gallon of rainbow-diesel from the nice man at the boot sale, strip your hands of flesh, bury their needle sharp fangs into and through your left thumb, right thumb or both thumbs and clamp their jaws till they meet.

To distract them from the job in hand, one must let them play swing-swong-grab-and-bite with the soft bits at the side of one's Adam's apple and the tender bits of skin just below one's ears. Then and only then will they allow one to remove the leaves, knots, twigs, clinging insects, yesterday's grub and that there stuff from the other end of their illustrious personages. We've found the best way to get rid of their fleas is to stand against the wall on the record player's turntable, spin it in a clockwise direction and as we whiz round we let the cats spray us with DDT. We did try at first using a cricket bat but my Dear wife somewhat over enthusiastically whacked one that had come to rest on my funny bone. Consequently, I lost the use of my left hand for a week and a half. And I don't remember laughing once but I do remember emptying my weeping vase a dozen or more times. To get fleas off the cats is a trifle difficult. We have to wait till they're sound asleep and not pretending to be asleep. Then we creep up on them and pick the critters off individually with a pair of blunt, rubber tweezers.

BATH TIME. They will allow you to bath them if the temperature of the asses' milk is exactly the same as the temperature recommended by the royal paediatrician for the bathing of royal babies. They will allow my darling and I to bathe them if having been in the asses' milk for three-and-three-quarter seconds you let them play JUMPJETKILLERWHALE. The rules of the game are simple. They leap to the ceiling howling in cat-speak we are orphans and Mr and Mrs Bumble are stabbing us with toasting-forks. As one of them goes up, legs thrashing, claws out, teeth bared and spitting asses' milk in ones face, the second one of Satan's foulest fiends, as if passing a mirror comes down. This whole sad procedure looks a lot like an invisible juggler, juggling animated wash leathers.

They do love to land legs akimbo in the milk. This game continues till the sink or bath is empty, or one of us throws a double-six or gets some wire mesh and throws it over the sink. When one has emptied the milk from one's wellies, the butter dish and sugar bowl and have no more dry towels or sawdust, (talcum powder sets like concrete on a wet cat) one must then let them use one's ribcage as a climbing frame and let them perch like a poltergeist on one's head. From this vantage point they are better able to see how far the milk splattered up the rubber plant. They retain this position with their claws embedded in the Morris dancer's grip through one's eyebrows and earlobes until the clock chimes. To remove them takes extremely deft manipulation and what seems like hours of eye watering agony. Pry a claw out and it clings instantly to some other tender spot. It's as if their tendons are made out of old lorry springs or one's head is an electro-magnet and their claws are shards of high tensile steel.

Being half bald down one side of my head, I no longer use this method! I have found the best way to get them off my head is, to bite through my tongue and lean over as far as I can towards what's left of the milk, as if to tip them back in. Then they spin round as only cats can, which is a hell of a lot faster than Torville and Dean even if they're wired to the mains. The cats are but a blur. When they finally let go they shout yippee and scrabble down my back then make a run for it. One of the down sides to this method is when they take their final grip for the long jump and just before they shout yippee! their front claws curl mercilessly into ones back, (even penetrating the divers' suit) then sink deep into ones buttocks, while the back claws search for the kidneys – then follows the leap. They clear the worktop by a mile and skid across the Regency dining table ten feet away. Even with patches of one's new fleece torn from the back and stuck like fluffy lime-green slippers to their claws, they still leave heartbreaking skid marks in its once highly-polished surface!

We long ago learned to remove the irreplaceable Yaki-Kraki-Saki porcelain urn containing my Dear wife's grandfather's ashes from the centre of the dining table and store it with everything else we have that weighs less than twenty kilos and are of any value. We keep them in a display cabinet screwed to the landing wall where the ceiling meets the sky. This safe-zone is three-cat-lengths out of their reach. I've often thought of fixing our bed up there!

After their so called bath, there follows the anointing of one's wounds with burny-stingy stuff and waterproof plasters. After the loss of a small amount of one's hair and even before it drops to the floor there swiftly follows a mad chase round the house to catch them and dry them down before they hide in my or my treasures pillows. Fortunately, we have some good but simple-minded neighbours who come round with tridents and nets to help in the chase. The kind neighbour from across the road is a specialist in dermatology; his presence among us greatly lowers the risk of septicaemia, or even worse, litter-tray rash.

I suppose we could do what Connie up the road does with her Persian cats. She straps hers to the handlebars of her husband's Triumph Thunderbird and rides it through the car wash in Leeds or through a sheep dip in Otley! The cats come home spotless, and she cometh home spotless and even better she cometh home without any visible scars. Her hairdo looks like an exploding thistle, but that's a small price to pay!

We once took them, on the recommendation of an ex-friend, to a chap in Skipton who was a specialist in grooming Persian cats, and our ex-friend assured us, this specialist doesn't wear armour. We understood he used some sort of anaesthetic to make the wash and brush up stressless. I must say it did. Within seconds of having the injection my beloved wife and I woke up to find the little beasts as clean as two new pins and back in their cage waiting to be off. We paid the bill immediately to what we thought was a mumbling Egyptian mummy from the museum on the floor above. But it was in fact the badly wounded specialist. I don't know what later happened to the specialist exactly but within a week the police found his punt by the canal lock, and a suicide note leaving everything he owned to a Martian and his family of caterpillar-like creatures who had, he said recently moved into his greenhouse!

To try and dry Persian cats with a hairdryer as we were once advised by another so called specialist, (even if their legs are clamped firmly in the cutlery drawer) is, if you think anything of your wallpaper, absolute madness; and don't get the idea Persian cats can't scurry across the ceiling upside down, because they can, and they still keep one claw free to hack-whack and defend themselves. The only scar-free method we've found up to press, is to herd them into a corner with a cattle prod, throw a car rug over them and weigh the corners down with a number of house bricks, (this number varies between the seasons of the year. You need ten per corner in winter time and twenty in summer), then leave them there till nightfall of the following Monday, or Tuesday if you bath them on the Sabbath.

FEEDING. They eat, as cat lovers know only too well, seventeen times a day, or twice, or never, or five times, or once. It depends on what they're doing that day. If they're de-fitting the lounge carpet, they eat when they're tired, or not at all if they are full-up with carpet pile. If they're playing in the potato box, the flour bin or the laundry basket, or playing cat quoits with the butter dish and sugar bowl on the breakfast bar, they eat quite often. For instance, once for every time they chip a bit off the sugar bowl or twice if the butter dish lands upside down in one of their litter trays. If they're un-decorating, they eat whatever they strip off the walls or ceilings. This meal is measured by yardage, not by weight. If they're re-upholstering an item of furniture, they seem to prefer the velour on the arms of the furniture to resemble the hind quarters of highland cattle huddled together in the foulest bitter cold of mid-winter, or a well-used floor-mop. We prefer it when the strands of material that are still affixed don't drag on the floor.

What do they eat besides their toys and flying insects? Today it was marinated beef and lamb, garnished with eleven grammes of lean boiled ham. The ham has to be fat free and sliced into one-eighth by one-and-seven-eighth strips. Before we knew better we used to roll the ham into six balls and sit each ball on its own modified egg-slicer. Then we'd wait for a visitor to call by so he or she could work the two central levers. Then when we were all set up, on the count of three we would all press together. But experience, a lack of coordination and the loss of a few fingertips has proven a paper shredder is safer and saves a fortune on sticky-plaster.

The little imps want this ham on a bed of sliced cucumber in baby mice shapes and bulked up with something they dragged in from the compost heap or where a warthog's been doing its number two's. Tomorrow they won't want it again, because they won't like it tomorrow. Tomorrow, in their opinion and after only one tiny sniff, they will decide it's laced with deadly chemicals or my darling wife's mother's face-pack stuff. Which looks to me like a good mixing of potted-dog and carbuncle ointment!

Tomorrow they might like medium roasted chicken breast and turkey necks with slivers of wild salmon on a bed of golden fried gizzard tips, but maybe not! Maybe it will be peacock tongue and trout garnished with herb de provence, or baby white rabbit, mushy peas and tinned rice pudding. Who's to know? One's a better chance of winning the lottery three weeks in succession than knowing what to feed our two.

Could be they'll want what we call a Beelzebub special, which is a delicately balanced blend of spiders, flies, sheep eyes, wood lice, six of the things that thrive on the moss in the cellar and two of the things that live under the bat box in the attic, but who knows? My darling wife or I will by two pm! It depends whom they find first; they will find one of us, they always do. Don't think that hiding in the loft or a neighbour's loft is any use. A ladder is no impediment to our two treasures and pretending to be dead is useless! I won't tell you how they check to see if you're dead but it takes ages to get the taste out of your mouth!

Whichever one of us they trap they stare at like two of those wicked wide-eyed children from the village of the damned, (or the Midwitch Cuckoos as the book was entitled), till the selected step-parent goes dizzy and the cats' desires are implanted in their subconscious. Seconds before feeding time, they remove themselves from their indoor-outdoor adventure park, which is half way up the velvet curtains; at the lounge window; drop like flying squirrels; use the front cushions of the settee as a braking strip; race into the kitchen to their Tang dynasty bowls with the wild bird motifs and howl like starving wolves! That's when one of us gets the evil-eye!

Their feeding time, (sticking their faces in their bowls time,) can be anytime between four in the morning and a minute past midnight – then at ten minute intervals throughout the day, or not. They like to surprise us.

When we first got them, they used to eat something that looked like vanilla and raspberry flavoured maggots. They didn't put up with that for long. That stuff only cost thirty pounds a bag. They soon discovered that fillet steak was nicer and minced rump steak wasn't that bad if you put it on a low light till it was the same temperature as mice innards. We use a jeweller's eyepiece now to spot any minuscule amounts of fat in the mince or they get the galloping sprids, which can reduce the value of your worsted Wilton by ninety percent before one of us can say 'don't vomit!' Or, in between gypping, yodel 'what's that stuck to your slippers.'

TOILETRY. I have heard dozens of euphemisms for the piles or pools of that there stuff from doting animal lovers such as my Dear wife and me. Little present, little accident, little whoopsy and that there stuff are but four. We have tried to eradicate the above by buying every type of cat litter on the market, even the perfumed ones. They smelled so nice we thought of using them ourselves. We tried the Pilkington formula in two litter trays in every room of the house. Relatives asked if we we'd gone into mushroom farming; of course we hadn't and it was a waste of good money. We even laid coloured photographs of ourselves in the trays; no joy there. So once more we returned to the dolly-peg on the nose bit and employed, at arm's length, various methods to clear it up, including an aqua vac and a snow plough. This was ok till we tried to remove the stuff from the vac's pipes, dust bag and workings. Alas we couldn't. So, in the dead of night when one of the cats was singing Nessun Dorma to some cats in the next village, and the other one was singing Brahms' Lullaby to the screaming kid two doors up or they were both playing shred the bed, we left it outside an Oxfam shop. It's still there! The refuse collectors refuse to take it! We borrowed, on some pretext, the neighbour's more up-to-date whizzy-whirly-whazy vac with the howling storm suction system, but without much success. It has a six horsepower motor with a spridoclismic converter, which clearly didn't work. It had a burr-walnut switch panel, a seeunderthesofa laser-light and a leather interior. The patented anteater snout attachment got it out of the corners and crevices perfectly but on an open patch of carpet it was another kettle of yesterday's fish in prawn sauce. The twin-spiral-diametrically-opposed-beater-bars instead of sending 'that there stuff' into the bowels of the vac where it belonged, peppered the fridge, the conservatory glass roof and the beige sacking folk weave walls. The place looked as though a child with a serious touch of flu and a mouth full of chocolate had stood on his head and sneezed till his nose fell off.

Later on that night when my beloved wife and I had swilled our mouths out with a brandy and vinegar wash, donned our gasmasks and opened the vac to clean it, the eight-interlocking one-micron filter pads, looked like Marmite on toast and the watch-the-muck-twirl dust collector, in dawn-light clear plastic, looked like a pebble-dashed gable-end. Both were beyond the cleaning power of concentrated bleach and our brand new garden rake. We took the useless thing back. The only good thing that came out of this was, the neighbour doesn't come round for cups of sugar anymore or invite us to her weekly séance. We've since found out, because of the pong that is, the poor soul thinks she's got ghost-cats living behind her skirting board or behind the coat cupboard where she keeps her vac. Last we heard, she was singing hymns outside the fish shop. I'm sure she'll end up as a day patient at the local psychiatric hospital where we go.

In a final desperate move, we tried a Karsher but it took ages to dry ourselves, the walls, the carpet and the family photographs.

No, experience has taught us that the only successful method of removing it is to scrape it onto a dust pan tied to a clothes prop with a fish slice tied to another clothes prop. (A long handled spade and a yard brush destroys the carpet pile.) Then we rub-a-dub-dub the affected area, or if it's worse than bad, scrub like hell-a-dub-dub, with a mixture of Dettol,

Stardrops and Jeyes fluid till one get pins and needles in one's fingers and elbows and the manufacturer's colours return to the surface! By using this method, visitors (when coming for a meal and entering the house) don't ask us if they can eat el-fresco! (whatever they are)? We usually have chips and peas for a treat every other Sunday.

BEHAVIOURAL QUIRKS. The smaller of the two cats is a flat face blue-white Persian and looks like a psychopathic gremlin. If she doesn't want you to sit in the same room as her, she explains it to you in various and lip biting ways (the cat doesn't bite ones lip, we bite our lips ourselves). If we didn't, our screams as the claws went in would shatter our Pyrex ovenware.

The other horrendous method she uses to get you out of the room is to purr, blink at one, then jump gently onto one's lap. Then after pretending to make herself comfortable she does a pile of that there stuff between one's legs and covers it within seconds with feathers from a favourite cushion or material from the trousers one is wearing. One instantly leaves the room in the manner of a person who's had the back of his thighs stitched to the back of his calf muscle. Trying to hold one's nose at the same time is stupid. You will find one needs both one's arms to maintain ones balance. She meanwhile has shot off to tell her friend what she's done.

If she doesn't want what's on the cat's menu for today she waits while we are eating our meal, creeps under the table, dashes madly up one's leg and even before one's eyes have started to water, she sticks her face in ones dinner or preferably, a guest's dinner. One can't help but laugh, can one? The other one, a silver pewter Persian, often uses a far more subtle method. If she doesn't want cat food, she sits by one's chair blinking intermittently, and gently swaying her head from side-to-side like a hooded cobra. Then when her eyes look as big as the moon she makes one think one wants to go to sleep. It's about then (for some unknown reason) one starts counting backwards from ten. By number seven one's under. Then before one knows what's happened, she's tucking into all the choice bits which one has laid neatly on the floor. We got round that by wearing blinkers at meal times. It's a bit of an imposition but we aren't losing weight anymore.

To repulse the blue-white, psychopathic monkey we stapled barbed wire to the edge of the dining table, trouser bottoms, and the hems of my Dear wife's "nothing to wear things". Then we sank a moat in the dining room floor. We take the plank up when we're safely across! Seems to be working. We had some friends round last week and they were quite happy to eat on an island wearing blinkers and some of my wife's "nothing to wear things". The up side to this arrangement is that after two or three bottles of Jacob's Creek, one's guests throw chicken legs over their shoulders and when they land in the water we can hear the piranhas munching away, which gives the impression we're eating beside a babbling brook! It could set a trend, perhaps?

SLEEPING. When they were kittens, they were perfectly happy to sleep in cardboard boxes from the supermarket. These, my wife and I fashioned into little houses with a front door, false chimney and carpets throughout. It was two days before the cats swapped houses with each other. The smaller of the two, (the blue-white) preferred the mock-Tudor box with the overhanging upper floor, and the big one, (the silver pewter) preferred the Swiss chalet box with the yodelling door bell. Naturally, and after clearing up the snow-storm of fur, we left them to it.

Time sped by and suddenly they were full-grown cats and it became clear that the box-houses were no longer adequate for cats of their social standing. This manifested itself when we were awoken, one frosty morning in late December, at ten minutes to three to what sounded like two, tone-deaf bulldogs playing Beethoven's violin concerto, not in D major (which would I'm sure sound acceptable,) but in H sharp flat minor. We found, as we shivered in our thermals, that the darling cats had demolished their houses and stuffed the remains under the settee and into the bread bin. As we lifted the settee back onto its castors and put the shades back on the wall lights, the cats disappeared.

We decided we would look for them in the morning, (even though it was morning when we made the decision) and went back to bed. I blew out the candle on the landing and the one on the tea chest in the bedroom and got into bed. I was shaken rigid when a dreadful threatening howl erupted from under my pillow and was instantly followed by a pair of furry claws doing sixty jabs a second! When I found my way through the storm of duck feathers, I realised my left ear and I had found the blue and white! When my darling wife suddenly leaped out of bed with something clinging to her little toe (which in the darkness she swore was a bear trap) and landed on the far windowsill, only then (by the light of the street lamp) did we realise she'd found the silver pewter! She was lucky I was a first aider and had the nut crackers to hand or we'd never have got her toe free that night. We slept fitfully the rest of that night as you can well imagine and swore long and hard that we would sort it out tomorrow, which I suppose in real time was today!

The first six cat baskets we bought for them were obviously in the wrong colour, material or design. These were stored in the bottom of my wardrobe awaiting the spate of summer boot-sales. I would have put them in one of the three of my Dear wife's matching double -wardrobes having been told four or five times that morning that she'd nothing to wear for some get-together that evening. But when I untied the sturdy rope holding the doors shut, all of them were packed tight with nothing to wear things, so I had to put them in mine. Why not? I'd loads of room! I'd just replaced my other wardrobe that had gone rusty and which, when the bedroom door is wide open is much closer to the bed. I've bought a six inch galvanized nail this time. It is well worth the extra three pence

From the thousands of samples we got through the post, the silver pewter finally settled for a cat basket in quilted thermotronic organza, patterned in Scottish plaid and deep buttoned with scarlet velvet tufts. The blue and white wanted exactly the same but in the plaid of the Macgregor clan and the deep buttoning in moleskin. We were able to order these from a firm on the Isle of Capri and fortunately on their five-year easy payment plan. The cats were happy with these for a whole week! Now at night they share the bed with my darling wife, and I sleep like a screwed up dormouse in the bottom of my wardrobe. It's quite warm and cosy and when closed tight the doors block out most of the noise from the nearby abattoir. But I and my right buttock are not over enamoured with the moleskin buttons!

During the day they sleep between the mountainous layers of ironing! Or having crumbed the four cut loaves in the breadbin they have forty or more winks in there. The pair also like to nap entwined like a couple of evil-looking spiders round the rubber plant. They sleep on the settee when they've ragged-up enough of the pile for their comfort. They'll nod off while clinging to the wall lights when catching passing flies. They'll have forty-winks while lurking under the garden shed waiting for the unsuspecting postman (weather permitting)! A minimum of eighty degrees and the gentle waft of a southerly breeze are obligatory. They nestle with delight in the neighbour's hammock, fluffy slippers, bread maker, silk flower arrangement, baby's pram, baby's face and behind the big picture in her hallway! They doze off on the bus to Filey, the taxi to Bridlington and all the way back home in the police car. They like to get as much sleep as they can in the daytime, which leaves their nights free to play racing and chasing, leaping and screeching, yowling and howling, spitting and the other thing. I dream of having nightmares!

PETTING. By appointment only or if they want a special eatey-treat! Special eatey-treats can be anything. They can be one's lunch; ice-cream; Mars bar; cuff-links; a St Christopher (it's best to take it off if they want to eat that!); the remote control (if anyone can tell me who won this years Ryder Cup I'd be grateful!); the daily paper and the evening paper; next door's letter-box-flap; the postman's stilts and whip; the Yorkshire terrier from across the road and it's ribbon and anything that crawls within their reach. That covers an area of about fifteen cubic feet! We know when they want a special treat because they scratch it in some sort of cat Braille on one's shin bone.

PLAYING. They play whenever they want but ninety-eight percent of their playtime is between the hours of darkness or when one's got a migraine or a broken limb. One game they delight in is Solo-chase-the-ball! Alas, a game of my own invention and one that can only be played by a mindless but caring idiot! I throw a rolled up biscuit-wrapper at some speed across the floor. From the comfort of my arm chair, they sit and watch me chase after it. If I can catch it before it goes down the cellar steps or under the piano, they stop yawning. They only purr or snigger during this game if I bang my head three times on some heavy obstacle.

Another game they delight in is Leap-toad. This involves them strolling through a pile of wet mud or other unmentionable detritus. When they are completely covered in this filth they dash back into the house and pretend to try to leap over one's head or throw themselves lovingly into one's lap. This game is only played when one is wearing one's pink Tam O'Shanter, pale beige tropical suit, tennis shorts, or wedding dress. They have a two-tier points system during this game. There are points for sticking for the longest period to one's head and points for depositing as much crap as possible on one's person wherever you were sitting. The smallest room in the house is not out of bounds during this game. Nor is the toilet. A recent game of their very own invention is "Scragarat". I will explain. Though it may take some time.

I had the misfortune the other week to be sent shopping. This, for me, was a harrowing and completely new experience. My darling wife, completely out of the blue, suddenly decided to try her hand (after some thirty years of marriage) at ironing. I was immediately sent down the cellar to find the said iron from amongst the other unused wedding presents we keep down there, and after a major search I found it buried under what I supposed were cooking utensils. I dashed back upstairs to the warmth of the kitchen and passed the iron proudly to my angel who in turn proudly scraped the cobwebs off it with a Brillo pad and dashed upstairs to the back bedroom to have a go with it. I proudly followed her up with the ironing in the neighbour's wheelbarrow. Alas, after struggling with a pair of my socks for ten earth minutes she developed a nose bleed, lost her temper and had to go and lie down for a week. I went over the road and reclaimed the iron from the neighbour's front room. They were lucky they'd drawn the curtains! I believe the lady of the house across the road works nights, or was it at night? I'm sure it's the same thing. So because my only reason for living had taken to her bed rather than risk being eaten in the night by our pets, I was sent off to Tesco's to stock up. Off I went with a note and some money in my glove. I'd no idea they'd changed the coinage. Had you? The last time my one true love gave me money, the coins were totally different. I preferred the old coins – they were bigger

If like me, you have the ability to pretend you are somewhere else when you are in dreadful danger or threatened with pain and confusion, you are among the fortunate. I use this ability quite often and I used it on this occasion. After fighting for a spot to park what was left of the car and entering through the occasionally automatic doors into Tesco's, and after entering further in I found myself in what can only be described as a disco for the walking dead!

I decided, because of the horrors of the situation I found myself in, to pretend I was in a better place. So I plumbed for being a tank driver on the Russian front. I, like the big lady with the moustache who followed me round, was also pretending she was on the Russian front and was driving a tank. Unfortunately for me her tank was much bigger than mine and much better armed. I think she was a colonel. She thought I was the invisible man or merely a private. I tried, after grabbing what supplies I could before the blood from my heels spilled over the sides of my hiking boots, to dash to the fish counter. This thing (I must explain to male readers) is not where they count fish. It's a cold long glass cupboard thing with dead fish inside. One points to the piece of fish you want and the nice lady painting her fingernails gives you the piece next to it, even if one's finger is nearly touching your preferred selection. I realised, after thinking for a moment, that if I was to get the piece of fish I actually wanted then I must point to the piece of fish next to the piece I wanted. Cunning hey! Unfortunately, I was thwarted from my true choice by being given the piece on the other side of the piece of fish I wanted. After this embarrassment (and with three lumps of fish in my possession) I decided to head for what's known as the check out. Again, rather than cause confusion for male readers this place is not the tollgate on the bank of the river Styx; it's where they take one's money. I'd just enough money to pay the bill after selling my Grandfather's gold hunter to the chap in the camel hair coat behind me in the queue. I looked for Black Bess to give her one of the gold plated apples I'd bought but there was no sign of her anywhere! Odd I thought to myself.

It was at the check out that the incident occurred, which set in motion the game of "Scrag-a-rat". I'd lined my tank up with one of the "Bird's eye" flags that signified in the distance the position of the check out, and I decided to close my eyes and make a straight-line dash for it. Sadly, by not having learned earlier in my life the ignoble art of queue jumping, I was no match for Colonel Grimbitch. Her tank, heavy-laden as it was with four-for-the-price-of-three ammunition, was expertly rammed into the small of my back and the bloodied heels of my feet. The back-arching impact propelled me at great speed and great pain into the trolley of a person who looked like Mike Tyson's big brother. As I offered what I though was a sincere and appropriate apology and as I pointed to the culprit (lady behind me in jackboots and with bosoms that ruled the world) he did some sort of Kung Fu movement. Then after the blur of the unwanted flying lesson, I landed on the cheese counter (a place not dissimilar in temperature to the fish counter but with lumps of cheese inside instead). All I remember clearly of this, my first unaccompanied shopping trip, is waking up in a litter bin with a piece of cod stuck in my mouth and a couple of haddock fillets somewhere else.

Being unable to spot where I'd abandoned the car, because of the uncomfortable angle of my neck and a rapidly closing eye you understand, I could only focus, or get a line of sight on things three degrees higher than a lamppost or seven degrees lower than an eagle. The kindly St. John's Ambulance man who had in a flash fitted my neck with a support collar and my now closed eye with a patch, saw my distress and despite my protestations and pleadings, put me safely on the first bus I limped to. Much to my despair it was the wrong one. He should have put me on the second bus or seen me safely to my car. Can you just imagine what terrifying thoughts went through the mind of a Yorkshire man while on a two-hour journey to Lancashire, and he without any form of disguise? Well have a try! The eye patch was no good; all the women in Lancashire wear them. I'd heard somewhere that some wear three! Luckily, and just outside a black pudding shop by the custom post, I was able to find a discarded pile of soot. I dabbed this about my face and clothes as quickly as I could and stood there with my mouth sagging. I soon blended in with the surroundings.

After deciding it would be safer to get under cover, I hid for most of the day in the Job Centre with the other bloke and made a break for freedom as soon as the moon popped up from behind a mill chimney. Crawling over the moors in the dead of night, wrapped in a lambs-wool rug I'd swapped for my bootlaces with the slack-mouthed chap in the Job Centre, was pretty nerve wracking. As soon as I saw what was surely a brigand or murderous gun runner I pressed closer to the nearest sheep and went baa, baa. Had I been captured without a visa, I could have spent the rest of my days bleaching tripe or polishing black-puddings in a freezing corrugated tin hut in Oldham. Or even worse, if I was no good at that job, I could (horror of horrors) have been sold on Bury slave market to some rich southerner and be something in the city! Perhaps the lid of a drain. Or even worse as an eel taster! You can't imagine what went through my mind (and the other end) those three nights I spent crawling over the moors to reach the safety of my fireside. NB (If you are reading this to somebody from Lancashire, please change Lancashire to Yorkshire and town names to Huddersfield and Batley. Otherwise the listener might eat you.)

After my week long period of convalescence I limped downstairs and sat in my favourite chair. The cats rushed in and up my person, both hissing and fighting to get to the highest point; it being my head. Then as one, when they saw the neck brace and eye patch, their wild eyes turned to slits. I thought at first that they wanted to play pirates but after wedging their back claws under the elastic of the eye patch, they focussed solely on my bobbing up and down Adam's apple and decided it was a fierce rat that needed to be killed instantly and taken outside to play with. They were soon after it. Their back legs now up my nose, their front legs probing and thrashing. That's how the cute little critters invented the game "Scrag-a-rat". I'm happy to say the stitches will be out next Friday and now we no longer possess an iron. My darling's nosebleed and fit of pique is a thing of the past. I thank the fates that my one true love seems to like going shopping!

TOYS. For Christmas and their birthdays we have bought them squeaky-creaky toys, ting-a-ling toys, dong-a-long toys, wind up toys, whack-along toys, swinging toys and roly-poly toys. We have bought them imitation butterflies that flutter and shimmer and squeak when they're torn apart and imitation moths that don't. We've paid out for plastic rats, plastic bats, plastic gnats and crab-stick plats and all for nothing! The cats just proddle their eyes out with my paper knife, swallow them, then pick up the remains and flick them into the Yorkshire pudding mix or push them under the rug where they bury most of the multi-legged things they slaughter.

The cats like to play with the two gigantic spiders who sometimes live behind the gas fire and who sometimes swim in my coffee. One has five legs now, the other has four, but luckily even in this semi-crippled state they're still pretty nimble! The cats like to play claws-out shadow boxing with my darling wife's silk flower arrangements or the net curtains. They love to play bouncy-bouncy or shoot the rapids. This involves pushing anything ornamental situated on the landing, down the stairs. If it's a huge ten litre vase of fresh flowers, that's terrific. Because they love to watch, not only the delicate petals floating momentarily in the air like a swarm of butterflies, but when the petals settle on the water which cascades beautifully down the stairs and out under the front door, these petals look like wounded baby salmon. When they see this, the cats go mental, and the wounded baby salmon are soon whacked and hacked into miniature confetti.

They take great, if not immense delight, in playing trip-n-flip! This is usually from the third or fourth stair down from the first landing, or when a draught has blown the candle out on the narrow curved steps from the attic. The Dear pair lurk like speed camera users, unnoticed and unseen, somewhere in the darkest shadows, and then when one sets off downstairs they race between one's feet like a Mini with loose wheels. One trips over them, screams in despair, and launches oneself towards the wrought iron grill across the front door, which is a mere three feet from the landing strip. We have lowered the emergency telephone to a point where it can be reached from the prone position. This game is played most often five minutes before sun-up when one's eyelids are still glued together, or when the stair lift is out of order, or even worse, the morning after a wild bout of wine tasting.

They love to play with the video recorder, not all of it, just the bits they bite off. They like to play ice hockey on the dining table with joss sticks and a pickled onion but their two favourite games are: This little piggy went to market, and rakey-scratchey for nits in step-mummy's or step-daddy's hair. We're not their real mummy and daddy but we don't want them to get stressed out so we haven't told them. God knows what they'd be like if they got stressed. They'd never be off the phone. These games start when the moon sinks behind the dyehouse chimney across the road and involves toes, heads and claws. Our toes and heads, their claws. Sleeping in wellies and pit-helmets put an end to this nightly blood bath. Needless to say they never found any nits and none of the little piggies ever got to market. They did get to A&E a few times though.

SCRATCHING POSTS. My beloved and I were told by yet another expert on such things when we first got the cats, that it was vital we supplied each of them with a scratching post or they would use anything to hand! So we did. We bought them each a pyramid-shaped thing with each side in a different texture. Fairly rough, rough, rougher and rough-rough. I could hardly keep my face straight when Mr Setter in the pet shop explained the surfaces. Unfortunately, these were soon in the bottom of my wardrobe. We thought perhaps the shape was wrong so we tried every geometric shape known to mankind and womankind. We even tried shapes we'd seen on the fourth repeat of Changing Rooms. We did this on a sale or return basis, or I would have needed at least three more galvanized nails! We persevered, and for the silver pewter, we fastened a carpet pattern securely to the newel post. As time sped by we had to re-fasten the newel post securely to the floor joist. She now uses a three foot tall cheese grater, which is concreted into the hall floor (just to the left of the landing strip).

The blue-white however was not so easy to please. She didn't like any of the scratching posts we fashioned. Not even the one that cries pitifully when it's clawed. Perhaps there was something wrong with the volume control! She prefers to use items of furniture made before the reign of Queen Victoria's dad but only then if they glow with pride, are priceless and have been drooled over on the Antiques Road Show. She will use other things at a push, or in her case at a pull. Rather than itemise these things, I will categories them! Anything woven or knitted and it doesn't matter to her if you're walking on them, sitting on them, drawing them on, or wearing them! At claw cleaning times, she's a little swine!

VISITING. Our two delights are now banned from visiting relatives and friends, their vehicles and their gardens. They are banned from the Palaeontology department of the local museum, the local park and the fish shop next door but one. The only places they are allowed to visit are Germany, where they buy collars with swastika's and SS badges and the vet's. The vet lets them visit because over the years we've bought him and his wife a Porsche each.

When they do visit the vet, we lure them into their mink-lined cat carriers with drugged caviar sandwiches. We have to drug them or they would get free and want to drive or sit on the parcel shelf and pull faces at following traffic, obviously a danger to other road users. They have, on occasions, got free by releasing the catch arrangement. This is secured by a dreadnought six-digit combination lock on each cage-cum-carrier! We did try loading them in the Black Maria back-to-back, but it was a hopeless waste of time. They'd wait for a sharp bend in the road, put their claws through the drain holes in the bottom, press down hard, and with the help of centrifugal force they would spin their carriers round until they were front-to-front! After that it was a blur of paws on spinning digits and they would be out in a matter of seconds and adjusting the rear view mirror, sparring with the gear stick or giving the V sign to the enormous Hell's Angel following behind on a rocket. I do let them out of their carrier and lower the car windows two inches if a traffic warden is foolhardy enough to approach the vehicle! We then drive round to the bank, ask for a loan, put the money in two briefcases and then we're ready to face the vet. When we finally arrive at the vet's we pass him the cages and the briefcases and go for a lie down in the reception suite next to the pool, which is across from the sauna and solarium. When he returns our little delights he also returns the briefcases and then with a smile, which mirrors that of the nice man at the boot sale, he says, 'I'll loan you these for a little bit longer. You're sure to need them again.'

We did, between you and me try once to leave them at the vets. In fact between you and me we've tried to leave them in a thousand places. How they got back from Kathmandu and the orphanage in Poland I'll never know. Anyway we tiptoed out of the vet's in our swimsuits and drove home by another route. We rushed inside but before I'd half-finished painting the front door and altering our number, a chap dressed in what looked like a leather beekeepers outfit walked up the path. It wasn't the vet because I could see through the mesh guarding his face. I, like a fool, accepted the two boxes and paid the delivery charge of thirty-five pounds, which I was told included the rental for the stranger's attire. Can you picture our faces when first one and then the other box hissed meeowm, meeowmtooo!

CAT-SPEAK. The following are a few examples of the sounds our two delights have made over the many blood-stained years and have now become known to us as cat-speak.

'Meeowgerup,' at ninety-five decibels. This means; you are sitting where I want to sit! It can also mean, WAKE UP ZOMBIE SLAVES, IT'S MORNING.

'Opoormemeow,' at less than one decibel and each of them with moist, pleading eyes and one paw lain across their chest and the other three pointing at the ceiling, means, pig-dog you are starving me to death!

'HEYOOMEOW,' at ear-bleed sound level, claws out and with eyes like a Chinese assassin means, you are still starving me to death!

'Meowgomeow, meowgomeow,' means, let me out, it's too hot in here.

'Meinmeinmeow,' means, let me in – it's too cold out here.

'Meowtmeinmeowtmeinmeowtinmeowoutmeow,' means let me straight out and straight back in twice or three times because selfish lazy mummy and daddy are having a minute!

'Meeeno,' means; no like that CD. No want bath. No want turkey twinkles. No want a thousand other things.

'Meenonononon,' means; no like that one for sure!

'MEEEEEEEEEOW SPIT SNARL HISSSSS STAB BITE SPIT MEOW,' means one minute past three, time to get up. We want to play shred the bed.

'MEEEEEEEEEEEEEEEEEEEEEEEEEEEEEEEEEEEEEEEEEEEEEEE OOOOOOOOOOOOOOOOOOOOOOOOOOOOOOOOOOO-W!' means; you've stood on my tail! You clumsy piece of pig muck.

'Yumwemeeow,' means; we've just eaten some baby Blue Tits!

'Medunitmeheeheemedunitmeow,' means: I've just been sick on the settee / down your back / on your pillow / in the stew pot, the coq au vin and the Boeuf Bourguignon but you won't know till you taste it tomorrow! It took quite a long time, a few sarcastic remarks about my beloved's cooking skills and a few new pan sets for us to find out what this one meant!

'Meeeeegetum,' means; the spiders have come out to play.

'Meeoavem,' means; I've eaten one.

'Meeyou, meeyou, meeyou,' means; they want to play pin-pong.

'Youmee, youmee,' means; they want to play chasing.

'Meemeemeemeemee,' means; they want feeding. This glass-shattering wail can continue until you get back home from the fish and chip shop. If the shop next-door-but-one's shut, luckily the other's only a threepenny tram ride away. But the thing that really chills the blood is when these two come towards you and they don't make any sound at all!

I can't tell you much more about them because my medication is wearing off and my one true love has just called me down to tell me the Valium soup is ready. So I'm going to stand up now and try to get the two monsters off my person and carefully make my way downstairs from the attic. Heck, I think the candle's just gone out!

'You, Rag-arse. Leave the printer alone and put my scissors back! And you, Whiningfatgreedybitch. Get your claws out of the scanner! And stay where I can see you! I won't be long my One True Love. If you'd just like to come up and give me a hand?'

"HARGH"!

'Hurry Dear! Grief, I hope they haven't left anything on the stairs.'

Richard Lee Wilson 2002

Black Bob

It was getting very noisy in the Golden Hind. There were a lot of raised voices and the atmosphere was not convivial to say the least. Black Bob leaned on his staff, which was shorter than a shepherd's crook, but longer than a walking stick. He didn't say much. He was a big-built, quiet sort of person. Some say he's as crafty as a fox! Some say he's worse than a fox. Others say he's even-tempered and difficult to upset. However, they all say he does like a good laugh and if at someone else's cost, the better he likes it. But at the moment and as far as Black Bob was concerned, there was nothing much to laugh at in here! He was surprised White Bob didn't put a stop to it. Robert Hughes (Black Bob's given name) decided to go and sit at a table by the door; at least he could get a bit of fresh air there. He would have preferred a table outside but it was raining. He knew it would be. In fact it was absolutely pouring down and the wind was gusting. He sat down and leaned his staff against the wall.

'Hey Bob!' he shouted to the landlord. 'Are you going to calm it down a bit? Noise is giving me a headache. It's more like a townies pub!'

He'd heard some young blokes moan. Then he heard them bragging about their orienteering skills and how many awards they'd got and how many times they'd won this and that, he was fed up of listening. They got plenty in here like them. I might take them on thought Black Bob.

'Got to earn a living somehow,' he muttered.

Bob, the white-haired landlord, called out to the instigators to hush it a little.

This was Black Bob's way in. 'There's nobody better at fell walking than I am! I'll take anybody on. There's fifty pounds in my pocket says I'm the best! And I'll tell you this! With a ten minute start, I could beat you lot blindfolded.'

He waved his staff towards the group sat round the massive centre table and sat back down. The locals grinned and looked knowingly at the young blokes who were having hysterics.

'He means it! If he said he'd do it blindfolded and if you give him a ten minute start, he'll definitely take you on,' said Billy the local gamekeeper. He gave them an odd enquiring look. 'He knows these parts like the back of his hand. Knows every path, every blade of grass and every stone and pebble. If there were any trees up there he'd know them an' all.

He's been a shepherd round here for seventy years or more,' offered Billy, nodding to confirm everything he said was true.

They laughed even louder. 'He looks more like sixty to me!' said the most vocal of the townies with a smirk.

'Looks sixty you say! I'll bet he wishes he was! He's eighty-four but he'll still beat you. Mark my words!' assured Billy dismissively as he went off to the bar chuntering and laughing to himself.

'Will a hundred pounds get you off your backsides?' challenged Black Bob, standing to his feet.

'If you want to give us a hundred pounds granddad, then we'll take it from you!'

'I doubt it very much sonny,' snapped Black Bob, who wasn't their granddad and didn't like being called it by strangers. 'I'll get my hat and coat and I'll meet you outside. Bob! Bring something that will do for a blindfold. I'll be at the bottom of the steps!'

Black Bob grinned to himself as he got his hat and coat. White Bob grinned and shook his head and opened a cupboard under the bar.

The rain had lessened slightly but rain didn't trouble him in the least, he was used to it. White Bob brought a bar towel and some string. The townies followed him out. Black Bob was leaning on his staff as he stood patiently a little way out into the road.

'Nasty weather,' said White Bob as he fastened the blindfold securely over Black Bob's eyes. 'How's that? Does it feel comfortable?'

'It's fine Bob, don't fret yourself.' Black Bob adjusted it slightly.

White Bob sniggered as he thought 'candy from babies!'

'I'm ready. Are the others?'

'We're ready.'

'Are they blindfolded Bob?'

'No, Bob they're not.'

'That's fair enough. Have they got a map?'

'Yes we've got a map.' There was much sarcasm in the leader of the group's reply that didn't go unnoticed by Black Bob.

'Right, the first to the Griff Inn in Blakedale wins the pot. If you don't mind I'd appreciate some of you locals going over there in your motorcars. That way you can make sure nobody does any cheating!'

'Hey, just a minute you,' snapped the same young bloke. 'Who's going to check on you?'

'Don't take that tone of voice with me sonny, and if you're worried about me cheating, one of your lot can come with me and a couple of your lot can go to the finish. I can't say any fairer than that can I Bob?'

'No that's fair enough. Right then who's going with Black Bob?'

'I will,' replied a tall sandy-haired chap of about twenty-five years of age.

'You'll have to keep up son!' laughed Black Bob. 'Because if you don't, you'll be on your own.'

'Don't worry about me old chap,' smiled the young man. 'I'll keep up.'

'So how many of them are left to go orienteering Bob?'

Black Bob burst out laughing. 'I've never heard such a thing.' He burst out laughing again.

'Three, Bob. Two of them are going straight to Blakedale with Billy and Walter.'

'Right off we go then. Make sure they give me a ten minute start Bob.'

'I'll make sure Bob.'

Black Bob set of at a steady but determined pace. He used his staff constantly to feel the ground and the edge of the road. The pair was soon out of the village and heading for the moor. The sandy-haired chap began to think Black Bob had the longest stride in the world. There were times when the young man had to run two-legged, crabwise, to keep up.

'How far is it to Blakedale?' he asked taking short, sharp breaths.

'Three-and-a-half miles or so. It's not all that far. Oh, and if you've brought your map, throw it away. It won't be any use up here!' replied Black Bob as if he was taking a stroll through the park. Off he went increasing the pace slightly and using the staff to feel his way over the rough terrain.

'If you need to rest, we'll be at the top in a few minutes. You can sit down there for a while if you like. You can always run to catch me up. It's downhill for a bit at the other side. And Son, don't get it into your head that I'll fall for any of your delaying tactics. I might be as old as old Alice's grandmother but I'm still right in the head!'

'I don't know what you mean by tactics! I'm fine. You can do what you like.'

'Whatever you say Son.'

He wasn't fine, he was far from fine and he wasn't using tactics. He'd never in his life been orienteering at this pace, and he'd never been this short of breath, and he'd only had four pints of lager! It has to be the two steak and kidney puddings that filled me up. His murmurings were swiftly collected by the cold wind and carried west. They reached the top. Black Bob a good first by at least a hundred yards. The young man followed and sank to his knees.

'I must have a breather, I'm gasping.'

'It's the air Son, it's thin up here,' called Black Bob over his shoulder. But he pressed on down the moor as if the air was pure oxygen.

Black Bob was a quarter of a mile away before the sandy-haired chap got to his feet then set off running down the moor like a mountain goat running to serve six lady goats in waiting. He hadn't run two-hundred yards when, with a loud yell of surprise, he tripped over a sturdy root, fell headlong into a hidden bracken-hollow and found when he tried to stand up that he'd sprained his ankle. He then found when he tried to get the muck off his face that he'd also broken his wrist. With gritted teeth, he crawled slowly out of the hole using his bad elbow and his good hand and leg. He knelt, easing himself onto one knee and looked into the distance searching for Black Bob. He was nowhere to be seen.

The young man threw a wobbler. Then, having realised that ranting and raving had achieved nothing, he set off limping furiously down the moor. The rain, which minutes before had been driven by gale force winds, almost horizontally across the face of the moor, had now almost stopped and he saw, much to his sorrow that the moor raised higher again. Yet this aspect was steeper, darker and wilder. He could see a belt of rain gathering on the skyline but he could see no sign of Back Bob or as he had begun to call him, Black-hearted Bob. How the old man, complete with blindfold traversed this mournful wilderness was a mystery to the young man. He told himself the old bugger must be an alien! He knew he himself wasn't one because his ankle was half as big again and his wrist was throbbing like hell.

Black Bob had slowed down during the storm but now he was pushing on again at a fair pace. The staff had swapped frequently from hand to hand but it had never stopped its 'to-ings' and 'fro-ings' as he checked the ground for the almost hidden sheep track across the moor. Once a shepherd always a shepherd he told his staff. He was three quarters of the way there and as yet he hadn't taken a breather. He didn't worry about the nitwits giving chase, after the sudden storm they would be lost or if they used their map they'd be climbing their way out of Cragston-old-quarry. Or worse they could well wander into Minging Mire. He would come back with a search party and find them; it had all happened before. He'd get expenses as they called them. He being a master of his craft new full well what the weather would do. Before going walking he always listened to the forecast on Radio Four. It was one of his golden rules! Another was 'make hay while the sun shines' and he was doing that now. In fact if he had checked his watch and counted his steps he would have known that he did the last mile or so in less than fourteen minutes.

He was with Billy and a couple of others in the Griff Inn. He was still wearing his blindfold and drinking a glass of Morgan's rum. He drank Morgan's because it had a picture of a pirate on the label.

'They'll catch you out one day mister and your cronies, you mark my words.' His wife Nellie was forever going on about the way he made his living. 'You lot are worse than pirates. Cheating people out of their money. And I'll bet you wore a blindfold and demanded a ten minute start. I know all about your tricks.'

Black Bob would ask what's for supper. 'Home-made steak and kidney pie,' she'd say. He'd reply, 'Are you having some?'

'Course I am.'

'Are you? Did you have the stuff given?'

'Of course not you silly old devil.' Then she'd fuss round the sink making as much clattering noise as possible without breaking anything. His parting words as he went through the door were, 'Well if you bought it with the housekeeping, you can give it a rest now because you're sharing this pirate's bounty!'

He was well through his second glass when the champion 'orienteers' traipsed in. What a sorry sight. They were dripping wet, covered in mud and slime and chilled to the bone. They'd brought the wounded soldier with them. 'You've got here then?' said Billy not quite with a smirk, and looked at his watch. 'You took more than an hour and three quarters longer to get here than Black Bob did and that's after deducting the ten minute start you gave him. I'd say he's the winner by a long chalk. These friends of yours will confirm what I say.' He looked across at them.

They nodded. 'He's been here more than an hour, Gary. He beat you fairly.'

'I don't believe it. He's supposed to be in his eighties!'

'I am in my eighties Son but I didn't have a map to follow so I kept away from Minging Mire! I take it by the smell in here you didn't!'

'No we didn't. And we've been laughed at in the Griffin that, as you well know, is half a mile to the east of here, which by coincidence is in the wrong direction.'

'I can't think why you went there lad, I told you plain enough we'd meet in the Griff Inn!'

The leader sniffed and wiped his muddy hands on his trouser legs. 'Oh yes you told us all right! No mistaking the Griff Inn from the Griffin. Oh and old man, while we're on the subject of places to avoid, I've marked (for future reference you understand) the position of that stinking bog-hole on the map.'

He's holding his temper pretty well thought Billy.

'You shouldn't have bothered,' said Black Bob, not intentionally rubbing salt in the wound. 'It's only there from late December to the end of March, beginning of April time. It's dry the rest of the time.'

'I'm sure you'll correct me if I'm wrong,' sneered the leader, 'But is it not mid May right now?'

'No you're right Sonny it is, but you see it's rained a lot lately so this year it's hanging on a bit. Like it is on you three.'

It was obvious to all that the leader wanted to strangle Black Bob there and then!

'Right then, settling up time!' said Black Bob happily.

'Before we settle up, I want to check that blindfold!' snapped the leader.

There was utter silence. Without a word Black Bob stood, took off the blindfold and dropped it on the table. Slowly, he sat back down. Gary picked it up and covered his eyes. Then like a stiff-necked puppet he searched for a source of light. He couldn't find one.

'Well?' asked Billy.

Grudgingly, Gary said he couldn't see anything through the towelling.

'Well then?' asked Black Bob with a scowl. 'Are you going to cough up or not? I can feel a thirst coming on.' He gave a wry smile to nobody in particular.

'You could have taken it off when you left Sandy in that state,' accused Gary nastily. '

'Firstly lad, I didn't leave your pal in a state. I'd no idea he was in a state. And him being in a state, as you call it, was no fault of mine. I told him before we left he'd have to keep up. Well he couldn't. Am I right Son?' growled Black Bob.

'Yes you are. Perfectly right. For goodness sake Gary pay up. We were beaten fair and square.'

'And secondly lad 'cause I didn't take the blindfold off. But you'll have to take my word for that.'

'If you say so!' Gary threw their money on the table.

Billy picked it up and gave it to Black Bob.

'I won't thank you lad; you're a poor sport. But you've learned a lesson; a bit expensive but well worth it. Drinks are on me lads. Pints mind. No shorts.' Gary declined and turned from the company.

Black Bob got to his feet, leaned on his staff and said, 'You come back here lad. You still think I took the blindfold off. It wouldn't have mattered if I had lad.'

Gary had turned to make some sort of apology and he'd seen Black Bob's blank gaze go straight past him.

Richard Lee Wilson 2006

Buried Treasure

During my lifetime I have experienced more failed adventures than one can shake a stick at. After each failure I unfortunately find myself in a rut. Although I must point out, it is often of my own choosing! I, like everyone else no doubt, have always found when stepping into the said rut it is no more than two inches deep. However, when I finally decide to step back out, I have found it to be sheer-sided and possessing a depth in excess of twenty feet! This I believe is referred to as the long slippery-slope and one is from birth to death warned to be wary of its perilous lure.

During one of my forays into the deepest rut imaginable, and while staring with boredom at the morbid reflection of my face in the clear depths of my third glass of cider, I heard a voice say, 'What the hell are you doing in here? I thought you were dead.' Having recognised the speaker as the sole cause of the present rut, I looked up in surprise to confirm the source of this uncalled for interruption to my musings and sure enough standing before me was Walter Winterbottom. His appearance (since my last reluctant foray with Walter) had most certainly altered for the better.

'Goodness me,' I exclaimed as cheerfully as possible and offered him my hand, which he accepted and shook warmly and firmly.

'What a remarkable surprise and coincidence. You thought I was aloft with the angels and I thought the same had happened to you!'

'Could have been old boy. I got decidedly close to the angels. Last little adventure near had me done for! Escaped by the very skin of my teeth. Damned aeroplane spat half the starboard wing off and the plane began to spin like the dickens. Couldn't reach my parachute because the damned thing had whizzed off down to the tail end. Thought I'd had it for sure! Mixture of umbrella pines and palm trees broke my fall and jolly-well most of my bones. Spent six months on my back don't you know? Went through damned purgatory.'

'Hard luck old chap. I am very sorry to hear it. But no, I had no idea. I heard some time ago from Ambrose that you were killed in a train crash somewhere south of Delhi.'

'No old boy, plane crash on the South Pacific island of Dahli. I can't think for the life of me where he got that from, obviously inaccurate or I wouldn't be here talking to you, would I, 'eh?'

'Most certainly not and I must say you appear to have made a most remarkable recovery!'

'I have George; it is in fact a miracle I survived the crash! The islanders got me out of the wreckage in the nick of time. Damned thing went up in flames within minutes. They took me to their witch doctor and he was an absolute marvel. He set each and every shattered piece of bone as if he was, in all honesty, doing a jigsaw puzzle. Frightened the life out of me when I first saw him. He wore some sort of mask in the shape of a giant red-beaked bird with huge staring eyes. Thing must have weighed half a ton. Bits of bone, ivory rings and animal teeth sticking out of his flesh! Thought the fellow was going to eat me. I was completely awake through it all, don't you know. Gave me a potion that tasted three notches below disgusting, but by George, if you know what I mean! Ha ha, it did the job. Never felt a thing. Do you know George, one looks like a good three-and-a-half pound of pork sausages when one's opened up! I still tip the scales at fourteen stones exactly and look at me, not a gram of fat to be seen anywhere! I've still got the extra bit under the chin old chap but that's been there for ever. My own Doctor has had a look at me, said although he found it incredible to believe, he couldn't for the life of him see any sign of the wounds I'd suffered. Not a stitch, not a bruise, not a scar, nothing! Utterly remarkable is what he said and he isn't one to fuss. Now enough about me. What have you been doing with yourself of late? You look as if you could do with a good square meal or two!'

'Do I indeed?'

'Indeed you do.'

'Well be that as it may and in answer to your question, I have been doing nothing much. Hardly a thing actually; so my appearance has nothing to do with overwork. I spend most of my time in here. I don't seem to have any enthusiasm or the thirst for adventure that I once had. I've got into a bit of a rut of late. Actually, I'm bored to tears most of the time, Old Boy.'

'Well George, if it's sympathy you want you won't find it in this quarter. Would you bring me a double whisky landlord? Chop, chop.'

'I'll just finish here and then I'll bring it over. Won't be a moment, Sir.' Butterworth, not used to being treated like a servant, scowled at Walter. Walter elected to ignore him.

Walter sat down uninvited and placed a rather crudely decorated, odd shaped medallion in the centre of the table. I for the moment elected to ignore it.

'What do you think of that George?'

'Is it some sort of tribal token?' I asked but without much enthusiasm.

'Why not pick the thing up and examine it closely?'

I sniffed and took it from the table. 'Where did you get it? And what the dickens is it made of? It weighs nothing at all.'

'I found it!' he said looking beyond me. I knew he was lying!

'I haven't the faintest idea what it's made of,' he continued. 'But...' Walter leaned across the table and in a hushed voice said, 'All the islanders' weapons are fashioned out of this. Their bows, which are only two feet long, can send an arrow over two-hundred yards. It is absolutely incredible what they do with the stuff. Knives that can cut through stone! Well not quite stone, but definitely good hard wood! Flunk only knows how they work it into the shapes they form. It's harder than tool steel. I've had it tested. I couldn't believe my own eyes nor could the engineer! I tell you Old Chum, there's a world wide market for this metal. Think what it could do for the aviation industry alone, never mind the military! Hilarious when one thinks about it. We've searched all our lives for buried treasure, hidden treasure, lost treasure and then – I fall from the sky and jolly well land on it.'

I looked at him as he laughed like a donkey and wondered, 'What exactly have you got on your mind, Walter?'

He took his drink from the landlord, took a swallow and leaned back in his chair. 'It's clear to me that you stole it!' He ignored the accusation.

After a few minutes of silence, it was obvious that he was having a good deal of difficulty making a decision. I assumed it was whether or not I was to be trusted with the knowledge of the metal's origin, or if I was to be involved in whatever scheme he had formulated to exploit this so-called buried treasure. Having placed his glass on the table, he gave a barely perceptible nod. I knew at that moment I was to be included!

'I can see a fortune in this George, a huge fortune. And contrary to what you think, I did not steal the token. This was given to me in exchange for my lighter and cigarette case. Do let me explain George.'

'I was merely interrupting Walter because I am curious as to why you are telling me all this and I was not aware of you taking up smoking!'

'I will come to that in due course George. When I was rescued I was carried to their village. I lost consciousness on the way and remember only very little before the operation. It was much later that I discovered they had gone through my pockets. They had laid the contents on a small decorated table; it being an altar to whatever deity they worshipped. Hadley's cigarette case and lighter were among them. But they had laid them out to match the design on the altar in perfect detail and the design you can see etched into this token. They took nothing from me and asked for nothing. I was with them for three years before they exchanged gifts. I thought I had drawn the short straw when they offered this in exchange for the case and lighter, but not when I realised the potential. This is better than a gold mine and I want you to be part of it! Well, what about it?' Walter relaxed and in a polite manner ordered another whisky.

'How do you propose we exploit it? Do you intend taking a cart-load of cigarette cases and lighters with the intention of bartering for the metal?'

'No, no, no. Come on, hardly that Old Chum. So you are with me then?' He looked excited I thought I ought to tread carefully, knowing how many of Walter's escapades had turned sour.

'Not at all, I want all the details before I even consider committing myself.'

'But you said "we." I thought…' He shook his head. 'Not to worry what I thought.'

Walter looked miffed but pressed on. 'Can you see the drawing on the token represents a volcano standing proudly between two smaller mountains?' He handed me the medallion.

'Yes, I can see it quite clearly. I think that is where the metal can be found!'

He smiled broadly. 'I take it you are referring to the volcano?'

'Indeed I am.' He smiled again. I didn't smile; I frowned and asked him why he thought the metal came from the volcano.

'They worship the volcano Old Chum. That's why it's drawn on the altar, and what's more when I asked Kalus the head man if I could accompany them to see the volcano close up as it were, he went spotty. "It is forbidden for strangers to enter the holy place!" he snarled. "You must not go near!" His face was like thunder and he threatened me with certain death if I disobeyed his command! I was extremely careful after that little episode. The funny thing is George, every time they go to worship at the volcano, a lot more of the metal appears around the village. That's why I am convinced it is somewhere near there.'

I downed the remains of my cider, rested my elbows on the table and cupped my hands under my chin before I answered. He could see from my attitude that I thought the whole thing was a crushing bore!

'I don't wish to be tedious Walter but it is to say the least, rather flimsy evidence. This additional metal appearing in the village could be a total coincidence. The natives could get the metal from any source, either en route to the shrine or on their return, or for that matter anywhere at all. What distance is it from the village to the volcano?'

79

'No more than five miles, George. The island is a mere thirty miles wide and forty miles long; it's an absolute dot on the atlas. One can just about see the volcano from just beyond the edge of the village. There are a few sparse trees and brown vegetation on the foothills at its base. It looked quite forbidding when I saw it through my binoculars!'

'I would rather not be a stick in the mud Walter, but I hardly think I am up to this sort of mad escapade. Why not approach Reginald with your scheme. He is more than well off and there was some mention of him looking for something to occupy his free time. Don't recall who mooted it but it was in the last week or two.' I stifled a yawn, stepped back into my rut and put the token on the table.

'But George, you are being a stick-in-the-mud, if I may say so. And an absolute one to boot and why do you suppose I need financial backing? Nothing can be further from the truth! I have more than enough capital to sponsor a dozen trips like the one I propose. I must say George, if you will forgive my being candid, but it was your wife Rosemary who suggested I speak to you; it would appear she is rather concerned about you. Now if I've put my foot in it you must tell me.'

'Both feet Walter. Rosemary is my ex-wife and has been for the last two years! My present situation is not my adulteress ex-wife's concern!' I gave him a baleful stare and ordered another glass of cider.

'Thank you Butterworth. Pop it down there.'

'No need for the glare Old Chum, you have only yourself to blame. You should have given her more attention. Lovely creature like that deserves better!'

'She's not a horse, Walter, and had I spent less time with you and your chums (as you call them) I have no doubt we would still be together!'

'That's all well and good and can't be changed but you can do something about this.' Walter waggled the token in the air. 'Think of it man, think of the lovely lolly!'

'I have enough capital to last the rest of my life and beyond. I do not need money Walter!'

'No need to snap at me Old Chum.' Walter looked peeved to say the least and remained silent for a time.

'Think then of the adventure George.'

I sighed.

'At least think of that, won't you? I've worked out a good old scheme. We hire a couple of helicopters in Jaluka, which is no more than two-hundred miles away. We fly in before dawn on a Monday. They worship on

Sunday, which will give us six days to find the mine. If we haven't found the mine by then, we just fly away and come back the following Monday and so on! Quick, clean and clever! It's as simple as that Old Chum. Well what do you say then?'

'I say it is difficult to decide whether the gleam in your eyes denotes enthusiasm or the first signs of insanity.'

Walter, for some reason, thought my remark hilarious.

'I was being serious Walter. How, for goodness sake, do you know the source of the material is a mine? How indeed do you know the natives will not just pop over to the volcano to ascertain what all the commotion is about? Do you intend to go in armed to the teeth as you did on the last little adventure we shared? You will remember the one I refer to. It was the one in which you shot me in the leg and the one after which Charles finished up in hospital for eighteen months. He still considers himself lucky to be alive. And further more he is a mere shadow of his former self!'

'I must say I take great offence to what you're inferring. My shooting you in the leg was an accident – nothing more. You make it sound as though I shot at you deliberately, and what happened to Charles was unavoidable. You know he was never one to follow orders. He always thought his way was better!'

'But you should have taken that into account before you sent him up there. I or one of the others should have gone with him.'

'I couldn't wet-nurse him George. It would have left our team another man short and we were few enough as it was. God almighty! Am I to be blamed for the weather? The rains came early. Hardly any fault of mine. Had he taken the grappling hook as instructed and secured it to the rock face, the accident would never have happened. It was his careless attitude that did for him George, not my lack of attention to detail. I really do think you go too far.'

'No use pouting like a schoolgirl, Walter. There were a number of serious incidents you could have avoided.'

'What serious incidents? I can think of no others?'

'The Reginald incident springs to mind.'

'My God! Do you put the responsibility for his drinking foul water at my door? Goodness me!' Walter huffed and shook his head.

'Do remember, George, that he had the same water purification tablets as the rest of us. Was I to follow him about like a shadow? Was I to sweep the bugs from his food? Was I to wash his hands and face? A nanny I am not! You give me no credit whatsoever for all the excellent effort I took for a trouble-free expedition. Hardly, fair Old Chum. I must say, not at all fair of you George.'

'Do have another whisky before you burst into tears. Same again, Butterworth, and bring the cheese platter over. Oh and some of those pineapple segments while you are about it! I need a nibble. How about you Walter? Because according to you I most certainly do!'

'If you have any humble pie Butterworth, fetch me over your largest slice please!'

'That's more like it Walter.'

'Really George, you are an absolute swine!'

The platter arrived.

'Here take a piece of the Stilton. Would you like me to sprinkle a dusting of sugar on it?'

'No I would not.'

He swept the crumbs from his handlebar moustache as though a couple of flies had landed on each end of it. We were silent as we returned to our nibbles and our thoughts. I wondered to myself whether or not to further rag him by mentioning the pearl diving incident. Because the only black, round and shiny object I encountered in that filthy lagoon that resembled a black pearl, was a disgusting venomous sea caterpillar. The vile creature was not worth the square inch of sea bed it occupied and after barely touching the thing it brought me out in a pox of a rash! I decided I ought not. Enough is enough.

'George?' asked Walter, leaning back and twiddling with his moustache. 'Do you remember the time when you picked up that black wormy thing? You thought it was a pearl! That was hilarious. Your face looked like a half-pound of potted beef.'

'No Walter, I have never given it a thought. I was thinking of the time you fell into the crevasse and was lost for three days. I certainly remember the colour of your nose at the time of your rescue, but not the exact shade. Was it signal-red or did we decide it was cherry-red?'

'If that was raked up to amuse you, and by the look on your face it has, then I tell you it has not amused me, George. What would cheer me up no end would be your agreeing to accompany me and two or three others on our trip to Dahli!'

'In truth, I am sure it would be more than a delight, Walter, but I have made other arrangements of which I thought you were aware. She is, after all, your niece.'

Walter looked surprised. In fact Walter looked astonished and stared at me for a good few seconds before saying with some sarcasm, 'The girl informed me that she was accompanying a handsome middle-aged gentleman on a motoring tour of the Scottish Isles. I wasn't told the handsome gentleman's name. Never dreamed it could be you. What with the age difference don't you know?'

'Thank you for that Walter, and no, I don't know,' I replied with equal sarcasm. 'But I would have thought my age is hardly any of your business!'

'True old chum, perfectly true. Well on that friendly note I will finish the last of the Stilton, George old chum and be on my way. I do hope 'accompanying' is not a banal euphemism for other things!'

Walter got to his feet.

'Poppy is more than of age, Walter old boy.' I stressed the old boy bit but he appeared not to notice. 'And, I am now a single man. She professes to be deeply in love with me etc and so on. She is a very beautiful, very intelligent young lady and as you must know, she is a lady in the truest sense of the word!'

'Indeed she is George, as all the Winterbottom's are. Do have an enjoyable tour. Now I must be off. Lot's to organise.'

'I will say have the best of luck and safe return. I do sincerely hope you unearth your buried treasure!'

'Goodbye old boy.'

'Goodbye old chum.'

Poppy and I had a perfectly magnificent six weeks touring the Scottish Isles before we turned south, crossed the English Channel and entered France. I did however have some reservations about the trip to Scotland. The main one being that I had always considered Scotland to be a bleak, rain-sodden land inhabited by rugged and surly barbarians. I was delighted to find that this was not the case. I found them most hospitable, helpful and exceedingly charming. Understanding their language at machine-gun-pace-delivery on the other hand was another matter, but even this small impediment spoiled our enjoyment not one jot.

Poppy and I remained in France where we discovered each other more fully, until the Sunday of the first week in August. The heat and the hustle and bustle of the tourist season around that time is more than one should be expected to bear. Poppy sports a delicate complexion and the strong sunlight (as with all fair-skinned people) unless fully protected against, can wreak havoc, and in the worst scenario, serious epidermal damage. I, being dark, was perfectly at ease with the glaring sun but not the perspiring crowds.

We were married within a month of our return and named our firstborn, George Poppy, in respect and in honour of my paternal grandpapa and Poppy's maternal Grandmamma; although Poppy refers to her with deep affection as 'that so-and-so-ing old witch'. I have remarked most forcibly and on numerous occasions that the expletive, whilst in company at least, should be replaced by a more suitable and far less taboo description but alas and to the chagrin of my older acquaintances this has not happened.

Poppy loves to ride. I, having lost my Dear father to a riding accident, prefer anything but. This all consuming hobby is not in any way detrimental to our marriage or our complete happiness, in fact I have a fine example of Stubbs's work hanging in pride of place above the mantel in my study. I, on the occasions that Poppy goes a galloping, go over to the nearby ruins of a monastery with my trusty short-handled 'digger' and my 'picking hammer'. I have over the last year or so unearthed numerous 'finds'; mainly, small pieces of pottery, roman coins and the like. But that was until yesterday! Yesterday, while inspecting what appeared to be some sort of Celtic or Stone Age headstone, I inadvertently broke through the thin surface of a rock-hard but small clay mound and tumbled headlong into a small underground chamber. Thankfully I had the foresight to take the crouched position before crashing onto the uneven floor. One can only imagine my utter delight when I noticed the glimmer of gold over in the left-hand corner, which fortunately was within easy reach of my grasp. Ignoring the amount of rubble that cascaded around me I calmly collected the 'find'. Had I laughed hysterically, which I felt inclined to do, I am positive I would have suffocated on the swirling clouds of dust. Having secured the 'find' on my person and having covered my mouth and nose with my handkerchief, I realised I would be extremely well advised to extricate myself from my present and dangerous situation. The rubble from what I assumed had been an arched roof was, I was quick to notice, still falling in at a pace. I also realised that the edge of the hole (even though I was standing in and on a heap of debris) was well beyond my reach! I refused to panic although I was seriously tempted. I considered taking my handkerchief from my mouth and bellowing at the top of my voice for help, but the thick, swirling dust put paid to that idea. The debris on the floor of the chamber by this time had reached three or four inches below my knees, and I was experiencing great difficulty moving my feet. I was beginning to think that I and my treasure would slowly but surely be entombed in this dreadful place!

I have always found it unwise to employ the use of superlatives whilst in the company of the recipient. When one is elsewhere it is (and of course if it is the truth) acceptable. I find it morally reprehensible to be informed that so-and-so is a delightful conversationalist, or so-and-so is beauty personified only to discover on meeting the said beauty that not only does she resemble Punchinello, she has a very similar manner of speech. I on the other hand, give praise only where praise is warranted. I was giving praise yesterday because it was deserved and I was using superlatives ceaselessly! Poppy was out riding at the time I was concerning myself with the serious predicament I inadvertently found myself in. With the kind of good fortune usually reserved for others, my precious angel came a galloping by the ruin. Poppy, thank God, saw the cloud of dust billowing from the underground chamber. Within minutes, Poppy had dismounted, alerted herself as to my position, alerted me as to hers and was off back to the Hall for a set of ladders and the gardener. Within twenty minutes I was out of the filthy pit and breathing the beautifully clean air of Rutland. On that occasion my beloved Poppy deserved every superlative known to man! Sadly, I lost not only my trusty digging implement but also any further desire to continue as an amateur archaeologist.

The buried treasure, however, was worth every moment of terror in what I found out later was indeed a burial chamber. I refrained from mentioning my 'find' when I gladly handed over the dig to the professionals from Westmunster. Finder's keepers and all that, and our thirteenth century golden chalice sits and gleams in all its glory on the mantel below the Stubbs in my study. The professionals appeared content with their 'finds' that consisted of a shattered skull, broken bones and some sort of belt buckle. It would appear from the caustic remarks of Professor Tinley that my fall into the chamber brought about most of the bone and skull shattering. He also stated in language unfit for the corporals' mess, that blundering amateurs ought to be kept under lock and key! Walter, no doubt would in the future get wind of my unforeseeable accident and use it to his advantage!

'Telegram for you darling, it's from Dear Uncle Walter.'

Poppy really does have the most melodious voice imaginable and when she laughs it is like the singing of an elfin choir.

'Bring it through would you Poppy. Oh, why have you not opened it darling?'

'Because it's for you George!'

'Silly thing. Stay with me if you wish while I read it. Here sit on the arm of my chair.'

She was wearing L'Air du Temp: perfectly apt. My first wife Penelope wore Scarlet Lady: also perfectly apt. Walter may be well travelled and he may have explored 'Darkest Africa', but he certainly has not explored the darkest side of Rosemary. At least not to my knowledge! I opened the wire with some misgivings. Nearly a month had elapsed since I last heard from him and the only information I got then was, 'Found it George-see enclosed sample!' He was tardy at the best of times but a month, even for Walter, was exceptionally tardy. This latest telegram read as follows.

'George.-Not metal- Do not put sample in water- Bloody savages - Unbelievable- Bodies interred below volcano-Bizarre chemical reaction-Material extremely well-baked human remains- team and I spotted- All hell broke loose-Heading out Tues 23. Must stay other side of Volcano-Weather atrocious.'

I laughed and laughed. 'Well that appears to be the end of that little expedition, Poppy my beloved!'

'What on earth does the telegram mean, George?'

'The finish to one of your Uncle's madcap schemes! And I do hope sincerely that it will be his last. Metal indeed! I should have known better.'

Poppy laughed and tapped my shoulder.

'What do you find so funny my angel?'

'He's also your Uncle now darling.'

'Pooh and double pooh to that my love and while you're up, would you pass me the paper-knife there on my desk.'

'This one darling?'

'No sweetheart, the weird-looking thing at the other side of my blotter.'

'This one with the handle shaped like a volcano?' Poppy held it up.

'Yes that one.'

'It doesn't weigh very much George, what is it made of?'

'Poppy my darling, you do not want to know!'

She handed it to me. I shook my head and smiled. There was barely a clatter as the dreadful thing disappeared into the waste basket!

'Actually my darling Poppy, our imbecile of an uncle failed to spot the greatest treasure of all! And I do believe it had at one time, stared him in the face!'

Richard Lee Wilson 2005

Fatally Fat.

What with over-eating, smoking and drinking in excess, lack of exercise and a dozen other ways to blow your heart to bits, it's a wonder we dare leave our beds. I am very pleased to say that I never over indulge in any of the former and I leave my bed at will. I have the build of the person who, when lying on the beach gets sand kicked in his face. Fortunately it has never happened, but I am of slight build. It doesn't bother me now and it didn't bother me then, not one bit. I was happy to weigh eight-and-a-half-stone then, and look like a healthy bag of bones. I am very happy to weigh about the same now, and I've every reason to be happy! My girlfriend at that time, was of a similar weight, perhaps two or three pounds lighter. It was never an issue between us, there was no competition. We are not of a competitive nature, not then nor now. She is my wife now and still about the same weight.

We suited each other down to the ground and thanks to lady luck we still do. She loved my impetuous nature and my not overly excessive spirit of adventure. I loved her gentle artistic temperament and her ability to create order from chaos. We, although being as far apart in character as the poles are in distance, came together like two deliriously happy magnets. She had and has the face of a solemn imp, haloed by golden hair cut in the pageboy style. Her eyes were forget-me-not blue and they are to this day. She even has those little yellow flecks in them like the centre of the flower. She has lips that would tempt the devil and a body that would tempt any man. I couldn't believe my luck then, when she fell for me, and I still can't! I have the face of a starving Jack Russell. My eyes are raw-umber and if they were any darker they would be black. I have never seen any flecks in them of any colour. My hair is as black as a coalman's armpit. I have it trimmed once a flood and it has always been in the hippy-style of the mid to late sixties. My lips are like everybody else's and my body, well it must have been good enough to tempt the loveliest girl in the world!

Being called every name under the sun has never bothered me in the least either. I've always felt in my life that I've never had anything to prove. Miranda is of the same opinion and is of a like mind. There is however one thing, other than our burning love for each other that we have in common. We are both vegetarians and find it uncomfortable to dine with meat-eaters. That is not to say we never do eat in their company, only that it is uncomfortable! Neither of us preaches, nor ever preached the gospel of vegetarianism but we long and often lectured our closest friends on the dangers of obesity. A lot of the time it wasn't always taken in the spirit it was given, and we did become distanced from some of our old friends… but that's life.

When Miranda was staying for a month with a relative in Paris and I was at a loose end, something happened which positively confirmed my opinion about the dangers of overeating. It didn't happen instantly then and there in the pub. Not at all. It happened in dribs and drabs, but when I think back, that's where the whole thing started. In retrospect I suppose it was a stupid sort of challenge and I was more than stupid for letting myself fall for it. It was crazy how it started. I was on my soap-box going on about animal fat and the harm it can cause; and how it can kill; and how I can run ten miles in a morning and ten more after lunch; and how barbaric and cruel it was to kill and eat God's critters. It was obvious I was missing my soul-mate or I might have shut my big mouth in time and let it all wash over me, but I didn't. I told the three of them they were well overweight and if the fat buggers wanted to live long and healthy lives, they should get rid of their flab, and the sooner the better. I could have put my point with more diplomacy but they were going at the beer as if it was free and I was saving for a digital video camera. Anyway, we were all in our early forties so we should be able to take it as well as give it.

Dan, was in his early forties, but because of his over indulgence in all things looked to be in his mid fifties. He'd reddish hair and a red face and he was the heaviest of the three of them. He'd just got rid of a pint without taking a breath and made a show of putting the glass down firmly on the table. Then he looked at me with a stupidly sly grin, put his hand in his coat pocket and took out a dirty, crumpled piece of paper. He leaned across the table and without a word he dropped it on my beer mat. I leaned forward to get the piece of paper and whatever was wrapped up in it, but he slammed his hand over it.

'Before you read that, Granny, (short for Granville) and before you see what's in there, I want to challenge you to a little test of fitness! You do think you're as fit as a fiddle, don't you? Your neck's about the same width!' Then he laughed and went to the bar.

I retaliated by saying, 'At least I don't buy scarves by the yard or glow in the dark like a stop light.' The other two laughed. I didn't say anything else till he came back with three more pints of bitter and a tonic water for me because I wasn't sure what was coming next. I do like a good pint, but there was no way on earth I could keep up with this trio! I would slot a pint in later on, at a ratio of three to one!

He lowered himself heavily into the club-chair opposite and continued where he'd left off.

'Well, do you think you're fit? Because you'll certainly need to be if you take it on!'

He laughed again but there was an edge to it. It seemed forced. The other two joined in but their laughter was real! I was soon up the ladder and mounting my horse.

'I'll accept any serious challenge you care to throw at me. I've nothing to prove. I'm as fit as the next man and fitter than some. But, I'm not an athlete and I never said I was! So if it's some sort of sporting event, well pal, forget it!'

'Shall we show it to him?'

'Why not?' Laughed Graham who had the haircut of a Marine but not the lean angular face to go with it. He did have, at one time. In fact at one stage I used to envy his looks and his physique but not now, too much sagging flesh nowadays. Dan took his hand away from the crumpled piece of paper and nodded to me to go ahead.

The crumpled piece of paper was a map; well hardly a map as such. The only reason I guessed it was a map was that north was shown in the top right-hand corner. There were rough outlines of trees, hills, rivers or streams and what I supposed was a cave in some sort of Lego building. It looked as if it had been built by a blind stonemason at the base of a cliff face. It could have been a rabbit hole in a banking behind some tree stumps because nothing was to any scale. There was a pile of something in the middle of the map that looked like lumps of grey coal. Perhaps the two intersecting lines outside the cave or rabbit hole could be a cross or a camp fire? But that bit was well-creased and dirty. The few legible place-names were scrawled like a child's scribble. In fact the whole thing looked like the creation of a bored child, who'd been told to go and draw something for his grandma! I supposed if I shut one eye, it could have been a monochrome Van Gogh landscape. It's what was wrapped up in it that made me burst out laughing. I had to laugh, because the three of them sat there with such looks of eager expectation and excitement on their faces. I'd expected something marvellous or unique to drop into my hand. Instead out popped a dull and dirty piece of broken glass the size of a flattened walnut! How the heck was

I supposed to know what it was? I'm not a diamond expert! Never have been.

'You don't know what it is, do you?' accused Dan. His smile had changed to a slight sneer.

'No I don't, and I don't know yet what the challenge is, either.' Graham and Jake were smiling at each other.

'Is it a broken bit off the bottom of a dirty milk bottle? That's what it looks like to me!'

They all laughed at that. Jake's rolls of fat flowed up and down his body as a seal's do when it's making a dash for the sea.

'A broken milk bottle? It's a diamond, you moron. Who in their right mind would want to wrap a piece of broken glass in a map?'

'How am I supposed to know this is a map?' I waved the piece of paper in his face. 'It looks like a child's drawing to me, and if that's a diamond my twonger's a daffodil!'

'It's uncut and unpolished, Granny! And in that cave there,' he grabbed my wrist, forced it onto the table, stabbed my finger hard on the map and said, 'There is over a thousand more of 'em!'

He let go. 'The challenge is, are you fit enough to get them out of there?'

I sniffed, frowned and massaged my wrist. 'Are there really a thousand of them?' They swore there was, and offered me a share! I sipped at my tonic and waited. One of them would, no doubt, come out with some sort of a yarn as to where they got it. And why they wanted me in with them. I didn't have to wait long. I could see they were bursting to tell me, but what I couldn't understand was why they wanted to involve me in one of their pathetic escapades. We'd all got married and gone our separate ways long ago. We bumped into each other on occasions when our eccentric orbits collided. We would re-live the past and exaggerate every happening, but we'd outgrown each other and fortunately we didn't meet very often.

Jake broke the silence. 'We were a great team at one time, but more than that Granny, we trusted each other and we need somebody who's fit and someone we can trust!'

He left it there, wagged his sausage of a finger at me and settled back. I didn't remember being part of any team. His expression told me nothing. The other twos' faces were a blank. They were hiding something, but I had no idea what it was! We chattered on about nothing in particular. I tried to hide my curiosity. It was my round so I went to the bar. We all had the same again. I'd hardly sat down when Dan suddenly leaned towards me and said, 'It's your build Granville. We need somebody who can squeeze through the entrance to the cave. It's cut into solid rock and we wouldn't have a hope in hell of getting through, but you would! That's why we want you in. It's no big deal. Equal shares for everybody.'

He'd called me by my Sunday name, so as far as I was concerned it was a big deal! I was about to ask how they'd got the map and the diamond when Dan held his finger to his lips and hushed me up. I must have shown surprise because it was getting sillier by the minute. He leaned forward and said in a whisper, 'If you want to know more about it, come round to my place after eight o'clock tonight, and we'll talk some more. It's filling up in here. Don't want the world and its neighbours to know, do we?'

'Obviously not!' I agreed. Then after about ten minutes of politically very incorrect, but hilarious jokes, I finished my drink and said I'd see them later and cleared off.

I went straight home and out for a run in the park. By the time I'd got back, showered and eaten and had a think, it was about seven-thirty. I could easily walk to Dan's place in half-an-hour so I decided that's what I'd do. I noticed as soon as I got there it had got bigger. It was difficult to miss. There was a two-storey extension built where the car-port had been and a double garage built at the other side where the lean-to greenhouse used to be. So he must be doing well! I didn't realise, until I was reprimanded later by Rosemary (Dan's stunning wife) that it had been two years since I was last here. I'm sure she fancied me; I could barely shake her off. I hoped Dan didn't notice, and if he did? He didn't let on. Petra and Serene were there. Both were made up to the eyeballs. I gave them both a peck on the cheek and came away with a fiver's worth of blusher on my lips! Neither of them needed splotch all over them, they were both lovely girls.

The lads got serious at about nine-thirty when I was ready for off. You can hardly hark back to the past for hours on end. Five more minutes and I'd have been on my mobile to Miranda. Instead we were sitting round a massive glass-topped table loaded with enough alcohol to send a spaceship to Venus, and enough food to hold an eating contest. No wonder they looked like Wobblies. The map appeared from somewhere with the diamond. Jake started them off.

'If we took this to Amsterdam and had it cut, we would have twenty grand between us. Less the cutting and polishing costs.'

I wondered how they were going to do that because to the best of my knowledge the origin of any diamond had to be registered. I believed it had something to do with the rebels in Sierra Leone or somewhere. I mentioned this. The three of them just laughed. I was getting fed up of being laughed at. Graham said that side of things had been arranged, and we've got a buyer.

'He'll take all we can get. So don't worry about that end, worry about your end. It's a hell of a trek to where we're going.' He raised his highbrows and nodded at the other two for confirmation. They obliged. I hate being patronised. The smug tullucks.

'Do I get to know in which part of the world your secret treasure is stashed? Or is that a secret as well?'

I thought secret treasure was a fair description for the not so famous four! And I kept my face straight!

'Ok, ok,' replied Dan 'let's get on, or this is going to take all night! Look Granny. We can all extract the urine till next Wednesday, but what we're telling you is the truth. There are diamonds, and they are in that cave. The next bit will sound crazy but it's true.' He didn't look me in the eye! He finished his drink and made a show of putting his glass down but I saw his hand shake.

'We got this last year while we were on one of those safari holidays in Kenya. This guy (Mike Crane) we got it from was broke. He approached us in a bar with a sob story about his wife and kids being killed in a car crash and his luck being killed off with 'em. We felt sorry for him. Brits abroad etc. He was half-drunk and would have been out of it if we hadn't got him out of the bar and into our hotel. We sobered him up, gave him a decent meal and got him to relax as best he could. It was obvious there was something on his mind.

'After the meal we went out on the veranda for a smoke and it was a glorious evening. The sunset was better than you see on the holiday programs. He almost ate his cigarette. Then suddenly out of the blue, he asked if we could be trusted. Well, how do you answer that? A complete stranger asks you a question like that. We looked at each other and wondered what was coming. He asked again. We all assured him we could and asked him what it was all about. After a few minutes he told us about the map and the diamonds. He told us about the cave and this hoard of uncut diamonds. He kept going on about it. Said he would swear on the grave of his children that he was telling us the truth. He couldn't raise the money he needed to get back there and have another go at the cave. Could we? We said we could. He told us how narrow the cave entrance was, and that on his last trip he'd no explosives with him. If he had, he said he might have risked blasting the entrance. I told him we could soon get hold of a few sticks of dynamite if that's all we needed. He said it might not be a good idea in case the explosion brought the whole cliff face down. I suggested we hire one of the locals to climb through the entrance if none of us could. He turned that idea down flat. Nobody local could be involved. Too risky! They might talk! And anyway the nearest locals were over a hundred miles away. We need somebody we can trust. Somebody who can keep their mouth shut. The other stipulation was: he's cock of the midden! He said without him the map wasn't worth shit, and without him we'd never find the place. We'd no objections. You've none, I hope?' He gave me a hard stare.

'I haven't said I'm going yet! And you haven't told me where it is, yet! But if I do decide to go, then no, I've no problem with that.'

He looked at the other two. They nodded. 'It's in Africa, and that's all I'm going to tell you. Do you want in? Because if you don't want to make a shed-full of money for a few days' work, there are others who do!' I looked at them and they looked at me. I thought about it. They looked at me. I said, 'I don't know why you keep calling it a challenge, but if you three are fit enough to go, I'm bloody sure I am!' They smiled. Actually, they grinned.

Dan said. 'We'll see!'

I rang Miranda and told her I was going to be away for three weeks. I told her I was going on safari with Dan and co, rather than tell her a downright lie so she wouldn't be worried about me. I also told her we'd be doing a bit of prospecting while we were there. She asked me what for and I answered diamonds. I promised I would bring her back a massive one. We blew each other kisses till our lips went numb, then reluctantly, I replaced the telephone.

I had nothing to do with the travel arrangements or getting the gear we'd need. Dan and the others saw to all that. We flew from Heathrow to Nairobi. When we got off the plane, the heat of the sun was dreadful! We cleared customs and went by taxi to a bar near the city centre where we met our two drivers. It was all very shady and storybook. From there we were driven four hundred miles north to a small scruffy village called Mahuti to rendezvous with Crane. He didn't look broke to me, or starving hungry. He was dressed like a memsahib and looked as fat as Dan and co. The introductions were made and his gear was loaded into the Land Rover that Dan and I were travelling in. Lucky me! I got half buried by the gear on the back seat! The drivers looked as if they'd been living rough all their lives. As we bumped and swayed further into the bush, conditions in the vehicle worsened. Crane didn't like me. I was wary of him. My beloved Miranda classes such characters as, 'Creepy'. I class them as sly. He didn't want to look anybody in the eye, and he laughed a lot. Everybody was his friend. It was great that we'd had a problem-free flight. It was great everything was running like clockwork. The weather was great. Everything was great. He was a great pain in the backside!

The rattling and banging seemed to go on for ever. But it was only three days. Every night the night sounds drove me round the bend. I felt like bait for every animal that howled and screeched. Every day the sun bored down without mercy. It was hell-hole-hot, and I felt as if my mouth and throat had been dusted with coarse talcum powder. On the third day I asked when we were stopping for a decent break. Dan grunted, 'Later.' That's all he said. I began to nod off. Land Rover-lag, I suppose. It was dark when I finally stirred. I'd been left asleep and I felt terrible. They'd set up camp on what at first looked to me (as I staggered like a drunk from the vehicle) an expanse of bare desert with a scattering of rocks here and there.

But when I got my bearings and set off away from the fire to have a pee, Dan shouted, 'Don't go too far, Granny! There's one hell of a drop over there.'

What, in the darkness I'd thought was desert extending away from me, was actually a black nothingness! We were on a plateau and not twenty yards away was a drop of God knows how deep. I didn't go and look. I did what I had to do, came back to the fire and swilled my face with cold water. I had a beer. The two drivers drove off into the darkness. They would return in five days, make camp and wait two more days. They wanted the money up front. If we weren't back in seven days, we were on our own! Nobody waved them off. After they left, nobody spoke. I ate a tin of cold rice pudding and a tin of sliced peaches, said my goodnights and went to bed. That night was strangely quiet. There was the odd bird call or whatever it was but it was a long way away. I was soon asleep and soon awake!

The morning sun burst through the material of the tent like a threat. It promised what was to come later. I was the last to rise and I got a few scowls. I hastily grabbed a bit of breakfast and a strong coffee. The others, supervised by Crane, were lowering ropes over the edge of the cliff and

94

securing them to the biggest of the rocks nearest the edge. All the gear had been unloaded from the Land Rovers and piled up by the cliff edge. Everybody's friend called me over and told me to lend a hand. I took my time. Since when was I his mug, and I didn't like being called, 'Chum' either. I finished my coffee and asked nobody in particular what needed doing. Mr nice guy told me to bring the gear over. I was happy to do that. I wasn't happy when a handgun fell to the ground. I had no idea what sort it was but it looked an evil bloody thing.

'Careful Granny, called Dan. 'That cost a bomb.'

He came over, took it off me, cleaned the dust off it with a handkerchief and stuck it in his belt. I asked him what it was for. He said, just in case!

I said, 'just in case of what?'

'Who knows!' he replied. Then he grinned, touched his finger to his lips as if he was standing on a street corner selling me a watch, and went back to what he was doing. I'd no idea who it was secret from. They'd all heard it clatter on the rocky ground and seen him stick it in his belt. We all had hunting rifles. Mine wasn't loaded and I don't think theirs were. None of us had fired at animals or anything else for that matter. I told them if they did I'd call it a day. Not the phrase I used, but it meant the same. In my opinion it's bad enough for antelopes and baby zebras to keep away from lions and the like, never mind high velocity rifle bullets! They hadn't kicked off about it. They had no desire they said of being big white hunters! I finished carting their gear over and sat down. The sun was doing it's best to toast my brain. I wiped the brim and stuck my hat back on. Wafting it back and forth across my face had been a waste of time.

They were checking the ropes and hoisting kit on to each other's backs; all of them were pumping sweat. I went to help Dan then he helped me with mine. It's a wonder my knees didn't buckle under the weight of it. I oyked mine higher up and tightened the straps. Crane had said we were responsible for our own kit and supplies. It would be tough titty for any of us who lost their gear.

'We need somebody down there to keep the rope tight. And another one up on that outcrop over there to keep an eye open. I don't expect trouble, but we might as well be prepared for it!' Crane looked deadly serious. Then I noticed he'd a handgun tucked in his belt. I'd had my suspicions about this trip all along, but now I was sure this was going to be dangerous as well as illegal. Dan and Crane kept looking back across the bush as if they were expecting someone coming after us. I couldn't see anything because of the heat shimmer. Crane and Dan opted to tie the boxes on the rope. I was elected as lookout; Jake and Graham were sent over the side to take the boxes off. They didn't say what was in the boxes. I hoped it was more tins of fruit. They would leave that rope fastened up here. The others would be coiled up and taken down.

It was hot on the outcrop where I was standing in the full glare of the sun, but they were a lot hotter where they were working. It took over two hours to get down. I said we should have unloaded the gear in the cool of the evening; Jake gave me the finger and told me to concentrate on what I was doing.

'It was only a suggestion,' I called back.

They ignored me. I left the silly sods to it. I was the last to go down. I untied the two ropes they'd lowered the boxes with, and threw them over the side. No way was I carrying those down. I've never done abseiling or bungee-jumping and I didn't like the look of this. I stayed away from the cliff edge till I'd taken a deep breath or two. It was a hell of a drop. The decent was a nightmare! The sides of the cliff face crumbled away every time I tried to get a foothold. The swaying rope dragged across the face of the rocks throwing gravel-like bits of stone in my face and eyes. My pack weighed a ton and the straps bit into what bit of flesh I had over my collar bones. I got a few snide jibes about my strength (well the lack of it) when my knees buckled after I let go of the rope. I couldn't have cared less. At least I didn't look like a baboon's backside, and I didn't have to bob up and down like a German Count at a regimental dinner to get my breath.

I eased the pack off my back and dropped it to the ground; they all did the same. I got a hanky out and coaxed most of the grit out of my eyes. I wasn't prepared for what I saw when my eyes stopped watering, or when I was able (without sneezing) to take in my surroundings! It sounds ridiculous, but we were in a tropical rain forest and we hadn't travelled due north. If we had? The sun was in the wrong place or I was totally disorientated. I pointed this fact out to Dan. He just laughed and said, 'What? Sure, we've come north, you div. Mike knows the way here like the back of his hand.'

'If he does, the moon's up and it's pretty bright!'

I couldn't be bothered with him. If he wanted to keep our whereabouts a secret it was ok by me! I didn't intend coming back, ever! I followed their example and hoisted my kit off the ground. They opened two of the boxes and concealed the other two in the undergrowth. I thought at least it would be our reserve food supply. It wasn't! It was ammunition, machetes and a bundle of brown candles. Now after hiding the empty boxes, the group was heading into a steaming hot jungle that shouldn't have been there; at the bottom of a massive canyon that wasn't on the map of Africa. How do they intend getting out of this place? I hadn't a clue! Climbing down a rope is not the same as climbing up! I followed behind into the steaming green sauna like a toy dog on a string!

Even with the dead weight of my pack and my machete bouncing against my leg it wasn't difficult to keep up with them. Within less than half a mile, Graham and Jake wanted to stop for a rest. They were pumping sweat that was visibly pouring down their faces. Dan and Crane weren't doing any better. Their chests were heaving and their shirts were wringing wet. They didn't want to stop, they made that clear.

'We need to be out of here and at the ruins before dark,' Crane growled.

I hadn't heard of any ruins! Mr everybody's friend was hacking at the undergrowth as if he was trying to kill a wasp and getting nowhere. Jake had dropped his pack and was sitting on it. He was steaming. We were all dressed in light-beige gear like big white hunters but without the funny hats. Now with all the patches of sweat and muck we looked as if we were the SAS wearing camouflage gear. Graham followed Jake's example and dropped his pack. Crane had embedded his machete in the side of a small tree and couldn't get it out. He began to curse it and yank hard on the small handle. Suddenly, he freed it and lost his balance and went over backwards into the undergrowth. As grim as the conditions were, I nearly kinked. Then the other three joined in. This little fiasco probably saved his life, because just above where his head had been, concealed amongst the tangle of creepers was a snake as long and wide as a drainpipe. Just seconds before he went backwards the thing had slithered out of hiding and swung at his head. It missed him by inches. We soon stopped laughing. I hate snakes. He was on his feet instantly – even with the weight of his pack. He went at it with his machete like a mad man but he missed it by miles. The thing was away into the vegetation like a rocket. I'd no idea they could move as fast as that. I shuddered. Couldn't stop myself! Graham and Jake were off the ground like they'd been shot up the arse. Their eyes were everywhere. So were mine. We were hacking our way out of there and on our way to the ruins (wherever they were?) before Jake and graham had got their packs on.

We reached the ruins (shown on the map as a pile of grey coal) at nine o'clock that night. We were to camp there till daylight. I'd never been happier in my life to see a pile of grey coal. The walls of the building were greyish but they were almost completely covered in creepers, moss and tall wide-bladed grasses. The highest of the walls still standing was no more than three feet high where, what was left of them, met like a letter T. The longest wall still standing disappeared into the undergrowth. The rest of the building was rubble. I'd no idea how old it was or what it had been, but it could have been some sort of shrine or temple. There were huge grotesquely-carved bits of statues lying broken on the ground on both the inside and outside of the building. Some had their heads smashed off, some their arms and legs. Some had half arms and legs sticking out of their great fat bellies. In the dimming light they all looked to be males! It wasn't a relaxing place to be. My clothes were stuck to me like they were made out of old wash-leathers. Dan could hardly peel his bush jacket off his back. We were in a foul stinking dump and now we were here, my enthusiasm was fading fast!

It came light at around four-thirty. It was bitter cold and my legs were as stiff as a board. I'd got out of the habit of living rough and awakening even rougher when I'd left Uni. But the memories of nights sleeping on bare boards or in some mate's bath came flooding back. I'd slept like a hunched old crone wrapped in my groundsheet. My arms were as stiff as my legs. I threw the groundsheet off and stood up. It was covered in bugs. I shuddered because I don't like bugs. I creaked and clicked like an old boat. If this is how they bivouacked in the forces, there's no way I'd ever volunteer. Crane was up and about somewhere because he'd got the fire going. I asked Dan, who was hunched against a wall and looked like he'd been trodden on, where Crane had gone.

'Gone for some more wood,' he managed to grunt.

Jake and Graham were making some coffee. I offered to fry some eggs but Crane said (as he came up behind me.),

'There isn't time! Get a coffee and a couple of these down you. They're a lot better than eggs.' They looked like dog-biscuits but they tasted pretty good! He swore there were no meat products in them.

'Fruit cereals, crap like that, but full of energy,' Jake said they were fine and took two more. Crane threw the bits of wood he'd collected on the fire; it wasn't so big but it soon warmed us up.

No sooner had he thrown the wood on when he said, 'Ok, put that out and let's get moving.'

It was five-past-five when we'd got our gear together and was on our way. It was cold and damp in the jungle and as silent as the grave, which seemed creepy to me. Every time I've seen a wildlife program shot in a jungle, it's been full of animal and bird noises. There wasn't a din round the shrine or whatever it had been but there were plenty of noises out here.

We made fair progress that day other than having to stop every hour or less for the Michelin Men to get their breath back. It was my turn to smirk. I'd got my second wind and could have gone on all day without stopping. The undergrowth wasn't as bad as it had been and there seemed to be more air and less damp. It became clear to me as we hacked our way through the vegetation that the ground was rising, not much, but we were definitely climbing. Our upward climb continued all day. We made camp at ten o'clock; they couldn't go any further. I could have gone on for another hour at least, but Crane was boss so we were calling it a day, ok?! He wanted two of us on watch for two three-hour stints. We would rotate and Crane would replace me tomorrow night. I would replace Dan the following night and so on, and no fire, 'Understood?!' Everybody understood. We did our three hours and Jake and Graham did theirs. The night was still and quiet with the occasional howl and screech but I slept like a baby.

Crane had got a fire going; he must like lighting fires. I woke up when Jake prodded me in the ribs with a staff he'd cut. I told him to go and do what his mother told him he shouldn't do till he was married. He said if I wanted a drink and some grub, I'd get out there if I was you. We're breaking camp in ten. I was soon out. I was hungry and thirsty! We didn't pack the tents and gear for half an hour. Seems all of us were hungry!

At midday we reached the top of an outcrop that reared up from the jungle like the back of a rhino when it lowers its head to charge. It was boiling hot. We were out in the open standing on its grey surface and I was wondering where we were going next, because stretching out on all sides was endless jungle.

I was about to turn round and ask when Crane, who was looking though a pair of binoculars at something in the distance said, 'See that Dan? At two o'clock. That's where we're heading. The temple is somewhere around three o'clock. It's built into the rock face. Not visible from here. But that's where they'll come for us! But I'm ready for them this time!'

What did he mean, they'll come for us?

'Who'll come for us?'

'You'll find out when we get there!'

Crane grinned and shrugged his shoulders but didn't enlighten us. I've been shown better respect at a supermarket check-out! Dan took the binoculars and followed Crane's finger. 'That's incredible,' said Dan turning to Crane. 'Absolutely incredible!'

I was last to get a look. I took the binoculars from Jake, nodded my thanks and looked where his finger pointed. It was incredible. No doubt about it. I could see a waterfall God knows how high and wide. It was impossible to get the perspective through the heat haze. It looked to come out of the rock-face, but I wasn't sure. I was sure about one thing though; it was a hell of a way off! There was something else besides the unanswered question of who will be coming for us that niggled me, but I couldn't work out what it was. At least, not with this heat bearing down on me.

The heat and the jungle noises were tremendous. I headed for the trees on the down-slope expecting the others to follow. Crane shouted me back saying, 'There's no way down there, chum!' They went over to the left and down – I followed their lead. He was right. The clump of trees I was heading for were clinging to a small ridge running across a rocky outcrop and below it there was a straight drop of at least sixty feet. The way we were going now was down a slope of about forty-five degrees. There was a good grip and thankfully it was well shaded by trees on both sides of the trail. It was narrow but it was obvious it had been used before! The going wasn't too bad. Though it still took us more than two hours to get to the bottom. We stopped for a half-hour break. By the way they were sweating and struggling for breath they needed it a lot more than I did. They were all two or three inches taller than me but they were all well overweight. Crane was the lightest, but not by much.

Our packs were dropped to the ground and Dan got his spirit-burner out.

Crane told him to put it away. 'Picnic time comes later, mate.'

His smile, as false as it looked to me, took the bite out off his sarcasm. Dan shrugged, smiled a similar smile back and put the burner away. He settled for a drink of cold tea. I went into the jungle for a pee. I saw the grey, stone statue on my way back; only this one was in perfect condition. It stood at least eight feet tall. Its belly was enormous. It looked like a woman in the last stages of pregnancy. But there was no mistaking the fact that the statue was male. Like the smashed ones I'd seen yesterday, this one had the shapes of arms and legs and heads poking out of its stretched belly. The face belonged to a race of people I'd never ever seen. It was like a fat, bulbous version of the faces of the statues on Easter Island. The fanged teeth were terrifying. Thank God it was stone!

I told them about it and they wanted to see it. Crane said there wasn't time but he was ignored. I took them to the clearing where it stood. Jake found another one not three yards away, then Graham found one. Then he found another. There were six of them in all. They were in a circle. Dan found what looked like an altar that was made of the same grey stone. It was stained black in places, and it was covered in red ants. I knew what the black stains were, but I wondered if the others did? Jake shrugged and wandered off; I supposed he was looking for more statues. This had to be something to do with fertility rites. It had to be a birthing platform. It was obvious. I'd heard of them. The giant statues were showing their ability to father future generations. The babies within their bellies with their arms and legs sticking out were obviously a display of masculinity. It seemed odd there were no female statues. Maybe there was a circle of female statues somewhere else?

We didn't get chance to find out. Two shots rang out in quick succession. Then we heard a crash. We ran back to where Crane was. I heard Jake curse. He was getting up off the ground and was about to put one on Crane. Crane pulled his gun and said if Jake moved a muscle, he'd shoot him. I could see Jake was debating whether he would or not. Dan stepped in asking what the hell's going on.

'Ask him,' growled Jake. Then he wiped his hand across his mouth, then saw the blood on the back of his hand and grunted at Crane. 'I owe you one, Crane.'

I'd never seen this side of Jake. Then after staring coldly at Crane for a full minute, he turned, picked up his rifle and pack, and then pointed at a weapon embedded in the trunk of a tree to his left.

'I shot at whoever threw that.'

The thing stuck in the tree looked like something out of 'Star Wars'. Crane didn't bother looking; he was in a crouched position slowly and carefully examining the area outside the clearing. His eyes searched very slowly one way then the other.

'Get down you morons!' he hissed. 'Are you suicidal? If there's one of them, there's bound to be more!'

He waved us down looking like a bird trying to take off with one wing.

I'd no idea who he was on about but I'd already crouched even though I was the most difficult target. I didn't want one of those things through my ribs. It was designed to go in and not come out. Whoever had thrown it had to be as strong as a bull for it to go so deep into solid wood. It bore a slight resemblance to a Fleur-de-Lis, but the blades on this thing were ten inches wide and two feet long. Running along the edge of all three blades there was a row of evil-looking backwards-facing barbs. All three blades, even the two swept-back ones had elongated oval holes cut down their centres and grooves that ran the full length of each blade either to lighten it or to allow blood to flow. I decided, both!

'What other surprises have you got for us Crane? You bastard,' snarled Dan as he crawled, commando fashion on his elbows to the very edge of the clearing and stared hard into the wall of greenery.

'You never said anything about this!'

'Be quiet,' hissed Cane. 'I'm trying to listen!'

Even though I couldn't hear a sound other than the buzzing hum of a million insects, I didn't move a muscle. We were sitting ducks if anybody was waiting out there.

'Right we're getting out of here. Keep low, keep your eyes and ears open, and don't shoot unless you're sure of your target. Because if you do and miss you've given your position away and these savages are merciless!'

The bastard knew about these people and now I knew what the rifles and handguns were for! If I could have stood the sight of blood I would have blown the scumbag's head off!

Graham and Jake edged up behind Crane and followed him in a crouched position down a barely visible trail leading at twelve o'clock from the clearing. I followed Dan about a yard behind them and a couple of feet behind Dan. If Crane had to suddenly stop we'd all go over like dominos! Going through there like that was grim, especially on the calf muscles. We kept in that position for no more than five minutes. The trail had widened but the vegetation on both sides was a wall of green. Crane decided it was safe enough to take a breather. I didn't. I thought he was mental. He stood up and wiped the dripping sweat from his eyes and from round his collar.

The others followed suit. Very reluctantly and as cautiously as possible I stood up. We listened for the slightest sound. It was impossible to see into the jungle or hear anything over the jungle noise. If a lost soul had come along and asked me where he was I would have said, twenty yards from the Amazon. This place was nothing like the Africa I'd ever seen on the box. This place looked like the worst scenery on Jurassic Park. The ferns (if that's what they were) had trunks woven like wicker baskets a foot in diameter and stood more than twelve feet high. There weren't two inches between them, and the stench from them would have felled a giant.

Creepers with blue-green leaves and strange brown tufted flowers hung like gigantic dead thistles in dripping clumps. Hanging somewhere high in the canopy (it was impossible to see where from) hung vines with purple and orange flowers crowded on them as big as dinner plates. They looked incredibly sinister. Not because they were grotesque but because there wasn't a butterfly or insect that would go anywhere near them. We could have been on another planet! We pressed on as best as we could.

At ten minute intervals we stopped at Crane's signal to see if we were being followed.

When we asked what the small packages were he was burying, he growled, 'Why do you have to question my every damned move!?'

'Because friend, you've been less than honest with us,' said Dan, coming out with the crappiest understatement I'd ever heard in my life! Jake and Graham burst out laughing till Crane glared angrily at Dan and told Graham and Jake, to shut their mouths.

'I'd better make one thing clear chums,' (there was nothing chummy about his tone of voice). 'If any of you are taken by these people, you're on your own. You'd better remember that now!'

'What people? You three never said anything about people!'

They said nothing.

'I told these guys all about them when we first met and what we were in for. If they chose not to believe me that's their lookout, and yours. But I'll say again. It's every man for himself if the crap hits the fan, and don't forget.' He sneered and pointed. 'They're explosives if you really want to know. If they come for us on the way out, I point this little gismo towards them, it sends a signal, then they go bang. We've got to get back out of here, and this is the best way out! Ok?'

Up to Jake and Graham having hysterics we'd been as silent as ghosts and watching in every direction for another attack but we'd neither seen nor heard anything. Could the weapon-throwing incident have been a warning?

He was off before I'd a chance to have a go at the others, or him for that matter. I wanted to know what I'd let myself in for and I'd damn well find out the first chance I got.

My chance came when the light began to fade. We'd reached another cave. It was obvious Crane had been here before because he knew exactly where it was.

We'd just crossed another stream when Crane stopped and said, 'We're camping here for tonight.'

We'd no idea where, because there was nowhere to pitch one tent never mind two. The ground went up at a fair old incline and we looked back down the trail but there was nowhere to bivouac there. He smirked, turned his back on us and disappeared through a curtain of vines just in front of him, and off to the right hand side of the track. It was well camouflaged. I wouldn't have found it in a hundred years.

He came back out. 'Get inside; we could be easy meat out here.' He disappeared again laughing his head off!

'Lunatic,' I muttered.

We got a move on and followed him. The interior of the cave was pretty good. He was flashing his torch up at the roof when we got in and I could see that the roof and the sides of the cave looked pretty well dry.

'Ok, same routine as last night. No fire, no light. Use a torch if you want to make yourself a target. Make sure your rifles are loaded and ready. Here you, you'd better have this.'

He gave me a handgun. I'd no idea how to use it.

'How do I?' I gestured with the handgun.

'Not now, I'll show you when the time comes. Ok. Now you two, one each side of the entrance behind those rocks. Don't stick your head out, you moron, they know where we are. All they need is a target. They warned us back there when one of 'em threw that Zangoo. I don't think they'll come at us tonight. But, you never know. It's more likely that they'll have a go after dawn. But I don't think they will. A, we haven't got to the shrine and B, they'll be more careful this time because we're well armed. Last time we weren't, and they know what rifles can do now they've had a demonstration! So stay on your toes. These guys are not friendlies!' he laughed, 'But I'm sure you know that by now!'

Dan threw his pack down and even in the dimness of the cave I could see he was having a hell of a struggle to keep his cool. 'You never mentioned there were others with you last time! How many know about the diamonds then?'

'None.'

'Why, what happened to them?'

'You don't want to know, friend! Now you, chum, sit on your gear in the middle there towards the back. You look down the trail, straight out in front. You two, you on the right, cover the left side and you on the left cover the right. Slightest movement warn me. I'll be asleep over there. Use your binoculars, you'll see more. Remember! The slightest movement and I want to know. Stay alert, these buggers don't mind sacrificing some of their own if it means them getting what they want.'

He laughed again. If he hadn't already lost his marbles, he was well on his way. And I was beginning to think I was! Like an obedient child, I'd sat where he'd told me to sit and inspected the gun. It was an odd shape and for the size of it, it was very heavy. I didn't know if it was loaded or not so I didn't put my finger anywhere near the trigger. I didn't ask Crane to show me how to use it because he and Dan were asleep, or pretending to be asleep. I'd have my say, later!

I stared into the gloom expecting to see a hoard of savages come screaming up the banking. Thanks to the moon, I could see a fair distance up the trail. There was nothing moving, no silent, shadowy figures, nothing. I couldn't fathom out why they didn't attack us before when we were in the open. We were easy targets then.

'Can either of you see anything?'

'No, not a thing.' Jake said the same.

Our watch seemed to last forever. Then Dan and Crane relieved Jake and Graham! I should have been relieved first. They were still rubbing their eyes when a hell of a din erupted outside. I began fumbling with my rifle because I'd put the handgun down and couldn't find it. Crane snatched it from me and told me to be bloody careful before I killed everybody.

'Hold it down towards the ground till you see something to shoot at, you arse!'

He threw it back to me and went to the cave entrance. Carefully, he eased himself beside the rock wall and looked out.

'Everybody can relax; it's only a leopard making a kill.'

I didn't want to see it and Jake didn't seem interested either. I went and sat on my pack, found the handgun on the ground behind it and tucked it in my belt. I might need it if only to shoot Crane! He let the creepers hanging down across the entrance drop back like a heavy bead curtain leaving only a small gap for me to see through. I pointed this out to him saying I could barely see twenty feet down the track. He told me to go and get some rest; we were going to need it. Then he took out his machete and cut half the vines away! Hell knows what for.

'Don't worry friend, even if they're out there, they can't see us in here. Well not as good as we can see them out there, and they don't have rifles!'

He laughed; I ignored him and unrolled my groundsheet.

I couldn't sleep a wink. The jungle noises seemed louder than they'd ever been. My mind was everywhere. Asking questions but not answering them. If Crane knew about these weird natives, why would he risk our lives and his own by coming back here? Not just for diamonds, surely? What happened to his friends last time he came? Why hadn't Dan and the others been completely honest with me and him with them? I knew there was a lot of money at stake. That's worth some risks. Risks I would take gladly. I could get Miranda all the things I wanted to get for her. But you can't do much shopping when you're dead. Another thing that annoyed and puzzled me was: why did he want to keep the whereabouts of the cave a secret? Nobody right in the head would want to come back here. I could only think he was hiding something else, but what?

It was obvious Crane had got money from somewhere, most likely off Dan and maybe Graham and Jake, but I wasn't sure. They said they'd helped him, but it didn't seem to ring true. There was one thing I was sure of though as I began to drift into sleep; we were going in a direction that would take us towards where we started from. I was positive about that, if nothing else. I have an uncanny gift for direction and I knew where east was. It's where the sun rises. Before we abseiled down the cliff, the early morning sun was behind me. Now, as dawn broke, the sun was coming up in front of the cave entrance. To reach here we had to go due west or thereabouts. This meant we were going in a big semi-circle towards the very cliffs we started from. If this was Crane's idea of keeping the whereabouts of the diamonds a secret, he'd failed big time! I estimated that we were four or five miles north of where we climbed down into the cavern. Six at the most!

I dreamed we were being attacked by the statues. I was lying prostrate on the ground and I couldn't get up. It was terrifying and real. Their mouths and their weird spears were dripping blood. It was drip, drip, dripping onto my forehead. I tried to stop it by putting my hand across my head but even more poured down.

Then a voice said, 'Wake up Granny or we'll leave you here.'

Startled and disorientated I nearly leaped off the ground.

'What the hell do think you're doing? You sad bastard!' It was Dan; he was using his canteen to pour water on my face. The rest of them thought it was hilarious. They were laughing like hyenas. I wasn't, I was raving mad. I knocked the canteen out of his hand and went to give him one. Graham grabbed my arm. Come on Granny, he was only having a laugh. You were muttering and twitching like you were lying on a bed of nails. Calm down, a few drops of water won't hurt you. Come on man, forget it. I called Dan a stupid tullock, shook myself free of Graham and wiped most of the water off my face.

'Nerds, the lot of you!' They had their packs on. I was starving hungry and thirsty. 'Anybody eating,' I snapped.

'Too late old chum, it's time to go.'

Crane threw his rifle over his shoulder as he left the cave. Dan followed. Jake shrugged his shoulders and said, 'Sorry mate, we didn't get anything other than water and biscuits. I'm more than starving. Can't live on bloody dog biscuits.' He rubbed his stomach.

'Let's hope it's worth it. Because I'm beginning to have my doubts.' I said.

'So am I. Bloody great big ones!'

'Jake, before you go out there, don't you think it's weird that they've just walked out of here as if they were going for a stroll through the park? How do they know the natives aren't waiting for them? They could be waiting anywhere for us, anywhere! You can't see five bloody yards into that jungle!'

'Crane said they won't attack us till we reach the shrine.'

'Hey?'

'That's what he said.'

'What shrine Jake?'

'The one by the waterfall. Come on or we'll lose 'em.'

'If he knew that, why the hell have we tramped round in a damned circle? You know we're going back to that cliff face we climbed down the first day we got here?'

'No I didn't Granny. What's his bloody game?'

'Surprised are you?'

'No more than I was when I realised where we were going! There's something wrong here, badly wrong. Do you have a gun?'

'Yes, Crane gave me one.'

'Let me have a look at it.'

I handed him the handgun.

'It's not loaded! What is his game?' Jake frowned.

'I've no idea. I'll load it. I've got a couple of spare clips. You should have some in your pack!'

'I don't know what the hell I've got in my pack!'

'Don't bother taking it off; it's a Panther sport the same as mine. I'll get them back off you later.'

We could see them now they were just up the trail.

'You remember in the pub when Dan showed me that diamond?'

'Yes, why?'

'Is it real?'

'Oh, yes,' said Jake sounding and nodding exactly like the Churchill dog. 'I was with him when he took it to Amsterdam. And it is worth what he said. The guy nearly drooled when he told him how many there were! It's real all right. If I had the slightest doubt Granny, I wouldn't be here! Here, it's loaded. That's the safety catch there. It's on. Push it forward like that. It's ready. Close it like that, ok?'

I nodded, took it from him and stuck it in my belt. '

I'm going to keep an eye on that bastard. And first chance I get I'll tell Dan and Graham.'

I nodded a reply. I was busy probing the walls of green on the sides of the trail. For God knows what!

The shrine, as Jake called it, was a hundred yards away. We'd just gone round a bend in the trail and there it was. The sun was on it. Even from here it looked superb but we didn't stop for a second. We couldn't. Crane upped the pace and was off. When we'd gone nearly half way, he stopped, crouched down and took what I thought were some of the candles out of his top pocket. Then he lit a cigarette. He was still crouched. I heard a fizzing sound. Then he spun round and hurled one of the candles down the trail behind us. There was a massive explosion. I hit the ground like I'd been hit with a hammer. Next minute he hurled another high in the air into the jungle. Screams tore from the jungle. They weren't bloody candles the lunatic was throwing. They were sticks of dynamite. The bloody maniac! He hurled another over to the left. There were more terrible screams.

Then he yelled, 'Run for cover, over there in the temple. Come on you morons run, or the bastards will have us!'

I went after him like a greyhound. It was a hell-hole and there were more dreadful screams from behind us. I didn't know if they'd got Dan or one of the others. I just didn't stop to look. I ran like somebody running in a bloody nightmare. I expected to get a spear through me any minute. I could hear somebody pounding after me and I hoped it was our lot and not theirs.

Although Crane was a flabby bugger, he could run. I'd trouble keeping up with him.

'Get in there!' he yelled at the top of his voice, pointing to the temple. He didn't need to point, it was massive. Twice as big as the ruined one we'd spent the first night in.

'Get in. Get your rifles. Come on, get your fingers out. They'll be on us in a minute! Dan, get behind there.'

He was gasping for breath but he was pushing Dan (who was near collapsing) over a big heap of bones. Then he pointed to another pile. You, Jake get over there and keep your bloody head down. Jake was grey in the face. Graham, you squeeze in there. Graham, staggering like a drunk, flopped behind a massive stone altar just to the right of the doorway.

'You,' he pointed at me, 'Get behind that and all of you get your packs off. Make sure you've plenty of ammo handy.'

I dived behind a solid stone bench (one of at least six) in a row running down the middle of the temple. It was bigger than I was but it wasn't big enough for my liking. One twice as big wouldn't have been big enough.

'Don't waste ammo. Shoot only when you've got a definite target, and don't aim for their heads, aim for their bellies. I'm telling you, make every round count. You'll need to! They think they've got us where they want us.'

I had to give it to Crane. Madman that he was, there was no doubting his authority. I'd never been in a situation like this. I wouldn't have known what to do if I had! I didn't know what to do now! I just wanted to disappear. How could I shoot a fellow human, it would be murder? I threw my rifle down and was about to tell Crane there was no way I'd be involved in murder, not even for a diamond for Miranda. We should talk to them and sort it out. I stupidly assumed they spoke English. That shows what state of mind I was in. Crane shot the first one to come racing out of the jungle, full in the chest. I watched as if I was watching something on

109

the telly. Then blood erupted from this huge man's mouth. He had the strangest face I'd ever seen. Then his strange face contorted as he choked on his scream. I vomited. I couldn't stop myself. The last thing I saw before I passed out was the dreadful realisation of death in the eyes of the dying man.

When I recovered there was a mound of bodies outside the entrance. Arms, legs, bent and hanging all over like broken toys. Crane was struggling to stack them up like logs on a bonfire, and that's exactly what it was, a bonfire he was going to burn them! He'd heaved the last one on the pile then he'd got a cart-load of dried creepers from somewhere and was ramming the stuff between the bodies. That's when I lost it. I didn't know Jake and Graham were hurt. I only found out when I staggered outside to hit Crane with a broken spear shaft I'd grabbed off the floor of the temple. He took it off me as if he was a school monitor collecting pencils. Then he balled his fist and said if I didn't get back inside and see what I could do for the two in there, he'd lay me out and throw me on the pile. I looked at him open-mouthed.

'Graham andJake are…'

'Yes' He shut me up. 'Now get in there!' he yelled it straight in my face.

I ran back in and tried to wipe his spit off my face.

Graham had one of those weird spears embedded in his lower thigh. He was trying to get it out but when he pulled at it, his skin stretched like an obscene sheet of rubber. Sweat ran down his face. His mouth was set in a horrible grimace as he held back what must have been searing pain. Jake had a gash in his side. He was trying to hold the flesh together but blood oozed from between his fingers. This couldn't be. I knew it wasn't real because it was Graham and Jake. I knew them. They were old friends. Things like this don't happen, not in real life. Nothing like this happens in real life I knew that for a fact! They would be ok soon. All I had to do was mop up the blood, bandage their wounds and they would be fine again.

My eyes must have been standing out of my head and Crane must have seen me staring at the blood. Next thing I knew I was staggering sideways after taking a right crack across my face. It brought me out of it. This was real. I was in it! I was here! We were fighting for our lives! I felt a surge of poisonous hate pour out of me that I couldn't in my wildest dreams think was possible. I grabbed my rifle off the ground and was ready to kill and maim anybody in sight.

'Put that down and help them you cretin!' bellowed Crane as he dashed outside with his pack.

'Help them! How can I help them you maniac?'

'You do it!' he screamed.

Crane must have found another body. He shouted Dan to give him a hand to get it on the pile. Dan was already out there with him. Between them they got the huge man's bloodied body on the pile. Crane ran round the pyre lighting the dry creepers or whatever they were. Dan, with his rifle ready, watched the jungle. His eyes were everywhere. Both he and Crane were more than twenty feet from the temple. They were easy targets – the crazy bastards. The fire took hold. I couldn't look. It was horrendous! Then from somewhere behind the wall of green, a chant-like sound erupted. It was louder than all the jungle noises put together. If this was a battle chant and they attacked now, they would have to circle the heap of burning bodies to get at us. They'd have no chance. I'd done what I could for Jake and Graham – it wasn't much. I'm no sort of a Doctor. Crane and Dan came back in. Crane got a box out of his pack and sod me, if he didn't have some ampoules of morphine in there. He gave them both a shot. It must have begun to slowly ease the pain because Graham's breathing was less laboured. It was taking longer with Jake! Blood didn't seem to bother Crane or Dan. I was ready for vomiting again so I left them to it. Crane told me and Dan to keep a lookout but to stay inside the temple, saying he'd need all the stuff he had to tend to these two.

There was no sign of attack but the eerie chanting continued. It had changed somehow. Now, although just as loud if not louder, it seemed more sombre than threatening. I couldn't look at the charred bodies. But it didn't seem to bother Dan. I was physically and mentally exhausted so what the others were like was impossible to imagine. I just wanted to lie down somewhere and go to sleep. Still no attack came. Nothing! Crane had swathed Graham and Jake in bandages. Jake's eyes were closed and he looked next door but one to where death lives. Crane said they were nothing but flesh wounds. Graham was sitting up even though his face was ashen. God knows what was wrong with me but I wanted to giggle!

Crane looked at me from where he was lighting the gas burner.

'Don't think I burned that lot for fun, chum.' He nodded in the direction of the cave entrance. I wanted to tell him he wasn't my chum. I wanted to tell him I hated his foul guts. He must have seen the hate in my eyes because he laughed before he started again.

'That should keep the hungry bastards busy for a few hours. They've only dragged one away. There's plenty more grub for 'em before they start on us!' Then he did laugh! I was sure he'd gone over the brink! Dan shook his head as though he was trying to get the words out of his head.

Crane's words didn't register at first, then when I realised what he'd said and what he meant, I sank to my knees.

'Yes chum, they're cannibals. Why do you think they didn't slaughter us in the jungle?'

I just shook my head. God's truth, I couldn't answer. He was mental. Why in God's name hadn't Dan told me? Nothing. Nothing would have got me to come to this place.

My mind screamed. 'NOTHING!' What could I tell Miranda? How could I ever hold my head up again?

'You filthy lying BASTARDS.'

'I didn't believe him Granny, none of us did. Do you think I'd have come here believing THAT?'

'Shut up both of you, you're pathetic.' He spit the words out. 'You're going to make a damned fortune. What's wrong with you? Did you expect to get it on a silver platter, you useless pieces of crap? Grow up and get a life!'

He turned his back on us. I should have shot him then right between the shoulder blades, the scum-bag; all four of them were scum. Worse than scum. I didn't want to be near them. They could all drop dead for me. I went to the back of the temple and sat on the floor and took hold of my rifle. If either of them followed me, I'd shoot them, and I knew I would! Crane made a pot of coffee. He handed it out with some cereal biscuits. I told him where he could ram it. He threw the lot at me. When I stood up to face him, he knocked me down. Dan jumped on him as he was about to put the boot in.

'Get away from him Crane! We need him. Instead of wasting time acting like hard men, we should be finding where the frigging diamonds are!'

'They don't need any finding.'

Crane pushed Dan away, laughed and pointed casually to the back of the temple.

'They're in there, you moron! They're at the back. Are you blind?'

He showed Dan a hole staring right at us. The hole was in the back wall of the temple. On either side of it were more of the statues cut out of

112

the solid rock. It didn't look big enough from where I was to get a cat through.

I went over to look. Crane shone his torch through. I gaped at the heaps of diamonds, if that's what they were.

'Shut your mouth before you start dribbling. Not bad eh? Do you think you can get through there? Or might you rip your nice jungle suit?'

I told him where to go, pushed my pack through, which took some doing and then my rifle. I had to take the gun out of my belt and throw that through. Then I threaded my arms through as if I was diving through the hole. Somebody took my legs and pushed hard to get me through. I tore the skin off my left forearm as I scraped against the jagged rock.

'Steady you clown; I've to get out of here!'

Crane's head came through. He saw the diamonds and said, 'Payment for their Gods I should think. Bloody expensive menu!'

Then he laughed and said. 'Throw some out then, let's have a look at them.'

I shone the torch round the cave which wasn't very big. I could stand up fairly easily but there were places where it was too low. It went a fair way back but I didn't want to go too far in; you never know what might be lurking in the corners. It looked to me like the perfect nesting place for every snake in the world! I shone the torch on the nearest diamonds, picked a handful up and threw them through the hole. I rested my torch on my pack, and threw some more out.

'Give me a hand out. I'll come out the same way I got in. Grab my hands and pull when I give you the word. Now!'

'Get your arms back in there and stay where you are. Empty your pack and fill it with diamonds then pass it out. I'll pass you my pack through; you can fill that as well! And get on with it.'

I got on with it. No point arguing. I didn't want to be in here all night. I didn't really want to be out there either; I wanted to be in Miranda's arms and she in mine! I emptied my pack, carefully. I picked five of the biggest ones. One for each of us then as fast as I could I filled the back pack. Then I had to get some out because I couldn't lift the damned thing; it weighed a ton.

'Can somebody get this, and don't go on about it not being full; it's too heavy to move when it's full.'

'Push it further through, you weed!'

113

Crane pulled as I pushed. I'd weed him one day and I'd wipe that sneer off his fat face. The pack was lifted clear. He threw another one through. I filled it half full and hoisted it into the hole.

'Grab that, one of you, I'm coming out!' I got part way in and asked Crane to give me a hand, when I heard rapid shots of fire. Then suddenly, Dan was trying to climb through the hole. He hadn't a chance in hell. I tried to pull him through, but he was miles too fat. Next thing he's wrenched from my grasp and Crane was trying to get through the hole.

'Pull you weakling, pull!'

A Shire horse wouldn't have been able to pull him through.

'Pull, will you!'

Then he was suddenly dragged out. There were more shots, more shouts, more screams. Followed by silence. Then the chanting started again.

'Where are you?' I shouted at the top of my voice. No answer. Only the moaning chant. I stood back from the hole and fumbled through my stuff. Thank God I still had my pack. I grabbed the torch again and shone it through the hole. Where the hell had they gone? I was beginning to panic. There was no way I could get out of here without help. I began to shout my head off when all hell broke loose again.

Then I saw something. 'Dear God almighty!' I screamed.

I leapt back from the hole and fell backwards over the contents of my pack, giving the back of my head an almighty crack. I got up, shook the pain away and scrabbled around for my rifle. I was shaking with terror. One of the cannibals had got Dan's head on a pole. They were parading round the temple with torches. They also had Jake's head on a pole. God, I couldn't stop shaking. I found the rifle, stood well back away from the hole, and as soon as I saw a big belly, I fired. The recoil from the bloody thing nearly tore my shoulder from its socket. But I heard the scream so I must have hit one of them. There were shouts and chaos, then the temple went dark; there was utter silence?

Still shaking, I ventured to the hole and shone the torch beam through. I had to hold it with both hands to keep it still, but I kept the rifle close to hand. They'd gone! Or were they standing against the temple wall on either side of the hole. No way on God's good earth was I going to put my head into the hole to look! There was complete darkness when I switched off the torch. I moved back further from the hole and sat on the diamonds. I hadn't the faintest idea what I was going to do. Still shaking like a leaf in a gale, I picked a couple off the ground and shone the torch on them. They looked like the one Dan had in the pub. I stuck them in my breast pocket, collected some more and put those in my other breast pocket. I filled all my pockets with diamonds. I'd buy the world for Miranda. Then still in shock I just sat there throwing diamonds everywhere, wondering what to do. I knew I couldn't get back through on my own, it was impossible. Then the realisation that I was going to die here hit me like a bomb blast. I don't know if it was the shock of everything that had happened but I fell asleep on the cave floor with a fistful of diamonds in each hand. I don't know what woke me up but when I finally got my eyes open I saw that the temple was lit up. When I crept up to the hole and looked out there were torches burning everywhere and there were fifty or sixty of the weird looking savages sitting like a congregation on the stone seats. They were chanting that dreadful moaning chant. There were bodies on the altar. I couldn't tell who they were because they'd been roasted.

The feasting started at nine o'clock by my badly-scratched watch. I don't know who they ate first. But I realised the significance of the arms and legs sticking out of the bellies of the stone statues we'd seen en route to here. It had nothing to do with masculinity. They were showing anybody who ventured into their domain what would happen to them if they were captured. That lunatic Crane knew and he'd told Dan, Graham and Jake but they hadn't told me. The lousy... There isn't a word in the English language foul enough to describe them! They knew that I wouldn't have come anywhere near this vile place if they had! What could I do now? Nothing, nothing, nothing! I was trapped here like a fish in a barrel. I could only stand at the hole like a peeping tom and watch, fascinated, as they walked to the altar, bowed their heads and solemnly took a lump of flesh each. They put it on what looked like a solid gold platter, bowed again, and then returned to their stone benches. I couldn't watch any longer and I couldn't stand anymore of their chanting – it was driving me mental. Then a foul, sickly stench wafted through the hole. It can't be what I think it is, can it? Yes it can. I gagged and I swallowed but I couldn't stop myself from being physically sick. I scratched among my kit for my water bottle. I daren't use my torch. I desperately wanted to swill my mouth out. Then my gun fell out of my belt. I'd forgotten I still had it. The chanting stopped. I held my breath. I crouched down and got the gun. Then as quietly as possible I began to creep towards the back of the cave. It was a nightmare in the dark. I fell over twice before I realised I'd left all my gear behind. Dare I go back? I was terrified but I had no choice. What food I had was there. I was beginning to sweat and shake with fright. I didn't seem to be able to move. God, was I that scared? Somehow I forced myself to go back. A torch, then a scattering of diamonds then another torch, then more torches were thrown through the hole. One of them had landed next to my gear. I ran and grabbed as much of my stuff as I could. I dropped some and grabbed it back up. I dropped something else. I was in a right panic. I grabbed the gun and hurled it at the hole – it missed by yards. I didn't care. That action snapped me out of my panic. With better control over myself I was able to pick out what I needed most. Water, dog biscuits and ammunition. I found the gun. I was regaining my self-control by the second, till one of those lethal looking weapons shot past my head. I didn't completely lose it but I was off with what stuff I was clutching and running like a drunk over the diamond strewn floor of the cave.

I had my rifle and my handgun. I found a cranny for Granny. I shook my head and stifled a giggle. God, I'd better get a grip. I squeezed myself into the niche. I could lean on a bit of a shelf at shoulder height and aim the rifle at the hole. I thought of Miranda and what my death would do to her. She might come to find me. No, God forbid. I had to get out of here. When I looked at the small boxes of ammunition I found I had plenty of big bullets for the rifle and small ones for the gun. I wasn't dead yet. I could take plenty of the cannibals with me if they tried to flush me out.

The torches had gone out and the smoke-filled cave was making it difficult to breathe. I wet one of my hankies and tied it round my nose and mouth. It wasn't perfect by any means but it was a hell of a lot better. The temple and now the cave were in darkness again. I didn't look at my watch to see what time it was because I didn't want to use the torch; the batteries seemed fine when I last used it, but they were the only ones I had and I didn't want to waste them. The good thing about the niche was: it hid me completely from their line of sight. They could hurl as many spears as they liked but I'd be ok. Then I realised the smoke had gone. I took the hanky off my face to make sure. It had, but where to? I was tempted to use the torch to explore the cave roof, but first I needed some food. I had twelve cereal bars, and four bars of Cadbury's Bournville. If I'd any tinned rice or fruit in my pack, I'd left it over by the hole. It could bloody well stay there. I ate two cereal bars and half a bar of chocolate. I hadn't much water! No more than half a litre. Buggering hell! I must have used more than I realised on my hanky!

The temple was still in darkness and as silent as a grave. My grave if I didn't find a way out of here! I didn't even consider fighting my way out, I wasn't that stupid. Besides I hadn't a clue how many natives were left. I'd counted more than fifty but there could be a hundred more. I could try and sneak out at night. I knew I was only five or so miles from where we climbed down into this hell-hole. If I could keep to the high ground, or if I could find Crane's dynamite. Maybe I could fight my way out, or at least have a fighting chance. I soon decided that was a crap idea.

I tried to sleep (not for long) just to rest my eyes but they were still sore from the smoke. I could crouch down and rest my back against the side of the niche and hide my feet with the groundsheet. It wasn't too bad. It must have been fine because I was asleep in minutes.

I'd no idea how long I'd slept. When I opened my eyes I was cold and the rock face was digging into the small of my back. I risked a quick look at the time. My watch showed four-fifteen. It had to be early morning because there was the faintest hint of daylight beyond the hole. I must have slept all night. I switched off the torch. I was hungry, very hungry so I ate one of the cereal bars, after I'd found the bloody things. I took only the smallest sip of water. Being short of water worried me the most. I debated whether or not I could sneak down to the stream for some, but gave that idea up straight away. Might as well shoot myself now, at least they wouldn't be able to get at me to feast on me. Not that I'd make much of a feast! I wasn't being rational. I was bloody losing it!

I must have been in a poor state to even consider such things, but I was in a hopeless position. I had to pull myself together and search the cave for a way out; the smoke must have gone somewhere. I'd nothing to lose. I could either sit here and starve to death, or I had to try to make a break for it. There was no choice so I got the torch. I couldn't see anybody by the hole. I got to my feet and stamped on the spot to get some blood into them. I checked the hole again and I still couldn't see anybody. I went to the back of the cave and started a methodical check of the roof. I was extremely careful when I got near or in line with the hole. The roof was solid rock. There wasn't a sign of the smallest crack or any tins of food. Maybe there was a way out in the wall. If there was a way out I would have to be quick as the torch was starting to go dim! After checking it best as I could, I found the walls were the same as the roof – solid! I could only think that the smoke must have vented back out of the hole. I felt absolutely sick. I cursed Crane and the others to high heaven, and the stinking cave, and the vile, lousy cannibals. Lot of good it did me!

I was going to get another cereal bar when I found it. I nearly fell down the bloody thing. The hole was in the floor and it was big enough for two to crawl into. I nearly burst out crying with relief. Maybe, just maybe there was a way out. God, I prayed there was! I went and bundled all my gear in my groundsheet, I stuck the handgun in my waistband and slung the rifle over my back. It was ten-past-five when I crept into the hole. I dragged my bundle after me, bobbed up, and took one last look towards the far hole. It was getting lighter and I saw a big, fat, ugly face staring through. I ducked back into the hole like a Jack-in-the -box in reverse gear and hoped beyond hope that this was a way out and they were all too fat to get into the cave!

I could feel a very gentle airflow, coming from behind me. The hole continued down at a fairly steep gradient for about ten yards then it more or less levelled off and very gradually started to rise. I had to creep on all fours in the dark. It was very slow going and my hands were bleeding where I'd caught them more than once on the rough surface. I had to wrap my left hand, which was the worst, in my hanky and that was no mean feat. It began to get steeper. I had no idea how far I'd gone, as I hadn't been able to pace it out, and now it was getting narrower and steeper. I sounded like a tinker's cart clattering along as I dragged my groundsheet behind me. But it was pitch black in the narrowing tunnel. However, I was making good progress.

The gradient now was bad, very bad! I'd gashed my knees, and my hands felt like they were pouring blood. I had no idea if the groundsheet holding my gear would last much longer. But, had the floor surface not been as rough as a bear's backside, I might have slipped back down the hole. Now there was a ledge sticking out above me; I only found it was there because I cracked my head on it. I had to find the torch and see how far it stuck out across the passage. I could get my hand over the ledge but it was impossible to guess in the dark how deep it was. I wedged my boots against the sides of the tunnel and knelt with one knee on the groundsheet. It was a nightmare getting the torch. I had to thread the hoop round my wrist in case I dropped it. I shone the beam up the steepening tunnel and saw there was room enough for me to get past on the left of the protruding ledge but it looked fifty-fifty whether there would be room for the groundsheet. Then I found by wedging my back against the right wall, I was able (after nearly bursting a bubble) to push the groundsheet up first. Then by pulling on the ledge as hard as I could, I pulled myself up and through. I was exhausted when I'd finished. There was a nice surprise waiting for me! The ledge was wide enough and deep enough to sit on and rest my back against the tunnel wall where it had widened out above the obstacle. I took a small sip of water. I desperately needed one. Always at the back of my mind nagged the realisation that I had only two days to get to the rendezvous point. I brushed it off. There was no point worrying about that now!

I rested on the ledge for ten minutes to get my strength back and ate a cereal bar and a bar of chocolate. Thank the lord they were in ring-pull cans because I'd lost the damned knife with the tin-opener attachment. I re-tied the groundsheet and shone the torch round the tunnel. It was at least two metres in diameter and the slope wasn't half as steep as it was below the ledge. I could stand up – brilliant!

I noticed as I moved along, that the floor of the tunnel was smoother, the bundled-up groundsheet was a lot easier to drag. Then I realised there was enough room in the tunnel to carry it. I twisted the corners tighter and oyked it onto my back. I used the torch as little as possible but shone it up the tunnel as I tried to remember any jagged bits sticking out. Then I turned it off and keeping my right hand on the wall I moved on at a fair pace. It was less than walking pace but better than crawling on my hands and knees. I moved on like this in half-hour stints. It was as long as I could go in the dry heat of the tunnel without a ten minute rest. The gradient kept swapping and changing. Sometimes it was nearly level sometimes it was fairly steep. The general direction didn't change though, it kept on spiralling left. It was like trudging up a giant corkscrew. The tunnel couldn't have been dug by hand. It had to be some sort of natural phenomena. Perhaps it was a water course formed over millions of years. I didn't give much thought to it; I had enough to worry about! I was getting low on water! I had to rest. I'd rest for an hour then go on. I don't know how long I slept but I suddenly woke up sweating from a nightmare. It was so real. They had come up the tunnel behind me and they'd grabbed my legs. They were pulling me back down. They were going to…Ugh, I shivered involuntarily. I got off the ground and shone the torch back down the tunnel. Thank God it was empty. I pushed on but I hadn't quite shaken off the nightmare.

I can't say for sure when I saw the first hint of light. I'd been staring hard into the pitch-black tunnel for hours; it could have been anything. When I first thought I could see the slightest contrast between the wall on my left and the wall on my right I passed it off because my eyes were so sore. I thought they were playing some sort of lousy trick on me, but now I was convinced the contrast was real. I'd just shut them and counted to eight; the time it takes (I'd heard) to normalise your vision! The contrast between the walls was real! God, I could have wept! I had to control the elation surging through my body or I'd have dumped the groundsheet and the bloody heavy rifle, then run up the tunnel like a madman. Instead I took a few deep breaths and sat down for a few minutes to take stock. I didn't sit for long; I was still too excited. I decided to go on till I could actually see daylight. Then I'd stop and sort myself out. I'd realised I couldn't just pop out of a hole in the ground somewhere, looking like someone who's fought in a war on the losing side! Using my torch, I moved at a good pace along the tunnel. It was definitely getting lighter. It wasn't yet light enough to turn the torch off, but it was getting there.

I wondered why there was a sort of red cast to the light, then I realised it must be sunset. I checked my watch; the crappy thing wasn't working. I shook it... nothing. I pressed on. There was definitely a red reflection from the wall. It had to be sunset. Twenty-five more paces and I knew it wasn't! The light was from torches, and lots of them. I nearly screamed out loud. My head nearly exploded in anger and utter frustration. I probably saved my life by not shouting out. The light was coming from an eighteen-inch wide hole in the left hand side tunnel wall. It was definitely from torches because the colours were like ghostly dancers flickering against the tunnel wall. I could hear Crane's voice. Holy crap, I had to be hallucinating! Crane was dead, wasn't he? I tried to convince myself, but I couldn't remember. I tried to visualise what happened in the temple. Dan was in the hole. He was in the hole trying to get in out of the way of the cannibals. I was trying to pull him through! Then he was dragged out and Crane was trying to get in. He had hold of my arms. He was definitely trying to get in! He'd told me to pull. Or? Was he trying to pull me out? Ridiculous. Why the hell would he want to pull me out? No point.

He was saying something about not getting them all. Next time he'd tie a bastard rope to the arse that went in for the diamonds.

Then he said, 'Tell 'em what I said.' My head was spinning, this couldn't be happening. I quietly lowered the groundsheet to the tunnel floor. It didn't make a sound. I crept silently up to the hole and listened. I could hear another man talking in a language I'd never heard.

Then Crane said, 'He'll be dead in a week. There's no way out of there. Tell 'em. They've got the others, what more do they want? The greedy bastards. Don't tell 'em that! Tell 'em I'll bring more sacrifices next time!'

Then one of the cannibals said something.

Then the other man said, 'He says bring more fat ones or they will kill you also. He's not kidding. Don't be fooled by his silly grin. Look at his eyes; you won't see anything funny in them! Nod and smile back and let's get out of here. We've enough diamonds to buy this f--ing country. Nod and smile then get up. Come on, we need to be out of here!'

Crane said, 'Give them something out of the kit. That should keep them happy for a couple of months. There's a couple of radios in there and a few knives. I should have brought 'em some coloured beads!'

Then Crane laughed. I didn't. I was the arse that went in for the diamonds. If I'd had a couple of sticks of dynamite I'd have lobbed them in there. I wanted to slit his foul throat and watch him die gasping for breath.

I suddenly realised, when my head stopped banging, that I had to find the way out of here, and then I could notify the authorities and get the bastard hanged. I went and got my gear and crept past the hole. I was sweating with fear as I silently went past. I heard a commotion but I didn't stop to see what was going on. I wanted to run like a deer out of there but I controlled my terror and took as much care as I could. The tunnel continued to turn left. I crept along at snail's pace. Just further round there was a doorway cut out of the tunnel wall. The commotion was louder now and I could see daylight ahead of me. Across the doorway was a huge iron door; it looked like the ones they had on munitions depots in the Second World War. God knows how they got it down here. There was a massive hasp bolted to the wall and a staple fastened to the door. Then I saw a pin lying near the opening. The pin was a six inch long bolt and it was at least an inch wide. Oh yes. Got you, you bastards every one of you! I picked up the pin, slammed the door shut and rammed the pin home. I hadn't even considered that there could be another way out. I'd only waited a couple of seconds before I suddenly thought there might be. I grabbed my groundsheet and rushed up the tunnel. Then in the distance I heard banging, loud and continuous banging. I knew then that there wasn't another way out! I put my gear down and retraced my steps. I had to use the torch but I didn't give a damn. I'd seen daylight. It was a long way off but it was daylight. They were trapped all right, and now I was sure there was no way on earth that the bastards would get out of there. There was screaming and shouting and banging and crashing. I left them to it.

By the time I'd reached the end of the tunnel, the noise had slowly faded to nothing. As soon as I was outside the tunnel and in the fresh air, I started to giggle. I told myself they might not have much to drink in there but they'd have plenty to eat! I giggled again. Then I began to shake. It had to be some sort of delayed reaction, some sort of shock. I tried hard to get a grip. I giggled again. Giggling like a loony, I told myself I mustn't. It took me a long time to stop, especially when I counted the diamonds in my pockets! It would be very tricky explaining to the two guys in the Land Rover what had happened but I'd think of something. I could tell them to come back for the others in ten days because they'd decided to stay a while longer. That should allay suspicion and give me plenty of time to make myself scarce. It would be even trickier getting the diamonds out of the country but I didn't give a damn, I'd find a way. I wouldn't dream of breaking my promise to Miranda. I think the first thing we'll do when I get back is have a fortnight in Amsterdam. Just to put a shine on things!

Richard Lee Wilson Feb. 2004.

Chief Inspector Granddad (Retired)

'You've got odd socks on Gada.'

'Have I Joe? Never mind, there'll be another pair somewhere exactly the same. I can wear them tomorrow.'

Joe's granddad bent forward and felt at his socks.

'What have you got for me today?'

'I've got all of them you asked for. Which do you want me to read first?'

'You pick one.'

'They've all got the same story on the front page.'

'Well read that one first; it must be important.'

'It is Gada. The famous financier, Lord Baron, has killed himself.'

Joe's granddad gasped. 'Never.'

'He has. He's shot himself in the head. It says he was found dead in his meditation room. They had to break in because he'd locked the door.'

'Does it say why he committed suicide, because I don't believe a word of it!?'

'It says he'd put a vast amount of his capital into a high risk venture and lost everything.'

Joe's granddad grunted. 'That doesn't sound like him Joe. I've always known him to be extremely careful with his investments. He didn't take risks with anything. No, never.' Joe's granddad shook his head in disbelief. 'That doesn't sound like Lord Baron at all. I think there's something fishy going on here. Read me everything there is in there will you Joe?'

'Ok Gada.'

'First go and get your orange juice out of the kitchen. I've left it on the side with two Penguin biscuits.'

Joe left the room. His granddad heard him laughing to himself. Joe eventually returned still laughing to himself.

'It's not orange juice Gada, it's barley water, and the penguins have been eaten by the Tiger bars. I'll be glad when Grandma comes back! You can have the barley water Gada, I don't like it.'

'It's good for you Joe; it swills out your kidneys.'

'I don't think they need swilling out Gada, I'm only eight!'

'Well get some orange then; that's good for you as well.'

'I've got some. Here there's the barley water.' Joe pressed the glass into his grandfather's hands.

'Come on then, tell me all about it.' Granddad felt for the table and put the glass down – he hated barley water. Joe pushed the glass further on the coffee table and began to read.

'At seven o'clock last Thursday evening an employee (a Mr Lattimer) had to break into the meditation room of Lord Baron. They call it his blue room Gada.'

'Right ho Joe.'

'He had called him several times but received no response. He was concerned because Lord Baron had an appointment at eight o'clock that evening. The employee decided to fetch Lady Baron. When they returned and after several more attempts to get some sort of reply from her husband, she told the bodyguard to break down the door. This took some time but when they finally got into the room they found him sprawled on the floor. He'd shot himself in the head. Police put the time of death between five-thirty and six-thirty. There was an old army issue Webley revolver close to the body with one round fired. Lady Baron's physician refused the press any contact with her, saying she was under sedation and would be for the foreseeable future. Once the police had finished their investigation the press were allowed to see the room. It says here. – "In a statement to the police, the bodyguard said Lord Baron didn't enter the room until six o'clock. He can swear to it, he says he saw him go in as he turned onto the corridor from the billiard room. He knew it was his Lordship because he was wearing his red and black tracksuit as he always did. And the only time he left his post outside the door was when he went to the lavatory. He took no longer than five minutes, six at the most. He checked his watch as he always did saying it was exactly six-fifteen when he returned. The lavatory is on the floor below. He assured the police that he didn't hear any gunshots during the time his employer was in the room or when he went to the lavatory, which is directly under Lord Baron's meditation room. He is convinced he would have heard the shot. He told reporters that a shot from an old revolver like that would have been heard in every room in the house. Because he left his post, this was considered by the family as a dereliction of duty, Mr. Lattimer is no longer in the employ of the Baron family and has gone abroad."'

'That's not fair, Gada.'

'No Joe, it isn't. It's rather unfair and very convenient.' Joe's granddad tugged at his ear. 'Does it describe the room anywhere?'

'I'll have a look.' Granddad heard the rustle of paper.

'Yes, it tells you here in the middle pages. It says:

"The Blue room didn't have windows and it was soundproofed so he wouldn't be disturbed. The room overlooked the tractor shed, that's why he had the windows walled up. The tractors were in and out of there all day long and he said they were a nuisance. The police found the key in his tracksuit pocket."'

Joe looked puzzled. 'Gada, so how could anybody get in to shoot him?'

'There's no mystery there Joe, there could be two or three keys for the room.'

'But the police say there was only one key. He never let anyone else go into his meditation room!'

'I wonder where they got that information from!'

'It doesn't say, but that's why they're saying he killed himself.'

'Well I disagree Joe.'

'Why Gada?'

'Because of what the bodyguard said and Lord Baron's character. A leopard doesn't suddenly change its spots young fellow.'

'But it says the room was soundproofed.'

'Yes it does, but it doesn't say how well, does it?'

'No it doesn't.'

'It's odd that the bodyguard should suddenly go abroad don't you think Joe? He's the only solid witness the police have. I'm very surprised at that, very surprised indeed!'

'He might have got fed up because they sacked him.'

'Bodyguards don't get fed up at things like that Joe; they usually fight their corner. No, I smell a conspiracy here. We need to know who is to benefit from his death. We need to know who gets the title and who gets the money. Money and power are at the back of this, mark my words Joe!'

Grandad went to his top pocket for his pipe.

'You're not going to smoke that horrible thing are you Gada?'

'No, not while you're here. I'm just going to suck on it while I have a good, long, think.'

Joe drank some of his orange then picked up another newspaper. He could hear the clock on the mantelpiece ticking. It was always quiet when Gada was thinking.

'His brother Horace gets the title Gada; it's in this other newspaper. He's the next in line, and he was at the house all that day and was giving what small comfort he could to Lady Baron.'

Gada said, 'Mmm,' and continued sucking at his pipe. 'Does it say who gets the money Joe?'

'No not really, but it says what's left of his fortune will no doubt go to his widow, Lady Baron. It also says in that other newspaper that no Will has yet been found. But then it says that this information has not been confirmed by the police or the immediate family!'

'That's another reason why he wouldn't kill himself Joe; it's totally out of character. I've known Lord Baron for a number of years; he was meticulous about his responsibilities. No way on earth would he neglect something as important as that. It's like I said before, a leopard can't change its spots, unless it's helped along the way! Let's see what tomorrow's papers tell us. Grandma will be back soon. Then we can have some lunch. When are you back at school?'

'In two weeks, Gada.'

'I don't know what I'll do then. Grandma doesn't always want to read the papers to me.'

'You could get those talking papers Gada! They're good.'

'It's not the same young fellow, they put me to sleep.'

'Grandma's here. I'll give her a hand with the shopping.'

'Right-ho, Joe.'

They had lunch and afterwards Joe played dominoes with his grandfather for an hour then he had to go home to see to his rabbits.

'You're early Joe, have you been to bed?'

'Course I have. I couldn't wait to bring you these. The headlines say there's been a new development in the Lord Baron suicide. There's a question mark after suicide, Gada. They say, Mr. Lattimer the bodyguard has been killed in a hit and run incident in Madrid in Spain. The Spanish police have issued a statement saying they do not suspect foul play. Two witnesses at the scene say the driver of the car appeared to lose control and mounted the pavement narrowly missing another pedestrian. It says Mr. Lattimer was killed instantly! It says he was an ex S.A.S. Captain. Gada, he's got all sorts of medals, did you know that?'

'No Joe I didn't, I only met him two or three times. He was a quiet man always there but always in the background. He was as straight as a die. I know that! Does it mention anything about the car? Have they arrested the driver?'

'No he drove away, and they haven't found the car yet but they are continuing the search. Spanish police are liaising with Superintendent Copperfield of Scotland Yard. Do you know the Superintendent?'

'Yes I do and his number two man, Chief Inspector Stansford. Good men the pair of them. I might have a word with Stansford later. Now what else is there in the papers?'

'I'll get a glass of orange first Gada, if you don't mind?'

'No. do I heck! Get me one while you're there.'

'There's some more about Lord Baron in this one, do you want me to read it?'

'If you would, we need every bit of information we can get. Go on Joe.'

'Well it tells you what he was doing the day he's supposed to have killed himself. He was shooting with a lot more people. Then he was called to the house at four-thirty to take an urgent phone call from America. Mr Lattimer went with him. One of the servants said he lost his temper on the phone and was on about heads will roll for this! Then he sent Mr Lattimer to see to his dogs and told him he wasn't going back to the shoot, he was going up to his bedroom to change and then for some peace and quiet in his meditation room. He said he needed to think.'

'What time was that did you say?'

'He left the shoot to answer the phone at half-past-four Gada, but it doesn't say how long he was on the phone and that's important isn't it?'

'It is Joe, very important but how did you know?'

'You started rubbing your feet together; you always do that when you're excited!'

'Well, I'll be a monkey's uncle. You don't miss much do you?'

'No, not when it's important.'

'So let's see what we know. Mr Lattimer saw Lord Baron go into his room at six o'clock. He answered the phone at four-thirty. That leaves a gap of an-hour-and-a-half, less the time he was on the phone; plus the time it took him to change into his tracksuit, say five or ten minutes on the phone; ten more to change at the most, but we don't know for sure so we'll say a maximum of fifteen minutes. That leaves just over an hour unaccounted for. I think it's then when their first moves were made. I don't know who made them but I suspect it started then.

'Mr Lattimer said he saw him while on his way from the billiard room. So why was he in the billiard room? We need to know the reason why he was in there Joe, that's one thing. Another thing we need to know is how many rooms there are on the same corridor as the meditation room.'

'That's easy Gada, there's a plan with a big arrow showing the room where he died. I'll get the other paper.'

Joe's granddad was deep in thought when Joe came back with the newspaper.

'Five Gada, not counting his room. Six altogether.'

'Right, thanks Joe. Now Mr Lattimer was away from the door for no more than six minutes. We need to know which room on that floor has had a thorough cleaning; it has to be one that's nearest the meditation room.'

'Why do you need to know that Gada?'

Joe's granddad tapped his nose and said, 'It's very important Joe. You're not looking at my feet.'

I need to make a phone call; it might be too late but we'll have to wait and see. They might have cleaned the rest of them. Or they might think they've got away with it and let their guard down. I hope they have Joe. Pass me the phone." Joe passed the telephone and then he searched for more information in the newspaper. His grandfather talked for a long time on the phone. Chief Inspector Stansford promised to ring him back as soon as he had the necessary information. Joe was handed the phone to put back.

'We'll have to wait now Joe, but I'm sure I know how it was done. Let's have a game of dominoes.'

'You always win Gada!'

'I should hope so; no point being in the local team if an eight-year-old can beat me is there?'

'I suppose not, but you should play with eight and me with seven, that would give me a better chance.'

'Get away with you; eight might help instead of hinder. Gives me more to pick from and stitch you up. You can go first, how's that?'

Joe played double six.

His granddad said, 'No surprise there then.'

They had to have fish and chips for lunch because Grandma was visiting her sister.

Joe cleared the table while Gada made a pot of tea. It was a slow process but he liked to do it. It was his contribution to the meal although he let Joe watch him like a hawk. Joe knew his granddad missed the job. He'd never said so but Joe knew he did. The criminal who did it only got five years; Joe wanted to smash him to pieces for shooting at his Gada. But it was more than two years ago and Joe was too small. That's what his mother told him but Joe didn't think he was too little; he'd wanted to get a big piece of wood to hit the man with.

The phone call came at half-past-four. Joe should have been home long ago but he asked his granddad to ring his mum and ask her if he could stay a bit longer. She let him stay but only until five o'clock. He had to feed the rabbits before tea; they were important and they relied on him. He promised he would.

'Thanks Conrad, it's as I thought. It's murder without a doubt and so I suspect was the supposed hit and run. But I can't understand why Lattimer left the country so quickly.'

'No, I didn't know, but thank you for coming back to me so soon.'

'Yes goodbye.'

Granddad passed the phone to Joe. 'Lord Baron had an office in Madrid. Lattimer had been there for some papers. Whatever they were and what information he got from them I'm afraid we'll never know. He hadn't any papers with him when he was killed!'

Joe didn't say anything for a minute then he said, 'I don't think they would have heard a shot if everybody was shooting nearby; they'd just think it was one of the other people shooting wouldn't they?'

'Yes Joe, the shoot would suit the killers perfectly.'

'Was there more than one person who killed him then Gada?'

'There had to be Joe, one person couldn't deal with Lord Baron. Lord Baron was a big, strong man; he was a mountaineer in what spare time he had. No, this little lot took more than one person. Two at least. I can't tell you who they are young fellow, but I can tell you how they did it.

'Conrad's just told me the room directly opposite has been cleaned from top to bottom, and it wasn't cleaned by the servants. That's all the proof I need. That's the room he was murdered in Joe, not in the blue room where his body was found. Lattimer saw somebody going in to the meditation room at six o'clock Joe, but it wasn't Lord Baron; it was somebody wearing a tracksuit exactly like Lord Baron's tracksuit. At some time between say half-past-five and six o'clock somebody got Lord Baron into the other room on some pretext or another, murdered him and waited for an opportunity to transfer the body into the meditation room. When Lattimer went to the toilet they had their chance. That was a stroke of luck; they couldn't have known he'd need to pay a call. I've no doubt they'd come up with some ruse to get Lattimer out of the way to give themselves time to get the body in there. The sad thing is that one of the murderers has to be close to him. That's the one who got another key made. Or just as easy, they could have had the tumblers in the lock altered so that any key will fit; I once did that with an old van I had. It's not difficult. I'll mention that to Conrad when I speak to him later. The other thing I will tell him is that one of them has to be about the same build as Lord Baron, that's the one who Lattimer saw going into the room. Lattimer didn't see his face but he swore it was Lord Baron so he had to be the same build and at the house on that day. It shouldn't be too difficult for the police to find him and the shop where he got the tracksuit. So, at the moment that's about all we can do Joe. Now you'd best go and see to your rabbits and I'll see you tomorrow young fellow.'

'Hello Gada, it's me.'

'Come through, I'm in the kitchen.'

'Gada, last night I thought of another way they could have done it!'

'Did you? Come on then, take the cups through and let's be hearing it.'

They went through and sat in their usual places. Joe laid the newspapers on the coffee table. His granddad felt his grandson's excitement.

'Are you going to tell me or what Joe?'

'Course I'm going to tell you. I was waiting while you got settled,' Joe laughed. 'You've found your other pair of socks Gada.'

'Never mind my socks. Get on with it,' he laughed.

'They could have put Lord Baron's dead body in the room when Mr Lattimer went to find Lady Baron, not when he went to the toilet. Couldn't they!? Because whoever was in the room pretending to be Lord Baron wouldn't open the door. Then when Mr Lattimer went to look for Lady Baron he could sneak out and then they could put Lord Baron's dead body in there. They could do it quick because the room's opposite.'

'Indeed they could Joe! And that way round the murderers wouldn't have needed any luck at all. Brilliant Joe and that would put Lady Baron in the frame! I think tomorrow I'll have to read the papers to you!'

'I wish you could Gada!' sighed Joe.

'So do I Joe,' smiled his granddad.

Richard Lee Wilson 2005.

Ghost Story

Their trail was done and gone, and the guilty scowled upon,
And no compassion would be shown for their foul deeds.
They were sentenced both to die and all the crowd let out a cry,
As the guilty trod the gallows heads held high.

Just a single lonely bell,
Tolled their passing into hell,
As the trap below their feet slammed open wide.
Though they knew their end was near,
Neither lover shed a tear.
Nor did their faces show the slightest hint of fear.

It was on the village green,
Where their ghostly forms were seen.
Then she vanished like a wraith within the mist.
But she didn't say goodbye,
To her beau who stood nearby.
She just took him by the hand then winked her eye.

They'd been lovers from the start,
And they swore they'd never part,
They never will, the judge he saw to that.
Their lost souls will roam this land,
Deep in love and hand in hand,
Till the seas run dry and shun the blackened sand.

Do they roam on Rowley Moor?
I've heard no one knows for sure,
But the sheep no longer graze on Gallows Hill.
Do they ford the old mill stream,
Where young lovers lived their dream?
It's a fact that there the fish no longer teem.

Who would want to take his place,
And to look upon the face,
Of a woman who's been dead a hundred years?

Who would lie in her cold bed,
Near her dreadful hairless head?
Her loved one would, was all they ever said.

Hear that rustle?
Hear that scream?
It's the night of Halloween;
See the moon creep up behind the old church spire.
Where the bell rang out their praise,
As their bodies swung for days,
Now they're silent like the thistles on the Leys.

They are not the ones who wail,
But they turn the locals pale,
When they glimpse them after midnight on the downs.
It's the breeze that blows the clouds and their satin burial shrouds,
And the screams are when they flit among the crowds.

They first met long ago,
But no person had to know,
For they were married each of them to someone else.
To each other they were true,
And their love just grew and grew,
But how they murdered their Dear spouses no one knew.

They killed them in the night,
When the moment was just right,
Then hid the bodies in a place they thought was safe.
They dug the hole so deep,
So no sounds would break their sleep
And the Lord could these poor souls in safety keep.

They packed their pokes and ran away,
Showed their love in every way,
But gossips came and spread the truth like fire.
They were captured by the law
And gained their freedom evermore,
When their bodies dropped like stone through death's trapdoor.

Now they roam on Fallow's Green,
Where no human's ever seen,
And they'll roam this land
Till the final trump of doom.
From their haunting they can't budge,
Till they come before the Judge.
And they pray that he won't bear a dreadful grudge.

So come tread the village green,
Bring your love,
But don't be seen,
And if she's someone else's no one here will care.
But don't flash your eyes this way,
Or to Satan you must pay,
Then your lost and lonely soul will rue the day!

Richard Lee Wilson. July 04.

Ghostly Goings On

I, being the eldest son, took over the burden of this beautiful old house from my father when he passed away. It's called Mollyfoll Hall. It's a lovely name for a house. He, being the eldest, took Mollyfoll over from his father and so on back to Elizabethan times when it used to be a nunnery or the like. It's a draughty house and it's noisy. Clanging and banging and moaning and rattling. Ghosts in every crevice. The din goes on day and night. I'm getting fed up with all of it. I don't get a minute's peace. But what can I do? It's been in the family forever, or so it seems. I can't leave it just because it's full of loony ghosts. It's been renovated and restored, painted and polished. My grandfather had the roof replaced with period tiles; cost a fortune! My father had the foundations strengthened under the two gable-end walls and four of the oak beams in the great hall had to be removed and strengtheners added at each end. That little lot cost him an arm and a leg. I seem to remember chasing up hill and down dale in the Land Rover looking for the perfectly matched pieces of wood.

In my lifetime I've had to have the eleven chimneys rebuilt because they were in danger of falling through the roof. I had to have three-quarters of the upstairs floors re-laid with English oak. This meant another chase up hill and down dale to find the right stuff. Luckily I found enough on the isle of Mull. It hadn't grown there; it had been shipped there from Carlisle. I've had the parquetry done in the great hall and six of the doors on the ground floor, all in the correct period materials because, of course, it's a listed building. I went to every salvage yard in the country. Listed building! The ones who make such stipulations should have to live here! There's hardly any of the original building left untouched. It's like when you hear someone say, 'careful with that!' That's my grandfather's hammer. It's seventy years old. My father replaced the handle and I replaced the hammer head!

"Keep the noise down will you? It's not midnight yet. And stop bouncing your head down the stairs. It's not funny anymore." They're a damned nuisance. I don't know who half of them are. It's Aunt Gertrude's head that's just bounced past me – I'd know that head anywhere! Now she's sent her legs to fetch it. Silly devils just kicked it into the Minstrels Gallery and it's rolling down the back stairs.

'Don't shriek so loud, you loony old crow. Do you want to shatter the window panes?'

She's no right to be here really. She only lived here for six months. I suppose in truth none of them should be here! Especially my wife's dearly departed relatives.

I've done nothing to the house since I came back. If there are any more repairs etc my son can sort them out. It will be his turn then. That's if he's daft enough to come back here!

'Great-Great-Grandfather, would you mind sorting Aunt Gertrude out? She's being a pain in the, you know what! And you don't need to wail and howl like that when you answer! Oh and for goodness sake do something with your beard. The thing's dragging on the floor. Don't float about please! Don't, you know it takes too much energy. Now look what's happened. That's what you get when you start showing off. No I won't come down and get them myself; I'm going into the walled garden for some peace and quiet.'

Ah, it's lovely out here. Perfect tranquillity. The sun's making the red roses glow like fire. Harry's a brilliant gardener. The flowers are superb, especially the white roses. The petals look almost transparent. He won't go into the house; my wife has to come outside to give him his instructions. He says he's scared of ghosts even though she's told him a thousand times that they are perfectly harmless. It's his day off today. Gad, I wish it was mine! I think I'll take a stroll down to the lake, across and through the orchard and then back up to the house. It's called Mollyfoll Hall. It's a lovely name for a house, but I might have said that before. Shame Mollyfoll's riddled with ghosts. Perhaps it's payment for the way my ancestors acquired it. I did read in one of the old parchments about murder, rape and pillage. If that was the case and the house was taken by foul means, well we're paying and it's a heavy price to pay. There's someone fishing over there. It won't be Harry, he's a vegan. It could be his brother. I believe he eats meat. Now the sun's gone in and it looks as if it might start raining. I might as well head back to the house.

Damn and blast! Gertrude and Great-Great-Grandfather are still at it. They only carry on like this when my wife goes out. She wouldn't put up with it. She'd have the vicar round to exorcise every ghost in the place. She's had him round once but he was too scared to come inside. Now there's a new vicar and I've heard he's quite young as vicars go. Perhaps she'll ask him round for tea on the lawn and sound him out!

It was hell on earth last month when she and the children went up to Cordwell for a week to stay with her parents. Luckily, her father made a full recovery or he might have been floating round here somewhere.

'Give it back to her. And put her eyes back in. No not like that! Put them the right way round. And take your fingers out of her nostrils. That's disgusting. I'm going up to my room now and if I see Great-Uncle Horatio on the way I'll tell him what you are doing with his wife's head! You can wail and moan and groan as much as you want. You can find something else to play with, right? Don't pull stupid ugly faces at me you're wasting your time! And put your horrible teeth back in and put Aunt Gertrude's teeth back in. No! Not funny in the least. Put them in her mouth. GREAT UNCLE HORATIO! Thank you. That's better. Now give it back. Thank you! I'll see you both later. Unless you decide to dematerialise before my beloved gets back.'

Whether they did or did not dematerialise is of no matter because my wife didn't come back yesterday and as yet, she hasn't come back today. She rang at about ten-fifteen this morning. Felicity, my youngest daughter who is twenty-nine and still living at home, answered the phone. It would appear from the conversation that the car had broken down and had been towed to the local garage. My daughter left immediately to pick my beloved up from the Golden Thistle Hotel on Rusden Street. As soon as she left the house, Bedlam! Unbeknown to me, Aunt Gertrude and Great Aunt Nellie had invited some friends over from a haunted castle in Risleden for a game of indoor hockey. I don't want to say what they used as sticks, and I don't want to say what they use as a puck because these items are irrelevant in the game. There are no known rules and no limits as to the size of the pitch or any disadvantages when the puck is off the field of play. I suppose if there is any rule at all it's that the game starts on the Shantung Square in the great hall. The puck lays dead centre of the rug and without warning every participant takes a whack at it. The game is over when all the players' heads have landed on the spiked railings by the rose arbour. They and the house went deathly silent when my wife and daughter entered through the gates! It was four o'clock in the afternoon; I went for a lie-down. The mayhem had sent my head spinning: Not a very pleasant experience.

It's Sunday again and all the family have gone to church. I don't go to church – it depresses me seeing all those gravestones. We have our own family vault over by the ornamental garden and the vault has a big iron lock. Harry's come in to prepare the flowers for tonight's memorial ball. My wife invites all her friends and I disappear upstairs out of the way. I can't do with crowds of people, especially when they're all dressed in black. They look like witches; makes me feel uncomfortable. Harry won't bring the flowers in here; he will leave them in neat rows on the drive by the front door. He will inspect them, take off his cap and scratch his head, put his cap back on, and rearrange the pots. Then once again he will take off his cap, scratch his head, rearrange them yet again, mutter something unintelligible put his cap back on shuffle his feet and disappear across the lawn. I've often wondered if he is aware of these subconscious actions.

It's Monday, the married children have gone home and my wife has gone to the market for fresh fish, meat and vegetables. These loonies around the house and around me are throwing multi-coloured slime at one another. Great Aunt Nellie is impaled, hard-fast against the library wall with a medieval lance through her ample chest. Aunt Gertrude is firing Party-Poppers at her (God knows where she found those). Great-Great-Maternal Grandfather Poulter has disembowelled himself and he and his innards are draped over the banister rail like an evil-looking octopus.

The nuns and the mother superior are sliding down the banister at some speed and squealing there heads off as they bounce over what's left of him. Two of them have picked up the wrong heads and now a fight has started. Great-Aunt Agatha who has just swung across the hall on the chandelier is chasing one of them with a carving knife. She was kept under lock and key in the attic over the west wing when she was alive; it's a shame she still isn't under lock and damned key.

Good gad she's caught up with her. Great-Great-Great Aunt Philomena, a forward thinker, has gone to the kitchen for a soup ladle and some catgut. Grief! Now one of our ancestors has decided to create a ghastly, ghostly stench. Now they're all doing it. The black and purple smoke is enough to sicken a saint. The noise is deafening. It's no good I can't take any more! My heads spinning. I can see all four walls at once. I'm leaving. They can do what they like with Mollyfoll Hall. I'm going to look for a tiny little cottage somewhere and do my haunting in peace and quiet!

Richard Lee Wilson. 2005

Herbert Wizard

The twins climbed the steps to the front door. They were careful because it was dark and they weren't sure what they were doing was a good idea.

They were on the second step from the top when a voice shouted through the letterbox, 'I know you're there. Get away from here. You're wasting your time. I know what you want. Now CLEAR OFF! You foul creatures!'

The two teenagers jumped out of their wits, and away from the door. 'We aren't foul creatures, we're runaway orphans and we just wanted a bit of grub and somewhere to sleep for the night. And anyway, how did you know we were going to knock on your door?'

'Never mind that. Orphans you say? I don't believe you. Come to the letterbox. Let me see you. If you're night-creepers I'll splatter you all over the grass.'

'What's he on about?' The fourteen-year-olds looked at each other and shrugged. 'What are night-creepers?'

'Mags, how should I know? They'll be nothing; he's trying to scare us away!'

'Col,' Margaret said as quiet as she could, 'He might be a psycho. We ought to get away from here.'

Margaret went back down the steps and called to whoever was behind the door. 'We won't bother thanks. We'd rather clear off home. Goodnight.'

'Come back here both of you, the barrier's up. You can't leave now.'

'It's ok, we'll climb over it.'

'You nit-wit. You can't climb over it. It's over ten meters high!'

'He is mad – I'm off.'

She ran down the path for about five strides, slammed into something and fell over backwards.

'The barrier (by the way) is invisible. So be careful. I've brought it nearer so you can throw a pebble or something at it. Then you'll know I'm telling the truth! But I'll have to let it go back to the boundary now because they're coming.'

'He's mad. We're trapped.'

'He doesn't sound mad to me. You stopped dead just then. Come on Mags. He'll see your hair. He'll know you're a girl. Come back, hurry up, it's cold out here.'

'I have to do all the risky things.'

'You've never done anything risky in your life.'

'Course I have, lots of things.'

'Such as?'

'I don't know. All sorts of stuff. He might throw something at me through the letterbox.'

'Why should he? Get on with it.'

Maggie hesitated. 'All right then. I'll come with you.'

'You're not a psycho are you?' asked Colin.

'Don't talk stupid. Come to the letterbox. Hurry you haven't much time! They're coming.'

'What does he mean? Come on Mags we'll both go. We're here!'

They climbed the steps to the door and the man opened the letterbox.

'I can see you now. You might be what you say you are but you can't come in and you should be in bed at this time of night. It's three minutes past ten! And after ten o'clock nobody comes in, nobody goes out. The place is sealed and I can't risk breaking the seal now!'

'It's cold and dark out here! You don't want to find us dead on your doorstep do you?'

'No I don't but if you don't stop interrupting you won't be found at all. So listen very carefully to what I say. I'm going to pass a wand through the door.'

'A wand? Are you a wizard or something?'

'Of course I'm a wizard. Who else would want to live in a crumbling old ruin? Now quickly, do as I say. Hold the wand above your heads and count to three. You'll feel a rushing through the air feeling then you'll be in the barn, which is behind you over there. Don't scream or anything because screams attract them. They're late as it is or you two could be, well anything? Right it's here, get hold of it.'

A shiny, black wand was passed through the letterbox. Colin reached forward and took it.

'Hold it above your heads and count to three or maybe four. But don't let go of it or you could finish up anywhere. And keep hold of it till morning.'

'You're having us on aren't you mate?'

'No I'm not you twerp. Get counting and get it above your heads before it's too late. They could be here any minute and they dart about as fast as lightning'

'This is stupid Mags.'

'Hey Col, maybe not? Look over there. There by the wood. What's that thing coming out of the woods? There's another. Oh blobs, there's another! Are those silver things its legs?'

'Quick Mags, hold the wand with me and count.'

'We're holding the wand!'

'Count as quick as you can.'

'Argh look at that!'

'One, two. Faster. Onetwothreefour. Wooow!'

'Where are you Mags?'

'I'm here. I'm right in front of you.'

'We must be having the same nightmare!'

'We must be.'

'We're in his barn! Wow! But did you see all those stars?'

'Of course I did. There were millions. They were brilliant. And I know we're in his barn, I've just got a mouthful of filthy straw. And I banged my head on something.'

Margaret couldn't see what it was. 'Well let's hope we're safe in here. Did you see how big their bodies were?'

'If you rub them Mags, they go.'

'What, the creepy things?'

'The bump you twit.'

Margaret looked towards Colin and said, 'Col get real.'

'They do! Dad says they do. It's the heat from friction.'

'Shut up Col, we're supposed to be orphans.'

'Tell me this isn't really happening is it Mags?'

'Be QUIET you idiots. They'll hear you. And keep hold of the wand, unless you want to waken up with all your insides and outsides missing!'

Colin didn't want to admit to Margaret that he was hearing things. But after a few minutes he said, '

Maggie!'

'What?'

'Did you hear anything a minute ago?'

'Yes it's him, it's the wizard. He's talking into our heads.'

'It's made me feel sick. It's weird. Have you gone dizzy?'

'No, I'm just tired and I'm starving and I wish we hadn't missed the bus!'

'At least it's warm in here and it's great in the hay.'

'You'll be covered in the stuff. "I don't ca…'

'I said hush you idiots. Can't you hear them? They're all round you. I'll give you something to eat in the morning if you're still in one piece. Goodness knows I've enough to do without worrying about you two twerps. Now don't say another word! And don't let go of the wand no matter what!'

'We could try and get to sleep Maggie.'

'Sleep? With those things outside. You're having a laugh aren't you?'

'For goodness sake you two, keep quiet! They can hear whispers! They've got ears like elephants. They're right outside the door!'

'Agh what was that?'

'Shush.'

Colin put his finger to his lips. He was wasting his time because it was pitch black in the barn. Neither twin could see each other.

'It's them creeper things!'

The door creaked, swayed and rattled again. They were scared now. Really scared. They crept as far away from the door as they could. Colin bumped into something. There was a thump, thump, thump, against the door and a sort of slurping sound. Colin stood dead still. He'd bumped into a hayfork. Without a sound, he took hold of it and held it pointing at the door. He waved his arm to show Maggie to get behind him. She could barely see a thing. 'PUT THAT DOWN AND PICK UP THE WAND YOU IMBECILES.' Colin's hair lifted when the wizard yelled into his head.

Maggie said 'Ouch that hurt.'

He stuck the hayfork back in the bale where he'd found it and scrabbled in the hay round his feet for the wand. So did Maggie because something crashed hard against the window right behind her. The loud bang made them jump and they banged into each other. Colin's head hit Margaret's then he stumbled, lost his balance and fell over. The door rattled, the boards rattled and it sounded like the whole place rattled and banged. Frightened to death, they found the wand, grabbed it and held onto it. Suddenly, everything went quiet. They daren't make a sound and they daren't move an inch. As quiet as mice they sat in the hay and held onto the wand tightly.

Their eyes slowly got accustomed to the dark but Colin wished his hadn't. He could make out strange, ghostly, grey shapes everywhere. Worse still, they looked as if they were moving towards him, but moving ever so, ever so slowly. He shut his eyes; Maggie's eyes were already shut, but she was trying really hard to stay awake. She didn't want to let go of the wand. Colin kept his eyes shut and tried his best not to hear the awful scratching sounds. He hoped the barn wasn't full of rats or worse still, earwigs. It was much later, or a minute later when somewhere nearby a screech owl called out. They were awake instantly and they were still clutching the wand.

Colin had cramp in his knuckles and was desperate for a pee. He let go of the wand and tried to massage his fingers back to life. Margaret's hair looked like a thatched roof. He decided to waken her up.

'Wake up Maggie. Wake up I can see daylight.'

'What? What is it?' Maggie yawned and rubbed her eyes. 'I am awake.'

All of a sudden she sat up. 'We must have fallen asleep. My fingers hurt like mad.'

'It's because you've been holding that wand all night. You can let go of it – they've gone.'

'How do you know?'

'I've let go of it and there's no rattling and banging. And I need a pee. I'm going round the back. Won't be long.'

Colin shot out of the barn as Maggie stood and stretched. She ached all over. She walked to the doorway and looked out. She saw a tall, scruffy-looking man with a mop of ginger hair coming down the garden.

'You're awake then!' '

'Who are you?' Asked Maggie still yawning and rubbing her eyes at the same time.

'Herbert Wizard is the name. I live here. Who are you?'

'I'm Margaret. That's Colin.'

Colin came round the corner of the barn. They were both covered in bits of straw and hay.

'Good morning. Sorry about last night. The night-creepers must have been pretty scary but don't panic, they disappear at dawn. You see I don't get visitors. You two obviously didn't read the warning on the gate, which says KEEP OUT WILD ANIMALS! Where's my spare wand?'

'In there. What are those horrible night-creeper things? They looked to have loads of legs.'

'They aren't legs. But more about those horrible things later. I've put the kettle on and there's some bacon and eggs waiting to be fried. I'll get my wand while you two get tidied up.'

142

The man went into the barn. Maggie and Colin picked the hay off their clothes and out of their hair. They didn't look any tidier when they'd finished!

'There's a brush in the house. You can use that. Come orphans, follow me,' he laughed.

The 'orphans' tagged along. They'd never seen a place like this before.

'He doesn't look much like a wizard does he? He's scruffy and so is this place. Wizards live in castles. This is no castle! There's rubbish everywhere!'

'I don't know Maggie. I've never seen a wizard before or a wizard's castle.'

'You've seen "Lord of the Rings" haven't you? Gandalf's a wizard! Wizards all have really long beards and cloaks.'

'That's a story, you drip!'

'I know it's a bloody story. It's how you picture wizards look, isn't it?'

'Hey, watch it. I'll grass you up to dad! You promised him you'd watch your language.'

'Shut it, we're supposed to be orphans! Orphans don't have dads.'

'You don't think he believed us do you? Come off it Maggie.'

'You don't know if he did or not!'

'You don't have to be much of a wizard to know we're not orphans, girl!'

'I don't know where you get that from?'

'It's obvious isn't it? Orphans don't wear designer trainers and Levi's.' Maggie laughed at him.

'You two aren't going to start whacking each other, are you?'

'No.' Colin shook his head. 'I haven't the strength. I'm starving!'

'Come in, the kitchen's through there.'

'Look Maggie, he's got a cauldron!'

'That's a stew pot.'

'Oh is it?'

'Do you want to wash your hands?'

He pointed to a sink under the window. Maggie sniffed but they went over. It was full of pots, pans and weird-shaped bottles. They were every colour on earth.

'It was cleaner in his barn!'

'Shush, he'll hear you.'

143

'Would you open the curtains while you're there please? Thank you.'
The place looked even scruffier with the light from the window.

The bacon sizzled away in the pan. He turned it over.

'How many eggs do you want?'

'Two please,' answered Maggie wiping her hands on what was once a white towel.

'Can I have three? I'm starving.'

'You may. Fried bread either of you?'

'Please.'

'Ta, two for me.'

'Well sit down, or are you going to eat standing up?'

They both sat down. Maggie dusted the seat of her chair.

He served up the food and sat down.

'I suppose you're wondering about last night?'

'Not half! Worst night I've had in my life!' Colin filled his mouth.

'It would have been worse had you stayed outside!'

'What are those creatures with all those legs? You called them night-creepers.'

'I call them that. But they're not legs Margaret, they're sort of suction pipes. Like an octopus with ten tentacles. Sometimes they creep about, sometimes they dash about. They're supposed to pick up all the rubbish outside. Trouble is they don't know the difference between outside and inside. Or people, or animals, birds or rubbish. So they collect everything. Somehow I got the spell wrong. Don't ask me how because I haven't a clue. I've tried for days to turn them back into old Hoovers but nothing seems to work. Look in here. I let them loose in here. They had a great time. They sucked up everything! But instead of tipping it outside, they spit it out in here. I don't know what half the stuff is. I keep shovelling the rooms out one at a time. The upstairs isn't so bad now. Goodness knows what Mira will say when she comes back. I only made the things to save her tidying up all day. She'll need another holiday! I'll just have to keep trying to get the spell right.'

Herbert Wizard looked more than fed up as he ate his breakfast.

I don't suppose you're any good with puzzles?' His eyebrows went up as he asked and he dipped a soldier in his egg. 'I've tried everything I can think of. Perhaps another head or two? Maybe see it from a different angle. The reverse spell's stuck on the fridge door.'

He chewed noisily on a piece of fried bread. 'I got a good mid-term report for comprehension. Seventy-five percent.'

'Not bad.'

'Wooo. I got a good mid-term.' Maggie kicked Colin.

'Shut your face. What percentage did you get?'

'OWCH. Now look what you've done. You've made me spill my coffee!'

'Don't be soppy.'

Maggie got up and went to the fridge. 'It's a rhyme.'

'For every spell and every un-spell there's a rhyme young lady. It's working them out, that's the difficult part. The first bit's easy.'

Herbert Wizard threw the cloth into the sink. 'Try not to spill it again young man.'

'Read it out Maggie. I'm still eating.'

Maggie looked at the piece of paper stuck on with a fridge magnet. The writing was weird but she managed ok.

See them twist, see them turn and soar.

These floppy things don't sleep on the floor.

Feeble-sighted they may well be,

But they never crash into house or tree.

Get two large grams of what they eat,

Mix it up with one gram of wheat.

Three stirs left and three to the right,

Mix them both on a moonless night!

'That means four grams of bat-droppings.'

'Do you mind Mr Wizard? I'm trying to eat here!'

Mr Wizard's eyebrows rose. 'It's normally girls who are squeamish, Colin.'

He turned to Maggie. 'Mixed with a gram of flour. The second one is easy. That's five small grams, which is two-and-a-half grams of salt and pepper.'

'How do you know it's salt and pepper?'

'Because of the sneeze bit there.'

The wizard's long finger pointed at the line in question. 'And that bit there where it says looks like it but it isn't sweet!'

'Clever,' said Colin putting the last piece of bacon in his mouth. He left them to it.

'It's the last ingredient that's giving me problems. I've already prepared the rest.'

Maggie read it out:

Four crescent segments,

Four hidden stones.
Half a pound of penny rice
And a pile of mouldy bones.
Mix it all with the sands of time,
Got from a clock that doesn't chime!

'The last bit's simple,' said Colin, as he wiped his hand across his mouth. 'It's an egg timer. They put sand in them don't they to time eggs?'

Maggie and Mr Wizard stared at him. For a good minute they were both speechless.

'It is simple, Colin. You are right. You are not only an eating machine you're a genius. I must be stupid not getting that one.'

Mr Wizard was over the moon. Maggie was quite impressed.

'Come on you two, I've got one through here.'

He shot out of the kitchen. He was searching through a cupboard when the 'orphans' came in.

'It's in here. I know it is.' More clutter joined that on the carpet.

'Got it! Come on. Follow me.'

They ran up the spiral staircase so fast Maggie went dizzy and Colin got indigestion.

'IN HERE!'

They followed his shout and went into a room that had everything a real or imaginary wizard could want. Including a skeleton and a stuffed badger.

On a bench that ran the full length of the room were at least a hundred cereal bowls. Each one had a mixture in it. There was orange peel, lemon peel, grapefruit peel and a dozen other kinds of peel. There were plum stones, apricot stones, peach stones, kidney stones and gall stones.

'I'm going to put a few grains of sand in every one of these mixes. Then we can tip them one by one out of the back window. Then I've got them.'

He threw his arms in the air and cheered.

'Come on one of you, empty the egg timer into that big bowl there. One of you grab a spoon. I'll put the sand in.'

'Where are they?'

'Where are who? What?'

'The creepers!'

'They're asleep in the garden at the back.'

'What! Asleep in the back garden! Why don't you just go and knock them to bits or something. You said they disappeared at dawn!'

Maggie was astonished.

'Not disappeared like that disappear. Disappear like go round the back of the house out of sight.'

'And don't you think I wouldn't have knocked them to pieces if I could you noddle-box? You can only break a spell with a spell-breaker spell. Goodness me, don't youngsters know anything these days? Come on we have a lot of work to do.'

Maggie didn't know what a noddle-box was but whatever it was, she was definitely sure she wasn't one.

It took them two hours to mix the sand with the disgusting contents of each dish. The mouldy, barbequed rib-bones smelled the worst.

'I'll open the window. We've done twenty mixes. We can start dropping it on them.'

Colin went to the window.

'I haven't unsealed the window yet.'

'Can you do it now? I'm beginning to feel sick.'

'Breathe in deeply Colin and put your head between your knees.'

'Breathe in deeply! You're having me on mate aren't you? I'd rather be sick.'

'Pass me that wand from over there if you're going to make a fuss. Sure you're not sisters instead of brother and sister?' Mr Wizard gave them a beamer of a smile.

'How did you know we were brother and sister? I've never said so.'

'Cyclops with grit in his eye would spot the likeness. And I know you're not orphans. I knew straight away. What I want to know is what you were doing out so late? You'll both be in big trouble when you get home.'

'No we won't. It's the weekend. We're sleeping over.'

'Won't your friends be worried about you?'

'No. Maggie rang them on her mobile last night.'

'We missed the bus back from Clayton. I told them we'd walk back or stay with Uncle Henry but he must be on holiday. Then we saw this place. We thought we'd pretend to be orphans and see if you fell for it. It's okay; I've told them where we are.'

'Oh, and what address did you give them?'

'This one. Thirteen, Bumble Wood Lane.'

'Did you indeed. You thought it was as easy as that!' The wizard laughed.

'I was going to ring them from the barn but my mobile wouldn't work.'

'No, it wouldn't because you were sealed in the barn!'

'That's about it really. Now can we dunk the creepers?'

'Yes we can. Come on, but I hope you realise how stupid you've been. I hope you don't do anything as stupid in the future.'

They both looked sheepish and shaking their heads, said, 'No definitely not.'

'Never!'

'Go on, tip one out and tell me what happens while I keep on mixing.'

He didn't believe they wouldn't do anything stupid again – not for one minute.

There was a loud whooshing sound. Maggie passed him the empty plastic bowl.

'Well, what's happened?'

'Nothing. I don't know. I can't see.'

'Stand back, let me have a look. No, they're still there. Pass me another.'

On the forty-first bowl there was a deafening sizzle then a massive explosion. Bits of purple and green stuff splattered against the top window and flew everywhere. Bits of silver foil were left hanging in the trees and on the washing line.

'Ha, that's done it! At last, at last!'

Mr Wizard began jumping up and down. His glasses fell into one of the bowls and one of his shoes came off.

'Excellent, excellent, excellent. They've gone. Suckers and all.'

He sat down and put his shoe back on and got his glasses. He was so delighted he forgot to wipe the stuff off them.

'Well thank you both very much. And for your brilliant help I'm giving you both one of my spare wands. You won't be able to work any magic with them but they will remind you of the time when you were so stupid. You could have been eaten alive you know.'

The wizard scratched his head.

'Actually you'd have been eaten dead. I suppose you can't be eaten and be alive.'

He scratched his head again.

'Well never mind that. Lucky for you two you weren't. Now if you give me the address of your friend's house, I'll whiz you over there. Each of you hold your wand above your head with both hands. Now say goodbye and count to three or four.'

'Goodbye Mr Wizard, thanks for the wands.'

'Goodbye and thank you very much indeed for your help.'

They counted, 'One, two, three, fou…' Then they were whizzing through the air. They landed in the compost heap in Ben's back garden. Then they staggered out and staggered about. Everything was so sudden and all was spinning round. They were well dizzy.

They were still a bit dizzy when a voice asked, 'Where have you two come from? And why are you creeping about? You're a bit old to be playing Ring-a-Rosy.'

'We're not creepers and we aren't playing Ring-a-Rosy, you dork. Can't you see we're dizzy?'

'Yes, I can! No change there then!'

'Get lost. Anyway you wouldn't believe us if we told you where we've come from, would he Col?'

'Nah, never.'

'We could show him though. The night creepers have gone. He might not want to meet a wizard.'

'Night-creepers! Wizard!' laughed Ben. 'You're having a laugh!'

'Come on then, we'll show you. Look.' They showed Ben their wands. 'Let's get to the bus stop.'

After a bit more convincing the three of them ran out of the garden and off down the road. They'd only five minutes to wait for the Clayton bus. The only problem was, they didn't know which stop to get off at.

'Just get the number three to Clayton. We'll watch out for the house.'

They jumped on the bus and watched for the house like hawks.

'We must have gone past it. That's the railway bridge! Come on Maggie, come on Ben, we're getting off here!'

The three of them got off the bus at the next stop and set off back the way they came.

'There's that big tree and there's the house!'

'That's not the house dip-head, that's a bungalow!'

'It has to be it Maggie. That's the wood where the creepers came from.' Colin pointed to the woods.

'It's gone. The house was here and now it's gone!' Ben smirked.

Maggie bit her lip and said, 'It must have been some mouldy cheese we ate.'

'Maggie what's that in your hand? Could it be a wand, the same as this one?'

Colin tapped Maggie on the nose with his shiny black wand.

'Stop it; I know what a wand is. And Maggie, we didn't eat any mouldy cheese. We didn't eat any cheese at all!'

The net curtains at the window moved ever so slightly. Had they looked at the window instead of arguing with each other, the trio might just have caught a glimpse of ginger hair!

Richard Lee Wilson 2005

Highwayman

He drove the car into a passing place and stopped.

'Ok, it's pitch black and you think we're lost!'

Tony massaged his temples. 'We might as well admit it Sam, perhaps we are!'

The storm battered against the screen and the side windows as the wind swirled round in ever changing directions. Even worse was the din it made when the rain pounded the soft top of the MG. It sounded like they were being bombarded with pebbles.

'Damn, damn, damn it!' growled Tony and slammed both hands against the wheel. Samantha didn't reply. She glared at the map and felt like tearing it to pieces.

'Let me have another look at the map, maybe I can find out where we are?'

'Take the thing. This farm-track-of-a-road's not a road at all, and it's not shown on the map!' she said angrily.

'If it is I can't damn well find it! Why we don't have an RAC road map like everybody else I'll never know!'

Samantha all but threw the map to Tony.

'Hey, I'm not the navigator, you are! And this, Grumpy, is an Ordinance Survey map. The best there is!'

He frowned at her, grabbed the map and spread it out across the wheel. She frowned back. He stared at it for a good five minutes. Then he muttered more to himself than his wife.

'We took the B1113 to Balan Falls. Then we turned off and came down that one.'

He showed the road to his wife. She showed no interest. Her head was back and her eyes were closed.

'We came over the moors on that one.'

Again he traced the twisty, thin white line on the map with his finger. Samantha only nodded.

Tony sniffed and said, 'The reservoir was on our left and if we could see through this lot it should still be on our left. I'll take the big torch and have a look.'

'You'd better get your coat or you'll get soaked.'

'Hosepipe ban!' she snapped.

'The greedy sods!' They were both tired out.

'Calm down. I'll put it on when I get out; there isn't enough room in here!'

'You wanted an old car, not me! We should have got a Vectra. Then we wouldn't have had to listen to this racket! And they have reclining seats. And they have a heater!' Samantha shivered.

'They didn't make Vectras in nineteen-forty-nine when this was made! And this has a heater, a good heater. So if you're cold put your sweater on! Hell fire, anybody would think I have control over the damned weather.'

Tony got the torch and his waterproof and opened the door. Although he was ready for it, the wind whipped at the door handle so suddenly it nearly tore it out of his grasp.

'You're right about the injustice of a hosepipe ban,' he shouted as he slammed the door and as the wind turned his coat into a sail.

He was back within minutes.

'The reservoir's still there.' He nodded to the left. He was wet through. Rain poured off his hood and the bottom of his coat onto the car seat as he dragged at his coat sleeve. He was doing his best to keep as much rain out of the car as he could.

He shook the coat. 'Well that was a waste of time,' he moaned as water went down his neck. 'Grab me a towel from behind there Sam, I'm wringing wet!'

Samantha rummaged as best she could behind the seats.

'Can you manage with that?'

'Anything.'

'It's your "Quo" T-shirt.'

'That's okay it's had worse treatment than this!' He crammed the waterproof coat behind his seat, wiped his face and hands and got the map. Keeping the T-shirt, he wiped the back of his neck and pointed to a right-turn about a mile along the lane.

'We need that next right. It's no more than a mile from here. It goes to Crag Vale. We can see if there's anything there.'

He dropped the T-shirt over his shoulder, gave Samantha the map and started the car. Before he drove off he pointed out the turn on the map.

'It's there Love, ok?'

'Yep.'

He looked at her and she smiled.

'I'm sorry I snapped at you. It's the weather.'

He smiled back and said, 'Keep your eyes open love.'

He put the car in gear and pulled out onto the road. The rain continued to hammer down.

'There's a nasty left-hander about fifty yards before our turn-off so be ready for that!'

She nodded.

Even with the main beam and the two spot-lamps, visibility was pretty poor but he drove with care. He'd no intention of finishing up in twenty or more feet of water on their first wedding anniversary. This was supposed to be a special treat.

They spotted the nasty left hander in good time and Tony slowed down even more. This bit of the road was nothing but loose gravel washed down off the moors. There were ruts and holes and some were pretty bad. He drove carefully.

'Good grief,' he shouted. 'I missed that by a millimetre. They could fill the damned holes with the rubble we keep bouncing over, the useless buggers!'

'Relax Darling, we're past it now.'

'I know we are Sam but I caught the front suspension on a rock or something. That's why I'm teed off! Not with you Love. Hope there's no damage!'

The surface improved but the weather didn't. Tony stared through the screen. He kept brushing his black, wavy hair back. A sure sign to Samantha that he was shattered. Restoring the MG every night until the early hours for at least eighteen months while starting their own design studio would shatter anybody.

They topped a rise and they could see a faint cluster of lights in the distance.

'They've got electricity then!' he said sarcastically and smirked. But he didn't take his eyes of the road, not for one second. It was a tarmac road but it could have done with a fair amount of tender loving care.

'Warm enough yet?'

'I'm getting there,' replied Samantha thinking of and longing for their roaring log fire at home.

'January's a daft month for a wedding. We should have got married in June or July.' She yawned loudly.

'Too late now Sam. Although we could always get a divorce and remarry. If, of course, you want to go through all that again. The endless tears, the tantrums and the foot stampings. And that was only your father!'

'Get lost! At least he didn't get rat-faced and puke up all over the place.'

'I have no control over your mother's drinking habits.'

'You shit,' laughed Samantha. 'I'll tell her what you said.'

'Please don't. Warts are hard to get rid of!'

'You two-faced pig, she adores you!'

'I know and I adore her.' He grinned. Samantha's mother was one of those rare women who a son-in-law would say is a great person and a good friend.

They drove up the hill and were soon amongst the houses. Ninety-five percent looked to be built of local dark-grey stone, which in the light of the street lamps and the foul weather looked black and unwelcoming. The couple would get the impression from their restricted line of sight that the main street ran through the centre of the village more or less cutting it in half. In fact there were far more houses on the right than on the left. Those on the right went up nearly to the edge of the moor. While the houses on the left only went back as far as the river. There were no houses on the other side of the river; there the moor rose too steeply and it was full of deep rivulets that fed the river which in turn fed the reservoir. Had the young couple not taken the right turn, a quarter of a mile further on they would have driven over a badly neglected bridge that spanned this same river.

Samantha spotted the hotel first.

'There's a hotel! There on the right we'll stop there. Its sign's lit up so it will be open, won't it?'

She pressed her hands together in mock prayer.

Tony glanced at his watch. 'It's only half-nine, it should be.'

Tony indicated, drove across the street and followed a sign that lead to the car park. The weather had eased noticeably but it was still raining steadily. Tony got out of the car grabbed his coat, threw it over his head, rubbed his eyes and stretched. 'Six-and-a-half hours to get here and we've another fifty miles or so yet. But I don't think we'll be going on tonight. No, not tonight. I'm shattered. How about you?' he said looking up at the rear of the hotel.

'I'm easy.' She yawned. It wasn't a very big building and there were none of the usual ugly kitchen or lavatory extensions tacked on at the back or the sides. The hotel, like the sign to the car park, was covered in ivy that gave it a genteel, Olde Worlde look. The hotel was detached from its neighbours by the wide entrance and exit to the car park.

'What's it called? I didn't see a sign or anything did you love?'

'Yes, it's called The Highwayman,' said Samantha pointing. 'There's a sign over that small door.'

'I see it,' replied Tony wondering how he could have missed it. 'Let's hope they don't rob us blind. Fancy some food if there is any?'

'Definitely! I'm starving.' Tony nodded, locked the car and they each took an overnight bag with them in case they stayed over. The rain now had stopped completely and they were sheltered from the wind. Tony, feeling far more relaxed than he felt earlier, pushed open the small door and let Samantha go in first.

'Thanks,' she said smiling.

'My pleasure.'

He followed her through into the front lobby. 'At last, civilization.' What they could see was tastefully decorated. The top halves of the walls were cream and the bottom halves, oak panelling. Each complimented the other, and there wasn't a curled up corner of wallpaper to be seen. But there was nobody at the small desk in the lobby to the right of the front entrance. There was a fairly large brass bell with a handwritten sign lying beside it that read: "Please ring for attention." Samantha rang the bell. It had the muted clang of a nineteen-fifty's school bell.

Tony looked round for the bar, took his coat off and hung it on a stand in the corner. Samantha followed suit, looked for a mirror, didn't find one so tidied her hair as best she could. There was a menu on a small side-table in a cubbyhole under the staircase. A pink-shaded table lamp illuminated this neat tableau. Tony picked up the menu and opened it.

It made impressive reading. 'How's your French today Sam?'

'The same as yours – average.'

There was a sound of heavy footsteps on the stairs and a giant of a man with a beaming smile across his face and using the newel post for purchase spun into view and bid them a warm welcome.

'Good evening Sir, Madam. Sorry to keep you waiting.'

'It's no trouble,' replied Tony returning his smile.

'Now what can we do for you?' he beamed again. 'If you want something to eat you'll have to shake a leg. Chef finishes at ten on the dot.'

A questioning rise of black, bushy eyebrows accompanied the smile.

'We'd like to eat and I think we'd like a room if you've got one,' replied Tony and turned to Samantha for confirmation.

'Yes I think so,' she said nodding.

'If it's just the one night mind, I can help you. We're quiet but we're fully booked after tonight till next weekend.'

'That's fine; we only want to stay tonight.'

'Right-oh then. We'll sort the room out once you've ordered your food. We don't want chef to go off on one do we?'

He beamed and they shook their heads because they didn't know what else to do.

'You can leave your bags behind the desk. I'll put your coats on them. Follow me and I'll take you through. You can have a table by the fire. It's a bit foul out there; you look as though a warm-through will do you both good.'

The big man led the way.

The dining room, from the floor to the ceiling was stunning. Victorian period tables and chairs glowed in the soft light of the converted paraffin lamps. Their soft flickering wicks, although not authentic, still cast dark dancing shadows around and about. The embossed Regency-stripe wallpaper was stunningly delicate with its pale blue, rose-pink and gold scrolling. This paper was not the same period as the furniture but no other wallpaper would have looked as good. The owner showed them to a table to the left of the fire and said, 'You can sit and look at the paintings.'

He held Samantha's chair and she thanked him. He asked if they would like an aperitif. Samantha asked for a pale dry sherry. Tony ordered a glass of the Australian red. The owner left them with the menu and went through a doorway at the other end of the room. He wasn't long before he could be heard coming back. The room didn't shake but you could certainly feel the vibrations. He placed their glasses on the table and asked if they'd decided what they would like. He looked relieved when Samantha ordered the duck and Tony ordered fillet steak and added before being asked, 'Rare please.' Neither wanted a starter. He thanked them and returned the way he'd come, calling out their order before he was through the kitchen door.

Samantha was staring at the pictures on the walls. Those "in the know" who seemed able to read the minds of long-dead artists would have called the scenes "Chocolate Box." Samantha, not being an art snob thought some of the paintings were beautiful. The one on the wall behind Tony, in her opinion, was the most beautiful piece of work she'd ever seen. What she didn't notice immediately was a price tag, the artist's name and that the painting was of this very hotel. But in fairness to her it was a bit grubby and it looked as if it had been painted a hundred years ago. The price and the artist's name were written in very small, neat script on an unobtrusive sticker on the wall beneath the frame. When she saw the tiny sticker, and when her eyes focused on the equally miniscule price her mouth dropped open and she had to slowly put her glass down because it was full. She was excited and any minute now her hand might shake. She didn't know the artist but to Samantha it didn't matter – she loved it.

'There is a picture on the wall behind you my darling.'

Tony's eyebrows went up. 'Don't look like that, you know you're my darling. I want you to buy it for me. If you love me as much as I love you, you will.'

'Is it a picture of an open fire?' he laughed.

'Very droll and no it's not!'

'How much is it?'

'Fifty guineas. That's fifty-two-pounds-fifty.'

'I know what a guinea is worth my love and if it was double that I'd buy it for you. Because you are my darling.' He gave her a dismissive grin and said, 'I'll call it your next birthday present!'

'No you won't. You can call it a love token like that extremely expensive Britool socket-set I got for you at that boot-sale! If you don't, I'll call you Ebenezer and get you some fingerless gloves!'

'If I remember correctly my socket-set was a tenner!'

'It's not the price; it's the thought that counts.'

'It's yours my love.' He shook his head. 'I can't argue against that sort of blackmail!'

Samantha leaned across the table and gave him a soppy kiss.

'Here we are! duck for you and steak for you.' The owner put their plates in front of them and took the sauces from a tray a young girl had brought to the table. She smiled, said bon appetite and left to go to the only another couple in the room who were sitting at a table for six by the window. The small jugs were placed beside the plates.

'Now is there anything else you'd like?'

'No thanks.'

'What about you sir?'

'No this is fine thank you. It looks delicious.'

'I think we have some crispy farmhouse rolls left.'

'No this is perfect thanks.'

'Right oh, enjoy your meal, but if you want anything just give me a call.'

'Wait there is one thing. I want to buy a painting; it's the one on the wall behind me.'

'It's the most beautiful picture I've ever seen,' interjected Samantha and smiled at the giant. 'We would like to take it with us tomorrow.'

Had she put a gun to his head and said empty your safe into this holdall the effect on him would have been less severe. He staggered back as the blood drained from his face and had to hold onto the adjacent table or he would have collapsed on the floor. It seemed to Samantha forever before he got a grip of himself.

'I'm sorry,' blurted Samantha. 'Are you all right? Can we call somebody?'

Tony was already on his feet and holding him by the arm.

'No, no, I'm fine. I'll be as right as rain in a minute. Touch of indigestion, that's all. Too much running about!' He smiled his beaming smile but there was a wild gleam of anticipation in his eyes.

'If you're absolutely sure?' asked Tony tentatively, letting go of the man's arm. 'I thought you were going to pass out.'

'So did I!' said Samantha looking worried.

'No it's gone. I'm as right as a bobbin now. I'll get a couple of Rennies. You two get on with your meals before they go cold.'

The young couple sat down as the man turned and headed for what Tony supposed was the kitchen or the bar. The big man certainly looked as if he needed a good stiff drink. Tony sat down and passed Samantha her sauce then reached for his.

'This one's yours.' Tony passed her the other and took the first one back.

'Bon appetite,' they chorused sending the incident to the back of their minds.

'Jinx, blue jinx,' laughed Tony.

'Get lost,' replied Samantha.

Neither saw a tall, serious-looking woman pop her head round the kitchen door and stare intensely at the young couple. They ate in comparative silence. This had nothing to do with "Jinx, blue Jinx." It was because the food was superb.

'You said she said the right words.' The woman looked worried.

'Did she say it was the most beautiful picture she'd ever seen?'

'Yes thank the Lord; she did. So that's it. We can be rid of the thing!'

'We can if you want but they seem nice people.'

'Of course I want, don't you?!' snapped the man. 'It doesn't matter to me who they are. We've had our time with it! And that's enough for anybody.'

The tall woman shook her head and said, 'They seem such a nice young couple.'

'I don't care what they seem. I want to sleep in my own bed in my own house Elsie. Not a stranger's bed,' the big man grunted.

'Do you think we've made it too cheap? We've never altered the price!'

'He's never said we had to.' The woman shook her head again.

'What's wrong with you woman, are you mad?' hissed the big man, taking hold of her by the shoulders.

'Of course I'm mad. You're mad. We must have been mad to agree to keep it, damn it to hell!'

The big man let go of her. He wasn't smiling now.

'Don't say that you fool.' He glared at his wife as if he hated the sight of her and she glared back at him. Neither spoke. He turned and left the kitchen.

'There must be something badly wrong with him, and it's not indigestion. He's got a face like the weather. Samantha turned to look.

'Wow, do you think he's ill?'

'He looks cross as hell to me. I don't think for a minute he had indigestion. I think it was some sort of shock reaction. I'm no Doctor. But I'd bet a month's salary that's what it was!'

'I bet it's the wrong price.'

'What's the wrong price?'

'The painting, Tony, it's only fifty guineas. It's worth ten times that, more in fact. I bet he saw the price. Somebody must have swapped them round for a change but forgot to swap the sticky-tags.'

'Not going by the dust behind it,' laughed Tony turning back to his wife. 'And there's dust on the cord. Odd really when you look at the rest of the place. Everything's polished and shiny. It's all as clean as a whistle.'

Samantha agreed with him.

'It is odd Tony.' She partially closed her eyes as if a deep dark secret was about to be passed on. 'That picture is from the eighteen-eighties or even before then. It's massively under-valued. The frame alone must be worth that.'

159

She leaned forward and said almost in a whisper, 'Especially when you look at some of the other paintings. The one above is five-hundred pounds. And it's not in the same class.'

Tony shook his head. 'I know. I've just had a look at it. Boring! But you don't need to whisper, we're the only ones in here now.'

'Oh', smiled Samantha as she turned to check. 'I didn't hear the others go.'

'I think they left when Goliath had his dizzy spell.'

'I think we ought to go up, Tony, and let them have a reasonably early night. I don't want anything else, do you?'

'No Sam, I'm well-full and well-tired. Let's go and find him and get to know which room we're in.'

'Have you realised yet what this is?'

Tony had turned to the picture. 'No but it looks familiar.'

'It's this place before there was a street out there.'

'No, I didn't but I knew it looked familiar. I just couldn't think why. It must have been lovely then. All those fields round it and those flowers.'

'Yes it must have been. Come on let's go and find him.'

They didn't have to look far; he was sitting at the desk in the reception area.

'Did you enjoy your meal?'

'Yes thank you. It was delicious.'

'Mine was excellent,' smiled Samantha. 'I won't need to eat for a week.'

He smiled at the couple but the smile lacked its earlier warmth. He appeared edgy and didn't seem to want to look them in the eye. His fingers fumbled for the key, he dropped it, muttered and picked it up.

'I've given you number thirteen, or twelve A if you're superstitious?' he asked hesitantly and leaning heavily on the desk.

'Not in the least,' replied Tony.

'That's good then. It's left at the top of the stairs, then third door on your left. No sorry, second on the left. Mr Videl's is the third door. He's a permanent guest. Your room's over the lounge. Here are your bags and your coats and I'll get you the picture in the morning if that's ok?'

'Yes, that's fine by us.'

'Well good night to you both. Sleep well.' Again he gave them a hollow smile. Their smiles and their "goodnights" were genuine.

It was obvious to them both that the big man wasn't well.

160

'He couldn't remember which door it was!' murmured Tony as they reached the landing. 'It's more than indigestion, I know that. He was still twitchy when he gave us our keys.'

'Perhaps a good night's sleep will do him good. It will me,' replied Samantha yawning and passing it on to Tony.

By quarter-to-midnight the young couple were in bed. There would be no joining of souls, because they were both tired out. Samantha didn't snore instead she made little hissing noises from her nose. Tony did snore, not loud enough to wake the dead but it disturbed Samantha and as she stirred she heard raised voices. She easily recognised the first voice; it was the hotelier's. The other was a woman's voice but she heard both voices distinctly. First she heard the big man say, 'They will have it.'

Then she heard the woman say, 'I won't do it. I won't have anything to do with it. At least my ancestors only stole their valuables!'

'They will have it,' the man shouted. 'You have no choice. Damn you! You stupid bitch.'

A door slammed. Then she heard the woman shout, 'A lovely young couple like them!' Then between sobs and even louder the woman cried out, 'We were once a lovely young couple. Remember!' Then complete silence.

She got out of bed and went and opened the bedroom door, but she heard nothing more.

Samantha got back into bed but she couldn't get back to sleep. She tossed and turned for nearly an hour. Her mind was everywhere. Should she waken Tony and tell him what she'd heard. No point she decided. I'll tell him in the morning. What had her ancestors to do with it? Had one of them painted it? Perhaps they'd realised the price was wrong and maybe that's why the couple had a go at each other? Yes, that had to be it. Samantha knew they wouldn't be able to pay the right price. Not with the outlay on the studio. She got back into bed and listened for the giant of a man stamping up the stairs. She heard nothing. She decided he must sleep somewhere downstairs. She'd tell the big man she'd changed her mind. She'd tell him the price was wrong and she couldn't afford it at the right price. She decided that would be the best way to sort it out. Or did his wife love it as much as she did? If she did, why hang it in public with a price on it? Samantha fell asleep leaving questions unanswered.

The alarm on Tony's mobile dragged them from their sleep at seven-thirty. Samantha's hair was a tangle of gold-coloured silk and she yawned as she sat up and rubbed her eyes. Tony was sitting on the edge of the bed pulling his socks on.

'Do you need the bathroom love?'

'In a minute,' sighed Samantha rubbing her nose. 'I hardly slept at all last night. You were snoring like a horse and they were having a right ding-dong downstairs about that painting. It must have been two o'clock in the morning. Well I think it was two. Could have been one o'clock.'

She pushed herself up and leaned against the mountain of pillows.

'I couldn't decide whether or not to wake you up. I took pity on you my love.'

'Thanks for that Sam. But you should have prodded me or something, I'd have stopped.'

'I couldn't find a cattle prod. No seriously Tony, I'm sure they've got the wrong price on the painting! Just my luck. Anyway after hearing what I heard I'm giving it a miss.'

'He can't refuse to sell it Sam even if it is the wrong price. It has to be sold at the price shown,' insisted Tony turning to her. 'Shoppers' Protection Act. You can demand it. Or at least I think you can!'

'I do love it Tony but It would be like stealing and she might love it more than I do. They might be the sort of couple who have his and hers things, and it could be hers. No, I'll tell him I've changed my mind. It will save trouble. I wasn't eavesdropping; I couldn't help but hear them. He was going at his wife about it. It must have been his wife because she shouted at him, that they were once a lovely young couple.'

'That's nice, whoever she is!'

'Yes it is. But I'm positive she loves it as much as I do if not more. She was sobbing. I don't think I could do that darling. It would be a crappy thing to do. And it would be highway robbery.' GIVE ME THE PICTURE! Samantha mimed the action of pointing a pistol at Tony.

'Especially when I know how much it's worth.'

'Your decision Sam.' He leaned over, kissed her and said, 'Better kick ass. Cheer up darling we might find you something the same value as my socket-set.'

'Yep, wish on!'

'I'm going for a quick shower and shave. Won't be five minutes. Where did I put my razor?'

'Black bag. Single side pocket! Your bath and face towel are folded neatly in the front pocket,' she stressed the word neatly.

'Thanks. Won't be long.'

Although the word had been neatly stressed, it flew straight past Tony. His thoughts were of breakfast.

'Don't forget you've put your socks on!'

Samantha slid her bum over the side of the bed, stretched, yawned again and went and got a change of underwear. Modesty sorted, she went over to the window. She pulled one of the brocade curtains to one side just enough to see out. She looked over the rooftops to the moors in the distance. There, standing as still as a lone shepherd, was the small stone tower depicted in the painting. Only the occasional meddlesome chimneys spoiled the view. She came away realising where she'd seen this tower or one very like it before. She sighed at the thought of giving up the painting and called Tony to hurry up she was starving.

She saw the carving of the tower as they went down. It was cut into the front of the newel post at the bottom of the stairs.

'I knew I'd seen it somewhere.' She bent down to look. 'The tower on the painting. It's there, look.'

Tony took a quick glance.

'There's a gargoyle dancing in the doorway and pulling a face at you. Very skilfully done, I don't think!'

'Don't sneer. You remind me of Nat. He sneers at everything.'

'Thanks a lot.'

'Well you do.'

'It's a long walk from here, lady, to Hundenly Falls.' He shook his head wondering what her interest was in the tower and the ugly figure dancing in the doorway.

They were sitting at the same table in the dining room at eight-thirty drinking freshly ground coffee. Samantha had taken the seat on the right next to Tony instead of the one opposite so she could get a better look at the painting. She noticed the man leaning against the door of the barn was a big man with black curly hair and a beaming smile. He appeared to be talking to a man in a dark suit and bowler hat. This man wore white gloves and he was leaning on a cane. She couldn't see the man's face even though he was pointing at a couple walking hand in hand across the field in the foreground. His body was turned but not his head; he was facing the big man.

There were hens and geese in clusters here and there. By the water trough was a magnificent cockerel, which for all the world looked to be crowing. Over on the left in the near foreground was the tall, gaunt-faced woman tending a vegetable patch. She looked sad, decided Samantha. She focused on the background and saw the moors and the tower. But there was no ugly demon in the doorway. She was just about to tell Tony when, with a beaming smile, the big man came to the table. He fussed about a bit moving the coffee pot and the hot water jug asking, as he served their breakfasts, if they wanted a refill, or more milk. They settled for more coffee. He then raised the subject of the painting.

'I'll take that and wrap it up for you. You can settle up when you leave.'

There was no suggestion of a request in the way he said it. The smile never lessened but there was a strange tremor of anticipation in his voice. Samantha wasn't given time to tell Tony about the demon. But Samantha had made her decision; as lovely as it was, the painting would not be going with them.

'About the painting, I've changed my mind Mr… er I'm sorry I don't know your name.'

'Coldhart, but everybody calls me Bill.'

'Coldhart,' she repeated in disbelief and frowned hard at Tony.

Tony had no idea why. But that's impossible she thought. How could he be the artist?

'Are you the artist?' asked Samantha, wanting to compliment him on his work.

'No I'm not!'

'But your name is on it!'

'I've told you already, I'm not the artist,' he snapped.

There was anger and frustration in the big man's attitude as he turned back to the couple. Samantha hesitated when she saw his face but only for a second or so. She wasn't going to be browbeaten by anybody.

'Look, I'm sorry but I've changed my mind about the painting Mr Coldhart. I think it looks perfect where it is. The room wouldn't look the same without it and I know your wife loves it.'

'What my wife likes is none of your business!'

Samantha was about to say, don't snap at me, when the man continued in the same tone of voice.

'This room wouldn't look any different to me. And if it did, it's nothing to you. The painting's yours now. I don't understand you young people. Want it, don't want it,' he growled.

Samantha suddenly stared at the picture. The figures of the big man and the woman were starting to fade. Impossible, she blinked, looked again and knew that they were.

'They're!' she exclaimed pointing at the painting. 'They're starting…' but she was interrupted by the big man. Tony was well angry with the big man's attitude and wondered what the hell was going on. The big man reached for the painting and yanked it of the wall.

'Don't seem to know what you want and what you don't want!' he growled as if she and Tony hadn't spoken.

Samantha couldn't believe it. The whole thing was stupid. Then the big man saw where Samantha's eyes were fixed, cursed under his breath and turned the picture away.

'Who the hell do you think you're talking to!?' demanded Tony.

'Are you mad?' The big man sneered at Tony and stormed out of the dining room with the picture held tight to his chest. The kitchen door opened and the gaunt-looking woman peered out. She rushed across to their table looking anxiously at the doorway that the big man had used a moment ago. She glanced again and there was fear in her eyes.

She quickly whispered, 'No matter what my husband says or what he does, for heaven's sake don't take that painting! The thing is cursed, and so will you be if you take it. I swear to God the thing is cursed!'

A door slammed somewhere close by. She snatched a quick glance towards the doorway again. 'Look I must go. For God's sake do as I say.' She almost ran out of the dining room.

The young couple were astonished. They stared at one another for a minute as if they were waiting for permission to speak. Samantha was bursting to tell Tony about the people in the painting and how she'd seen two of the characters fading away but Tony got in first.

'This is crazy Sam. Come on, finish your drink. We're off. He can stick his hotel where the sun don't shine and every picture in it! Come on let's go before I lose my temper.'

He got up from the table, took a gulp of his coffee and waited while Samantha stood up.

'We'll get our bags and get out of this bloody madhouse.'

They went through the lobby and up to their room. The big man was nowhere to be seen but they passed a man on the stairs. He was wearing dirty white gloves and carrying a battered old silver-topped cane.

Samantha caught hold of Tony's arm. 'That's the other man in the picture.' She turned and he turned, but when they looked over the banister rail there was nobody there.

'He was quick. Where's he gone? I just saw him!'

'Come on Sam, don't worry about it. He probably ran down the last few steps thinking he'd be late for breakfast. Not as genial as we thought our host was he?'

'He couldn't run anywhere Tony; he looked twice as old as the car and he had a bad limp,' she argued.

'He must have gone somewhere, people just don't disappear, Love. Come on, forget him Sam. I want to be out of here.'

Tony went to their room, picked up his bag and checked he'd got everything. Samantha looked a bit miffed when she collected her bag but she didn't say anything. Tony went into the bathroom, splashed his face with cold water and said, 'Have you got everything?'

Samantha nodded.

'Come on let's be off.' He took her hand.

They left the room and went downstairs. The big man, moving this and that on top of the desk and looking terribly uncomfortable, was waiting for them.

'Look, I can't apologise enough for what happened earlier.'

Tony tried to say something.

'Please,' said the man shaking his head. 'I can't think what came over me. There's no excuse for bad manners.' He fiddled with their bill on the desk. Tony again tried to speak but the big man stopped him with a gesture of his hand.

'I've knocked twenty pounds off your bill. It's my way of...' he looked embarrassed. 'It's my way of apologising properly. And please forget all about the painting, I've hung it where it belongs. And you were right young lady; the room didn't look the same.'

For all his talk, he never once looked them in the eye. 'I hope you'll call again sometime. Whenever you're passing.'

He knew they'd never come back; well, not in this life. The big man tried not to burst into hysterical laugher as he took the ninety-five pounds-fifty and handed Tony the bill. Tony checked it, decided he'd bought shares in the hotel and settled it. But, for the big man, try as he could, it was a waste of effort. As soon as he heard the rear door close, he roared with laughter.

The couple didn't speak as they walked to the car. Both were trying to think why Samantha's change of mind had got such a reaction from Mr Coldhart.

Samantha said suddenly, 'Did you hear him laughing? He must be round the twist. Hey what's that tied to the parcel rack Tony?'

Tony went to the back and looked.

'It looks like another sweetener. It's a parasol with the name of the hotel on it. There's a note. It's says, "Compliments of the establishment"!'

'It's just another little bribe, Love. I'll throw it in the bushes.'

'No don't, that's a silly waste. We'll leave it somewhere. Someone else might want it. There's always Oxfam.'

'Yes, good idea!' Tony left it where it was.

The gaunt woman, although supposedly sweeping the paving stones, was in fact watching them safely off the premises. She heard what Samantha said about the parasol. She dropped the sweeping brush as if it had turned into a snake and dashed into the hotel. Two minutes later she came running out shouting, asking them to stop! Mr Videl and her husband watched her from behind the curtains of Mr Videl's room. She was too late, they'd gone. The pair smiled at one another (if such a facial expression could be called a smile).

The young couple left the parasol on the parcel rack, got in the car and drove off, vowing they'd never come back to the place. Without thinking Tony turned left out of the car park and drove the way they'd come. He'd gone more than a mile before he realised he was going back the way they came.

'Damn it. I've gone the wrong way Sam.'

'Look's like we're going back quicker than we thought.' Samantha said, 'Do you want the map darling?'

'Get lost,' he laughed.

He turned the car after three shuffles and headed back.

'Can you smell something?' she asked sniffing. 'Smells like something's burning.'

'No I can't smell anything.'

Samantha sniffed again. 'No, I can't smell it now.'

The gaunt woman ran into the dining room and went straight to the picture. It was a copy.

'You've copied it!' she screamed at the top of her voice. Her husband, who was blazing mad, slapped her hard across the face and shouted, 'Shut your noise.'

Mr Videl tut-tutted, tapped his battered cane on the floor and hissed, 'You can do nothing now woman. Soon you will be free.' His laughter was hellish.

Suddenly, she cocked her head to one side and listened. Then, with a cry of triumph she lunged for the copy. There was no mistaking the roar of that exhaust.

She dashed through the front door and into the street. They were fifty or sixty yards away. Plenty of time to stop them. In desperation, she ran up the road waving the picture at the young couple. She could see the panic on their faces. The young man was shouting at her. She screamed at them to stop. In an instant she realised the car wasn't going to stop. They had to stop. She'd make them stop. She had to get the picture off them. There was no time to waste.

Tony blew the horn. She stood like a statue challenging him to run her down. He swerved hard to the right. She threw herself in front of the car. Tony slammed his foot on the brakes again and swerved the opposite way. This time the brake pedal went to the floor. He knew as he desperately swerved the other way what the collision with the rock had caused.

'I must have split a brake hose last night! Brace yourself!' he shouted at Samantha. Mrs Coldhart threw her arms across her body and screamed. She looked, then suddenly folded herself over the front off-side wing. The terrific impact threw her spinning backwards and rolling sideways across the street. The picture was shattered to pieces under the car and there was a horrible noise when her head finally smacked into the edge of the kerbstone.

Tony dragged the handbrake as far back as he could and at the same time tried to crash the gear stick into first. It wouldn't have it. He hit a lamppost and the car spun round, mounted the pavement backwards and crashed into a garden wall. Tony was thrown backwards then as he rocked forwards, his forehead smacked into the steering wheel. Samantha, not knowing what would happen, had her feet braced hard against the bulkhead and her hands pressed hard against the dashboard. On impact she was knocked about like a doll but not thrown forwards and though badly shook up, she clambered out of the car. She got round to the driver's side and yanked open Tony's door.

'Are you all right? Are you hurt?'

She saw the gash on Tony's forehead.

'Oh God,' she gasped.

He straightened up slowly and said, 'Give me a hand, Love. I'm ok. Just a bit stunned. Must have hit my head on the steering wheel or something. Better see how Mrs Coldhart is. I hope to God somebody's rung for an ambulance. See if you can open the door wider, it's crushed against the front pillar.'

Samantha pulled the door back as far as she could and Tony eased his way out. Samantha let the door spring back. He leaned against the car.

'See how she is Sam. I'll be fine in a minute.' He thought he was going to be sick.

Samantha got across the street but kept turning to see if Tony was all right. He was leaning against the car and pressing a bunch of paper handkerchiefs to his forehead.

He half staggered across the street as Samantha bent to see how Mrs Coldhart was doing. There was a small crowd of people standing round but she couldn't see the big man.

'Has anyone rung for an ambulance?'

'Yes, I have. I saw it all. I rang as soon as I saw it happen. It's on its way.'

Samantha feeling a bit sick and holding back tears knelt down and told Mrs Coldhart what the man with the beard had said. The woman suddenly opened her eyes and looked at Samantha. The half-conscious woman was desperately trying to remember something.

'It's in the parasol.' Her eyes shone. 'The picture. He's hidden it in the parasol.'

'Please don't try to talk. Wait for the ambulance to come.'

Samantha rushed back to the car and brought her coat. Gently, and ignoring the blood, she placed the folded coat under the woman's head. Tony tried to help her but he stopped instantly when a terrible stab of pain shot up his arm. He had to go and lean against a gate post.

'Please don't try to speak,' begged Samantha as the woman tried to move. 'The ambulance will soon be here.'

'Never mind the ambulance,' she gasped with a fierce urgency.

She tried her damnedest to sit up, coughed horribly and sagged back. Blood dribbled from the corner of her mouth.

'Get the parasol, she said as she coughed and clenched her teeth. 'For God's sake get it back inside the hotel. Do it now! Or that foul place will be yours for the res…'

A tremor shook her body as she tried with all the strength she had to continue but her eyes glazed over. The fire in them faded and she passed out.

Tony (even though he was standing away) heard what she'd said. He limped back to the car as best he could and with one hand he tugged at the cord holding the parasol to the parcel rack but it wouldn't budge. He pulled and wrenched on the handle till the cord snapped but the pain in his shoulder was hellish. He took a breath and dragged the thing up the street towards the hotel. He tried but he couldn't lift it off the ground.

Samantha ran to help.

'Sorry, Love, I think I've broken this arm and this shoulder's killing me. I heard what the woman said. We have to do it. I saw her face Sam. She looked desperate. I've never seen such fear and desperation.'

'It's dreadful. That poor woman. And all over a damned painting!'

Tears ran down Samantha's face.

'Come on, Sweetheart, don't cry, It's bloody grim what's happened, Love but it's not our fault. How the hell were we to know we were getting involved with a lunatic? It should have been him, not her. Take the parasol will you Sam, I'm going to drop it.'

'Oh darling. I'm sorry. Give it to me.' Samantha took it and said, 'There's something tucked in here, I can feel it. Mrs Coldhart was right! He has put something in it.' They got to the hotel.

'Can you chuck it in there Sam?'

'Watch me.'

Samantha yanked the door open and threw it in. It hit a big brass handle on the inner door and fell to floor. She was going to slam the door when she heard a dreadful moan tear through the building. Then as she watched, a piece of the picture frame fell out then another until all four were on the floor. Wide-eyed and with her mouth hanging open, Samantha turned to Tony. She couldn't believe what she was seeing.

He nodded, 'I see it Love.' He couldn't squeeze her hand but he desperately wanted to. With odd, twitchy movements the frame had joined back together. Then another dreadful moan echoed and the picture wafted out of the parasol and landed in the dead centre of the frame. Samantha screamed and clutched Tony's arm. He saw what she saw and he was as terrified as Samantha.

The woman had gone from the picture and so had the big man. But the man in the bowler hat was there. He was pointing his cane and looking straight out at Tony and Samantha and his red snarling face was that of a demon.

Samantha turned away. 'Oh God, did you see that?'

The door suddenly slammed in their faces.

'I saw it. Come away, Love! Quick, come on. Hurry. We're in real danger here!'

Samantha gave what support she could as Tony tried to limp away as fast as he could. The pain in his foot was chronic but he made a tremendous effort and they got to Mrs Coldhart. Tony sank onto a low wall to take the weight off his foot and took deep breaths. A mingled stream of sweat and dried blood covered one side of his face, which he wiped at it with his T-shirt. He said he'd be ok now and asked Samantha if she'd see how Mrs Coldhart was. She wasn't sure. She didn't want to leave him there. He assured her he was fine so Samantha hurried off. She wasn't gone long before she returned to tell him she was still unconscious and sat on the wall with him. She stood up when she heard the duelling sirens of the ambulances. Everybody turned to watch as they raced down the street. The passenger door flew open even before it screeched to a stop. The other followed within seconds. The Doctor was out and at Mrs Coldhart's side within seconds.

The paramedics cleared the crowd then helped the Doctor. The middle-aged man with 'Doctor' stamped in black on the back of his glaring green coat had his fingers probing gently at the side of Mrs Coldhart's throat. He held them there for a time then shaking his head, he looked up at one of his colleagues and said, 'She's gone, Raymond.' Raymond gnawed at his lip, shook his head and went for a cover.

There were gasps and mutterings from the small crowd.

'Does anybody know who she is?' asked the Doctor getting to his feet.

'Yes, she's Mrs Coldhart,' murmured a woman at the front. 'She and her husband have the hotel there.'

She pointed.

'Right, thank you. Do you want to go along there Bruce and tell him what's happened? He should be here.'

When he turned and saw Tony he said, 'Hurry will you. I need to have a look at this chap.' He went over to Tony and Samantha.

'Would you like to come over to the ambulance? No onlookers there. And you young lady, you're as white as snow. Climb in, you're both in shock.'

They followed the Doctor and climbed into the ambulance. He sat them both down while another paramedic wrapped a blanket round Samantha and draped one over Tony's shoulders. The Doctor saw to Tony first.

'I'm afraid the laceration will need stitches. This is obviously broken.'

He gently lowered Tony's arm and he moved the blanket, checking the left shoulder.

'This is going to give you some pain. It's very badly bruised, but it's not dislocated.' He replaced the blanket. 'You've sprained your ankle or torn the tendon. I need to take your soc…' they were interrupted by Bruce.

'Sorry to break you off, but her husband's dead. I've checked him over. There was an old man in the hotel. He told me the dead man was her husband. Look's like a massive heart attack. Terrible facial contortions. Must have died when he lifted that big picture off the wall. There's an empty space. Modern art. It certainly didn't fit in with the others. It's lying there beside him. It's completely blank except for some sort of gnome or something. Honestly, that's all there is on it. And you can barely see the gnome. He's still clutching it in one hand. I've left him where he is till you look at him.'

'Ta. I'll be a while yet. Better see if the old man's all right.'

'He's all right. I asked him. He said people die every day. He was really off hand. Said he wasn't related to the dead man and he was going for his walk. He didn't say where to.'

The Doctor said thank you and was about to continue with Tony when Bruce stepped out of the ambulance and said, 'Look, that's him there,' he pointed. 'He's there, halfway up the moor! He must be fitter than I am. You can see his bowler hat!'

'Yes I see him,' replied the Doctor popping his head out of the ambulance. 'There can't be much wrong with him.'

Neither Tony nor Samantha bothered to look. They knew where he was going.

The weird old man turned, waved his cane at the hotel and laughed. In the hotel dining room a blazing log rolled out of the open fire and came to rest against a table leg. Another followed and another. Then two more. They soon began to do his work.

Richard Lee Wilson 2006.

Is there anybody there?

'You're not going to a spiritualist meeting tonight, Shirley, surely?'

Arthur frowned and wondered if she'd forgotten what day it was.

'Of course I am, Arthur,' she called from the other room, then smiled a sneaky little smile to herself. 'Mr Greybone's speaking tonight. He's very good. One of the best according to Alice.'

Arthur's face dropped a mile. He looked as if he'd just seen Bobby Charlton sent off the pitch for head-butting the referee!

Surely Shirley hadn't forgotten their special day? Surely not? He hadn't seen her open her card, he'd put it on the mantelpiece in full view and he'd taken so much time over which one to pick.

'There are hundreds,' he'd told the young woman with the purple lips and spiky hair. She'd nodded, pouted, sighed and wondered what time it was. He'd finally picked one of the first one's he'd seen. The card with the big bunch of white roses on, and a verse which was lovely and sloppy! The young woman had sighed again, taken his money, and given him his change (what little there was) thought Arthur, as the worthless nickel coins were piled on the glass-topped counter. She smiled then, but only because Arthur's arthritic fingers had a big problem picking them up. When he'd got them she said, not looking the side he was on, 'Ta-ra.'

Arthur said, 'So-long,' to the cluttered counter and went for a cup of tea, a butterfly-bun and to people-watch in the market hall. He hadn't stayed long. He'd muttered to one of his cronies, 'This stuff tastes like maiden's water. They must have used that tea bag all day today and yesterday!'

Lenny had replied, 'They used it in mine, I can tell you that. You can see right through it.'

They'd parted grinning. The half-drunk pots of tea had been left on the table along with the empty sugar sachets and the dreadful plastic spoons that Arthur said were only fit for feeding drooling babies.

Hadn't she noticed he'd washed-up properly and put the pots away?

'She knows I only wash-up on special occasions,' he moaned to Puddle. Puddle ignored him completely and continued grooming his nether-regions.

'You only bother with me when you want something, you selfish, greb.' Arthur gently prodded Puddle with his toe end.

The big tabby didn't make a sound, it just gave him a foul slit-eyed glare, got up and sauntered into the dining room where Shirley was getting herself ready – well, doing the final touches. She'd already spent over an hour in the bathroom!

Shirley's final touches involved standing far enough from the dining-room mirror to keep her hair in focus, but near enough to the mirror to check her roots. She turned her head from side to side and stared hard at her reflection. Puddle, meowed and brushed against her legs until he got what he wanted. She patted him, patted her hair and decided with a few more discrete tilts of her head, that her hair-do was more than satisfactory for a spiritualist meeting! The dark-chestnut coloured dye had blended perfectly with the grey, leaving the whole a sort of medium auburn colour. She decided the ladies would have to look very closely indeed if they wanted to see her ever encroaching spread of grey hair.

Puddle sauntered off into the kitchen for the last bits of his food. Shirley went into the sitting room. Arthur thought she looked very nice.

He said, 'Her hair was perfect and it looked exactly like it did on the day they first met.'

This small attempt, by a still frowning Arthur to jog her memory, was either ignored or unheard, because she was singing the praises of Mr Greybone before Arthur had even finished speaking. She does that a lot these days he thought to himself as he gnawed at his bottom lip. At one time she'd have hung on my every word. That thought whizzed off to be replaced by others more pertinent and a bit louder.

'I don't know why you go? It's our special day. Bloody spiritualism, and bloody spiritualists. Phoney as a nine-pound note! They're creepy, the lot of 'em,' he muttered these thoughts under his breath.

'Damned Ruby wedding next week,' he griped.

'Will you stop muttering Arthur? I can't hear what you're saying.'

'I said. Are you going to be out all night?' He turned his long narrow face to her as she headed for the door. He looked fed-up.

'I'll be home between nine and half-past.'

She threw him a kiss as he said, 'I'll be between the sheets at a quarter past, and get Mr Greybone to contact your mother and ask her where she hid the key to the treasure chest buried in the garden.'

'You can mock Arthur Tanner, but Alice said he's had marvellous results.'

'Why, does he sell double glazing?' Arthur's eyebrows went up and he made a noise like, fla-fla at such silly talk.

'The ladies say he's the best there is.'

'It's a lot of codswallop. Anybody with a bit of common sense knows as much. They only do it to make money out of gullible women. Surely, Shirley, you don't believe that rubbish?'

'Course I don't, I'm not stupid!'

'Well why are you going then?'

'Because all the girls are going, that's why!'

'I'll bet you won't find many men there.'

'Well that shows how much you know, doesn't it!'

The front door slammed shut before it was explained to Arthur, by a miffed Shirley, just how much he didn't know.

She didn't bother telling him it wasn't really a spiritualist meeting, or that it wasn't in the spiritualist church or anywhere like that.

Alice had told her, 'She wouldn't have seen anything like it before'. But she wouldn't tell her anything else. Alice said, 'It would spoil it all!'

Arthur turned the television on. Puddle strolled back into the room and leaped up onto the easy chair opposite Arthur's.

'And you can clear-off as well!' grinned Arthur.

Puddle ignored him and started to tread the cushion. Arthur scratched what bit of hair he had left over his right ear, lit his pipe and settled down.

'I'll make Shirley a cup of tea for when she gets back,' he muttered. 'That should cheer her up a bit, eh Puddle?'

Puddle didn't look the side he was on, he'd had his meat so at the moment he didn't need anything from Arthur or anyone else and Puddle was concentrating on making his bed. He was busy clawing the remains of a cushion to death! Arthur didn't mind, it was the cat's cushion, and he was part of the family. Puddle stopped kneading the threadbare cushion. He'd had enough kneading for now, but he didn't settle there, instead he cleared off upstairs to one of his other beds. He settled for the one by the radiator on the landing. He'd left the cover Shirley used to wrap his cushion in a crumpled mess and hanging forlornly over the front of the chair. Arthur got up, smoothed it back out and flicked it back onto the seat as he went to turn the television off. It was Top of the Plops, (as he called it) and put a Caruso record on.

'That's singing, you bunch of Mary Annes!' snapped Arthur poking a finger in his ear. The Mary Annes had already disappeared into the white dot on the screen, but he told them anyway.

Shirley caught the bus at the stop opposite the off-licence on the corner. She sat next to Bernadette who didn't stop telling Shirley and Alice how good Mr Greybone was until they got off the bus at the top of Cornhill Road. Shirley had told Bernadette as soon as she'd sat down what Arthur had said about spiritualism in general and spiritualists in particular and she'd regretted it no end! Shirley hadn't been able to get a word in. Alice, sitting on the double seat opposite, didn't even bother trying. She was busy staring at the terraced houses along the route, as if she'd never seen them before!

As the bus negotiated the rather narrow streets through the town centre, Shirley thought about the beautiful card Arthur had got for her. She'd sneaked a look at it. She thought the verse was lovely. She'd give him hers when she got home as she was going to be home early to give him a nice surprise. She'd made the cake the day before yesterday and decorated it with a great big heart with an arrow though the centre with an, A on the pointed end, and a, S on the end with the feathers. Then she'd sneaked upstairs and hidden it and Arthur's card in her wardrobe behind her pile of abandoned handbags. Arthur never looked in there! She smiled and nodded to herself at her cunning and thought longingly of the day she and Arthur had first met.

She could see him now, standing straight as a rod outside the Curzon cinema. He looked as smart as a general in his uniform with all that braid and all his medals. She fell for him then and there. Then, when he called out, 'Seats in the circle and the rear stalls,' in that soft, sort of gentlemanly way, my goodness, she went funny all over. Shirley smiled a silly little smile again at the thought of it all. Bernadette, who was still chatting away, saw the silly grin and asked Shirley if she'd got a touch of wind. Shirley, unaware of her own facial expression wondered why she'd asked, but automatically tipped her feet on end and looked down at her shoe soles. There was nothing stuck on them. Alice, who'd got fed up of the view she saw every time she went to her daughters, wondered why Shirley looked at the underneath of her shoes but she didn't bother asking. They were nearly there!

Shirley noticed there were more men than women in the queue outside the hall, she wished she'd her camera with her, then Arthur would have to eat his words. Some of the men and women were quite young. This strengthened Shirley's opinion that Arthur knew a lot less than she did about spiritualism.

He was always moaning, 'It should be banned. They're a bunch of charlatans. They should all be locked up!'

She'd only been to two other meetings before and they were three or four months ago! It wasn't as if she went every week! He was getting grumpier by the day. She loved him as much as ever, maybe even more, but some times she could strangle him. And that stinking pipe was getting fouler by the day as well. She wondered, as they walked up the steps into the hall, if all ageing husbands and pipes got like that? Pointless asking Bernadette, Shirley decided, as she paid one of the nice men at the door, even if she could get a word in! Bernadette was single and she never listened to what you were saying anyway! Alice hurried off up the steps and left Bernadette yapping away at Shirley. Shirley wasn't very impressed by Alice's downright selfishness.

As the gathering took their places and after a few minutes, no more than three or four, Mr Greybone strode onto the platform at the end of the hall opposite the door where Shirley and the rest of the hopefuls had come in. Shirley found herself plonked next to Bernadette on the fifth row back. Alice was on the third row from the front, two seats to Shirley's left. They waved to each other. They'd have a chat during the refreshment break, if she could escape from Bernadette. She might ask Alice about her husband; see if he was getting like Arthur. She felt sure Alice's husband was about the same age, if not older by a year or two.

Mr Greybone, a tall distinguished man with greying hair at the temples, smiled broadly, looked round the packed hall and waited while the chatter faded away. He didn't ask for silence or give any indication that he would if the talking didn't stop, he simply stood and smiled. Then suddenly, as if the gathering had received some sort of sign, there was complete silence!

He nodded his thanks and said, 'Good evening, ladies and gentlemen.'

He had a rich, strong voice and although he looked relaxed and at ease he still let the gathering know he was in control. He certainly had the presence and the personality to match his six foot-two frame.

'First let me thank you all for coming along. There are quite a few faces I recognise and plenty that I don't.'

He smiled again and focussed his smile on a group of young men and women on his far right. Shirley noticed that most of the young women, though very self-consciously, did manage to return his smile.

'For those of you who haven't been to one of our meetings before, please don't be alarmed by what you see and hear. You are in no danger whatsoever.'

His dark earnest eyes swept the congregation once more, then he turned to two gentlemen sitting on his left and asked them to dim the lights a little. Shirley thought the "no danger" announcement alarming, and wondered if it would have been wiser to stay at home with Arthur and Puddle on this, their special day. There had been no mention of danger at the last meeting she'd attended, but the chap on that occasion had been a bit of a let down. She did feel a bit mean, her going out in a huff and leaving Arthur all on his own but Puddle was with him she told herself.

Mr Greybone returned to the centre of the platform and closed his eyes. His head twitched from side to side as if he was listening to the scratching of a mouse. Although the lights had been dimmed there was hardly any difference in the brightness around the platform. Shirley didn't think they'd done anything to the lights, but there was some background music playing that she hadn't heard a minute ago. Was it, "O for the wings of a dove"? It was so quiet, Shirley wasn't sure.

He turned to his right as if someone had tapped him on the shoulder and said in the same rich voice, 'Do we have a Penelope here? I have a message from someone called Eve. Sorry, Evelyn. Her name is Evelyn. She's asking me to tell you,' he waited a moment, nodded his head very slightly and said in a very different voice, 'You must see your Doctor, Penny.'

There was another slight pause before he continued in the same soft feminine voice. 'You must go and see Doctor Edwards. You know what it's about.' There was a muffled gasp from somewhere behind Shirley but she didn't look round. She'd gone all goose-pimply, and besides, it was none of her business. No doubt Bernadette would tell her later who Penelope was, and all about her.

The next person to gasp was sitting two seats away from Shirley and he gasped so loud it made her jump. Mr Greybone had come to the front of the platform, and had searched for a face on Shirley's row. He'd kept turning his head slightly as if he was following instructions from someone, but Shirley couldn't be sure. She thought he might have a nervous affliction. When he found the person he was looking for, he didn't mention his name; he just pointed at him, glared and said in his own voice, 'Helen

178

says, she has no pain now and she forgives you. I won't repeat here what else she's just said.'

He was getting angry. 'I don't want you in my congregation! Now, or ever again. Get out of here! You should be ashamed of yourself!'

Mr Greybone was extremely angry now.

The man got up from his seat and started mouthing off at Mr Greybone. He ignored the man. His two assistants moved quickly, one down one side of the room, one down the other. They would have closed in on him but the man having got what he no doubt wanted, didn't give them a chance. He hurried out of the hall as fast as he could. Mr Greybone consoled someone only he could see! This time he did demand silence from his congregation but only by raising his hands with his palms facing out! Shirley was out of her depth and she wished she hadn't come. She thought they were playacting!

'Please accept my apologies for that. I should not have lost my temper.'

He mopped his brow with a big white handkerchief, then said quite curtly, 'Yes, yes. I am listening.'

Then he said again, 'Yes, I am listening.'

He turned to the congregation and asked, 'Is there a John Herbert here?'

If there was he was behind Shirley somewhere but she didn't hear a reply. Mr Greybone must have seen some sort of acknowledgement because he turned and looked over Shirley's left shoulder and said in a high pitched feminine voice, 'Please take your medication my darling. Please take it. You know it's absolutely essential. I put your day-box in the kitchen drawer. The top one in the set by the tumble dryer. You do understand, don't you?'

Shirley didn't hear a reply; she was busy scratching her neck where the hairs had suddenly stood on end. Bernadette turned to see who the man was. Shirley nudged her and she turned back.

'Yes I ⑨⅓✚⅝ passed on your message! Yes, for goodness sake! Your husband is nodding. He has definitely promised to do as you say.'

The handkerchief came out again. Shirley could see the sweat dripping off his chin.

Shirley hadn't seen a meeting conducted like this before. Not even when that very famous, foreign lady came. She asked the congregation lots of questions but took a lot more time with her answers. And she was quite vague with her answers as well. It could have been a problem with the language, but Shirley didn't think so. This meeting was more like those American ones they have on the television and they hadn't said any prayers yet. Shirley thought that was a bit odd. She would ask Alice about it later, if there was time? Mr Greybone announced the break. 'There are various drinks and snacks available at the back of the hall. If you would start with the back row and so on to the front you will all be served efficiently, thank you.' The back row filed out like obedient zombies.

Arthur was conducting, "On with the Motley", from the comfort of his armchair. He'd listened to it three times. Twice by Caruso and once by Tauber. He decided to let Tauber have another go and then he was going to look for their, "Special Day Cake". He knew Shirley had made one, she always did, she always hid it, and Arthur always found it. Shirley wasn't a devious person, Arthur knew that. Had she been she wouldn't have hidden it in the same place for the last umpteen years. He went upstairs to the airing cupboard. The cake wasn't there! Arthur rubbed his chin.

'Surely, Shirley hadn't forgotten their special day,' he muttered to Puddle.

Puddle yawned and stretched his front legs taking three pounds off the value of the carpet as his claws dug deep.

'Stop it, you bloody monster,' snapped Arthur, clearly frustrated at not finding the cake in its usual place! Puddle took another three pounds-worth off the same piece of carpet then strolled arched-backed half a yard across the landing and curled up there. Arthur was tempted to prod him but instead, he went into their bedroom to search for the cake.

Shirley had returned to her seat but hadn't managed to shake off Bernadette. She'd had a natter with Alice over a cup of coffee during the interval and had said the meeting was more like a visit to the theatre than a service! Alice had said Mr Greybone always did it like this. Shirley wasn't keen, she didn't believe any of it, but she didn't say anything to Bernadette. The only difference between this meeting and the other two, in her opinion, was that at this one there was more playacting! Shirley was beginning to nod off. For the last three-quarters of an hour, Mr Greybone had been doing the same sort of thing. She wondered if she could sneak out and get home to Arthur. Her eyelids drooped.

Silence fell once again as Mr Greybone moved to the front of the platform.

'Is there a, Shirley? He paused a moment. 'A Shirley Anne Redcliff.'

Shirley nearly had an ep! She thought he'd meant her for a minute. Bernadette told her to calm down. Shirley gave her a cold stare and pulled herself together. Harvey says the garden is beautiful, especially the rose arbour. He also says, 'Go steady with the wine or you might be seeing him rather sooner than you think!' Mr Greybone smiled and nodded at the unseen Harvey or in the direction his voice was coming from. Then he smiled at Mrs Redcliff. She looked acutely embarrassed but managed to blow her nose quietly. Alice looked to be nodding off. Shirley wished she could join her but Mr Greybone had made her jump out of her wits when he'd asked if there was a Shirley here, and now she was wide awake.

Arthur had found the cake in the wardrobe. He did a little jig across the bedroom floor but kept a firm grip of the plate it was on. He thought it was magnificent. 'It's the best cake yet Puddle. I don't know how she found room for it in there!'

Puddle got up and strolled out of the bedroom and across to the landing. He was feeling a bit peckish. Perhaps he could try and wheedle a few biscuits from his master. He meowed and looked up at Arthur with that starving-orphan look on his face. Arthur softened as he always did. 'Come on then and don't get under my feet, you monster.' Puddle meowed again and fussed around Arthur, brushing against his legs like he always did when he wanted something. Arthur gripped Shirley's card between his teeth, bent down slightly to fuss Puddle, then he set off with him to the kitchen for some Meetytreets. He decided that when he'd fed Puddle he'd set the table with the cake in the middle and a couple of those purple candles at each side. All he had to do was to find out where the blinking candles are. He wondered where she'd hidden them.

Shirley was getting fed up again. She knew Arthur was right. She'd seen nothing special yet. She shouldn't have come, not today of all days. Not one manifestation as Bernadette called them. Bernadette had told Shirley that last time she'd been to see Mr Greybone; she'd seen at least three manifestations. Probably pink ones thought Shirley. Pink ones with trunks and great big ears. The only bit of excitement was when that chap scurried out of the hall. But he could have been anybody. Obviously a stooge of Mr Greybone's, concluded Shirley stifling a yawn. Shirley yawned as Mr Greybone started twitching his head again.

Shirley was half asleep when she thought she heard a voice she recognised. Alice or someone with a voice just like hers had heard the same voice and had shouted, "No it's impossible." Then still half asleep she heard Mr Greybone say, 'I have someone here beside me who says he's tripped over a Puddle. Well that can't be right, can it?' he smiled. 'I must have misheard. Trod in a puddle, perhaps?'

Shirley's eyes shot open. There was Arthur, her Arthur covered in cake standing next to Mr Greybone. Why was Arthur glowing and shimmering like that, she wondered and why was his neck bent like that? He's never had his neck bent like that before. Suddenly, and as if she'd run face first into a plate-glass door, she realised why! It was a mere breath of time before her hands flew to her face and her dreadful cries of anguish were stifled by her falling to the floor like a broken doll.

'We were wrong My Love, well wrong,' said Arthur to Shirley who suddenly appeared at his side clutching a shimmering hand to her heart.

Richard Lee Wilson 2004

Keeping up Appearances

'We must go and see them, Joe.' Beryl fussed and fiddled with her glasses as they were digging into the bridge of her nose. Joe watched her and shook his head. Why the hell, wondered Joe, did she wear them? There was nothing wrong with her eyesight. 'I said we must go and see them Joe, regardless of what's happened.'

'I heard you the first time.'

'They've gone to a lot of trouble to make the place comfortable for us. Larry told you he'd completely re-done the guest room and everything. You know what Larry's like. He won't put a nail where it needs a screw! So it will be nothing but the best. And he said Beryl, who's not one for bragging, told him how much she'd spent on the curtains alone. And what's more! They'd come and see us under the same circumstances.'

'Stop going on about it Freda, I never said we wouldn't be going, did I? Good grief, you're doing my head in! Of course we're going. The plane tickets are paid for and upstairs. You don't expect me to throw good money down the drain, do you?'

'Of course I don't. When have you ever done that?'

'There's nothing wrong about being careful with money. So we'll have none of that.'

'If you hadn't been so careful with money, as you put it, we wouldn't be in the position we're in now!'

'What sort of crazy logic do you call that? You're rich aren't you? Hell fire! I noticed you never moaned about it when you were swanning around in the South of France!'

'If you're going to start a row, I'm going to do my face and go down to the parish church to say a prayer!'

'Bit late for that!'

Freda left the room without a word. Not because of what Joe had said, it was because her face was itching. She'd have to recite a few more prayers when she'd finished cursing her makeup and asking herself why they'd ever got involved in the robbery in the first place.

'Damned robbery! Damned diamonds!' she muttered under her breath.

'They'll definitely be coming, Beryl. You know what Joe's like. He throws money round like a man with no arms! Last time I spoke to Martin, he told me he'd spoken to Joe and Joe told him he'd be on his way for the tickets as soon as he got off the phone. That was more than a month ago.

There's no way Joe will waste them. Even if he's to fly out here, get some duty-free, and then fly straight back!'

'Don't be rotten Larry. I used to like Joe. I still do. He used to make me laugh.'

'He'd laugh if he knew the circumstances we were in!' Can't leave the house without makeup! And I'm not being rotten, I'm being brutally honest!'

'You aren't, you're being mean! And why should he or Freda find out? They'll never know till we tell them! Nobody's found out yet. Anyway, there's nothing we can do about it. So we'll have to do the best we can. We were on the stage, Lovey. So it's on with the motley, the paint and the powder, and that's an end to it!'

'Are we going to meet them at the airport?'

'No Larry, we're not. We'll send a taxi like we did the last time we had visitors. We don't want to be seen with them, do we? It would be suicidal!'

Larry slowly shook his head.

'Twenty-five-pounds-fifty for that taxi fare. I should have asked him for the registration document. We as good as bought it!'

Joe looked pained. 'Put your face straight!'

'Why, has it slipped?'

'No you ninny! My makeup's perfect, I mean smile a bit for goodness sake, we're going on holiday.'

Now Freda looked pained. 'I will if you will?'

'That's more like the Joe I used to know.'

They smiled together and headed for the desk. Everything went like clockwork. In two hours or so they would be in the South of France again. Freda could barely contain herself. Joe wasn't that bothered. He'd always found it to be too hot for him in the South of France. They didn't eat on the plane. Couldn't face it!

Everything went like clockwork for them at the French end. There were no delays at the airport. Their small amount of luggage hadn't gone missing and wasn't searched. Even better, their hand luggage that Joe and Freda clasped to their bosoms like long lost children, wasn't searched either! It would have been difficult to explain about the things that were in there.

They tried not to hurry away from customs. The diamonds were perfectly camouflaged as a massive, cheap necklace. The diamonds had been lacquered every colour under the sun and the three-stringed gaudy necklace looked typical of what rather frumpy women wear. In fact it bounced about like a coil of onions as they sauntered away. It wouldn't have mattered anyway even if they had rushed; the customs officers had already decided that this elderly couple were nothing more than air-sick holiday makers. The two uniformed men were now giving their complete attention to a young blonde thing in a short-cut top, and an even shorter skirt! One was fascinated by her cluster of bellybutton rings and the other one by her long, shapely legs that to him, seemed to reach the sky.

It had been hot when they left the plane but it was even hotter outside the terminal. Joe began to worry about his make-up. He didn't say anything. He didn't need to; Freda had seen the start of panic in his eyes. She took his hand, squeezed it and did her best to smile. It wasn't easy! There was a taxi waiting for Joe and Freda at the exit. The driver held a small white board saying Mr & Mrs Crow. They and their luggage were soon in it and on their way to Larry and Beryl's isolated spot in the foothills behind Nice. Now they were nearly there, the couple were beginning to relax, only slightly but it was a start.

Unfortunately the driver wasn't relaxing!

As they sped along the twisting, winding roads at twice the speed of light, Joe asked the driver if he had a death wish and if not, would he fazing-well slow down? Joe was ignored. The driver's mind was on his lunch and Marie – in that order.

Seconds later and even louder Joe said, 'It's boiling-hell-hole-hot. Slow down!'

The driver, being French, hadn't a clue what Joe was saying but he smiled and gave him the obligatory Gallic shrug. Joe's hand luggage that looked like your everyday overnight travel-bag rested between the pair on the back seat. Freda's was behind it. Joe's left hand was through the handle, while Freda's right hand was through the handle of her travel bag. They were valuable pieces of luggage to the couple and they didn't want to lose their contents in a head-on crash with a cork tree or a heavy lump of farm machinery. The taxi sped on but neither the road nor the driver improved. Joe kept hold of his bag even when the taxi turned into the short drive leading up to Larry and Beryl's place. The smiling, but pasty-faced couple were waiting on the front patio for their friends.

Joe, holding his bag, got out and went and opened the car door for Freda. She got out of the car holding her little bag, straightened her dark blue skirt and made a big fuss of waving hello and smiling. Joe didn't wave, but he smiled a lot. The couple on the patio smiled back quite a lot.

Neither couple kissed, embraced or shook hands. It had been a long time, and there seemed to be something holding each of them back. Joe said what with all this sunshine he thought they'd both be the same colour as David Dickenson, if not darker! Larry smiled and said they stayed out of it as often as they could, then asked them to come inside where it was cool.

The taxi driver, in one swift movement, dumped the two small cases from the boot to the ground. Lunch time was fast approaching and it was a fair way back to Nice. Marie's husband was home at sixteen-thirty; a good hour back to Nice, an hour-and-a-half for lunch. Yes, he could do it! The fare had been pre-paid by debit card and he wasn't offered a tip.

'Les Anglais,' he moaned. Then without a backward glance or another word he got back into his taxi. Without effort he spun the car round in the drive and raced off to Nice and to who knows what delights. It was Monday; perhaps it would be steak and chips?

Joe and Freda settled in the big comfy chairs offered by Larry who'd brought the suitcases in and put them by the big stone fireplace. Beryl had gone off to the kitchen to make a drink of tea. Both Joe and Freda had declined a glass of local wine. Larry didn't have a glass either and neither Joe nor Freda wanted anything to eat. They both said they'd eaten on the plane! Freda said it and the ride in the taxi had made her travel sick. She said she wouldn't be able to look at food for a week if not longer. Joe said he thought he had a stomach bug. That and the drive from the airport with that madman was enough to put a person off food for ever and a day! Still the same old Joe, thought Larry. He'd still moan if he lived rent free.

'You two look ashen, perhaps when you've had a nice cup of earl grey you should go and have a lie down.'

'Do they have that here, Larry?' asked Freda, looking greyer than ever.

'You'd be surprised what we have here, Freda. We've a dozen tins of baked beans if you want some on toast in the morning? I don't bother with them nowadays.'

'I never eat in the mornings. Sometimes I don't eat all day!'

'Is that why you look so grey Freda?' called Beryl from the kitchen.

'No paler than you two look,' answered Freda a bit miffed. 'And you have all this sunshine!'

To change the subject, Larry asked them what they'd been doing for the last fifteen years.

'Shouldn't we get the passwords over with first, Larry?'

'If you like Joe. Is that tea ready, Beryl? We're ready to exchange passwords!'

'Coming up, I won't be a minute.'

'It's better to wait till we're all together before we start.'

'I agree with Freda.'

'So do I Joe.' Beryl came in with the tea.

'I was just saying we should all be together when we exchange passwords.'

'I heard you when I was in the kitchen, Larry.'

Larry looked up at his wife and smiled. 'This one doesn't miss a trick!'

Joe got the ball rolling. 'Mine's Robert the Bruce meets old mother Riley! I couldn't guess a phrase like that.'

'Well mine's, Danny La Rue meets Spiderman. There. That's mine! And I had the same face job as Joe. Well he was Tony then!'

'You don't need to give more information than you need to Freda. Be as tight with your info, as I am with my money! Or so you all make out!'

The four of them laughed like hyenas. 'What about you Larry? Or should I say Albert?'

Larry hesitated for a split second, scratched his head and grinned.

'As far as I can remember my name was George and my password was, The three little pigs meet superman's mother.'

He settled back in his chair.

'Mine is little Bo-peep meets the three musketeers. I know we all look totally different to how we looked then, but none of us could have made up those dozy passwords! Now can we all relax with this lovely pot of tea I've made? And they're not silly tea bags!'

'Yes my girl, we can.'

'I'll second that!'

'And I'll third it and pour, if you like Trudy!'

'Call me Beryl, Christine, I've got used to it.'

'Ok, you might as well call me Freda.'

'And we'll both call you ladies, pains in the ar…er bum if you don't get on with it, won't we Larry?'

'Definitely!'

Relaxed sounds of laughter filled and bounced round the room. Joe and Freda wondered how long it would be before they could, 'come clean', as it were. Larry and Beryl thought it was going to be very difficult to explain what had happened to them since they last saw each other.

'Well, it's been a long time.'

'It has – fifteen years to the day. Larry, you wanted to know what we've been doing for the last fifteen years. The same as you two have, no doubt. We've been dodging the damned law and half the snouts in England. We've moved house six times if not more! We've had a few close shaves I can tell you.'

'I thought they'd got us six months ago,' Freda burst out. 'They'd had our faces on "Crime Watch". Not our new ones. Then on the Thursday, they knocked at the house next door with a sheaf of photo-fits. Some before we were done and some after we were done. They didn't know for sure we'd had plastic surgery but somebody had come up with the idea. No doubt some young copper trying to make a name for himself. Anyway, we were out of there like a shot. We moved across to Birmingham for a while, then up to Scotland, then down on the south coast. That was a lovely little place. Charming people. I wish we were still there. But then...' Joe coughed loudly,

'Then... well nothing really! Except Joe and me have been looking forward to seeing you two for ages.'

Freda looked deadly embarrassed. She sipped her tea and tried to hide her face behind her cup.

'Was it the same carry-on for you two?'

'Yes Joe it was. Well at least till we came over here. We got sick of moving from one place to another. It put years on us. Especially Beryl, what with her heart murmur and all. The doctors never sorted it out you know.'

'No we didn't know, how could we when we were on the run all the time?'

'We wouldn't have found you but for your phone call and you sending a taxi for us. We walked on eggshells after that phone call.'

'Well we're sorry about that, but now you know how it is with us Joe, Freda.'

Larry smiled at Freda. Freda thought he, and especially Beryl looked as rough as she and Joe looked, but that would be impossible. Their circumstances were completely different. Well that's what Freda thought!

'How did you get our number, Larry?'

'We didn't get your number. We rang Bert'

'Who's Bert?'

188

'You know him as Martin. He's a bit of a lad.' Larry grinned. 'We left a message with him. He contacted you, we didn't. Besides, he wouldn't give us your number no matter what we said.'

'It sounded exactly like your voice.'

'He can sound like anybody. You, me, Tommy Cooper, Ken Dodd. He was an impersonator in a previous life. We used to work with him in cabaret. He's good, bloody good.'

'He must be! I always thought Martin was a builder or a plumber, something like that!'

'Well there you go.'

'I'll take your things through. Your room's at the back.'

Beryl didn't wait for a reply. She took the cases and went through a curtained archway. The beads rattled like so many dry bones as she let them fall back into place.

'I think we'll go and have a lie down for a while. Must be suffering from jet-lag. What about you Freda? Fancy a nap, do you?'

'Yes Joe, I think I do.'

'Cheers mate. See you later.'

Freda smiled at Larry as she led Joe and the travel bags through the bead curtain, then lowered them back carefully. She didn't like the rattling noise as the sound reminded her of something else!

Joe and Freda didn't get up for dinner or supper. In fact they didn't leave their room at all that night and they didn't get up for breakfast the following morning. It was twelve-thirty when they finally showed their faces and they looked pretty relaxed. The colour (if their hosts didn't look too closely) had returned to their cheeks. In all, the couple looked fine. They found Larry and Beryl sitting at the dining table. They looked a lot better than they did the day before. There was what looked to Joe and Freda, to be the remains of a meal on the table but appearances can be deceiving.

'Would you like something to eat you two? We've some fresh fruit and chicken breasts in the chiller-cabinet. It's going to be a warm one!'

'What is? The day or the chiller-cabinet?'

'The day is Joe, you silly thing!' There were smiles all round.

'Look it's already above the cork trees. They're a member of the oak family you know.'

'No I didn't.' Joe shook his head.

'Why is the bark that funny shape?'

'It's where they cut the cork from. They can't take all the bark or the tree would die. So they just cut them like that and leave it to grow round again. They do look funny though. Now, what about something to eat?'

'Not for us, Beryl thanks. We've just this minute finished off the sandwiches we brought with us.'

The lying old devil! Thought Freda. 'What about a nice cup of tea to wash them down then?'

'That would be nice, Beryl. Shall I go and do it?'

'No, I'll do it Freda.'

'I notice Larry didn't offer. No change there then.'

Larry didn't rise to the bait. But as tired as he was, he managed a little snigger! Joe received the small compliment with a slight grin in return.

The pot of tea and Beryl duly arrived and was poured out. Nobody spoke. The only sounds the four could hear were the pouring of the tea and the buzz of countless insects in the garden. Joe was watching Freda like a hawk. She couldn't keep this pretence up-much longer and for that matter neither could he. For one thing, her make-up was beginning to soften in the heat. And if hers was, his was. But he certainly didn't want her to blurt it all out or pull her make-up off his face in front of them. It would scare Larry and Beryl to death.

From behind his cup, Larry kept casting sly glances across at Beryl. He was dreading her spilling the beans and frightening Joe and Freda to death. He should get it over with and tell them now. Break it gently before his make-up melted all over the floor, because if his was melting, Beryl's must be melting and when his friends spotted that happening, it would definitely be too late! He put his cup on the table and went into the kitchen. He dabbed his face with a wet towel then called Beryl into the kitchen. As soon as she walked in he told her to get that crap off her face. He was doing the same. The layers came off like plasticine and the stuff was thrown in the waste bin.

'Listen you two,' called Larry from the kitchen. 'We've got a bit of a shock for you. Are you sitting down?'

Joe, who was pulling the same sort of muck off his face and trying to help Freda do the same, called back, 'Yes we are, and we've got a dreadful shock for you! So for God's sake be ready for it when you come back in here.'

As soon as Larry and Beryl entered the dining room, the two ladies screamed and flung their hands across their faces. The two men looked open-mouthed at each other. For one whole minute they just stared at each other. Then they began to laugh, and they continued laughing till the ladies lowered their hands and joined in. Joe was the first one to recover; well to recover enough to ask for some food.

'I'm starving. We haven't eaten since we left home. We daren't in case our make-up slipped.'

'We haven't eaten all day either and for the same reason.' Larry started to laugh again.

'I can't believe that scumbag of a quack gave you my face and Freda, Beryl's.'

'And the lunatic gave you mine and Beryl, Freda's. Pour us all a good stiff drink Freda. No not you Beryl! The other Freda. I'll throw these make-up kits in the dustbin.'

'Take ours with you, will you? I'll be glad to see the back of 'em. They're in those travel bags in the guest room!'

'I don't suppose you want to throw that God-awful necklace in there with them do you?'

'Not on your life!'

*Richard Lee Wilson Feb.
2005*

Peas in a Pod

It was a glorious sunny day. The birds were singing and I could hear the gentle cooing of doves. If asked, I would have said it was the perfect day for a funeral. There was quite a large crowd gathered round the graveside to say their goodbyes to me. I recognised most of them. And there were quite a few flowers and wreaths kicking about. The black marble headstone would read David South, Rest in Peace etc., or something equally banal. There would be no mention on the stone of my being murdered. Most cruelly cut down in the prime of life. I sneered ironically to myself at the thought of it. It took only a single shot. The bullet hit me dead in the heart. I smiled again. They left me lying in a pool of blood on the bedroom floor. Or so they thought. There would be no record of Detective Chief Inspector Ford's implication in my murder, or the slimy sod's affair with my wife! No! There would me no mention of any of that. Well not yet!

The crowd couldn't see me; I was dressed in dark grey and I was twenty or more yards away hidden in the dark shadows of three magnificent Yew trees, which because of their standing, seemed to be at odds with the strange angles of some of the gravestones scattered about like rotten teeth. I could see the mourners. All of them were dressed in black or charcoal grey – all of them other than the vicar; he was the odd man out. His spotless surplice fluttered in the occasional gentle breeze like the wings of a huge but feeble butterfly. All of them were standing like respectful statues. I could see them, even those standing in the shadow of the church tower. I liked the sorrowful tone of the single bell. It tolled for me. A nice touch. I smiled an ironic smile and waited. I only stayed there to see if my darling wife was going to play the bereaved widow and throw a single red rose into the hole. I didn't have to wait long. In it went. I couldn't hear what she said but I saw the black handkerchief go to her eyes. The two-timing bitch should have followed the rose in. Ford wasn't there to comfort her but there were plenty of others turning to her with the usual platitudes. Ford was only the latest of her lovers, and he'd be her last! I'd make damned sure of that. I'd seen enough. I disappeared from the churchyard. Nobody saw me leave.

I suppose I ought to explain from the beginning..............

A few months ago I had to go to a meeting. It was late Thursday night when the boss rang. For him to call was unknown so I knew something was up.

'It was imperative,' he said. 'I want you and two of your engineers to get to this address.'

He'd heard rumours; we had to get the work done before ten-thirty Friday morning. I couldn't refuse so that was that. He was taking over yet another failing company. The boss was good at that, in fact he was extremely good at it. He had spies everywhere. I wasn't one of these nameless men, I was Head of Security and one of his many "step and fetch its". Perhaps there was something about this deal that the boss wasn't prepared to share with us. I didn't ask him. I do what I'm asked to do and no more!

Clara didn't seem too concerned about my going even though we were having some very close friends down for the weekend. She said she would put them off. 'It was no big thing, they can come another time.' Then she smiled and swept her hair over her right shoulder. She smoothed it into place and blew me a kiss. I smiled back at the devilish twinkle in her big brown eyes, shrugged my shoulders and left. I returned unexpectedly on Saturday night instead of Sunday night. The boss told me I wasn't needed at the kill. I'd supervised the installation of the eyes and ears which was critical. Nothing could be left to chance. There was no point in me and the engineers hanging about for nothing. They could dismantle the equipment at a later date. The boss didn't want too many of us there, it might create suspicions in the minds of the other party. I was very happy to leave.

I checked out of the hotel at seven o'clock. The hustle and bustle of Birmingham was behind me by eight and I took the scenic route, expecting to get home no later than ten, ten-thirty. It was just after ten when the timing belt decided enough was enough. It went with a terrific clattering and banging and a pall of blue smoke, dead opposite Mellor's Garage. I left it there, scribbled a note saying I'd give them a call in the morning. I wedged the note behind the wiper blade and went for a taxi. He dropped me off around ten-forty-five but he wouldn't take his car down the lane. He said it wasn't fit for a horse and cart. That little remark cost him his fiver tip.

I walked down to 'Old Farm' skirting the potholes. For some reason the house was in darkness and all the exterior security lights were out; including the one on the side of the barn. It was when I turned into what was the farmyard that I nearly collided with the car. It was parked half way under the holly bushes by the mistle. I recognised it as soon as I saw the registration number. I couldn't think of any reason why he should be here at this time of night! Never in my wildest dreams did I think he was having an affair with my wife!

I opened the front door and went in. I wasn't even being particularly quiet. The downstairs rooms were in darkness so I turned on the light, threw my jacket on the chair and my night bag next to it. I went through to the kitchen and got a beer. Clara hadn't called me so I assumed she was asleep. Maybe Ford's car had broken down. We were good friends. He often called round when I was away because the farm was fairly isolated. I thought it was good of him! I didn't give it another thought, well not then. I did a second later when I heard the sounds from upstairs and there was no mistaking what those sounds were. I stood deathly still.

A searing white flash burst in my head. I went dizzy. I couldn't bear the stabbing pain pounding away at my temples. I wanted to go upstairs and kill them. I can't for the life of me think why I didn't. It was as if I was completely comatose. Obviously I was in deep shock but I didn't realise it at the time. Nothing registered. It was like I was standing in outer space. I must have just stood there for ages as my head whirled – completely uncontrollable. I do remember calmly and slowly reading the beer label in a whisper and wondering why I was reading it. I remember putting the unopened bottle ever so carefully back in the fridge and turning the bottle till the label faced me. I remember shutting the fridge door and pretending to blow the light out as it shut. I remember tip-toeing into the room and getting my jacket and bag. And I remember silently locking the outside door and inspecting the key as though it had performed some sort of miracle.

I got a grip when I found I was walking in the wrong direction down the main road. I'd been telling myself I should go back and kick the living daylights out of 'em. I rang for a taxi instead. The good kicking would come later! It was after midnight when I got to the Crown and Sceptre. I knew there'd be one or two still hanging round the bar. I went round the back and knocked. Peter let me in. I told him the car had broken down and asked if he'd a room.

Just for one night. I said, 'I want to sort the car out first thing in the morning'.

He said its Sunday tomorrow! I said I'd learned the days of the week. He gave me an odd look but didn't comment any further. He could read nothing from my face, or at least I hoped he couldn't. I followed him through to the bar and asked for a double brandy. I nursed it for long enough. The others in the bar didn't leave until after two. I went up to my room at half-past.

I didn't sleep much; my mind was all over the place. It must have been four o'clock when I finally decided what I was going to do. I woke at seven.

Peter was knocking and asking if I was having breakfast. I shouted 'Yes I was'. I was in the dining room at seven thirty and away before eight-thirty.

Mellor's house was next to the garage. I went round there. He was doing paperwork in his office. I knocked on the window; he looked up, frowned but waved me in. We shook hands. I told him what had happened and he said he'd get his son to bring it in but it would be Monday before he could have a look at it. He said if it was the timing belt it could mean wider damage. He wasn't one of these rip-off merchants who are everywhere. He said he would give me a price before he started the work. I asked him for the loan of a sales car. Gordon Mellor is a good old-fashioned bloke in his early fifties. I asked him to put the hire charge on the bill. The boss would pay; it was one of the perks! He removed some keys from out of the safe and took me round to the front. The only car he had was a Renault and I was happy with that. One can't be picky on the Sabbath.

Over the next two weeks I devised a very simple plan as to how I could keep my eye on the lovebirds when I was away. I would fake an attempted break-in at the farm. Then to protect my darling wife in case it should happen again, I would have sophisticated security cameras fitted outside the house that she could activate each night. Then I would get my lads to build a safe room in the attic where she could go if burglars did break in. I'd make sure it wouldn't be found. There would be a mobile phone in the room so she could phone the police and I would ask Ford to pop round as often as he could to keep an eye on things. The bitch was all for it! It's a wonder her eyes didn't light up.

What I didn't tell her was when my lads did come round they would fit hidden cameras everywhere, especially in our bedroom.

The work was finished within a fortnight. She assured me she would be 'as safe as houses'. I had to make some arrangements in Glasgow (the bosses' euphemism for eavesdropping). I was back from Scotland in three days. Yes she'd been fine. Yes Ford had called round. No sign of intruders? No, none, she'd said smiling sweetly. I couldn't tell if she was laughing at me! The trigger-kneed slapper! She should have been in Hollywood!

I looked through the tapes as soon as she left for town and there were about two hours maximum but I only needed five minutes. They'd had their frolics and then they'd planned my death. Planned my death in my bedroom! I could barely control the stomach-knotting hate. The pair of them had got it all worked out. They were going to wait till the middle of the night. She would wake me up and say she'd heard a prowler. Ford would be waiting for me by the bedroom door to shoot me as soon as I got out of bed. He'd leave and she'd call the police saying her husband had been shot by a prowler. She could tell them what the hell she liked but it definitely wouldn't be her husband who got shot. Not on your life!

I hid the tapes in my office upstairs and re-loaded the ears and eyes with new tapes. I had three weeks to prepare. Not much time but I'd sort it out, and them.

Ford was going to Greece until the middle of July. I rang my twin brother and I was put through to a male nurse. I gave him the code words and told him I wanted to know how my brother was progressing. He put me through to Doctor Hayes. After repeating the code and after a long and boring lecture he told me he was progressing extremely well. The new medication he was on had worked exceptionally well. Indeed, Simon was soon to be released under the 'care in the community' system. God help the community I said to myself.

He told me my brother had recently returned from an unaccompanied (and more importantly) a totally problem free holiday in Scotland. I asked if I could speak to him. 'Off course you can', with this medication he's as sane as you or I! He said he'd put me through to his room. After a few clicks and buzzes, I told him I wanted him to come to Old Farm for the weekend. He chatted on about nothing but finally agreed. I arranged for a home visit. Within the week he was on his way here. I arranged to meet him at the railway station in Morton. Seeing him after all this time was like looking in a mirror. He hadn't changed much, at least no more than I had.

I told him I wanted to go away for a week with my latest girl-friend. He could have what fun he wanted with my wife. But he must not let her find out who he was or we wouldn't be able to do it again, ever. He fell for it. I knew he would. It would remind the sex maniac of the old days when we used to swap girlfriends for a couple of nights. They never found out that they'd slept with both of us. And I didn't find out that sometimes he gave them a hiding.

It was just after Christmas; in fact it was the day after our nineteenth birthday when he disappeared. It turned out he'd raped then strangled a teenage girl. The police called it a ferocious attack. He was caught and arrested. He was advised by his barrister to plead insanity, if not he could well face a life sentence. He didn't need advising, it was clear to everybody he was as mad as a hatter. He was put in a mental institution. I wasn't there to see all this but my father wrote to me. He told me everything that had happened and the effect it had on mother etc. I was trekking through India at the time. I stayed away as long as I could. I didn't want anybody to know he was my twin brother.

I was in Tibet when I found out about the death of my parents. Now there was only me and the maniac left. They were killed in a freak road accident. I'd been away three years and when I returned to England, I changed my name and married Sally. For some reason I never told her about my twin brother.

I met him at the station and drove him to a hotel in Nuneaton. He was to stay there and out of sight till I got in touch. On the way there I gave him his instructions. He laughed a lot. There was a glint of brightness in his eyes which I must admit made me feel pretty nervous. He said it would be a piece of cake. I dropped him off up the street thirty or so yards from the front entrance and stayed in the car. I checked with him that he had his medication. He said he had and told me to relax! He laughed and walked off down the street still laughing. It was like watching my reflection walk into the future. I hoped he would do better when he met my loving wife! I went to a solicitors' and made my Will. I left everything I owned to my brother, Simon North. Now all I had to do was wait till Ford came back.

Well that's about everything. Ford came back – I stayed away. They murdered my brother thinking he was me but that's no great loss. I probably saved a few innocent lives by setting him up. They've just committed his body to kingdom come and I'm going home to retrieve the tapes and replace them with tapes as fresh and crisp as chilled lettuce. I want to see their ashen faces when they play them back. I want to see their eyes pop out. And the best thing of all is! – they will have no idea where they came from! It's hysterical but I mustn't laugh too loud, even if I have got Ford and my widow just where I want them!

I watched the tapes last night; they are perfect in every detail. I just can't seem to stop laughing. I'd no idea my widow was so athletic. They should have got them by now. I posted them copies and enclosed a brief but succinct threatening letter three days ago. I'm at Mellor's enquiring about my supposed late brother's car. The house should be empty and they should be well on their way by the time I get round there. I don't know how far they'll get because I've sent copies to the nationals and Ford's Chief Superintendent.

I'm sitting in the lounge watching the second lot of tapes. The ones that are as crisp as chilled lettuce. Their faces are a picture of horror and disbelief. They're panicking like mad. It's hysterical. I think I'll play them again. I've never seen her fill a suitcase as fast! No neat folds, just stuff em in. It's funnier than the two Ronnies. Damn, I'll have to answer the door.

'Mr North? Mr Simon North?'

'Yes.'

'I'm Detective Chief Inspector Holmes and this is Detective Sergeant Stow. I think you already know Doctor Hayes.'

I didn't but I said I did. Didn't want to blow my cover. I laughed.

'Of course I know him! He's my Doctor.'

'Good. The reason we are here is because we want to ask you some questions regarding the murder of a young girl near Edinburgh. You were the last person to be seen with her. Do you mind if we come in?'

Richard Lee Wilson c 2005.

The Boss's Hat

The huge early Victorian office block had seen better times – much better times. The cornices and ornate lintels were grimy and fouled by pigeon droppings. But worse still in Mr Dowley's opinion, as he gazed at them from across the street, they were badly blunted and weathered by over a hundred years of Mother-Nature's fickle temperament, and eighty or so years of heavy traffic pollution. The cherubs, which at one time used to grimace down on the pedestrians below, were now faceless lumps of sandstone. It's possible, thought Mr Dowley as he crossed the busy street, that perhaps granite would have withstood the test of time. He held his breath as he passed through the vestibule then let it out and climbed the stairs. The drizzle had set his mood, or at least for the moment.

Mr Dowley, the last surviving member of Billton Hewet and Dowley Solicitors, even under these difficult circumstances, did try to maintain a degree of an age passing if not long gone. It was a pointless effort he often told himself. What could one do about the scruffy facade of the laundrette on the ground floor, and the dreadful pervasive pongs wafting up like malevolent spirits from both the laundrette and the newly opened Indian restaurant next door to it? Precisely nothing, he told himself. He remembered when both of them were owned by Carters Jewellers; it was elegant and tasteful then, but that was twenty years ago, if not thirty and the exterior of the building hadn't been touched since.

The brass plate and the front door were polished Mondays, Wednesdays and Fridays but not of course with the same polish. The mosaic-floored entrance hall, shared by the customers of the Taj Mahal was cleaned on Tuesdays and Thursdays. He often thought it might be a good idea to have the floor done on the same day as the nameplate. But he let it be. Smithies, the porter, had enough on his plate. He was in his mid-seventies and only a month younger than Mr Dowley. Twice a week on each task (the often pensive Mr Dowley concluded on Smithies behalf) was adequate.

He entered his inner sanctum; for latterly that's exactly what it had become. He went quickly through the case notes on his desk and wondered how people in general could ever get into such a tizzy over the most trivial of matters. He was reluctantly studying the bundle of instructions on his desk and was, after reading them for less than a few minutes, undecided as to whether he should contact Mr Crossley on the telephone and explain in words of no more than two syllables, that the Laburnum tree he wanted removing from the roadside corner of his neighbours drive (simply because it partially blocked the light to his greenhouse) would without doubt (if it ever came before the court) cost him more than it would to move his silly greenhouse! Instead, he muttered under his breath and pushed them with some annoyance to one side. Then realising the time pressed his buzzer. It was five-to-eleven; he would have a cup of tea and a couple of chocolate digestives.

He frowned inwardly but managed to smile outwardly as the latest of the many 'Temps' popped her multi-coloured head round the door and said, 'Did you buzz, Mr Dowlow?'

One day he promised himself this nincompoop of a girl would surely get his name right!

'Yes I did. I would like my tea, Miss Simpleton!'

'Miss Singleton, Sir,' she whined. 'My Name is Singleton.'

'Oh is it? Of course it is. How silly of me. And my name is Dowley. Mr Dowley. Should I spell it out for you yet again? Do try your best to remember it, and I will do my best to remember yours.'

The multi-coloured head and the bemused, pretty face disappeared.

Mr Dowley removed his spectacles and massaged the bridge of his nose. He was troubled. Even though he had good reasons not to do so, he had finally decided to retire. He was not an indecisive man, in fact he was the very opposite. But on this subject of retirement, the critical decision had been made with great reluctance. He wondered how he could break the news to his staff. Especially the senior staff, who over the years had become if not firm friends, close colleagues. He leaned back in his chair, closed his eyes and gave more thought to the problem. Suddenly his thoughts were invaded by the sound of a woodpecker drilling into his door. Miss Singleton had returned. She quick-marched into the office and placed a vivid yellow tray, with bright red triangles and green circles in its corners on his desk. Mr Dowley thanked her for the tea and biscuits. He hated the garish tray and wondered what had happened to the wooden one that he used to consider as his own personal tray. She did a swift about turn and click-clicked towards the door.

Stuck on her back was a sheet of A4 that read, 'If found return to the parrot house, London zoo.'

Mr Dowley stifled a laugh and let her leave. No doubt it had been stuck there by Archer, the office clown. He would have a word with him later.

He had once overheard Archer telling Simons the other junior, 'that he'd had a real giggle at a party the night before.' The gist of the conversation was; Tom Archer and a bunch of the lads had gone partying. It was his chum Graham's stag night, so they were going to have a laugh. Archer had somehow got hold of a roll of cling film from one of the kitchen staff. Then half a dozen of them had hung about the ladies lavatories. As soon as the opportunity arose, he sneaked into three of the cubicles and stretched the cling film across the lavatory pans. Then he lowered the seats and lids and waited with his cohorts at the bar for the outcome. Within five minutes two girls went in. The lads waited. Suddenly they heard the squeals and shouts, and saw the half-hysterical girls storming out of the powder room. He and his chums had a right laugh. He said, the highlight of the evening was when the Neanderthals on the door got hold of Graham (who was well wrecked) and threw him into the street. Then they all went for a kebab! Brilliant night, he'd told Simons. Simons agreed and told Archer how he'd fallen headlong down the stairs of the same nightclub, but hadn't felt a thing.

'I was absolutely spannered,' he'd said grinning.

Mr Dowley, angered, astonished and disgusted by such talk had shaken his head in disgust. He'd decided earlier that both of them were mentally deficient and would be better employed on children's television, rather than employed as junior solicitors in his practice. This latest incident had confirmed it. They were immediately summoned to his office. They stood like statues and in his sternest manner, he outlined their many failings and short-comings. He said he didn't think they were benefiting from this practice, or befitting to this practice. He then told them that perhaps they really ought to consider their future. They were dismissed from his presence without having said one word in mitigation. Mr Dowley (according to some) was an out of it old twonger. He wasn't. He was a gentleman – in all senses of the word. When in the office environment, Mr Dowley kept his thoughts to himself. To each his own and never ever the twain shall meet.

It was Friday. The day was overcast and threatened a poor weekend but it was of no import to Mr Dowley. He wouldn't be going anywhere. The boss's hat, a small Lovett Tyrolean with a couple of Jay's wing-feathers in the band, was hanging in its usual place. The top-most peg on the hat stand. Archer was the second person to arrive at the office, while Mr Dowley was always the first. Archer put the hat on the bottom peg, sniggered and put his own on the top peg. This action didn't go un-noticed by Mr Dowley. He was, at the time, sitting at his desk in his office with the door slightly open. He also saw the sneer on Archer's face and made a mental note that if this silly feud was to be re-ignited he would not only shred Archer's hat, he would also find him something extremely boring to do. Perhaps, Laburnum versus Greenhouse? Yes indeed, he decided. With deliberation he put the file in his out-tray, and then he switched on the huge shredder. He waited patiently until Mrs Driver had sorted the nincompoop out, then he popped out, took the bowler, smiled at Mrs Driver and returned to his office. The hungry plastic monster ate noisily.

Mrs Driver, the most senior of Mr Dowley's staff both in age and qualifications, had seen Archer's childish act and told him, crossly, to put the hat back at once and to act his damned age. Then, to put him in his place, she sent him to the sandwich shop. She smiled at Mr Dowley as he popped out and took the bowler hat. Fetching the sandwiches was Miss Singleton's daily chore. Archer was seething and as he banged down the stairs, he bumped into Simons at the door.

'The Medusa's sent me for the bloody sandwiches, can you believe it? Me a junior partner! I moved the boss's hat and she saw me.

Simons smiled and said, 'That gag's old, dare I say, that chummy, and I'll have a ham salad please?' He burst out laughing.

Archer told him to take a hike, and strolled off down the road. Simons hurried off upstairs; he was more than two hours late and Mr Dowley didn't like it when anyone was late.

'Damn the tube, and damn these stairs!' he muttered, slightly out of breath and with a touch of pink to his moon-shaped face, which at his age he shouldn't have.

Mr Dowley rang for Miss Singleton and she arrived. He didn't know clothes were made in such conflicting colours, and was glad it was dull out or the effect in strong sunlight would have given him a migraine. 'Put those on Mr Archer's desk would you, please?' He passed her Laburnum versus, Greenhouse and a bag of what looked like funereal confetti. 'And ask Mr Simons to come in when he arrives.'

The colour chart left the sanctum as Mr Dowley's gaze returned to the papers before him. Rankin versus Poole! His thoughts as they often did these days turned to the meandering trout stream in Fenaybeck Woods. Rankin versus Poole and the contested boundaries were momentarily abandoned.

'You wanted a word with me, Mr Dowley?'

Startled from his reverie by Simons, Mr Dowley placed his imaginary fly rod onto the imaginary banking and sat forward. He cleared his throat and said rather more sternly than he intended.

'You were late this morning. That's the third time this week. It really isn't good enough, Simons.' He Paused. 'Well? What was it this time?'

Simons face simulated mortification and he said, 'It's the tube, Sir. Got held up at the Elephant and Castle. Faulty brakes, I was told! The damned thing stopped a hundred yards short of the platform. Nobody could get off.' Simons pushed his hair out of his eyes and waited.

Mr Dowley didn't have a problem with his own hair falling across his brow. Mother Nature had seen to that, long ago. He scratched at the bit over his right ear and decided this would be the last warning for Simons. He scratched over his left ear. Sure indications (for those who knew his mannerisms) that he wasn't in the least impressed by his junior's excuse.

'Did the earlier train have faulty brakes, Simons?'

'I've no idea Sir!'

Simons dropped the, I'm very sorry Sir. It won't happen again Sir, look from his face, but didn't go on the offensive. He wasn't that stupid. If Mr Dowley was ever challenged over a matter of discipline, it turned into world war three. Mr Dowley, in his quaint but somewhat antiquated mind, was utterly convinced that when he disciplined his minions, he was character building. He was safeguarding their future. It was for their own good! Surely they understood. Had he asked Simons or Archer their opinions on this matter? And had either of them been brave enough to give it? Mr Dowley's world would have shattered like a crystal bowl being whacked with a coke shovel.

'Every evening next week, you will stay behind and do fifteen minutes extra work. Thank-you Simons. That will be all.'

'I do have some engagements next week Sir,' explained Simons, tight-lipped, as he subconsciously rocked on his heels.

'Then you must re-arrange them. You are a salaried employee and so must honour your commitments to this practice! That will be all, Simons!'

Mr Dowley laid heavy stress on the, will be.

'Thank you, Sir.'

Simons didn't quite storm out the office but he did close the door with some venom. Mr Dowley smiled and went back to the solitude of Fenaybeck Woods, to that special place where the trout stream did a wide, nearly circular sweep through the Willow Grove. The same willows under which he and Maureen had spent many a glorious hour. Those were delightful times. He would (he swore to himself) when he retired, stroll again beneath those willows, regardless of his domestic difficulties.

Archer returned with the sandwiches. He begrudgingly handed them out and took his own and Simons' to their office. Simons grinned and pointed to the bag and instructions on Archer's desk.

'Mr Dowley sent you those.'

When Archer saw the contents of the bag, he glared and swore he would get his revenge!

There were four private offices in the suite of rooms on the first floor. With the passing on to a better place of the two other partners, Mr Dowley had become the sole owner of the practice and the property. The smallest of these adjacent to Mr Dowley's office was furnished but not occupied, and it remained so. Mr Dowley (one of the founders of the practice) occupied the largest of the four offices, and had done from the start. Mr Billton had occupied the second most spacious. He was the first to enter into partnership with Mr Dowley and because (according to office gossip) of his over indulgence in the pleasures of life and his excessive weight, he was the first to exit the partnership. Mr Hewet (even though he was older by ten years than Mr Billton) was the second of the partners to be called before the only judge that matters. Mrs Driver occupied the late Mr Hewet's office; Simons and Archer shared the late Mr Billton's; the two secretaries, Mr Crumb, Ms Audrey Allan and Miss Singleton shared what became known as 'The moat'.

'The Keep' would have better described its location in the first floor suite. Their desks were surrounded on the south by the outside wall, on the north by the unused office and Mr Dowley's office, on the west by Simons, Archer's and Mrs Driver's offices and finally, by a small reception area to the east manned by Delia (the recently appointed but despite being a mere eighteen years of age) very efficient telephonist. The hat-and-coat stand lived a hermit's life three feet into the Moat from behind Delia and next to the door of the unused office. The boss's hat (unless Archer was being silly) was the hat-and-coat stand's only regular summer visitor. In the winter it had more visitors than it could cope with. On these occasions, the overflow of winter apparel went into the toilets that were reached by way of a small flight of steps (ninety degrees off to the right) at the top of the stairs from the road. These, like a small built-on afterthought of a tower, were the only two rooms that marred the perfectly square symmetry of the first floor.

Not one member of staff had seen Mr Dowley wearing this hat or entering the unused office. He was always first in the office and the last to leave. In the last umpteen years, neither the hat nor Mr Dowley had missed a day at the office other than holiday periods. Nobody gave a thought as to whether or not (on these occasions) the hat went with him. The only problem the hat created was for Archer. He had a thing about it. He'd been told more than a dozen times by Mrs Driver, but only once by Mr Dowley, that the topmost peg on the hat-and-coat stand was for the boss's hat. In fact, Archer had never worn a hat until the day after he'd asked Mr Dowley the reason why that Tyrolean hat was always hanging on the top peg and why nobody used the other office. Mr Dowley had told him there was a perfectly simple explanation; it being the boss's hat, the top peg was its proper and rightful place, and must not be interfered with. Mr Dowley said nothing about the unused office. Archer had for some odd reason taken Mr Dowley's explanation about the hat as some sort of challenge!

The following day he'd come in to the office wearing a bowler, casually swinging a brolly. This was something he'd never done before. He'd stood beside the bentwood hermit and removed the boss's hat to the bottom peg and placed both bowler and brolly on the top peg. Both were there when Archer (his jelled hair in a scruffy mess) left to go to court that morning but on his return, they were in his own wastepaper basket. On his desk in Mr Dowley's own hand was a piece of paper that read, 'If you wish to advance your career within this practice, you will do as instructed, and nothing more.'

When asked, Simons couldn't shed any light on how the note, or the bowler and brolly had found their way onto the desk and into the waste bin. There was a very simple explanation. Mr Dowley himself had put them there.

Archer had tried various tricks to usurp the hat's authority. But each time he tried, he had always found his items of subterfuge in his waste bin, other than on one occasion when he had cunningly replaced the boss's hat with what he thought was an exact replica of the afore-mentioned. On that occasion, and on his return from the magistrates' court to the office, in the distance, he spotted the thing that had cost him a fair amount of his leisure time to find and fifteen damned guineas, blowing away across the forecourt of the Shell station down the road. The hat had been crushed under at least two sets of uncaring wheels before he caught it. After that he left the boss's hat where it was. Well, at least for a time!

It was Monday and Simons was working late. He appeared to be doing the fifteen minutes extra demanded of him by Mr Dowley and had exceeded the set detention time by a further ten minutes. Although showing no sign of calling it a day, he was not there at Mr Dowley's behest nor was he working. He was looking for another position, after deciding, even before the latest carpeting to go elsewhere. Mr Dowley, in Simons' opinion was out of touch with modern practices and should have retired, or at least gone the way of his partners long ago. His opinion was shared by Archer, Mr Crumb, and at times by Ms Audrey Allan, mainly when Mr Dowley had his perfectionist's head on. Mrs Drivers, Smithies and oddly enough Delia, worshipped the ground he walked on. Mrs Driver's reasons were professional. She knew of his exceptional and outstanding legal skills. Mr Smithies' reasons were for his caring attitude and Delia's were known only to her and her best friend, Fern! Miss Singleton, having only worked there a matter of weeks, didn't like or dislike Mr Dowley. She was impressed by him, and a little wary of him, but only in a boss-man to new kid on the street relationship.

In the utter silence of his office, Simons continued to search amongst the appointments pages. There were three positions that looked very promising and three more, quite promising. He disregarded those out of town no matter how promising, underlining the preferred ones in red. He would do his best to get one of those. If he could get in with Carter, Bright and Hollywell, it would be terrific, as they did a substantial amount of, no win, no fee. Very lucrative! He would apply to the ones underlined in blue as a last resort. He put the journal in his briefcase and left the office. As the door closed behind him and as the lock clicked home sealing the prison, he realised he was the last to leave and the boss's hat was still on its peg! That's odd, he thought. Perhaps the boss was coming back? This brief thought was instantly replaced by the picture of a vodka and lemonade on the bar of the Henry the Eighth in Bradshaw Street so he hurried off. On the other hand Mr Dowley did not hurry off home. He called his wife and said he would be working late. She hated him to stay late and she made her feelings perfectly clear. He sighed audibly as he put down the telephone situated in the corridor between the saloon bar and the trophy room. The Golden Lion was always quiet before eight o'clock. He took his sherry into the trophy room.

It was nearly nine o'clock when Mr Dowley arrived home and Maureen had gone to bed. There was a turkey salad on the table that was uncovered! A sure sign that yet again he was in her bad books. He picked up the curtly worded note lying beside it and grimaced at the contents. He frowned hard at the curled up edges of the sliced turkey and picked up a piece of limp lettuce with his fingers. There was no salt on the lettuce! As he chewed, he wondered (as he often did) why the bright, sunlit smooth road of their marriage had turned into a dismal boulder-ridden cart track. He took his place at the table and made the best of his meal. A generous splash of salad cream livened it up. He finished the meal and left the plates and things on the table.

'Two can play silly games,' he told the kettle, out loud as he made himself a cup of tea.

He took the weak, but very sweet tea into the sitting room, popped it momentarily on the glass-topped coffee table, and turned on the television. He wouldn't particularly notice what was on as it was only for company. He left his cup of tea to cool a little.

His mind (as it often did) went unbidden, back over the years. Maureen was smiling at him as she relaxed in the long grass beside the trout stream and willingly shared his happiness. His heart raced at the very sight of her with her gorgeous green eyes that put the most glorious emeralds to shame, as did her tumbling, copper-coloured hair that stole the sunshine and refused to give it back. And her figure! What could one say about a figure so perfect. He was in paradise. He sighed out loud with some sadness as he came back to the present and reached for his cup of tea.

It was well after ten when he took the stairs to his separate bed! Her decision, not his. It was the day after her thirtieth birthday that it happened. It was sudden and without reason, or without a reason she was willing to disclose. Their second child was only one week old and like his sister, he was an absolute angel. She didn't want him near her.

'I don't intend to discuss the matter', she'd said. And then she'd coldly turned her back on him.

They should have gone their separate ways immediately, if not for the love of his children and the heartbreak it would cause their respective parents, he most certainly would have done. She refused to take medical advice and as far as she was concerned, that was the end of their relationship. On that day the dullest, palest emerald would have outshone her eyes, and he wouldn't have noticed if a thousand suns had been shining in her hair. He'd ignored the look of pain on her face and looked past her into the garden with sightless eyes seeing only a totally unjust nothingness. The whole episode had come like a bolt out of the blue and he was hurt beyond measure. He could think of nothing that could have provoked this bombshell. Had he asked, she couldn't have answered? She shared nothing of his life after that dreadful day. She never worked again and he wouldn't under any circumstances ask her why! But for some inexplicable reason, he still loved her!

He made the announcement the following day… he was to retire. Mrs Driver would take his place at the helm, but he would be available in an emergency, if required. He would arrange a small celebration, nothing extravagant, just a small get-together for those who wished to attend. It would be in the trophy room at the Golden Lion a week on Friday. He thanked them all. He had not intended his announcement to be so melancholy.

On the Monday of the week before that of his retirement the boss's hat went missing. Mr Dowley as usual, was the last to leave. He had a good idea where the hat would be. He entered the trophy room at the Golden Lion and sure enough, neither Archer nor Simons were there. He wasn't surprised, in fact he was delighted. They were not of his age, they were from the present and Mr Dowley wanted nothing to do with that!

The little get-together was a rather sad affair. The vol-au vents lacked imagination as did the petìt-fois. The conversation was hesitant and at times embarrassingly forced. They would miss him and his expertise. He would miss them and their companionship. He left when they left at eight o'clock and walked determinedly to the Henry the Eighth in Bradshaw Street. Archer and Simons were both standing at the bar and Archer had the boss's hat on his head at a jaunty angle, making fun of the feathers in the hat band and Mr Dowley's (in his opinion) quaint manner of speech, saying, 'Who's the boss now?' and 'I would wish to bring to your immediate attention the matter of, etc, etc.'

They both laughed liked hyenas and didn't see Mr Dowley till the hat was knocked from Archer's head. As the hat fell to the floor Archer heard Mr Dowley's stern voice say, 'Not you Archer, you haven't the intelligence to be the boss! I will have your resignation on my desk on Monday and my wife's hat now! If you would be so good.'

Richard Lee Wilson 2003

The Butler did it!

Dawn had stretched, yawned and rubbed its eyes and gone about its business. The ormolu clock on the bedside cupboard pinged eight o'clock. It was peaceful in the bedroom and the sun shone gently through the drapes. Jeeves entered and stood silently by the side and a little towards the bottom of the magnificent four-poster bed. He awaited instructions. The breakfast tray (although alien to him) was held firmly in his grasp. He felt uncomfortable playing this role and wondered why Madam would want breakfast on this, her last day? He coughed and took a short pace forward to make her aware of his presence. There was no need as she was well aware of it.

'Good morning. That smells good Jeeves. What is it?'

Her voice, soft and sweet, pierced his heart as surely as a blade of finest Sheffield steel. Had he not been in full control of himself he would have wept.

'Good morning Madam.' He dipped his head slightly. 'Today it is the full English breakfast.'

He smiled gently and made some small fuss of arranging it on the bed-table. It was the very least he could do.

'Yummy, lots of black puddings!' She smiled as she ate delicately. 'Mm, delicious,' she fussed in turn.

'Will that be all, Madam?' enquired Jeeves, barely able to enunciate.

'Stay awhile would you Jeeves?'

'If you wish Madam.'

He stood almost at attention and she resumed eating.

'What's your real name this time round Jeeves?' she asked looking up at him with eyes that would melt ice.

Jeeves had to turn away. This was wrong – she shouldn't be asking. He fussed about with the drapes. After swallowing as unobtrusively as his pain would allow he replied, 'If you insist Madam.'

'I do insist.'

Again the delicious smile. He'd no armour against that sort of weapon.

'Bracknell, Madam, as always.'

'No Jeeves, your Christian name! Not your surname.' She smiled again.

'Bracknell, Madam. Bracknell is my Christian name. My surname is August.'

Jeeves looked extremely uncomfortable. He found it almost impossible to hide his love for this beautiful woman when in such close and intimate proximity. Why on earth had she insisted he bring her tray up? He was also having difficulty restraining the recurring spasms of pain in the pit of his stomach. Why could he not die twice in her stead? Could it be arranged at such short notice? Would the boatman know? Would the boatman care? These thoughts and many others of equal melancholy slowly marched through his mind.

He took another pace back as if this slight distance would be some sort of miraculous salve for his discomfort. It wasn't!

'Will that be all Madam?' he asked softly. There was a perceptible pleading tone in his voice.

'Do relax Jeeves. We were both well aware this day would come. The piper must be paid!'

She smiled over the rim of her teacup. Her head was tilted slightly to one side as she said almost coquettishly and not quite looking him in the eye,

'Or would you perhaps prefer to be elsewhere?'

'Never Madam.' He willed the brightness from his eyes.

'Please forgive my slight impertinence. I merely wanted to say I would not wish to be anywhere else.'

'I don't think we need pretend on my last day Jeeves, do you? You can't suppress your feelings forever!'

'I am most sorry Madam but I am unaware of what you mean.'

'Oh come now. You no more want to be a butler than I do, although I must say you look tall, dark and very handsome in those clothes. And I know you love me and you know I love you. Do we have to play this silly game?'

'Please stop it. Stop looking at me like that. You know we must play this game Madam! Otherwise he will say we have reneged and we would grow old. He may even destroy us!'

'He would not destroy us Jeeves, he's too selfish to do that. Don't be so melodramatic. We would grow old like everyone else, nothing more nothing less!'

'I do not wish to grow old. Nor do I wish you to grow old.' Jeeves turned away and went to the window.

'Look at that. The blue of the river reflecting the glorious blue of the sky. The lush summer green of the fields and the majesty of the wild woodland, Madam. Would you throw it all away?' He turned and faced her. 'And you are the greatest reason of all. What more could I want? What more could anybody want? And think of this Madam. We might be allowed to return as ourselves next time!'

Jeeves looked desperate. This silliness had never happened before. Madam laughed. The sound of her laughter made Jeeves want to go to her, take her in his arms and keep her there forever. But he stayed where he was.

'You make it sound one-sided Jeeves. I ache for your love, as you ache for mine.' She gazed into his eyes.

Jeeves was totally at a loss. He now began to pace the floor and wring his hands. Then he stopped and said as forcefully as he could, 'Please Madam, you must get all such thoughts out of your head. He will be here shortly and if he gets the slightest hint of your state of mind we are done for. He will never again let us be ourselves.'

'One long passionate kiss Bracknell and I will say no more.'

'Behave yourself Madam! Such a thing is out of the question. Please Madam! Clear your head. Or at least hide the thought deep, deep down somewhere. He will be here any minute.'

'Why should we deny our love until the end of time Jeeves? We might as well be dead! It could be no worse than this.'

Madam waved her arms to encompass the whole room or as Jeeves stared into her eyes and saw such sadness there, it could have been a gesture to encompass the whole world. Jeeves was terrified. If he were to loose her now what would he do?

'Madam I beg of you. If you love me body and soul as I love you, you will do what we agreed to do. I can have no life without you.' Jeeves looked as though the endless years of his existence had suddenly caught up with him. Madam wept silently even though Jeeves had said something very funny.

'Think of the first time we came back and you were a whore in Soho and I was your pimp. We had fun then! Think of the time when we first married! I implore you. Think of the magic we shared.'

'Why did you say body and soul? That was so funny!'

'It was a manner of speech nothing more. It was not supposed to be funny.'

211

Jeeves was annoyed. 'You exasperate me sometimes Madam. I am being deadly serious. We must play our parts!'

'I know you're being deadly serious, and I know we must play our parts.' She was silent for a moment, then sighed deeply and said quietly, 'I know we must.' She frowned and would have thrown her covers off the bed but she was naked and that would have been much too much for Jeeves. 'So if we are going to continue this charade, you may take the tray away Jeeves.'

'Thank you Madam. I do hope you enjoyed it.'

'I certainly did. Especially the black pudding.'

Jeeves grimaced, took the tray and left the room. Madam waved a little wave and again sighed deeply. If only he would take her in his arms! He was better than all the black pudding in the world.

It was two in the afternoon when she made her entrance. Jeeves stopped to gaze on her as she swept with elegant grace down the stairs. She was dressed in red and looked magnificent. Her chestnut hair shone from the crown of her head to halfway down her back. It swayed like meadow grass tantalized by a summer breeze. She stopped for a moment and rested her hand on the curving banister rail and did a half-twirl. 'Will I do Jeeves?' She continued down the stairs. Jeeves could only stare. He was transfixed and bit the inside of his lip to keep control of the primitive urges that were coursing through his body.

It was some time before he spoke but at least when he did speak he said exactly the right thing! With the slight aloofness butlers assume, he intoned, 'Lunch is served Madam. Unfortunately your guest has not yet arrived.' He now gnawed at his lip. The guest must not be late. He knew this but he was! Maybe, just maybe the guest would not call. Perhaps he'd miscounted the leap years. Perhaps it should be next year. But if he had forgotten and such a thing was unprecedented, it would nullify the agreement. Oh, thought Jeeves (longing for night to come rushing) if only!

It was as these tiny pearls of hopeful thought sped through his mind that the vision of loveliness standing before him shimmered into a cascade of tiny sparkling red stars. The stars spat, sparkled and hissed nastily. They swirled, then spiralled and crackled loudly. Finally, they reformed and solidified. The nasty evil things took her place. There in all his dreadful glory stood the guest! Jeeves bowed low and he stayed head bent.

'It is done. She is dead. I will stay for lunch and you will serve.'

Jeeves bowed even lower. He dare not look at the guest.

'Be gone, about your business.'

Jeeves, eyes down, hurried off to the kitchens. The guest ate in silence even though the cinder toffee pudding was lukewarm. Jeeves was relieved when the dreadful meal was over. He had to be extremely careful. He had to keep all thoughts of love out of his head. It was hellish. Jeeves went to remove the empty dish.

'Leave it and go to her. Now!' snarled the guest.

Jeeves dashed out of the kitchen and ran upstairs, while the guest departed with a sneer on his face but without another word.

This was the bit Jeeves hated. He hated it because he could never be sure what method the guest had used to kill her. He took a long, deep breath and entered her bedroom. She was lying on the bed with the covers pulled back and he didn't immediately see the evil-looking dagger pinning her slender neck to the pillow but when he did, he cried out in anguish. He flew to her side and tried to pull it out but the more he pulled the firmer it became. It was as he was doing this, that the police suddenly appeared.

'Don't move. Stand away from the body,' ordered the Chief Inspector.

'I can hardly do both Sir,' replied Jeeves who was by this time, utterly distraught. He stood, shook his head slowly, blew his beloved a kiss and sank into the nearest chair.

'I take it you are the butler?'

'I am the butler.'

'We received a call from a Mr Guest saying you had threatened to murder your mistress. You also threatened to kill a Mr West or Mr Guest if he didn't mind his own business. The caller sounded (according to the officer who took the call) to be terrified. And Sir, it would appear he'd every reason to be terrified.'

The Inspector looked hard at Jeeves.

'His body, with a dagger in the heart not dissimilar to the one there, is lying in the hall by the telephone and the cord is tight round his neck. Have you anything to say?'

Jeeves looked at the policeman and smiled a wry smile.

'Nothing I say or do will alter the circumstances of Madam's death. I could no more murder Madam or Mr Guest than I could murder you.'

'Be that as it may Sir, but under the circumstances – I am arresting you on suspicion of murder.'

'Do as you wish.'

After the formalities were concluded the police and their suspect left the house and journeyed to the police station. He was formally charged and remanded in police custody until the following morning when he went before a magistrate. He was further remanded in Wormwood Scrubs to await trial. On April first nineteen-forty-nine he stood in the dock at the old Bailey. He elected to represent himself, even though he knew it would be a complete waste of time, but he did his best. For his first witness he called for Mary Brown, Madam's personal maid. She would swear they were deeply in love. It wasn't much but at least it was something. The jurors would believe Mary. Jeeve's hoped she would have recovered by now as her wounds weren't that bad. The usher left the courtroom and could be heard shouting, 'Calling Mary Brown. Calling Mary Brown.'

There was some commotion at the back of the courtroom; a buzz of murmurings could be heard. The usher who looked slightly flustered came down and whispered something to the Clerk. He in turn whispered to the Judge. The prosecuting council was whispering to his number two. The Judge demanded silence then turned to Jeeves and said, 'Your witness, I am afraid, died of blood poisoning over two weeks ago.'

Jeeves smiled but pressed on. He asked that an envelope and its contents held by the Solicitors Grebe, Blaine and Partners be offered as evidence for his defence. Mr Blaine, called as a witness for the prosecution, took the stand and the oath but swore he knew nothing of any envelope lodged for safe keeping by the defendant. When questioned about the defendant and the two victims, he swore he had never met any of them. The guest had covered everything. Jeeves gave up. 'I have no more evidence to offer Your Honour.'

The evidence against Jeeves, to say the least was overwhelming and the jurors were soon returned. When asked the Foreman stood slowly and pronounced clearly and solemnly a verdict of guilty. The judge, equally solemn, donned the black cap. Jeeves was ordered to stand. He stood with the same wry smile on his face.

'Prisoner at the bar,' intoned the Judge. 'You have been found guilty on two charges of murder. There is only one sentence for such heinous crimes. Bracknell August, I hereby sentence you to be hanged by the neck until you are pronounced dead and may God rest your soul.'

Jeeves laughed, he thought that was funny! The Judge didn't.

'Take him down! I see no remorse on that man's face.'

There was no appeal. Jeeves went to his death without a murmur. He remembered nothing after his feet went from under him and he heard a sharp snapping sound.

''addock three an' a tanner a parnd.'

It was a bitter cold morning and the fishmonger's fingers were blue. He rubbed them and blew on them and stamped his feet but it didn't do much good.

'Cam orn laydys. Cod farve bob a parnd. Caught 'em wi'me own 'ands this morning. Fresh Atlantic cod. I'll let you 'ave this an' the 'addock for seven an' tanner. Laaarvely fresh fishes,' he shouted in his strong cockney accent.

He stopped his bellowing and reached for a steaming pint pot of tea then clutched it in his hands. Soon he would be able to feel his fingers. A poorly-dressed woman approached his stall and looked longingly at the shellfish at the front. 'How much are the cockles there?' she pointed.

She was very hungry, very cold and very beautiful.

'Ta you me love tanner a gill.'

She leaned forward, stared at him for a moment and said, 'Bracknell?'

'Darn that way me darling. Battom o' the street, turn left, number seven bus right rarnd the cowner!'

'No, I'm sorry… I meant…' She looked embarrassed. 'I'm sorry,' she said and turned away.

'Carm orwn lady. Farl English breakfast only 'alf a crawn. Miles af black puddings, done em myself larst night.'

'Er, no I don't think…' She spun round and ran back, arms wide shouting, 'Jeeves. Jeeves! It's you.'

'You rang Madam? Nha, I ain't Jeeves now Madam,' shouted the fishmonger laughing as he held out his arms to grab her. 'Come here my sweet darling, it's going to be dark in a hour. Mary's on with our wedding supper!'

Richard Lee Wilson 2006.

The Corner Shop

'Good morning, Sir, what can I get for you?'

'The cash out of the till, and be bloody quick about it!' The eyes of the would-be thief were cold and held a cruel glint.

'But there's nothing in the till Sir. I've only just opened.'

'There must be something in there, where's your float?'

'Float, Sir? I don't know what you mean. This is a sweet shop and the angler's shop is along the road.'

'Money from yesterday, change to give to your punters; you stupid old pillock!'

The shopkeeper gasped. 'There's no need for that sort of talk in here Sir, as I said, this is a sweet shop not a public house!'

The shopkeeper removed his glasses, polished them as if they were filthy and glared at the would-be thief.

'If you don't hand over some money now pal you'll wish you were in a public house.'

'P'fuff,' replied the shopkeeper dismissively. 'I don't frequent public houses no matter what the circumstances are; I am a teetotaller as is all my family.'

'I don't sodding care what your family is!' snarled the would-be thief. 'If you don't give me the money you won't have a bloody family!'

The shopkeeper looked back at him with contempt.

'Bad language denotes a lack of education Sir, and I deplore bad language in all its forms. I would be grateful if you would restrict yourself to using the King's English.'

'The Queen's English, granddad!' sniggered the would-be thief.

'I am not related to you in any way whatsoever,' he was about to add, and I wouldn't wish to be for all the tea in China! But a bell rang as the door opened and the shopkeeper turned to see who'd come in.

'Good morning Mrs Draper, what can I get for you?'

'Good morning Mr Peter,' smiled a tall, elderly woman with a kind smile lighting up her face. 'I'd like four ounces of Dolly Mixtures please.'

'I won't be a moment; I've got a new jar in the back.'

'I'm not in any hurry Mr Peter.'

'Perhaps you'd like to come through and see which ones you want. I've got some giant ones that only came in this morning.'

'She's not going anywhere pal and neither are you, not till you've coughed up!'

'Not you again,' sighed Mr Peter. 'We don't cough in here Sir as we don't want nasty germs flying all over the place, do we Mrs Draper?'

'Not at all Mr Peter, this shop is a hygienic shop.'

Mrs Draper turned to the young man and frowned. 'Not like those supermarket places. I couldn't do with shopping there for sweets.'

'You'll not be shopping anywhere missus if he doesn't hand over the lolly and pretty sharpish.'

'Who on earth are you? You ill-mannered lout, why don't you ask for a lollipop in the proper manner. Young people these days are so rude; I blame the parents Mr Peter.'

'So do I Mrs Draper.'

'Well are you going to ask for a lollipop in a proper manner? You won't be served until you do. I know you were first in the queue, but you didn't act as if you wanted anything; facing the wall like that. Have you forgotten to shave? Scruffy devil, I blame the parents Mr Peter.'

'So do I Mrs Draper! I won't be a minute.'

Without a glance in the direction of the unshaven young man, the shopkeeper disappeared.

'Hey, where do you think you're going?'

'He can't hear you when he goes through there young man, so it's pointless raising your voice like that.'

'How would you like to eat through a tube missus?'

'I don't eat Smarties anymore; I've had to cut down on chocolate. Doctor's orders you see.' The tall woman nodded to make him understand. Craig wanted to whack the stupid old bag.

'I've found these Mrs Draper, I know you like Rainbow Crystals. Don't they sparkle?'

'My goodness they do indeed. I'll have a quarter of those while I'm here.'

'These are the giant Dolly Mixtures; do you want to try some of those?'

The smile broadened on the tall woman's face. 'I think I will. But I'll just have two ounces though if you don't mind. I don't want to make a pig of myself.'

'Oh I don't think you'll ever do that Mrs Draper.'

'Hey you, I aren't standing here all bloody day, give me the sodding dough.'

217

'How dare you talk to Mr Peter like that you ruffian. If you don't control yourself I'll slap your face.' The tall woman glared at the young lout. 'Mr Peter doesn't sell things like that. Go next door and ask for it there; that's a bakers' shop. But be careful how you speak to Mr Gabriel he's a big strong man and he isn't as patient as Mr Peter.'

'Give me the bread you stupid old bugger.'

'ARE YOU DEAF, THE BAKERS' SHOP IS NEXT DOOR?'

'Don't shout at me you loony, I want the dosh, the mazooma, the cash. Get it you stupid old bitch!'

'OOOH, how dare you talk to me like that! Get out of here and don't you ever dare come back. You're an absolute hooligan; your parents should be ashamed of themselves. Go on get on your way. You won't be served in here, will he Mr Peter?'

'No he won't be served in here today Mrs Draper.'

'Now is there anything else I can get you?'

'No thank you Mr Peter.'

'That will be one-and-eleven-pence-ha'penny then Mrs Draper.'

The tall lady fumbled in her leather purse as she was having some difficulty opening the clip. 'Got it,' she beamed as if she'd worked a small miracle. 'Can you change a ten shilling note Mr Peter?'

'Oh yes, I've plenty of change. Unlike this young man here; he hasn't a penny, not even a chocolate penny to his name! That's funny isn't it?'

'It is, it's very funny. Hasn't a chocolate penny to his name. That's a good one Mr Peter. Goodness knows how he got in here.'

It was the shopkeeper's turn to frown. Puzzled, he scratched his head. 'I can only think he must have taken a wrong turning Mrs Draper.'

'Yes he must have done.'

'I don't think that's funny and you won't think this is funny. Now you either pay up or you're dead.' The thug pulled a gun on Mr Peter.

'Ooo, look at that Mr Peter,' mocked the tall woman. 'He's got a gun. Has it got any bullets in it you coward?'

'Ignore him Mrs Draper, he's a thief but he won't get anything worth having here. He's got a gun but I've got lots of torpedoes, should I give him one?'

'I've got lots of torpedoes!' laughed Mrs Draper. 'You are a one Mr Peter. I'm partial to liquorice torpedoes myself. I'll have a quarter of those while I wait. My tram should be along soon.'

'Shall I put them in with your Dolly Mixtures Mrs Draper or do you want them in another bag?'

'No don't waste a bag; you can pop them in with these.' Mrs Draper passed the Dolly Mixtures back to Mr Peter.

'Wilful waste, eh Mrs Draper, brings woeful want. That will be tuppence-ha'penny please.'

'Yes it does Mr Peter and there's lots of waste nowadays. Goodness knows where they put it all! There you are.'

'Thank you Mrs Draper.'

'I'm counting to five, and if you don't give me every penny you've got – and I don't mean that rubbish – you're dead meat! That's not legal tender. I want real money, now get on with it.'

Mr Peter put the money in the till. The till went ping.

'Was that my tram?'

'No Mrs Draper, it was the till. Your tram isn't due for another five minutes.'

'Did you hear what this thief said?'

'No what did he say?'

'He said my money isn't any good. He said it isn't legal tender!'

'Did he? Well you'd best have it back then Mrs Draper; we'll have to start again. Do you have any gold sovereigns or diamonds you could settle your account with?'

'Ooo, you are a one. I haven't had any of those since I can't remember when. But you can have this watch if you like, it's solid gold.'

'I'll have that you old bag.' The thief snatched the watch from Mrs Draper's hand.

She slapped him hard across the face and snatched it back. 'I warned you, how dare you call someone an old bag. I'll bet he can't tell the time Mr Peter.'

'I think you're right Mrs Draper.'

The thief pointed his gun at Mrs Draper and pulled the trigger. There was an almighty bang but instead of the bullet blowing Mrs Draper's brains all over the place, it just dropped out of the barrel and rolled across the floor.

'Not much of a gun is it Mr Peter?'

'I must say I have seen better ones Mrs Draper.'

The thief had his hands over his ears.

'I think that's your tram I hear. See you tomorrow Mrs Draper. Here don't forget your sweets.'

Mrs Draper took the sweets. 'Thank you Mr Peter. I'll be in at the same time tomorrow, Cheerio.'

The would-be thief was trying to say something about loony old buggers and that he didn't want chocolate pennies and there are no trams nowadays. But he couldn't form the words as his ears were ringing and ringing.

'What time is it?' Craig, even though his eyes were closed, knocked the alarm clock off the bedside cupboard. It shot off across the bedroom floor and clattered against the wardrobe.

Charlene woke with a start. 'What the hell's wrong with you? You scared me half to death!'

'Nothing's wrong with me. Go and make me a coffee and don't set the bloody alarm clock again. It isn't seven o'clock yet, why the hell have you set it, you moron!'

'Don't call me a moron you pig! And for your information I didn't set the thing. You did, and you can make your own bleeding coffee – I'm going back to sleep!'

Charlene tried to go back to sleep.

'Go and make me a coffee you lazy cow, I've had a right nightmare. Look at me I'm sweating like a pig!'

'What else would you sweat like? You are a pig!'

'Don't get smart with me or I'll give you a good slapping.'

Slapping, he thought? A little bell rang deep in Craig's mind but he couldn't think why. He knew there was something, something about slapping, but he just couldn't put his finger on it. He tried to find it but it was just out of reach. He dug Marlene in the ribs and told her to go and make him a coffee. Marlene snarled and got out of bed. She threw on an old nightgown her mother had given her and turned both lights on then left them on.

'Sleep now you lazy pig!' Marlene had a bit of a temper but unlike some, she was never violent. She stamped down the stairs; there was no carpet on them to deaden the sound. Craig grunted and turned over. But he couldn't get back to sleep so he got out of bed.

Craig followed her down. He'd tried but he couldn't get back to sleep and he couldn't remember his nightmare, not one bit of it.

'Are you going to shave someday?' She filled the kettle.

'You look a right mess.'

'You've a nerve, look at you!'

He lit a cigarette and coughed his head off.

'When did you last run a comb through your hair? You've turned into a right slag.'

'If I have it's thanks to you!'

'What do you mean it's thanks to me?'

'I mean it's because I'm getting like you. I don't give a damn anymore! We've no sugar and the milk's turning. The damned fridge is like you; it's packed up working!'

'Stop whingeing you sad cow. How can I get a job with my record? Give me my coffee.'

'You won't get one if you sit on your backside all day, will you?'

'Like you, you mean.'

'Go to hell. I'm going back to bed.'

'I'm going to get some money.'

'Dream on, and get some sugar while you're out; that's the last of it. And if you take the heap don't forget it's not taxed and the brakes are crap.'

'Not as crappy as you!'

Charlene ignored him and went back to bed.

Craig went through to the front room and opened the top, left-hand drawer of an old sideboard. He snatched a rolled up piece of oiled linen. The bundle of cloth held something heavy. He smiled and took out his gun. He'd show the sad cow. She didn't know about this. He'd get some bleeding money. He slammed the drawer shut. There's that sweet shop on the corner. That old giffer must be rolling in it, the place is never empty. All these thoughts went through his mind as he stormed out of the house. He pulled the wire fence back and got in his car then he stuck his 'Tax applied for' sticker in the corner of the screen and switched the ignition on. He tried the footbrake, it felt okay; it was a bit spongy. So what, it had always been spongy. He decided he'd park up on the waste ground across from the shop till it opened he could have nap in the car. He drew out onto the road and left the fence as it was, he'd be back in a couple of hours. He didn't see the lorry coming down the hill as he made to turn onto the waste ground. He was pumping the brakes like mad to slow down, as he didn't want to finish up going through the churchyard wall. He yanked at the hand brake and tried to drop a gear all at the same time but the handbrake only worked on one side. For Craig, the right side wheel was the wrong side wheel. The rear tyre screeched as he lost it and skidded out of control across the road. He hoped to God he could stop in time but everything seemed to be in slow motion. He didn't seem to be able to move his hands fast enough! The lorry hit him head on and he never felt a thing.

Charles sat bolt upright in bed. Sweat was pouring down his face.

'Molly!' he yelled at the top of his voice. 'Wow, what a night.'

'What on earth's the matter?'

'Nightmare, darling, two nightmares Molly. I don't know how many nightmares. Wow, no more strong cheese for me last thing at night! What time is it?'

'Ten-to-seven. Time to be up darling, you mustn't be late on the first day at your new job. And don't be eating your samples; I've seen all your chocolate pennies! Too many sweets are bad for you.'

'Don't worry I won't. Oh by the way Pet, I'll have to use your car today if you don't mind? The people from the garage are taking mine in this morning. It won't be done till after lunch; there's a fault with the handbrake.'

'That's ok, take it. I won't need it. I'm not going out. Draper's are coming to fit the new stair carpet sometime today.'

'Of course they are, I'd forgotten it was today. Oh and don't for goodness sake be wearing that raggety old dressing gown when they come, or they'll think we can't afford a new carpet,' Charles laughed.

'You stop riffling through the sideboard-drawer and be on your way!' laughed Molly in return.

Richard Lee Wilson 2006

The Exhibition

Arabella Smythe, Lady President of the Huntsford Ladies Charity Guild and for sometime now a sixty-year-old widow, loved all things sweet. Fresh cream chocolate éclairs being her favourite. A very close second was her love of butterfly buns. Not the disgusting butter-cream ones; they were soon returned by a more than frosty-faced Arabella to the bakery. The ones Arabella loved were the ones filled to overflowing with fresh double-Devon cream! She also loved her late husband, Dear Henry, her nephew Richard, and raising money for charity. It was difficult for friends and casual acquaintances to ascertain which of the four held pride of place in her more than ample bosom. Meanies said it was fattening food but they were wrong. Richard had been a close second until he decided to live in sin with a young woman who wore more make-up than the Mikado and displayed her navel. Arabella considered the term 'Partner' to be a euphemism for bed-mate. Maud called Richard a 'Clever Dick', but never in front of Arabella.

Cynthia, a senior committee member, was a shy but artistically gifted young lady with neglected hair. When it wasn't tied up with something she'd found in a corner of one of her many paint boxes, her hair was long and auburn. She loved art in all its forms. Her own work was excellent, sometimes bordering on more than magnificent. Jeremy and Karl loved Cynthia and both would have crawled nine miles over broken glass tipped with rancid butter-cream to win her heart. Alas, Cynthia's heart was already spoken for! Her art owned it. Melanie, one of the models, loved Karl and would have gladly thrown herself bare-bottomed onto the same broken glass to win his heart. It appeared, alas, that her wish would never be fulfilled either. Melanie a life-class model, although a friend of Cynthia's was not a member of the committee, junior or senior.

Maud, a frail-looking spinster but by no means a vestal virgin, was the oldest member on the committee and second only in authority to Arabella. Maud's love was her garden and everything in it. Although seventy-something she was not a deeply religious woman but she thanked God many times for the strength he gave her to maintain her beautiful garden. She should have thanked the kindly and conscientious professionals at the arthritis clinic or the distillers of her fine medicinal brandy, which contrary to wicked rumour she used only very sparingly. Was it they perhaps who kept her going? Although cowed somewhat as a child by her father's strict regime, she never got over his early death. And as no man she'd ever met could better him or even get close to him, Maud never married.

Scatty Mavis, another senior committee member, loved her husband and her three darling children – Stephen, Simon and Daisy the youngest. Dreamboat, as she called her husband Ronald, was the best thing that had ever happened to her. Scatty Mavis or Sugar-plum as he often called her was the best thing that ever happened to him although their children were a very close second. Stephen and Simon (they often told Daisy) and contrary to all behaviourists' advice, were good boys and did as they were told! This was usually spat out when rescuing Fluffy the cat from Daisy's clutches or the washing machine, confiscating her slug collection or searching for her in the coal cellar. Arabella thought four-year-old Daisy was some sort of angelic poltergeist and especially so when she pulled a face like Witch Lotsawarts. In all fairness to Mavis, her rather unjust nickname was given to her because quite often during committee meetings, her body was *in situ* but her mind was often at home or on the bus somewhere. This circumstance did not distract her from the good charitable work she put in. Well not a great deal!

Margaret and Betty, two more senior members were uncomplicated ladies. Both were married with teenage children who often helped their mothers at some of the charitable events, and in fairness to the youngsters, not always unwillingly! While one or two committee members ran about in all directions, these two plodded to the front line, in a straight line; an ability not unnoticed by the perceptive Lady President, who, from her vantage point at the end of the committee room table noticed and noted everything. Perhaps her eyes were not what they used to be, but they were still plenty good enough! She only popped her glasses on when, as she put it, her eyes were extremely tired because on Sunday night she'd been going over the minutes of last weeks meeting and hadn't noticed the lateness of the hour. Neither Betty nor Margaret was foolhardy enough to question this fiction! They didn't ask why Arabella wore a size six in shoes either, when it was quite obvious (what with the strange mincing gait of hers). They'd both agreed she'd be more comfortable in a size seven, or even a seven-and-a-half. Margaret and Betty didn't concern themselves with trivial matters of vanity! They were both working mothers.

The lovely Lady Marion was not a working mother or a mother at all for that matter. She was another senior committee member albeit a recent one. She loved men; sporty; big; strong and handsome men in particular. Her husband, Lord Percy De Glynn, loved her with all his heart. She thought him a wealthy twit with the brain capacity of a six-year-old but she was entirely wrong about him. Fortunately, Lord Percy knew nothing of her nasty habits, or of her earlier life. Thanks or no thanks to the crystal ball, Arabella did. She still hadn't fully recovered from the dreadful shock of witnessing one of Lady Marion's sordid entanglements at the Golden Crab Hotel. Maud knew of Lady Marion's nasty habits; she'd heard her grunts and squeals over the two-way radio during the treasure hunt. Perhaps other members of the committee knew. It was well understood, however, that not a whiff of this knowledge should get back to Lord Percy as it would destroy him. The protection of Lord Percy's happiness was the only reason she remained on the committee and was tolerated by the other members! Arabella often questioned how long this state of affairs could continue?

Martha, a more than plump lady and the most recent senior committee member, loved clothes. Her favourites were those designed and marketed by Rainbows End. These creations, according to Betty were well over the top. Margaret said they and the monocle were a distraction. Martha's favourite was an ensemble called Tribal Feathers. It was everyone else's least favourite. None of the committee members would even consider hurting her feelings by airing their views within earshot of Martha. Betty, just for fun, came to one committee meeting wearing sunglasses. Fortunately, Martha didn't put two and two together. Arabella did and suggested she should remove them unless she was wearing them for medical reasons. A suggestion by Arabella being equal in strength to a court order had Betty whipping the glasses off and into her handbag. Arabella had thanked her and further suggested that clowning is all well and good at a circus but not here Dear! The Lady President then glanced quickly at Martha's latest multicoloured get-up called, Evening Sunburst on Venus, and decided it had been designed by Daisy, Mithter thlippery and her horrible toy octopus! She considered telling Betty she could put them back on! But it was only a thought! Arabella hoped Martha would wear something less eye-piercingly dramatic at the next committee meeting.

The ladies came early, although Arabella was late for the meeting leaving them wondering if the clocks had gone back an hour. No, it was showing seven o'clock exactly and it was late June. Had she been run over? Had she been kidnapped? Maud said if she'd been kidnapped it had to be by a suicidal gang of more than four. Mavis was late, and Margaret was late too. No one could think of any reason why, Arabella, for the first time in her adult life, could be late! She was never ever late!

Mavis came dashing through the door at twenty-past-seven and Margaret followed her in.

Margaret spotted the empty teacups first and turned to Mavis, 'You forgot to tell them about the later start, didn't you? Her Ladyship won't half give it you if she finds out!'

'I'm sorry but Daisy was…'

'No time for that,' interrupted Margaret. 'If I was you I'd be clearing that lot off the table before she gets here! You've only five or six minutes.'

The others gave Mavis a hand and there was no sign of the previous clutter when Arabella arrived ten seconds before half-past-seven. All the ladies except the lovely Lady Marion, who hated Arabella, were sitting, backs straight, with their pads and pencils at the ready. Maud didn't have a pencil; she had a blue biro and also a red one because she took the minutes.

'Good evening ladies. I see you got my message. Thank you Mavis,' Arabella acknowledged.

'Er, I…' Margaret glared a warning at Mavis.

'Did you want to say something, Dear?' asked Arabella. Her perfect crescent eyebrows raised themselves almost an inch up her forehead.

'Nothing important Arabella.'

'Well don't let us waste time with trivia then Mavis. Perhaps one of you will make a pot of tea. There seems to be a tantalizing odour of it about the room.'

She popped her big brown handbag on the floor by her chair and sat down. Her blue rinse came into full view as she bent to look at her neatly arranged notes on the table.

'When you're ready.'

The tea was quickly passed round and Arabella began shuffling her notes; a sure sign to the gathering that she was ready and waiting. She gave them all a cursory glance and after seeing Martha's new outfit, Arabella realized her hopes had been dashed. Maud sat with her blue biro at the ready.

'Firstly, I would like to sort out the over-sixties paper chase this evening and,' her gaze fell on Cynthia, 'Secondly, I would also like to make sure the arrangements for your art exhibition are on song! Cynthia.'

'They are Lady President.'

'Thank you My Dear.' Arabella was quite surprised by Cynthia's positive reply. She'd half expected her to say no, then hang her head and let her thoughts go to one of her happy places!

226

'Now ladies, the paper chase.' Arabella passed each member a sheet of A4. 'The date before you has been confirmed with Lord Percy and the start-off point is the same as last time. I have also listed your duties. Because of last years fiasco we are going to use dolly-pegs to mark the route. Then if the wind does pick up like it did last time, the dolly-pegs won't be blown to kingdom come and halfway back, and more importantly, we won't lose any of the entrants… oh and we need to collect their entry fees before the start of the chase rather than after. Then if any entrants choose to fall by the wayside it won't matter.'

Maud made a note.

Arabella paused for a second as though chasing another thought and said, 'Do you think we ought to change it to the over-fifties paper chase? I'm sure we would get a lot more entrants than last time. Well what do you think?' No one answered immediately. The committee members were not used to being consulted on such things. 'Well?' She asked and up went the eyebrows.

Maud was the first to answer. 'I think we should. The more the merrier!'

'I wasn't thinking of merriment, Maud, I was thinking of the extra money we could make Dear!'

After Arabella's fairly barbed response, there were no more opinions forthcoming.

'We will vote on it then,' suggested Arabella nicely. 'Time and tide wait for no man, nor women. Are you still with us Mavis Dear?'

Mavis returned but nearly replied yes Miss! She nodded instead.

Arabella shook her head and said, 'Those in favour?' She counted the hands. 'Unanimous, excellent! Then I think these posters I prepared yesterday can go up. Usual places.'

Maud nearly laughed out loud when she realised they'd been had. Each member was given three posters to position round Huntsford.

'Now Maud Dear, finances I think. Margaret and I,' (she looked pointedly at Maud), 'have had the good fortune to win a few pounds at the races. We were very lucky with our selections. Between us we won a total of sixty-four pounds.'

Maud, who looked like she'd just eaten a spider, entered it in red in column A.

'Which I think for a couple of novices isn't bad.'

The applause that followed was genuine even though Arabella's little speech had been a bunch of lies. Maud dropped the scowl from her face and decided then and there that she must put a stop to this as soon as possible. This supposed lucky streak had gone on long enough. She would speak to Arabella about that damned crystal ball after the meeting. Margaret thought it very generous of Arabella to include her in the glory. After all, the Lady President had picked all the winners!

'Now future events. I thought we might try our hands at a boot sale. Although I haven't been to one myself, I have heard they're well supported. Volunteers?' She glanced up. 'No? Well I'll leave the arrangements to you two.' She elected Betty and Margaret. The two ladies smiled as if they'd just met somebody to whom they owed a stack of money.

The ship's crew offered their thoughts on boot sales as the ship approached the port. Martha asked if she could bring some of her old outfits along to sell. Without thinking, Arabella said she didn't think anyone from the theatrical profession would visit a boot sale. The monocle fell from Martha's eye like an alien teardrop. Soon everyone hoped the ship would anchor and they could get off home. In due course it did. They were off down the gangplank at a good rate of knots as soon as the huge handbag was raised from the floor, and before the captain could come up with something else.

Maud couldn't catch Arabella's attention. Her hip was giving her grief and Arabella seemed to be in a big hurry. Maud knew why as well! She sat back down, had a spoonful of brandy to ease the pain and swore she would call round at Arabella's in the morning. Maud didn't rush round in a morning; she liked to take things easy till she got warmed up. Firstly and at snail-pace, she made toast with lashings of butter and marmalade while the percolator bubbled away on the Aga. Secondly, and without fail after taking two pieces of toast, she'd go and look out of the big window at the back of the house. On the mornings when it wasn't cold or raining, she'd pop out onto the patio, sit cross-legged on the top step and watch the birds hop about on the lawn. Maud liked to watch the magpies best because they marched and hopped, nearly at the same time. It was while she was watching a territorial conflict between two cock robins that she nearly had a heart attack. The more aggressive one had just chased the smaller one into the rhododendrons and was about to peck its eyes out, when someone suddenly said, 'Good morning Maud. Bird watching I see, I thought you would have been dressed by now!'

'Arabella,' gasped Maud, who was now pulling her toast up off the paving stones at the bottom of the steps where it had stuck like a bloodstained poultice. 'You frightened the life out of me.' The startled robins flew up into the silver birch tree and continued their war up there. 'What on earth are you doing here at this time in the morning? Why didn't you ring or something to tell me you was coming round? My heart's going twenty to the dozen!'

'Stop fussing Maud. I knew you'd be up by now.'

Arabella didn't join Maud on the step. She took out a handkerchief and flicked a miniscule speck of something or other from one of the patio chairs.

'Don't you fuss Arabella, the chair's spotless.'

'It is now Dear,' she replied rather snootily.

It was perfectly clear to Arabella that Maud wasn't herself. She sat for a few moments as though she was watching the birds before she replied, 'Calm yourself Maud. Take a breath, I'm not fussing. I don't fuss as you call it. This skirt is my favourite; I would hate to get bird droppings all over it!'

Maud's eyes turned to the heavens. 'Well?'

'Well what Dear?'

'You didn't tell me you were calling so it must be something important Arabella.'

'That's true Maud and it is important. Going by the look on your face at the meeting last evening it was obvious you were less than delighted with our small efforts at the races! And I got the distinct feeling that you would call on me first, and without forewarning. Isn't that so?'

'It is so Arabella! That damned crystal ball is having a bad effect on you.' The grey-haired spinster was clearly annoyed with Arabella. Then she sighed and let out a breath and said, 'Sorry for snapping at you but you should chuck the thing in the dustbin and stay away from the races altogether; nothing good can come of it.'

'I'd say four-hundred-and-twenty pounds was good Maud, Dear, wouldn't you?'

Arabella had adopted her superior tone of voice as she often did when she was in the wrong and the chips were down, but it didn't impress Maud.

'No I wouldn't, not under the circumstances, and we've been over all this before. All you're doing is taking money by false pretences, and don't try to use the excuse you're only taking it from bookmakers! That won't wash, and where will it end Arabella?'

Maud picked at her piece of cold toast. She was agitated because she'd gone through this argument more than once.

'You ask me where will it end: Here Maud, here and now!'

With much drama, Arabella fished in her huge handbag and brought out the crystal ball wrapped in its red, velvet shroud.

'I am leaving this with you Maud. I know you won't use it and that it will be in safe hands. Here Maud, take it.'

Arabella handed her the crystal ball.

'But what the dickens am I supposed to do with it?' Maud looked stunned.

'Keep it safe somewhere. You could pop it in your mouth at the moment Dear, it's certainly hanging open.' Arabella's soft thud of a laugh erupted. Maud closed her mouth.

'There must be a safe place in a house as big as this; find somewhere. You've seen the effect it has on people even intelligent, strong-willed people such as you and I.' Arabella stood up. 'I won't bother with a nice cup of tea and a piece of your delicious looking toast; I must be off. See you later Maud, Dear.'

Maud didn't know what to say. Arabella not bothering to eat! She stared at Arabella and Arabella stared back.

There was a very serious look on Arabella's face when she said, 'Promise me you won't look into the crystal Maud! Promise. If you do, you might just see something you don't want to see! I'll say no more.'

'I won't touch the damned thing again I promise you that! But if something's worrying you Arabella, you must tell me.'

'Nothing's worrying me in the least Maud, Dear. Now I must dash so see you later.'

Arabella strode off round the corner of the house watched by a very pensive Maud.

'Bye,' said Maud to the house corner. She was sure something was worrying Arabella, but what?

She knew what she must do with the crystal ball lying like a lump of lead in her small hands. She got up from the step, threw the remains of her toast for the birds and went inside. She took some newspaper from the rack on the kitchen door, wrapped it round the crystal ball and went upstairs. She put the thing in her bedside cabinet and locked the door. Her bedside cabinet, like the rest of her furniture, was early Victorian and made of solid walnut. She'd decided a grizzly bear wouldn't get it out of there! She went downstairs to her writing desk in the sitting room and took out an envelope.

She wrapped the key in some scrap paper that was to hand, secured it with sticky tape and put it, and a little note asking her cousin Sarah's eldest daughter Fern, to keep the key in a safe place. She addressed it to Fern's holiday home in Scotland. There would be no visitors at the cottage until the second week in August. If Arabella softened and demanded its return she would tell her it was impossible until the middle of August and she wouldn't be telling lies. Maud was so pleased with herself, she went and threw the rest of the cold toast to the birds and made some fresh pieces.

Cynthia was working hard to get every picture finished in time for the exhibition. She'd been up since a quarter-to-six and had gone down to the river to capture the early morning light on the water and the fresh pale-green of the weeping willows. She'd called the picture Dawn Chorus and she would put the wild birds in later. There weren't many birds on the river these days; there were too many noisy factories and too much pollution but the two hardy swans she'd seen over by the far riverbank would get pride of place. They might not have pure white feathers now but in the painting, the grey-green slime on their lower feathers would be replaced with the palest of pinks and yellows.

Karl, who lived in the same big house as Cynthia but in the flat upstairs, had volunteered at least three times to go with her to the river, even at that time in the morning. Having rarely seen that time in a morning unless he was returning home, he thought his offers were on a par with martyrdom. Jeremy, who shared the flat with Karl, suggested four times that he should go instead. He pointed out to Karl that three of the paintings he'd offered to do for Cynthia's exhibition lie unfinished on his bedroom floor. 'Sitting on his backside and lusting after Cynthia wouldn't get them done!' Only he didn't quite put it so delicately.

Cynthia was used to foul language having been at university herself but she pretended not to notice it. Instead and after wondering what was wrong with them she declined their offers saying, 'Thank you but I don't want any distractions.' Then after sweeping her hair from her elfin face, she'd hurried off before they started arguing again. Cynthia could see at a glance the delicate complexities of dawn light on a gently flowing river, but alas not the laser powered love-light ripping from their eyes.

Later in the day and long after Cynthia had daydreamed most of the day away (other than a two hour spell when by some sort of wizardry she'd converted the gate house of Craven's shabby paper mill into a two-hundred-year old pristine windmill complete with a family of swans). Betty was having a drink in the Unicorn with Clara and Connie. Like Betty, her two friends worked flexi-hours. She hadn't gone in there on a whim or for the need of a gin and tonic (even though she was sipping at one) she'd gone in to get hold of Harry the head butcher at the Co-op supermarket and as Mr. Longbottom was soon to retire, Harry was soon to be the Manager. She needed a favour. She knew he came in here most evenings on his way home from work and she was lurking at the bar to catch him at his most jovial.

Her glass was close to empty when one of the many clones of friar tuck bounced through the door. As soon as Harry saw Betty he waved and she waved back and called him over. As ever, he had a big smile on his ruddy face and a friendly greeting on his lips, which as soon as he was within reach he transplanted onto Betty's cheek. She returned his greeting but without the yum-yum slurp sound Harry made. Clara and Connie each got a kiss and a big smile.

'When are you going to leave that miserable husband of yours and run away with me?'

Betty said if he could keep up with her and if he'd a wallet as wide as his braces they could set off now!

Harry didn't take offence he just laughed out loud and said she was a cheeky bugger. Harry ordered a pint and offered the three a refill, which they declined.

'To be honest Harry, I only came in to ask you for a favour. Her Ladyship wants Margaret and I to organize a car boot sale and I wondered if we could use the Co-op car park. We could get a load of cars in there. It's no use asking the others; those grabbing devils open on a Sunday.'

'I'll find out and let you know. When is it?'

'We haven't set a date yet. Perhaps early Jul – there's the gala soon and there's still a lot of work to do for that! I don't suppose you two would like to help?'

Connie and Clara said they would have a word with their husbands, which to Betty meant no they wouldn't.

'Is she going to tell fortunes again? She was dead right in what she told me last year.'

'I don't think so Harry, not after the scrap she had with Madam Zina last year.'

'Aye, I remember that. What a right carry on that was, eh?'

'She's got over it Harry. Nothing stops Arabella bouncing back.'

Betty finished her drink and told Harry she had to go but she would be calling in later. Harry said if she was coming on her own, he'd still be here.

But he added there's no point waiting Lass if you're bringing Keith with you, is there? Betty laughed; she liked Harry. He was a flirt but all talk.

'Wait till I tell Angela about your offer.'

'Hey don't tell her she'll knock me down and kick me up for falling,' replied Harry. Then laughing like a drain, ordered himself another pint.

John pulled him another and told him he was wanted over there. He turned to where John pointed and saw some of his cronies from work. They called him over to where they were sitting round a massive oak table at the far end of the room. They wanted to know if he was any good at general knowledge and if he was, they wanted him in their quiz team. Harry said he'd come over, then turned to Betty, Connie and Clara and said, 'See you later my lovelies.' Then clasping his hand to his heart as if it had shattered, he left Betty and her friends at the bar. Connie called him and told him if he had a heart at all it was on the left. Harry swapped hands. Betty waved and blew him a kiss as she left. Then Harry and two of his friends made a pretence of catching it and putting it their pockets.

Arabella finally arrived home and the car was tucked neatly away in the small attached garage where it lived. It never lived outside on the small intricately-paved drive with the three diamond shapes positioned equidistant from the sides and ends. It had camped out there when Dear Henry was alive but it was only for two nights and two small patches of oil. The patches of oil and the car soon disappeared from view, not quite at the speed of light but getting near it. One was removed by Dear Henry at six o'clock in the morning while still in his dressing gown. A start on the other two began at three-minutes-past-six by Fairy Liquid in one rubber-gloved hand and a wire brush in the other. Henry said the pink gloves were a bit over the top but he'd wear them if she insisted. They will protect your hands Dear she insisted. He wore them. The oil stains were a thing of the past by seven-thirty. Arabella wanted neither oil stains or the rubble nor those hulking great slabs of stone on her drive. Maud was welcome to them. They looked far too quarryish for Arabella.

As she walked from the garage to her front door she saw a stone the size of a milk tooth marring the eighteen-inch border of topsoil. She bent down and confiscated it without breaking her stride. It would be banished to the waste bin with the fragment of paper she'd picked up beside it.

The neighbour's foul creature of a cat had swiftly abandoned the comfort of Arabella's greenhouse roof as soon as it heard her car turn into the top of the street, but even though it was bent-legged and creeping away like a spy, it did sneak the odd glance back till it was a safe distance from the house. It knew the sound of Arabella's car very well, once having disregarded it as perhaps being another of the same make. But it wasn't a car of the same make it was her car and being caught napping once on the greenhouse roof is one too many. It never ignored that sound again. Luckily, on that occasion as it leaped sideways to dodge the water, it landed feet first in next-door's rhubarb patch and like the latest fad in tomatoes, it soon dried in the sun.

When Arabella had finished adjusting her favourite photograph of Dear Henry (on the gleaming surface of the piano) from doh, to-ray, ray to me and back to doh-a thing she did when trying to repel thoughts of doubt – she said to the photograph, 'You were better where you were Dear.' The truth was she wasn't feeling quite as resolute about her decision to give that crystal ball over to Maud's care. Perhaps, thought Arabella, it might have been a better idea to throw it away and scrap her devious little plan completely, just in case something untoward happened. What if Maud found out? Dear Henry's photograph was moved an inch to the right. This thought had nagged her even in the Baker's shop where she'd stopped to buy herself a small reward for her guile. She'd been so distracted from her purpose by the same nagging thought that she'd nearly bought those dreadful coffee-flavoured éclairs. It was only after Mr. Ball asked her a second time that she realized what was in the paper bag on the glass counter top.

'Are you sure those are the ones you want Mrs. Smythe?'

She said, 'definitely not, I didn't ask for those.' Then she wondered why he gave her an odd look. She returned it. He thought perhaps she'd a headache. She thought he was trying to rid himself of yesterday's buns!

'You know I detest those things. If not, you ought to do by now!'

He thought she was being totally unfair and as soon as she'd gone he went for a cup of tea and a coffee éclair in the back room to cheer himself up. She adjusted Dear Henry's photograph one last time, gave it a smile and went to make a cup of tea. Perhaps if she ate two of the éclairs she'd feel more settled in her mind and less conscience stricken?

The lovely Lady Marion called Lord Percy who was exercising Theodore on the drive to tell him it was time to go for her tennis lesson. He waved back, patted Theodore and told her, 'To have a good lesson my darling.' Alas the only running about this Darling would be doing would be a ten second chase round the huge bed before the actual tennis match started. Lord Percy's mother, Lady Audrey, who'd forsaken her bed for some reason, heard this exchange as she wandered over to the drinks cabinet in the morning room. She was pouring her first gin of the day and pecking at a scotch pancake she'd found on the kitchen table when the budding tennis star flounced past the window. Lady Audrey whose deep worldly wisdom and foul vocabulary were second to none called the lovely Lady Marion a something-something. Two things that even Cynthia, her two would-be boyfriends and their university lecturers, had never even heard of. Luckily, the Hall had been brought up-to-date and had triple glazing on the ground floor or there might have been a scene! Lady Audrey, having 'strutted her stuff' at the Windmill Theatre in its naughtier days knew from experience that her daughter-in-law suffered from 'trigger knee syndrome'. This is not a medical term as Lady Audrey, who was on her third gin and tonic once explained to Arabella (who was already on her second gin and tonic). But unlike that slut, when I found the man I wanted to spend the rest of my life with, my safety catch was locked firmly into place. Arabella's thud-thud of laughter and Lady Audrey's screeches had the chandeliers shaking on their hangers.

Lady Audrey kept the lovely Lady Marion in her sights until she turned the corner to the stables. Lady Audrey wondered if she should follow her. She decided not to. Instead of a full-frontal attack she told the sparkling fountain of bubbles trying to escape from her glass, I shall try the more subtle shot of the green-eyed monster with just a dash of blackmail. A good name for a cocktail (she told the wicked little bubbles as she went to the telephone). She called Lady Eleanor, a very close friend of hers from the so-called golden era at the Windmill. They arranged a get-together at the Royale Hotel in Huntsford Old Town for the following afternoon. Lady Audrey explained she didn't do mornings and after lunch would be preferable.

'I don't rise until ten-thirty Darling!' If ten-thirty followed two-thirty, she wasn't telling lies.

Just over a week later Belinda (one of the many nieces of Lady Eleanor) called at the hall. Belinda had the kind of beauty men would die for and some had fought hard and long to gain her favour and still did – but not of course to the death; the odd broken limb or two on the polo field or a manly, facial scar during frenzied sword play between rivals was as serious as it got. Although this visit was supposedly on the spur of the moment her arrival was timed to coincide exactly with the lovely Lady Marion's departure for her tennis lesson. A stunned Lord Percy, who was in the middle of saying his goodbyes to the one, and his welcomes to the other, suddenly found himself in the embarrassingly close and cushioned embrace of this glorious creature, this very angel, saying, 'It's so lovely to see you again Percy my darling. It's been too, too long!'

While his Lordship tried to take all this in, the girl turned to Lady Marion and said, 'You must be his elder sister Gloria. I've heard so much about you. It's rather great to meet you in person.'

The Lovely Lady Marion couldn't decide whether to give her a forearm smash over the head or a backhand smash under the chin. Instead, she put her racket under her arm and after a begrudged touch of the visitors' fingers said, 'I'm ever so sorry but I must go. The court's booked but I will see you again!' She turned to go.

Lady Audrey came out of the house and said, 'Can't stop, must go and see Toni, she's had one of her fits again.'

Belinda (without any sign of recognition) passed Lady Audrey on the steps and went uninvited into the hall. Lord Percy followed like a tour guide on his first day at work in a labyrinth. The grim-faced Lady Marion didn't know who Toni was but she did know what a fit was and when she got back, she was bloody well going to have one! For a mile or two the car tyres and gearbox paid on behalf of Lord Percy; he would pay his share later.

Lord Percy, who was still in a bemused state couldn't decide where to sit. After half-sitting in various places, he settled for leaning on the mantelpiece. He had tried four or five times and from discreet angles to discover exactly who Belinda was and where they'd met and was now offering her the hospitality of the house. He got Mrs. Walker to do tea and perhaps some of her cucumber sandwiches. His frugal request was delivered on one huge plate and the tea in a pot with two matching cups and saucers. The maid put the tray of sandwiches on an occasional table standing between the armchair occupied by Belinda and another one facing it. Then without offering to pour, or so much as a, 'will that be all Sir', she left the room.

Good manners and Mrs. Walker's deliberate tardiness in providing side plates soon had the reluctant host placed in the chair opposite Belinda and well within range of her alluring perfume, much of which had been impregnated upon his Lordship's jacket by her extremely friendly greeting on the Hall steps.

'I'll pour darling as you poured last time in Katanga,' offered Belinda at a volume loud enough for the maid to hear. Lord Percy, although widely travelled had never heard of Katanga. Phyllis, having heard the first course was on its way, waited silently by the door in case there were any more titbits coming her way to pass round. She was surprised and delighted when the next morsel was cast her way.

'It was only last month Percy darling while we were camping on Mount Tugoo. Surely you can't have forgotten already? You were so, so wild and romantic!'

That was meaty enough for Phyllis; she was off. Not only had she heard Mrs. Walker's footsteps marching nearer (and nearer and you don't cross wands with the Wicked Witch of the West,) but she was bursting to gnaw the bone with young Henrietta. Had she stayed she would have found out that it had all been a silly mistake. Belinda had forgotten her lenses, and as Lord Percy knew, she was as blind as a bat without them. Lord Percy, didn't know but he offered her a beaming smile as a fibbers yes.

'I must have muddled the addresses somehow. We didn't camp on Tugoo; it was the other Lord Percy. Do you have blond, wavy hair Percy?' She made a small pretence at peering close up at him. 'No damn it, you don't. 'What on earth must you think of me? I'll pass on the refreshments, if you don't mind; I'm sure they're delicious. I do feel a bit of a twit. Perhaps another time?' She gave him a quick peck on the cheek and left as fast as Phyllis had done.

He didn't wonder how she drove to the hall; he didn't wonder why she didn't recognize him on the front step; he didn't wonder about a lot of things. He was only too pleased to wave goodbye as she skilfully manoeuvred the Aston Martin at some speed round the tight curves of the drive. He should have wondered because the lovely Lady Marion would and she'd want to know how the smell of Belinda's perfume got onto their bed sheets! But if she wanted the answer to that puzzle, she'd have to ask Lady Audrey and if she did ask her, Lady Audrey wouldn't have a clue. She would reply, 'Don't you remember Marion? I left the house as the beautiful young lady arrived. My calming presence was required at Toni's bedside.' The two ex-windmill girls had set it up perfectly.

Lord Percy was still thinking about Belinda when Marion arrived home. She flounced through the door and threw her racquet into the corner where muddy boots are left to dry.

'You look flushed my love. You must have had a terrific two hours!'

Her reply wasn't as tender as his question. 'I did, what about you?'

'Me? I've been with Theodore to check the pheasants. Not as energetic as your spell on the grass but he did break into a trot when he saw a rabbit. I'd let him off his lead you see.'

'Did Belinda go with you to see the pheasants?' Her tone had a courtroom tinge about it.

'No my love, she left not long after you left. I wasn't the Lord Percy she thought I was you see. Silly girl forgot her contact lens things; thought I was somebody else. Since when have I shared a tent stuck on a mountainside with a lovely young woman? Those were the days eh, Marion!'

'It's only three weeks ago, Percy, that we were in Snowdonia National Park,' pouted Marion. 'Where I believe you shared a tent with me.'

'One could hardly call it a tent, Old Love. A three-bedroom log cabin with hot and cold water with a bidet is not camping out My Love. Had it been so when I was in the Scouts, I might have kept at it, especially with a brace of Girl Guides in attendance?' He laughed, slapped his leg and said he was going to see to the horses. The scowling Lady Marion went upstairs to change. He was either innocent or a bloody good actor. She kept this thought and other more daring thoughts to herself as she had decided earlier that next week's lesson was going to be even more energetic. Had her outward appearance mirrored her inner being she would not be referred to by all and sundry as the lovely Lady Marion.

Cynthia's inner beauty was reflected by her looks. Those who thought her shy and retiring didn't understand the whole picture. She was self-conscious and had been since a child, mostly because her parents (who were no Venus and Adonis) told everyone, and proudly, what a beautiful girl she was. Even when she blossomed into womanhood they didn't stop. Consequently, she adopted a rather shy smile and a mildly introverted nature. This was her protection and it helped her drop out of discussions she found utterly boring or mind-blowing. It also helped her drop out of the school choir and hockey team. Cynthia wasn't a team person. She did find some empathy with her arty friends at college but not with their morbid and self-harming excesses. Now her only remaining friends from college were Karl and Jeremy but though their feelings for her were honourable and perfectly genuine, each had his sights on her. In fact they both had their sights on her now while she was inspecting Dawn Chorus and subconsciously rubbing her nose at intervals of twenty seconds. Karl was going to lean forward and rub it for her himself; he desperately wanted to but Jeremy spoiled his chance by saying, 'Stop rubbing your nose Cynthia, or you'll rub it off.'

They were more than rewarded by the smile that followed his remark. 'Am I doing it again? Sorry. It's that colour there. It's a bit green.'

'Most summer grass is green, and it looks perfect from here.'

'Fine then, I'll leave it as it is.'

She stacked the picture against the wall with eleven more. She was now ready for the exhibition. If Js and Ks were ready she could catch her breath and try to wash some of the oil colours out of her hair.

'How are you two doing with yours? Are we going to beat the deadline?' She smiled again.

'I've a couple of finishing touches to put to mine but they'll be done by the weekend,' promised Karl.

Jeremy sniffed and hoping to win Brownie points said with a grin, 'Mine are finished. They're over there.' From behind her back Karl imitated the grin perfectly and mimed Jeremy's words exactly. Jeremy ignored him. Cynthia asked to see them but he refused saying he didn't want to spoil the surprise for her.

She didn't seem to mind and she said, 'That's ok; I want to go and do something with my hair.'

The real reason Jeremy didn't want Cynthia to see the paintings was because there were twenty in all. Four of his and some that had been done by friends of theirs. They hadn't told Cynthia about this, it was to be her surprise. Unfortunately it would be more of a dreadful shock than a surprise!

Cornelia called to see Lord Percy within an hour of Belinda's departure. The furious Lady Marion, having gone up to change and having registered the pong of a strange perfume about the bedroom, was stamping towards the stables as Cornelia's coupé scrabbled to a stop outside the front door. She got out and called, 'Hi there, is Lord Percy about?'

'Who's asking?' spat Marion.

'I am Darling. Cornelia Portman-Sidney. Promised I'd call in if ever I got up this way. Haven't seen him for weeks.' She turned and glanced across at the copper beeches. 'God knows what keeps him in this neck of the woods?'

'I do!' snapped Lady Marion.

'I'm so sorry; I thought his mother was an invalid. I do beg your pardon.'

'I'm his wife, not his mother you silly…'

The stream of abuse didn't materialise, for just at that moment Lord Percy came thundering round the corner of the house on Whirlwind, bellowing, 'Can't stop the damned thing My Love. I'll have to let him tire himself out!' He bravely tried a quick wave at Marion's visitor as he flew past. 'Shouldn't take more than a couple of…' The rest of his words were lost to the wind as he headed for the laurel hedge bordering the lake. The spiteful Lady Marion prayed for Whirlwind to jump it by a mile and throw his rider into the deepest slime-infested part of it.

Cornelia's attention was not diverted by this drama. She was screeching, 'You didn't tell me you were married!'

Then she began waving a delicate fist in Percy's direction and calling him a scoundrel, a bounder and other things too vile to mention. But before Lady Marion had a chance to get her inquisitor's claws into Cornelia and find out what her game was, she was in her coupé spitting gravel all over the place and speeding down the drive. It did nothing for Lady Marion's mood when a good handful of hot gravel rattled off her person. Luckily there was nothing smashable to hand and after a few foot-stampings, the tight-lipped Lady Marion vowed to wait for her husband's return!

He returned on foot and in the gait of someone who'd found the darling buds of May had suddenly sprouted from their rear. Marion didn't notice his discomfort as he hobbled past the window bellowing for James to come and see to 'this bloody creature'. James heard His Lordship even though he was over in the far orchard exercising Nellie (the old grey mare). He ran to His Lordship's aid. Marion didn't hear him because for some reason she'd answered the telephone and done Mrs. Walker out of one of her duties. This was all arranged by Lady Audrey. The timing of the call from the bar of the tennis club had been perfect.

'No,' said Marion in answer to the female caller's question, 'Lord Percy is unavailable at the moment. Who is that?'

The caller had a young, la-di-dah voice. 'It doesn't matter who I am. When you see him, tell him I'm a good friend who has some information about his wife and her close friendship with the club professional!'

Unable to answer due to the sudden constriction in her throat the sheet-white Lady Marion let the handpiece drop from her hand as though it was a viper. She watched it spin even more snake-like as the cord twisted back to its correct shape and then, with a sort of argh-sound, she fell in a heap on the floor. Mrs. Walker (who was lurking outside the door) dashed into the room and went to her aid. They hadn't expected this; Mrs. Walker was only to hand in case Lady Marion had a fit of temper and began hurling priceless heirlooms round the room. Lady Audrey had not anticipated this reaction. Helped by a platoon of maids, Mrs. Walker had Lady Marion in the comfort of her four-poster within minutes.

Lord Percy sought the comfort of a long, hot bath and a well-known soothing cream. Lady Audrey suggested he sleep in one of the guest rooms for a couple nights, just until his Dear Marion was herself again. Lady Audrey was a wise old owl. That very night Marion wanted to know why her husband was not sharing her bed! And why did everything in this room smell of Belinda? Lady Audrey told her she was imagining things, 'unless you mean my perfume Dear?' And Percy will be in his rightful place as soon as he felt she was up to it! 'No more than a week at the most Dear,' smiled Lady Audrey from the doorway.

The following morning and after dreaming she'd been chased round the tennis court stark naked, while Percy umpired, she rang the club and cancelled her so-called lessons. Lady Audrey (flushed with success) was already working on a scheme to blunt the sword of Marion's fencing instructor. She was soon on the telephone to congratulate Lady Eleanor and her delightful nieces, to ask for their help a second time.

'More than pleased, Audi Love,' offered Elli-pet.

Within ten days of the second meeting between the two canny schemers, the fencing instructor's sword was rusting away in its scabbard.

The posters for the exhibition were everywhere. Arabella had seen at least twenty on the high street and they were bright, bold and looked very professional and very expensive. She would have to corner Cynthia as soon as possible and find out where on earth the money had come from, or worse still, was coming from to pay for them. She'd no need to worry; the taxpayer would foot the bill. Not knowingly or voluntarily, the guys at college had done them on the latest stand-alone printer, copier, scanner, laminator etc. The taxpayers were lucky the thing didn't crush grapes or roll joints. Arabella spotted Cynthia outside the dry cleaners whilst holding the last of Dear Henry's suits, which was bound for the Oxfam shop on Lower Firth Street but not before it had been cleaned and pressed and was as good as new.

'Cynthia My Dear, how on earth are you going to pay for those?' She indicated the posters and put the debt in Cynthia's court in the same breath.

'Hello Arabella,' replied Cynthia stalling for time while she considered her answer. 'They were… they were donated by some friends of mine. We don't have to pay for them.'

It rushed out faster than she intended but Arabella let it pass as she was in a hurry – the betting shop closed in ten minutes.

'God, very good well done Cynthia, My Dear. Keep it up. I'm sorry, I would lend a hand but I'm in a hurry, I'll see you Monday if not before. Bye for now.'

Cynthia watched her hurry down the street with that strange walk she had and breathed a sigh of relief. She wasn't frightened of Arabella but she did find her domineering. Anyway, the posters had been donated by friends. Cynthia had friends who were taxpayers and was one herself. Conscience appeased, she went about her self-imposed task.

Maud was having a salad in the Wimpy Bar across the street from the bookmakers. She'd done her posters as they'd only given her six to do. They'd said most of the others were done. Maud liked Jeremy and Karl; they seemed very nice. It was obvious to her that they more than liked Cynthia and they didn't half make a fuss of her. She smiled to herself and wondered which one Cynthia would choose. She was about to pop the last of her sandwich into her mouth when her hand stopped two inches from it. It wasn't that she'd seen the two slices of tomato wink at her; it was because she'd just spotted Arabella leaving the bookmakers. Her sandwich hovered there for a moment till the man sitting at the table opposite asked her if she was all right and after an embarrassed, 'Yes thank you, I thought I'd just seen a friend of mine,' he returned to his crossword.

The sandwich finished its journey as Maud left the table. By the time her hip had stopped protesting at such sudden movements, Maud had let go of the door handle and entered the street. Arabella was nowhere to be seen. Maud said damn and slowly went for her bus. She felt she'd been badly let down. Then as she neared her bus stop she had a terrible thought. Had Arabella listed the winners of future races? Would she do such a thing? Yes, she damn well would, Maud told the pigeon strutting along the pavement at a better pace than she. She ignored her twinges and the enquiring looks from the nearby pedestrians and hurried after the pigeon. It turned left, Maud turned right, her bus was approaching. She was in good time and she would find out later that Arabella did have such a list! But what Arabella had also done was far simpler and far more devious than merely making a list!

The first day of the exhibition came; there had been a flurry of movement from early morning and all through the day till eight o'clock on Friday night. Some of these preparations, the surprise one in particular, continued on Saturday till an hour before the first public showing in the afternoon, which was from two-forty-five until eight forty-five. Or as Arabella insisted, a quarter-to-three, to a quarter-to-nine. The public room, which once upon-a-time had been the mayoral banqueting hall, wasn't a massive room but it was more than adequate for an exhibition of this size. The room had cost nothing thanks to Arabella's friendship with the Council or more particularly, the Mayor. It was theirs for two days: Saturday and Sunday, subject to it being returned to its original state of cleanliness. The room looked to Arabella as if it hadn't been cleaned since doomsday, but she didn't say so. Free of charge is free of charge. On Sunday, visitors would be welcome all day from ten o'clock in the morning until nine at night. Moderately-priced refreshments would be available throughout the duration of the exhibition. Twenty-percent of all monies raised from the exhibition would be donated to deserving charities. Arabella, the ladies of the committee, the Mayor and the press were all there for the grand opening. They were lined in tiers on the front steps of the Town Hall like rows of Aunt Sallys. Margaret asked Betty if she could see Uncle Tom Cobblers among the crowd and Betty burst out laughing just as the first camera flash stole her vision. She turned and pushed Margaret for making her laugh as the second one went off. Arabella gave them both the evil eye as the third went off but for the press photographers, all seemed to go well. The Mayor said a few words of thanks to the three artists (not knowing there were six more upstairs) and the ladies of the Huntsford Ladies Charity Guild before declaring the exhibition open.

He led them all upstairs like an Alpha Male and after opening the big double doors and bowing like a ballroom dancer with a back problem; he waved them all past him into the room. Mavis followed at the back with Daisy, who had had a fistful of feathers (that Mavis hadn't seen) in her hand when they left home. Mavis demanded to know where she'd found them. 'That nithe lady there', she pointed the fist full of feathers at Martha. A small patch on the lower back of Martha's favourite creation looked like a battery hen's bum. To avoid what could be a later confrontation with Martha, Mavis tried to confiscate them so she could hide them somewhere, but Daisy's little fingers curled tighter and held onto them with her hand held as far behind her back as it would reach. They were for Mithter Thlippery and Obbledy. They wanted to be Gerominos like Thteven and Robert. Mavis begged baby Jesus to not let it turn into one of those days! Perhaps baby Jesus was busy that day because more feathers would fly later and they would see a side of Cynthia her doting parents had never seen!

As Cynthia came into the room she was greeted by warm applause. She wished only two things as she shook her head and tried to form words (meaning their thanks weren't necessary). Her first was that J and K and their friends would stop it and the other wish was to be beamed up by Scotty. As beaming up hadn't yet been invented she had to stand there and wait till the blood that had rushed to her face cleared off and went about its business round the rest of her body. By the time her mind had shot off to one of her happy places and back, the applause had stopped. Happily, she went about her business, which at the moment was taking Arabella and the Mayor on a guided tour. She would speak to J and K later!

Cynthia's work had been given top billing on the wall by the door. Everybody had to pass there to get to the rest of the exhibits. The Mayor looked at Dawn Chorus. He looked again and thought it was the best painting he'd ever seen. Ignoring the price tag of one-hundred-and-fifty pounds he bought it immediately. He said every one of her paintings was beautiful, but Dawn Chorus was the one he wanted. Cynthia thanked him as best she could and to conceal her delight she marked off the sale in her little peach-coloured notebook. Arabella complimented him on his choice as Cynthia led them to the next array of paintings. These were Karl's and Jeremy's she explained. Arabella was impressed, so was the Mayor and so were some of the ladies who'd tagged-on behind. Maud wanted the one with the three wild rabbits peering through the bramble bushes while one on its hind legs nibbled away at a clump of big, shiny blackberries. It was the rabbit's innocent appealing eyes that did it.

'Surely they will die if I don't take them home with me young man!'

Karl, the recipient of this old loony's remark, stepped back a pace. He watched with care as Maud opened her handbag and pulled out her purse instead of sharpened-steel knitting needles. Only then did he manage a grin.

'Only kidding young man,' said Maud as she passed him the modest sum of thirty pounds and crossed her eyes. Karl had no answer to this. Brave as he was he let Cynthia collect her money. Cynthia ticked it off then Maud giggled as they moved on; Maud had a wicked sense of humour.

The room was getting fuller and fuller – small groups were forming and chattering and it was all getting rather hectic. Martha was haggling with Jeremy for a picture called Illusions. It was every colour under the sun and some from over the sun thrown in for effect. Arabella was convinced it was done for spite by those monkeys she'd seen playing in paint on the television. Martha finally coughed up the fifty pounds after being told by Arabella she wanted to get the refreshments under way.

'It's all for charity Martha, Dear. And we must get on with our duties.'

Cynthia thanked her as J gave the thumbs up to K.

Arabella made her excuses at this stage saying, 'We must go and prepare the refreshments before they've all spent up. I'll leave Mavis to give you a hand should you need one.' She collared Maud, Martha, Betty and Margaret and led them across the passage to the committee room.

The lovely Lady Marion hadn't yet arrived. This fact had not escaped the notice of Arabella, or even Mavis for that matter and she'd plenty to think about; her plenty to think about was just squealing a loud hello to Aunty Thinthia, then having to have her mouth wiped by her mother, who was still trying to get the feathers. She hadn't a chance. Daisy was already showing her 'pluckted thems' to Aunty Cynthia. 'They're for Obbledy and Mithter Thlippery as well. Geromino!' she squealed. Cynthia picked her up gave her a kiss and patted hello to Obbledy, that Cynthia had made for her and for which Mavis cursed the day. The demon kissed her back but Cynthia wasn't a bit bothered by the instant splatter.

'Are you being a good girl darling?' asked Cynthia who thought the world of this little imp especially, and all children in general. A fact that her two supposedly-perceptive and intelligent housemates had missed.

Daisy looked at Aunty Thynthia as if she'd spoken in a foreign language and said to her mother, 'Obbledy's hungry Mummy.'

'Will you be all right for a bit if I go and get her something to eat?'

'Course I will, there's plenty of us to sort things out.'

Mavis grabbed Daisy before she kissed Cynthia again and after another session with a tissue, she took her for some grub, half of which was pushed into Obbledy's beak-like mouth until by some secret sign he told Daisy he was full up now. She passed this on via a very clear signal to her Mummy. This time Mavis was having none of it. Daisy either got it off the floor or she was going straight home to bed. Daisy said Obbledy did it and he should go to bed. Mavis put her foot down. Daisy and Obbledy picked most of it up but Margaret did it properly when Daisy took Obbledy for a drag across the floor on his fat belly. It was supposed to be a walk but she had short arms and he had long legs or were they arms? Mavis, knowing of her small daughter's speech limitations had never referred to Obbledy's limbs as tentacles.

While Mavis was cleaning Obbledy's arms or legs, Cynthia went over to thank J and K for the great surprise. She was a bit premature with her thanks as she, like Arabella who'd just returned to see the last of the exhibits, hadn't yet been to the far end of the room! The lady President was heading in that direction now.

J and K still hadn't told Cynthia of the real surprise they had in store for her. They were trying to get publicity for the art classes at which attendances were more than diminishing. It was an image and cost thing, which the local education committee had washed their collective hands of. Art to them was the first step to vandalism or debauchery. K and J had cleverly drawn the photographers over to where they wanted them and were now luring Cynthia in the same direction. Arabella had stopped at a sculpture most people seemed to be avoiding. It was called Birth Cry. To Arabella it looked obviously like a six foot tall woman made out of twenty miles of black spaghetti. It had all the attributes of a woman but they were grossly exaggerated. The statue had one ear covered by one hand and something like a blue rubber chicken coming out of the other ear. The statue was trying, with its other spaghetti-like hand, to push it back in.

A rag-tag of an individual approached and without being asked told Arabella the statue signified a blindness and refusal to allow the birth of a new idea!

'Does it?' she replied while at the same time wondering if he was going to make a grab for her purse. 'Who, I wonder, came up with that? I would have thought the chicken thing would be more pertinent coming out of one her eyes, wouldn't you?'

She moved away without waiting for an answer. The rag-tag individual watched her go and wondered why he even bothered trying to educate the masses. He thought one of his major works was well worth three thousand pounds. Arabella didn't. She'd already valued it at no more than tuppence-ha'penny and that was for the blue rubber chicken thing to throw at that creature if she ever caught it on her greenhouse roof again. She heard Cynthia call and went over.

All the ladies of the committee were there including the lovely Lady Marion who should have been on the door taking voluntary donations. Luckily, Connie had come to the exhibition and after a few moments of Arabella's moral blackmailing techniques, said she would be happy to stand in for the miscreant. She was wondering now whether she'd be better off at home doing the washing; a chore she hated second only to ironing. Ronald, Thtephen and Thimon were keeping Daisy occupied in the committee room. It was obvious from the whoops and squeals that the Red Indians were attacking a wagon train. Cynthia began to speak and the room went quiet.

'My friends would like me to unveil this picture as a thank you for the committee members of the Huntsford Lady's Charity Guild for allowing them to display their work here.'

'It's we who should be thanking you for donating a very generous portion of it to good causes, My Dear,' interrupted Arabella, and indicated in no uncertain terms that sincere applause was due. Both parties paid their dues.

Cynthia gestured to the rag-tag man. The string was pulled and the veil dropped. First there were flashes going off like a night-time bombardment then somebody sniggered and then somebody joined in. Within seconds everybody in the room was laughing except the Mayor and the hard-working ladies of the Charity Guild, including Cynthia. Arabella didn't need her glasses to see what the disgusting swinish louts had done. There before her and half the world by morning, and in full colour were the faces of the committee members on the naked bodies of nubile dancing women of the worst sort. Cynthia gasped and with a yell ran from the room. Karl and Jeremy, realizing what a crass and stupid mistake they'd made, ran after her. They would be sent packing by a deeply hurt and stone-faced Cynthia.

Maud giggled once, but only once, and then she saw the look on Arabella's face. Betty said they were childish, Margaret said they were a load of silly buggers and if they finished up in the papers she'd take them to the cleaners.

'And don't think I don't bloody well mean it!'

Margaret wasn't one to beat about the bush unless there was a leopard hiding in there that had stolen her fish and chips. The noise abated.

Arabella hadn't said a word; then she slipped her glasses on but only for a moment. The shock of her seeing herself in a state of undress (even though it wasn't her body) was too much and not in the least bit funny. Not in the least bit funny at all! Letting go of her huge brown handbag and making a noise that Geronimo and even Daisy would take years of practice to achieve, she leaped towards the offensive object on the wall and although she felt a terrible shock of pain in her right foot, it did not deter her from her goal. Neither did the rag-tag man who tried to block her way to protect what he thought was a stunning work of art. He was swept away by Arabella like one of Daisy's feathers up a Hoover, but there would be no dust bag to soften his landing. He staggered backwards at some speed and fell on his Birth Cry followed by a birth cry of his own.

What Arabella thought was black spaghetti was actually welding rods and the rubber chicken thing was cast lead. None of this concerned Arabella, nor did his injuries; she was ripping the picture to pieces. It was only when it was the size of confetti did the throbbing pain in her big toe register. Suddenly, she felt sick and had to sit down. The ladies were round her in seconds. Maud had rescued Arabella's handbag and was about to hand it to her when she noticed a red velvet something or other just like the one shrouding the crystal in her bedside cabinet. Maud instantly put two and two together. She drew it from Arabella's bag like it was a live hand grenade and offered it to Arabella's restricted view. It only took the blink of a tear-filled eye for Arabella to realize she'd been rumbled. She tried to make out she couldn't see what it was.

'What is it Maud, Dear. Is it important? You can see that I'm in some pain, I think?'

'I have the thing here that caused the pain Arabella; it landed on your toe. Should I lock it away with the other one for you so it doesn't cause any more pain?'

'Yes. Yes, if you must. You'd better lock my jotter away with it while you're at it. It's got next month's winners in it. Help me through there; I need a strong cup of tea and a medicinal brandy!'

There were congratulations galore at the next committee meeting. Cynthia hung her head and went to the fairy dell where the pixies play, swelling with pride as Arabella congratulated her for her magnificent efforts. The exhibition had been an enormous success. They'd raised over five hundred pounds! Arabella's head was up in triumph and her big toe was up in size. She was wearing one of Dear Henry's size nines on her left foot and she'd only been two seconds early for the meeting. Maud had locked the crystal ball in her bear-proof bedside cabinet at the other side of the bed so that thing was safely away! Martha, having seen the back of her favourite creation, flung it in the bin, ordered a replica and bought two dozen mothballs – six for each wardrobe. She also bought a small lavender bag to hang on her husband's coat hook on the back of the bedroom door. Daisy had found a magpie feather on her way home and she and Obbledy had decided it would look nither if it wath pink and yellow. Mavis's nail varnish stuck to the feather perfectly. It was the amount of water that Daisy and Obbledy mixed with the custard powder that caused all the problems!

Arabella brought Mavis back to the meeting with her strong contralto tone, when she barked, 'Well we can't rest on our laurels ladies. Betty, Margaret, how's the car boot sale progressing?'

The lovely Lady Marion looked absolutely fed up!

Richard Lee Wilson January 2005.

The boot-sale

Betty and Margaret were looking forward to the boot sale, not for the work it involved but so they could get rid of a load of old junk. Not their junk; they'd both agreed they hadn't any. They wanted rid of their husbands' junk. Women don't collect junk, every woman knows that. Their husbands' didn't know they had a load of old junk. Their precious collections of old spanners and car parts. Boxes full of valuable second-hand nails and rusty but still useable screws were theirs! They had nothing to do with wives!

'Good husbands don't interfere with the washing, ironing and cooking, do they? So why should good wives interfere with our treasured collectables?' They were lucky their wives were elsewhere or they'd have got a good slapping for that remark.

The two men had been discussing this over the din of the cascading water through the lock gate where it was warped with age and the occasional accident. Other pertinent subjects discussed were the miserable weather, the troubles of the world, politics, health, the redundancies at work and which bait was best for catching Perch. After two hours of fishing by the neglected canal and suffering the drizzly rain and too much chat, they'd both come to the same conclusion; if they were going to catch anything at all before dark they'd have to chuck a few good handfuls of ground bait in and shut up about politics and the rest of it!

'Nothing we say will cure a damned thing will it? No matter how long we talk about it'.

They agreed it wouldn't.

Within ten minutes of silent concentration, and if their manic excitement was anything to go by, Keith, (Betty's husband) had caught a twenty foot roach and Bill, (Margaret's husband) had caught a mermaid and the men kept glancing every so often at the keep-net to make sure the one didn't rip its way out and the other didn't lure them onto the rocks. They packed it in when the barely-visible sun went behind Quarry Hill. They freed their two captives and went home. Neither of the captives made much of a splash. All in all they agreed fishing was a waste of bloody time.

Unlike their husbands, Margaret and Betty hadn't wasted any time. In only five days Harry had got them the Co-op car park, and thanks to Arabella, a small but free advertisement in the Huntsford Bugle had been granted. And even better, the two ladies had allocated more than half the pitches. Some of the applicants did boot sales for a living and they were the first to book. Arabella Smythe, the tenacious Lady President of the Huntsford Ladies Charity Guild had suggested that perhaps they should have charged a larger fee. With Arabella's 'perhaps' being a synonym for definitely, Betty and Margaret had looked slightly piqued, but only slightly – it didn't do to show open rebellion when in Arabella's company.

Connie and Clara had a word with their husbands and proved Betty's assumption wrong! They would help at the boot sale and if the Huntsford Ladies Charity Guild wanted a couple of new members, the pair would be glad to join! Margaret, who was also a friend of Clara and Connie asked Betty how she thought the two free-spirited women might get on with Arabella and her strict regime. Betty had replied, 'I think they'll knuckle under after a few cracks of the rope's end.' Over the years the senior ladies had likened their position on the committee to that of crew members on the Bounty, and even though most of the ladies were Christians of varying degrees, they had never harboured any thoughts of mutiny!

To test the water as it were, Connie and Clara were invited to sit in at Monday's committee meeting. It started at half-past-seven on the dot! Both the newcomers couldn't help but admire the Lady President's efficiency. Item one and one A and item two had all been dealt with without deviation or hesitation. There was a bit of repetition but that's perfectly understandable. Both women had been on committees in the past but none ran as crisply as this one. There was no chit-chat between members on this committee. Arabella's steely glare soon put any hint of that to the torch. Clara noticed every minute was so packed with such a varied amount of information that it was difficult to take it all in.

Connie was doing what she always did when she found herself on the peripherals… people watching. She wondered how this motley crew had ever got together. They seemed an odd mix. There was Maud, she must be touching seventy and Connie was sure there was a bit of privet leaf in the lady's hair and her fingernails looked as if she'd clawed her way out of a gravel pit! She looked frail and had a slight limp yet she'd seen her lift that big tea-urn onto the side table as though it was a china cup.

There was Mavis sitting next to her; she was sure that's what she said her name was. But during the introductions the name Daisy and Obbledy kept being mentioned. Connie wondered if she was all there. She'd watched her closely since then. It seemed to Connie as if every so often Mavis' eyes sort of glazed over and then she appeared to go off into some sort of trance. Then there was that lovely blonde young woman with tired eyes. Perhaps she was somebody's daughter. She didn't look as if she was enjoying herself very much. Then there was Martha who looked as if she'd been dressed by a child. Connie's thoughts were taking over but she soon dashed back up the gangplank at the speed of light when Arabella's strong contralto voice demanded to know if Mavis was with us or on the way home to her family. Her excuses were partially drowned by gentle laughter. This, in its turn was strangled to death by the Lady President's eyebrows disappearing heavenwards and a rapid shuffling of papers. These papers, or so it seemed to Connie, were spread out on the table for that purpose only.

'Maud Dear, would you put Connie with Margaret, and Clara with Betty; I believe they're all good friends.'

Arabella smiled at the four ladies. Maud smiled, nodded and scribbled away!

'Now ladies item three. The paperchase. You will all remember that we were to use dolly-pegs for the paperchase? Although I suggested it, I'm now in two minds whether we should. I'm having great difficulty in finding enough of the things. Every place I've tried only have the plastic ones and the price they charge is ridiculous. I can see no point in throwing good money away, can you?'

The ladies agreed they couldn't!

'So with profit for the charities in mind I have arranged for Arnold from the Bugle to drop off two bundles of last Saturday's newspaper. If some of the entrants do get lost then I'm afraid that's their misfortune. We have no control over the weather. I did think about moistening the shreds of newspaper so the wind won't blow them about as easily, but would that be worthwhile? What do you think? I myself think it will. What about you?' Arabella's arms went out to encompass all at the table.

All the ladies thought it would be a good idea and they all hoped silently that they wouldn't be the one to get the 'wetting the paper job!'

'Good then. I think everybody should muck in to give the shreds a decent soaking; we'll do it next Saturday morning. That will give us all plenty of time before the start at six o'clock. You all know your duties, yes?'

The ladies nodded, some more enthusiastically than others.

'As usual, I will be at the finish to give out the prizes, and please dress sensibly this time. I would suggest Wellington boots and a light-coloured anorak or the like. We don't want a repeat of last year's unfortunate confrontation with one of Sir Percy's gamekeepers, do we Margaret?'

Margaret shook her head but wondered what all the fuss was about. All I did, she thought, was threaten to knock his block off and smack his gun to the ground. Mavis going head first into the stream was funny though. Margaret chuckled quietly to herself.

'Now item four, oh before we move on, would all of you bring a torch? I will let Margaret and Betty do item four.'

Arabella sat down and eased her shoes off; her feet were on fire. Size six shoes on size seven feet is not a good idea. Maud scribbled furiously.

Betty stood up and told them how far they'd got with the arrangements. She also suggested through the Chair that they ought to have a stall of their own. Arabella excused her interruption and suggested they should have two. The ladies voted for two. Maud made a note. Clara and Cynthia would run one stall; Martha and Lady Marion would run the other. Arabella sat down again. Martha was dressed in what looked like a trawl net with seaweed and roses glued to it. The effect on whoever surveyed it was stunning. Not in the glorious sense of the word, but stunning as in cattle prod stunning! Rainbows End the fashion house that created Martha's exclusives had a lot to answer for! Martha had told Mavis earlier her ensemble was called Ocean's Hidden Depths. Mavis had kept her face straight and her eyes half closed against the dazzle and said the name was perfect.

Martha looked delighted at being selected to co-run a stall. The lovely Lady Marion De Glynn looked as if she'd been told to scrub the stone floor of the long dining room up at the Hall. Arabella didn't give a hoot. It's about time she pulled her weight thought Arabella.

'What about refreshments Maud?' asked Betty but looked at Arabella. 'Are you going to deal with that?'

'Yes,' said Maud laying her pen down to cool for a moment. 'I don't think a few cakes and biscuits will do any harm. I think we've some left over from the exhibition. The tins are unopened so they'll be fine.'

Arabella nodded. 'Good idea Maud. Has anyone any questions?'

There were no offers.

'Well then, I'll let you all know how well we get on at next week's meeting.' Betty sat down and Arabella stood up.

'Now, item five, Maud.'

'Item five is the donation from Lady Audrey, Arabella.'

'Ah yes. Lady Audrey has donated fifty pounds to the unmarried mothers' fund. On everyone's behalf I have dropped her a few lines expressing the committee's deepest gratitude.'

Maud made a note.

'Item six is the Gala. I have given a lot of thought to what we can have as the central attraction at this year's gala. It will not, I can assure you, be a fortune teller!'

Arabella's perfect, crescent eyebrows crumpled into two gyrating centipedes as her thoughts went back to last year's fiasco. But that was best forgotten. She swept the thought into a tiny cupboard at the back of her mind.

'I had thought of some sort of amusement-arcade, hoopla, and those little plastic ducks with numbers written under them. Similar stalls to the ones at the fair in Holderby. Not as big obviously, but on those lines. Will you all give the idea some thought during the week and see if you can improve on my idea? Nothing's written in stone yet, but I have sharpened my chisel!'

Arabella smiled nicely and she turned to the minutes. The ladies all began to murmur and mutter. It was obvious they didn't think much of the idea of a funfair. The murmuring and muttering stopped as the papers began to shuffle. Arabella liked a disciplined crew. She certainly didn't like background chatter!

'Item seven Maud, what's item seven Dear?'

'There isn't an item seven Arabella, you told me to remove it from the minutes. You said it was a bad idea.'

'Yes I remember, it was a bad idea. I was going to recommend we as a group buy a lottery ticket. It would appear it's taken the country by storm. I thought each committee member would select a number and we'd use those numbers each week. I know it's a new thing and we would be gambling with donations, but a pound each week doesn't seem much...'

'I think it's a good idea Arabella,' interjected Margaret, 'Without going through the chair.'

'Do you Dear? Well perhaps we should vote on it then? Those in favour?'

Arms were raised.

'I do believe that's unanimous. Are you voting Lady Marion?'

'Yes, I've raised my arm!'

'I would have spotted it Dear had you struggled to raise it from the table!' Arabella's accompanying smile would have curdled milk.

'So would you all like to pick a number. I think we need six numbers don't we Maud?'

The lovely Lady Marion sulked.

'Yes Arabella.'

'So if we all pick a favourite number and pop them in this bag, and the first six to come out of the bag we will use. That seems the fairest way possible. I have some paper here if one of you wants to cut it into small squares?' She handed the paper to Mavis.

Everything was done and dusted within minutes. Connie and Clara were elected to pick out the bits of paper. Maud entered the numbers in the minutes in red biro, but her thoughts were elsewhere. Arabella was up to something and she couldn't yet work out what it was. Arabella's suggestion regarding the amusement arcade smacked of gambling. Maud would have to keep a beady eye on her. No way would Maud give her back the crystal ball, never!

'Thank you ladies for your attention and as there's nothing more on this evening's agenda other than to hope Clara and Connie have had an informative and relaxing evening.'

The two ladies acknowledged the sentiment.

'Thank you both. Now we may all jump ship.'

Arabella smiled and after saying her goodbyes she hoisted her big brown bag off the floor and put her papers away; she was the first through the door! Arabella went straight home; she'd a lot to do and she'd got enough fresh cream éclairs to help her do it.

Mavis went straight home but she didn't know she'd a lot to do, at least not until she got there and found Ronald scrubbing Daisy's hand prints off the lounge carpet. He explained to a distraught Mavis that beetroot vinegar is a nightmare to get out of carpet pile.

'I know I should have cleared the table before I went to get the lawnmower from the shed, but I swear to you I wasn't more than five minutes. The boys had gone upstairs to do their homework. I thought Daisy had gone up with them. She must have been hiding under the table. She's an absolute monster. She's forever wanting to paint things. I couldn't get it off her face and her hands, or Obbledy's; I've had to put her to bed as she is. Bathing her and Obbledy was a waste of time! I've hung it on the line and it should be dry by morning!'

Mavis gave him a hand with the carpet. It was after midnight when they decided it would need professional treatment. They went to bed and had a short business meeting to cheer themselves up. At two o'clock in the morning, Daisy was singing twinkle, twinkle little thtar to Mithter Thlippery. He couldn't applaud because cloth snakes don't have hands so each time she finished her version of the song she applauded herself. Fortunately by this time the rest of the family were sound asleep. They were fortunate because they knew from previous night-time renditions that Daisy had no control over her vocal chords or if she did, she didn't let on?

Betty and Margaret called in at the Unicorn on their way home having decided to have a swift tipple before going round to Betty's to make a sop-supper for Keith and Bill, but only on the proviso that the men-folk had cleared enough clutter out of the attic and got it ready for either the dustbin or the boot sale. The men went misty-eyed when the one thought lovingly of the mahogany teapot stand he'd made at school. The other stared with obvious melancholy at the thought of his burr-walnut pipe rack, but reluctantly they'd signed the contract, and after all they agreed, a sop-supper is a sop-supper. Betty had suggested to Margaret they should call in for one to give their husbands more time to sort out their clutter because the pair of them hadn't seemed keen, even though they'd agreed to do it; Margaret said it was a good idea and they might as well have two while they were there, then their husbands would have even more time! Connie and Clara went straight home; their houses didn't have an attic and Richard and Harvey, their husbands, didn't store things that might come in handy for the day before the world ended.

Maud drove straight home. Her hip was giving her grief and she'd forgotten, for once, to take her medicinal brandy along to the committee meeting. She wasn't thinking only of her medicine as she negotiated the tree-lined road home, she was also wondering about the mad idea Arabella had mentioned. There had to be some connection between the crystal ball and the amusement arcade, no matter how tenuous. There had to be something, but how could she use the damned thing to influence a fruit machine or one of those silly ducks? Maud's mind went back to the time when she used to go to the local fair with her father. She wanted him to make the bell ring with that huge hammer, but he never would.

'That's a silly thing to do Maud. Such antics belittle one and make one look stupid.' She thought that was the only reason for going to the fair; to be daft and have fun. She sighed and washed these thoughts from her mind as she gave her full attention to reversing her car into the garage. Maud liked to get as near as possible to the left-hand side to give herself as much room as possible to swing her bad leg out.

The lovely Lady Marion did not go straight home. She went to see Mr Granger on the recommendation of Lady Audrey. Lady Audrey had a cruel streak and knew Mr Granger, and the number of steps there were to his top floor classroom. Lady Marion had made an appointment at the computer centre on the High Street. He had explained on the telephone that the class finished at eight-thirty, but if she wanted one-on-one tuition he would stay behind until nine o'clock. The lovely Lady Marion liked his voice; it was deep and masculine and sounded as if it resonated from a huge manly chest. The truth was she no more wanted computer lessons than she did a Sunday morning paper round, but thanks to Lady Audrey and her chum Lady Eleanor, Lady Marion's supply of sporty men had vanished like polar bears in a snow storm!

She arrived at the premises slightly before the deadline and climbed the narrow spiral stairway to heaven and stopped for a moment on the top landing to get her breath back. After a dab or two of perfume and after making sure she was at her best, she knocked and upon hearing his deep manly voice say 'enter' she opened the door and swirled in. Within five minutes she swirled out! Mr Granger was a big let down. He was a slightly-built studious man with sloping shoulders and a pigeon-chest. Her beauty had made no impression on him whatsoever. Perhaps if she'd been silver and black like everything else in the huge room he might have paid her more attention! Lady Marion began to wonder why Lady Audrey had suggested she go and see Mr Granger in the first place. Why on earth, she muttered to herself, would that witch send me here? She'd never find out from the old witch (as she called her) because Lady Audrey was plotting other wild goose chases, or gander chases in Lady Marion's case. She was making the strumpet pay for making her son look like the village idiot!

Cynthia went straight home: she was working on a commission from the Mayor. He liked Dawn Chorus so much he wanted her to do another painting on the same subject but in the shades of early evening, and he wanted it to be called 'Fading Light'. He offered her two-hundred-and-fifty pounds to do it and Cynthia jumped at the chance. The money would help her to move out of her flat and maybe, into a better one? It would be a gamble but after the dirty trick they'd pulled at the exhibition she wanted to be well away from Karl and Jeremy. She'd miss them as she'd known them quite a while. She liked them a lot, but she'd already decided to find somewhere else, and the awful embarrassment with those pictures at the exhibition had been the final straw. There was another reason why Cynthia wanted to go but she didn't want to talk about it. She knew the depth of her feelings for Terry, and they were very different to those she'd felt for other men. She wanted Terry to be part of her life and not only as a friend.

Terry had been at the exhibition and Cynthia saw him as he saw her. He smiled and for her that was it. She didn't go to hide in one of her many happy places, but she was happy! She smiled back then he came over and said how good her paintings were. She thanked him and even though she felt extremely self-conscious she still didn't go to one of her happy places. He said he was no expert but he'd heard others say the same thing.

'We can't all be wrong can we?' he'd said. Then he'd shrugged his shoulders and smiled again. He'd asked her out and Cynthia had said yes. They had a good time and the meal was excellent. Cynthia wasn't into wine but quite out of character she tried some and said it was fine. They arranged a date for the following Saturday and even though Cynthia thought his term, 'date' to be a bit quaint Cynthia didn't mind in the least! He was two or three years older than Karl and Jeremy and he wasn't a student. This latter fact alone had to be a plus as far as Cynthia was concerned. She was really looking forward to their 'date'.

On the Wednesday morning Martha took the train to Broomsferry. Earlier in the week and after her temporary loss of control she'd rescued Tribal Feathers from the dustbin. She was going to see Harriet, Martha's favourite and one of the more free-thinking of the Rainbows End designers. Martha wanted to know why the feathers had detached themselves from Harriet's creation. Or as Martha's husband had said earlier, 'Your dress arrangement's moulting!' This earned him a swift removal of her monocle and a two-eyed stony-faced glare. She was well aware of the bare patch at bum level.

She arrived in Broomsferry in good time and took a taxi to 'The House of Rainbows End', which wasn't a house at all. It was a modern but dreary-looking factory. After being met at reception and after much darling-ing and lovely to see yous, Martha was taken through to the design workshop. There, with a cup of strange-tasting tea in one hand and what looked like a dead ostrich over her other, she explained her dismay at the obvious lack of attention by Harriet's seamstress.

Harriet explained in detail how skilful and meticulous her people were and as the bald patch was in the area it was in, 'that perhaps Martha had sat on some rough or very uneven surface. Perhaps in a rowing boat or sitting on a splintered park bench?' Harriet's suggestion instantly brought to Martha's mind the day she'd spent selling raffle tickets and the incident with the suicidal policeman who'd suggested, because she'd fallen asleep on a park bench, that she was a lady of doubtful morals. Martha remembered lambasting him and sending him on his way. Since then Martha had steered clear of park benches and street corners. A rowing-barge would have been more suited to Martha's bulk. Martha knew nothing about Daisy plucking them so she could make a headdress like Geronimo's. Martha sniffed loudly and gave Harriet a glare.

'Only examples darling! And as you can see only this small area is affected.'

Harriet showed the affected area of the dead ostrich.

'Had we been negligent in the making surely, Darling, a lot more of the feathers would have detached themselves?'

Martha wasn't impressed. Martha in truth was totally unimpressed. This she pointed out, almost thrusting the garment up Harriet's nose. 'This is not a special offer outfit! Nor was it an end of season garment! This was an exclusive. A model! There isn't another one in the world! And I am a client of long standing.'

The result of this short game of ping-pong that had it gone on much longer, would have been concluded with a forearm smash Harriet was saying. 'We will repair the cloak at cost! How does that sound, Darling?'

Martha replied. 'If that is the best you are prepared to offer Darling, I don't have much damned choice.' Martha laid heavy emphasis on the word 'Darling' and without seeing any sign of a crock of gold she left Rainbows end. She also left the odd-tasting cup of tea and the dead ostrich.

Betty didn't buy designer clothes unless there was something in the Oxfam shop that was as good as new. She didn't need to. She looked good in most things. She was in good shape with a well-moulded figure and good legs. She was using these good legs now! She was out collecting donations for the boot sale. Margaret was with her and although she had a fine pair of legs they were beginning to ache.

'Haven't we enough rubbish yet, Betty? We've only got two stalls and Arabella's forgotten Marion's on holiday so she won't be running one.'

'It's cancelled.'

'What's cancelled?'

'Marion's holiday. They're not going now. It's been put back to November. Lady Audrey isn't so well so Lord Percy won't go.'

'Nobody tells me anything!'

'I thought you knew?'

'You know what thought did? Followed the muck cart, thought it was a funeral.'

'I don't know where you get such things from?' Betty laughed.

'From Granddad Robinson,' laughed Margaret. 'Where else?'

'Come on, let's call it a day. We'll stick these in your garage till Saturday.'

'Our garage is full Betty. You couldn't get a pint of milk in there unless you poured it out of the bottle! We'll stick them in yours!'

'Ok,' Betty nodded.

The ladies put the stuff in the car boot with a pile of other 'priceless' things and called it a day. Betty's garage, although she didn't know it, was already quite full because Mavis had sent Dreamboat round earlier in the evening with a stack of Daisy's part-worn toys. Most of the dolls had been operated on by Daisy and Obbledy, and the rest needed plenty of TLC. But if all else failed there was always the dustbin!

Arabella had offered some of 'Dear Henry's' ties and shoes to be sold at the boot sale; not his favourite tie or his favourite pair of shoes – to get rid of those would be unthinkable. Maud gave a dinner service and a cutlery set, both were unused and had been in the family for years. Arabella told her it was a disgrace to give family heirlooms away. Then as Arabella reached for yet another fresh cream éclair, she further explained that Maud must put them on one side. 'It would be far better to send them to the auction room Dear. You'll get a much better price there!' Maud conceded and wondered if God had suddenly turned to her page in his big black book.

Things were arriving at Betty's and Margaret's in droves. They rang Arabella and told her they had enough stuff for half a dozen boot sales and that they must call a halt.

'There's nowhere to put it,' said Margaret. 'And half of it is rubbish!'

'We'll have three pitches. That will solve the problem Dear. You and Betty won't mind running it would you?'

The phone was put down with a chortle.

'Three pitches! That's what she said, Betty. Three pitches. Guess who's running it?'

'Who?'

'You and Me!'

'She knows best Margaret,' replied Betty, pulling a face.

Margaret sniffed as she always did when unconvinced.

For the paper chase Maud (accompanied by Arabella) had driven and at times walked the route. From this hellish hip-clicking experience Maud, with the aid of a couple of medicinal brandies, had drawn up the position of the marshals and a plan of the route. These would be photocopied free of charge by the helpful young reporter at the Bugle. Entrants must have all four signatures on this sheet. Along with the marshals' sheet, a copy of the route in a sealed envelope would also be given to each entrant at the start.

These were to be handed in at the finish unopened and no later than nine-thirty. If by mischance someone did get lost, he or she would be allowed to open their envelope and refer to the map inside to find the quickest way back to civilisation. Any opened envelopes handed in by entrants would lead to disqualification but anything would be better than wandering through the woods in the dead of night. This ploy of Arabella's would put the responsibility of getting lost firmly on the entrants' shoulders, rather than on those of committee members.

The day of the car boot sale drew near, but in case Cynthia wasn't at her best she'd been elected by Arabella to man the overflow pitch. This decision was reached not by the usual democratic show of hands but by remote control. 'If one of your student friends could be kind enough to give a hand?' She waited a split second before saying. 'That would be more than helpful Dear. It is Clara's first time and the more the merrier.'

There followed a slightly longer pause. Arabella knowing well of Cynthia's reluctance to be 'front-line active' was waiting for her to return from one of her happy places. Cynthia was actually wondering if Terry would mind helping. An em sound floated down the phone line.

'Is that a yes Dear?'

'Yes, it's a yes, Arabella!' replied Cynthia (her mind elsewhere).

'Well done! I will ask Connie to help Mavis and Martha. I'm not convinced Marion will turn up. I will speak to you later Dear!'

Arabella was so surprised by Cynthia's fairly positive reaction she forgot to sprinkle pepper on her tomato salad.

Betty was trying to sort the wheat from the chaff and there was a lot more chaff than wheat. She wondered if she dare put some of the chaff in the dustbin. She rang Margaret for advice. Margaret suggested she wait for nightfall and throw it away then, which was exactly what she intended doing. Unfortunately Betty was cruelly thwarted from her goal by Arabella who chose that very evening to call round and lend a hand.

'All hands to the pump Dear,' said Arabella climbing out of the car. 'We've come to help.'

Betty who was just about to stuff a bag into the bin was caught in the act as it were and said rather too quickly, 'That pile of bags there is for Oxbin.' Then quickly said, 'I meant Oxfam.'

Arabella smiled and put the chaff in the boot of Maud's car.

'Come along Maud we'll pop round to Margaret's and see what she's put on one side for Oxbin!'

Arabella smiled, Maud looked uncomfortable and Betty looked sheepish. They said their good evenings' and drove off. Fortunately for Oxfam Margaret didn't have any chaff in sight when Arabella and Maud got there. Oxbin had already got it. Maud decided that she would call at the Oxfam depot in the morning and donate the contents of her boot, and she hoped none of the volunteers would think any of it had ever belonged to her! Arabella went home and as she entered the spotless lounge her thoughts had, without wish or request, gone back to her childhood days when 'wilful waste brings woeful want' was intoned by her father at every sorry meal! 'If only these people knew,' she told Dear Henry's photograph. Dear departed Henry smiled back at her as he always did.

The day of the boot sale arrived in its turn. The crowds came in droves. Margaret asked if the council had opened the cemetery gates. Connie said it looks like it and returned to her 'bargaining' with the skill of a one-eyed Casaba trader. 'But Sir!' she said resisting the urge to swing the toaster round on its wire and belt him at the side of the head with the crumb filled thing. 'Where else could you buy a toaster for two pounds?'

The man dipped his hand into his pocket to prove to the grinning bystanders that he wasn't the tight-fisted skinflint they thought he was. 'We'll throw the crumbs in free of charge and thank you very much. That's only two-pounds-fifty for the lot,' said Betty who'd appeared from nowhere and without taking a breath offered the fistful of cutlery to a young woman with a yowling child. The man tucked the toaster upside down under his arm and left with his super bargain and a warm glow! Had Hansel and Gretal been about they would have followed the trail of crumbs to his car. The young woman didn't want the slightly tarnished knives and forks, at least not at full price! Connie said over her shoulder and as if to no one in particular, 'It's for charity you know.' Betty accepted the woman's offer but that was only so she would clear off and take her wailing-machine with her.

Arabella, eyes going everywhere, patrolled the car park like a botanist looking for a scotch plaid tulip. As she collected the fees she noticed how well some of the stalls were doing and wished she'd charged them a little more. Maud accompanied Arabella and entered the amount against the reference name and number of the stall.

'We should have made the pitches a little more expensive Maud, Dear. Some of these people obviously make a good living! Perhaps a pound extra would have been fair.'

Maud nodded and scribbled away. Her hip was bothering her and Arabella's feet were beginning to twinge.

'I think that's the lot Arabella,' said Maud as she checked the list. 'Some of the pitches were paid for through the post. I listed those in green.'

'What about that one there with that good looking young man on the stall?'

'That one's ours Arabella. It's Cynthia's helper. Lady Marian cried off if you remember?'

'Yes Maud, Dear, I do remember.'

Arabella sniffed. Maud shook her head and made a barely-audible tut, tut.

'Well you do say the oddest things Maud. Why would I forget such a thing?'

'Well with you asking…'

'Never mind that Dear,' interrupted Arabella. 'Let's see how they're doing. You know what a shrinking violet Cynthia is.'

Arabella's soft thud of a chuckle disturbed the still of her ample bosom as the ladies threaded their way between the cars, the vans and the more professional stalls.

'I should be at the refreshment stall Arabella!'

'Don't fuss Maud it's only a quarter-to-eight.' Puffed, Arabella squinting at her watch. She'd bought one with bigger numerals but it was still difficult to see them without her glasses, which she said she didn't need but most of her friends knew she did!

'I think we've got everyone's' money. Check your list Dear and then you can make a start.'

Maud checked as recommended, said see you later and left Arabella to circulate.

Arabella didn't stay very long at Cynthia's stall. She was introduced to Terry and she found him charming. But one visitor she wasn't expecting appeared from under the table and spluttered, 'Hello mithith Thmythe, me and Obbledy are helping Thinthya and Terry and Clara on thith thtall. Mummy thed I could. And I'm being good but Obbledy ithant. Heth's been thouting at the cuthtomerth.'

Cynthia could barely keep her face straight. Terry thought Daisy was magnificent. Arabella thought Daisy was something, probably some sort of angelic poltergeist. And that dreadful octopus that Cynthia had made for her was just as bad. Clara was trying to sell a pale blue suit to a man half as big as the suit. Arabella didn't want her favourite bottle-green skirt spraying by an excitable Daisy so she kept well back, waved and told them all to 'keep at it' and she would see them afterwards. Cynthia nodded, smiled and wiped Daisy's chin. She also wiped Obbledy's chin because Daisy said, 'Ith full of thpit as well.' Mr slippery was draped round a heavy brass candlestick keeping two beady eyes on a cabbage-patch doll. A woman asked how much the knitted snake was and Daisy said, 'It wathn't a boot-thale bargain. Ith mine and he bithes.' She bought the cabbage-patch doll and Daisy glared at her. Both Cynthia and Terry were enjoying themselves. Clara's customer had wandered away without the suit. Daisy had fallen asleep under the table with Obbledy as her pillow and a table cover she'd found to lie on. The sun came out again and the day ticked on.

Maud was doing pretty good on the refreshment stall. She'd been and got a canvas-seated chair from her car but hadn't had a chance to sit in it. She made herself another special. Her hip was giving the occasional twinge but she hadn't much medicinal brandy left, perhaps enough for one more later on, with a nice strong coffee. Arabella suddenly appeared from behind a clothes rail on the next stall and ordered a cup of coffee.

'I'd like one of your specials Maud if you've got enough ingredients. I'm exhausted.'

'Just about,' replied Maud. She hoped not too sadly for Arabella to notice. Arabella thought Maud's expression was caused by a pain in her hip.

'I'll sit on this chair for a moment.' Maud turned to make a special, hoping Arabella would get it down her throat and go about her business!

There was a disturbance on Mavis and Martha's stall. Somebody had dropped a china plate and it had smashed to pieces. Mavis had told the woman she'd have to pay for it but the woman refused. Arabella gulped her coffee down, thanked Maud and set off with that strange mincing gait of hers to the source of the trouble. It didn't take her very long to elbow her way through the thinning crowd.

'Now what's the problem, Mavis?' Arabella straightened her back as she always did when preparing to go into battle.

'This woman picked up a china plate and dropped it! Now she refuses to pay.' Mavis had her lip out.

'Oh, is that so,' crooned Arabella at her most dangerous. 'Isn't that one of the plates I donated? It certainly looks like it.' Arabella stooped and selected one of the larger pieces off the ground. 'Yes. I'm sure it is. Now we were asking four pounds for that but because accidents do happen and because it's neither use nor ornament now, is it Dear?' The woman wasn't given chance to argue the point. 'We will accept two pounds. In that way we all pay for your clumsiness. I'm sure you'll think that's the fairest way to do it! After all we are not doing this for profit; we're doing it for charity, Dear!'

Arabella didn't exactly surround the woman but she certainly blocked her escape. 'Well Dear?' asked Arabella, as pleasant as a school bully. 'Are you going to accept half the responsibility?' The woman coughed up. Everybody was looking at her. 'Thank you,' said Arabella. 'Now are there any another plates you fancy?' The lady President picked a nice willow pattern from a group of three. 'These are only six pounds for the three. A bargain if I say so myself. Look, they are so fine you can almost see through them.' Arabella held it up to the light. The woman bought them and scurried off before she had to buy anything else.

'Well worth the walkover,' said Arabella ready for heading off back to the refreshment stall.

'We were only asking a pound for that plate,' said Martha releasing her monocle in surprise. 'And I donated it.'

'Did you Dear? I could have sworn I donated it. Perhaps it was that one there.' She didn't point to any plate in particular. 'But if that was a pound and the other was a pound, all's well that ends well. See you after,' smiled Arabella and off she went.

'That woman doesn't miss a trick Mavis!' said Martha now Arabella was out of earshot.

'Tell me something new Martha,' laughed Mavis.

Some of the regulars began to empty their stalls and load their vehicles.

'Are you all right if I go and fetch Daisy? I think we'll be packing up soon.'

'Yes I'll be fine as it's thinning out now.'

Arabella watched them from the comfort of Maud's chair, whilst Maud was sitting on the corner of the stall and she wasn't comfortable. She wanted to call it a day.

'I think we should do the same!'

'Do what Maud Dear?'

'Shut shop!' she replied, wondering why Arabella needed it spelling out.

'But there are still a few people about, Maud. Why not offer everything at give-away prices. I'll go and tell the ladies to make a last effort.'

Arabella strode off and Maud reclaimed her chair.

Arabella was gone for quite a while and when she returned, her face was flushed and she was wearing a beaming smile. Maud had loaded most of the left-over refreshments in her car and was stripping down the tea urn. 'You look happy. Have they sold all the gooseberry and rhubarb jam?'

'Better than that Maud,' chortled Arabella. 'Cynthia and Terry have got engaged.'

'Excellent,' said Maud and beamed in return.

'They haven't set a date for the wedding but I'm so happy for her. The bad news is they've asked Mavis if Daisy can be one of the bridesmaids. That should show them what life's all about!' Again Arabella's soft thud of a chortle erupted.

'Arabella! Sometimes you can be really mean. Daisy's a lovely little thing. She makes me laugh at the things she does. And when she gets that face on and speaks so seriously, well it sounds hilarious.'

'It won't be when she wants to carry that daft-looking doll of hers down the aisle,' Arabella laughed. 'I've just been listening to the little monster and I must say Maud, I never noticed before but everything she wants she says the doll or that ridiculous snake wants. She's just said Mr Slippery needs a drink of orange and Obbledy needs a biscuit. She offered the doll a biscuit and said, "He says he isn't hungry now. He wants me to have it." She did the exactly the same with the orange juice. She's a crafty little Madam.'

'She'd have got them anyway,' Maud smiled. 'She can twist Mavis round her little finger.'

'True Maud, true Dear. Here let me help you with that! It's heavy.'

Then Betty's husband rolled up with his van.

Arabella didn't mention anything about the lovely little tea set that matched her cake stand. She'd bought the set for ten pounds, after explaining to him that she hadn't come to buy.

'That is all I have with me! It's as much as I can offer.'

In Arabella's opinion it was worth fifty. She would use it on Wednesday when Maud popped round for elevenses. He'd asked for fifteen but the most she would offer was ten. It was one of the few things he had left and he was almost ready for going. Arabella loved the dark green and gold fleur de lys on the plate, the cup and the saucer and it was in exactly the same place as the one on the cake stand. They looked to be hand-painted but she would wait until she got home to have a closer look. She didn't want the stallholder to think she was too interested in it.

Everything was packed away by six o'clock. Arabella thanked everyone for their tremendous efforts and asked them to hang on to their takings till Monday night's committee meeting or if they preferred, they could pop round to Maud's with it. As she hadn't been consulted, this came as a surprise to Maud! 'Arabella, I won't be in this evening. I'm going to see an old friend of mine who's just retired from the church. I'm sorry everyone but you can give it to me now or leave it until Monday!' Mavis was holding Daisy and Martha was holding the cash bag so she handed it to Maud. The others did the same. 'I won't sort it out this evening Arabella, I'll do it in the morning. Now I must be off! See you all on Monday. Cheerio,' sang Maud walking to her car.

They all answered and said their goodbyes. Cynthia went with Terry and Daisy, who was still asleep, went with her mother. Arabella watched all of them go and there was no mistaking the look of contentment on her face. Maud thought she would be desperately lonely when Dear Henry passed away and for a number of years she was but now she had a different family and a different goal and they'd made a big difference to her life. Arabella checked to make sure there was no litter left behind and then left. She would write a sincere thank you letter to Harry for his help in getting them the use of the car park: Arabella was nothing if not thorough!

After her usual breakfast of lashings of jam on toast, Maud counted the money. There was four-hundred-and-seven-pounds-fifty. As she crammed it all into one bag and tied the string she thought how delighted Arabella would be when she told her the total at tonight's committee meeting. She put it in the bureau and locked the drawer. She also thought about last evening and the supper she'd shared with Reverend Harris. She also thought about his parting words, 'We must do this again very soon!' Maud had said, 'It would be a pleasure.' And she'd meant it.

Arabella ate alone but it didn't dampen her spirits or her appetite. As usual she ate a bit too much. She finished the pork casserole and had two fresh cream éclairs for pudding. This mini feast didn't give her indigestion but it did make her feel a little uncomfortable. She decided, after wriggling about for long enough in her favourite chair, to go for a walk. She removed an empty crisp packet that she spotted instantly as she went down the path. It had blown into the garden and she saw more or less at the same time, that something had disturbed the soil beside her Snapdragon. The thing was picked up in a small plastic bag and in the dustbin within seconds. The disgusting creature was not on the greenhouse roof!

Her next-door neighbour was working in her garden but she stopped as Arabella passed.

'Hello Arabella.'

Arabella smiled and asked if all was well.

'Fine, yes everything I've put in this time has taken really well.'

'Good.'

Arabella popped her head over the hedge and complimented Christine on her efforts. This garden, although the same size as Arabella's, was arranged far more casually than Arabella's pristine geometric paradise.

'How did the car boot sale go?' asked Christine returning to her weeding.

'I don't have the final figures but there were no problems whatsoever. I think we did very well. There were a lot of people there. I'd no idea car boot sales were so popular! I'm thinking of having one at this year's gala. I'm going to put it to the committee tomorrow evening. I'm convinced most people prefer to give odds and ends rather than money but it's all the same to us in the long run. I think it will be a good idea, don't you?'

'If you've done well with this one, yes I do. In fact, Arabella, I've been doing some sorting out. It's all in boxes in the garage. I was going to give it to Oxfam but I'll keep it for the gala if you want me to?'

'Yes do. All proceeds go to local charities and there are no administration fees!'

Arabella's soft thud of a chortle filled the air.

'Well I must be off but thank you very much indeed Christine.'

'It's nothing Arabella. See you later.'

Arabella said, 'Cheerio,' smiled and went on her way. We could squeeze quite a few stalls up by the refreshment tent, thought Arabella as she turned for home, the telephone and a good night's sleep.

Monday came as Mondays do. The weather was changeable; it rained in the morning and was sunny for most of the afternoon. Then just before five o'clock it began to rain again. It was raining when the ladies set off for the committee meeting and it was raining when they got to the town hall. Mavis had got Daisy's Postman Pat umbrella because she couldn't find her own. Maud had her sombre beige and black paisley. The lovely Lady Marion was escorted up the well worn stone steps to the main entrance under Lord Percy's red golfing brolly. Harper, their butler, opened the sturdy door and made sure not one drop of evil rain assaulted her ladyship. He was rewarded with a tiny smile and for Harper that was enough to cheer him up no end. He hadn't been long at the Hall!

Arabella hadn't bothered with a brolly. She'd parked right outside the main door and skipped up the steps like a twenty-year-old and there was good reason for this brief exhibition of athleticism; Arabella had been told by her chiropodist that if she continued wearing shoes a size too small, soon, she would in the long term pay dearly! And she had already paid a deposit! The bunion on her big toe was pushing her joint sideways. Not only must she wear the correct shoe size, she must also get a wide-fitting shoe. The wider the better he had insisted. She'd taken his advice (although reluctantly) and the difference in comfort had been tremendous. She felt as if she could jump over the moon but before she tried anything like that she would have to bypass the bakery for two or three years. Arabella had been over indulging lately and it showed. Maud had been brave enough to mention this on two occasions and Arabella had taken note.

The committee meeting began on the dot. Arabella's huge brown handbag was laid at her feet like a posh sack of King Edwards and her papers were before her ready to be shuffled around if the need arose. She stood and checked the attendance. All the crew were present but because there were no handsome dashers there, the lovely Lady Marion didn't look quite as attentive as the others. Arabella didn't expect her to. Maud the first officer, the secretary, and at times second assistant to the organ grinders monkey, passed Arabella a sheet of paper showing the takings from the boot sale. Arabella was impressed. This was clear to all because she suddenly beamed, 'This is excellent Maud, ladies. Four-hundred-and-seven-pounds-fifty-pence! I propose we do this again at the gala. What do you think?'

There were murmurs and mutterings. There was a shuffling of papers. The chattering was soon stopped.

'Ladies!' announced Arabella. 'Please address your remarks one at a time and through the chair. We all know the system. If you wish to give an opinion please raise your hand! But before you do let me tell you how far we've got. Last night I spoke to Lord Percy and he said he was all for it. He offered with the help of Lady Marion to not only run a stall but to sort out some bits and bobs for us. I thought that was very generous of him, don't you?'

There followed some enthusiastic applause but not from the lovely Lady Marion. She was hoping for a Saturday afternoon 'Spanish lesson' with her brown-eyed handsome man. Sadly for the lovely but not so chaste Lady Marion, Lady Audrey had already put her cunning plan into place.

'Good, now are there any questions before we go on to item two, the paper chase?' She waited but not for long. 'Good. Now Maud and I have outlined the route and there is a copy for each of you. Now who are the marshals, Maud?'

Maud stood.

'Mavis at post one, Cynthia at post two, Lady Marion at post three and Martha at post four. Connie will be with me at the start to mark their route and Clara will be with you at the finish to check them in!'

Maud confirmed these arrangements and ticked them off.

'Good, that's settled then.' Arabella took over. 'Gordon at the White Owl has made a donation for having the finish in his car park!' Arabella had had to wring it out of him. But she was an expert.

She had explained in mitigation that he would do a good deal of business when the competitors got there. 'They will all want refreshments, won't they?' she'd smiled nicely. 'And there's a well above average profit on soft drinks or so I understand!' He'd reluctantly agreed. But he did get chance to tell Arabella and in the sorrowful manner of someone who's rabbit's just died, that since the breathalyser had been brought in, trade in country pubs had plummeted. Arabella wondered if the price of BMWs had plummeted too, because she noticed a new one parked in his parking spot. She didn't mention the car when she said goodbye while thanking him for his generous donation of a cheque for twenty pounds!

The weather forecast for Saturday was perfect. Warm, some mist or slight drizzle at times but only in the late evening and best of all, no wind. For the paper chase these conditions were ideal, so much so Arabella decided on Friday night to wet the paper would be an unnecessary waste of time and effort. She let everyone know and suggested Betty and Margaret should lay the trail starting at half-past-five. If they wanted any help shredding the paper on Saturday morning they should let the others know as soon as possible. They said they would manage with the help of their husbands. They borrowed Maud's big guillotine and Keith's small one and by two o'clock the shredding was complete. They decided over a gin and tonic that they wouldn't put loads down, just a sprinkling every ten yards or so.

There were eighty-two entrants at the start and after announcing the first prize was a silver-plated trophy the size of an eggcup and ten pounds there was a lot of jostling for position. Maud had to give a few of the more boisterous ones a good talking to. When she was satisfied no one had a particular advantage over the other entrants, she blew the whistle for the

270

off. The first scattering of paper was fifty yards or so from the start. This, according to Arabella, would stop them all from following one another. Unfortunately, Betty and Margaret's fifty yards was nearer a hundred so there was a lot of confusion and shouted accusations of, 'There's no trail been left. Where's the bits of paper?' These kept flying back at Maud at intervals and from deep in the wood. Maud shouted back that there was plenty. Then having had enough she and Connie got in her car, headed for the finish and a brandy and lemonade and a gin and tonic with lots of lemon!

Three entrants who thought Maud, after the evil stare she gave them, was on a visit from Pendle decided to get their revenge and have a bit of fun at the same time. These were fit young men from the rugby club and the three of them (after only a few minutes) were well ahead of the rest of the field. As soon as they found any bits of paper they grabbed every scrap. Once they'd got the lot, one ran off to the left and one ran to the right in great sweeping arcs scattering two false trails. The third one followed the trail. After three quarters of an hour of this deception there were people in every corner of the woods and they were well lost and well peeved off. Some were doubling back to try to pick up the trail again as others ran passed in the opposite direction. Others called out from somewhere in the distance and quite a few gave it up as a bad job. Over half the entrants went home vowing to complain to the local newspaper.

Cynthia, accompanied by Terry at post two, signed the cards in the second square of the three sweating rugby players and thinking that other entrants would be due any minute, were ready with their check board. Nobody appeared. They waited and waited but after twenty minutes or so they decided something wasn't right. Cynthia radioed in!

The lovely Lady Marion at post three took her time with her check board. She was deciding which one of these hunks should get the come on. After trying for all three and seeing her signals fall on stony ground she finally signed her name in box three and hoped, as she watched them tear off into the distance, that the rest of the idiots would get a bloody move on. She waited thirty minutes exactly and then abandoned her post. She took the two-way radio with her.

Martha spotted the three rugby players before they spotted her. She was ideally (but not deliberately) camouflaged. She was wearing a pair of what looked like ex-army overalls. This attire was also a creation of Harriet's mind wanderings. She'd called it rustic tiger. And in fairness to Harriet she'd got it dead on! The belted suit was patterned in an all over haphazard blend of brown and green irregular stripes on a khaki ground. Martha, who was resting against a fallen tree, was invisible! The three miscreants ran straight past within six feet of her. She only woke from her nap because one of the trio went head-first over a protruding tree root. She watched him struggle to his feet while the other two abandoned him and jogged off in different directions. It was only then and with the aid of her binoculars that she saw them laying the false trails!

'YOU!' she shouted at the top of her voice. 'WHAT DO YOU THINK YOU'RE DOING?' They turned, saw they'd been rumbled and put a spurt on. The one who'd tripped was bleeding from a gash in his knee. He couldn't escape Martha's anger. 'It serves you right you hooligan. I KNOW WHO YOU ARE,' she bellowed into the trees. 'I knew there was something wrong when Cynthia buzzed me on the radio. Here, wrap that round your knee. We'll take the car. It serves you right; I've no sympathy for you whatsoever. You realise the three of you have ruined all the work we've done and some pleasure for a good few kind people!' Martha was truly angry.

'That needs cleaning and stitches!' she snapped.

'It was supposed to be a joke, a laugh,' offered the wounded rugby player.

'Well it's not funny in the least. And you can see I'm not laughing, can't you?' Her monocle dropped and she glared at him. 'Come on the car's over there.' He limped and was obviously in pain. 'Put your arm over my shoulder that should make it easier.'

He towered above her and replied through gritted teeth, 'I'm ok, it's no problem.'

'Don't be so soft!'

She took his arm and draped it over her shoulder. He had to bend to reach her height. They got to the road, she helped him into the car.

'Don't you get any blood on the seat or I'll make you walk to the finish!'

The lad of about twenty didn't know whether to laugh or cry. He was being threatened by a camouflaged barrel. There would be a lot more aggravation for him and his two cohorts when they got to the finish. They'd have Arabella to face and Arabella now knew what had gone on. She also knew about Lady Marion leaving her post! 'Bugger!' she'd said under her breath, resorting once more to Dear Henry's favourite expletive.

'Why does everything have to be spoiled Maud? Why does everything go wrong? All those people who've supported us over the years!'

272

Maud shook her head at each statement.

'All the work the committee's done to get things absolutely right. Then some damned louts come along and wreck it! And that Madam Zena or whatever her name was. They'll get a damn-good telling off if they dare to show their faces here!'

'Nothing they don't deserve! Arabella,' replied Maud sadly.

'It was just the same at the exhibition, Maud Dear, wasn't it? That disgusting painting. I'm glad Cynthia has nothing more to do with those students. I know all about students and their nasty habits.'

'Do you know Maud, I can still see that dreadful painting and the leering faces of the visitors. Had I been a man I would have flattened the damn lot of em! And faced the consequences.'

'I know you would Arabella.' Maud smiled and took a sip of her brandy and lemonade.

'Yes, I know you would.' Arabella got herself together. 'We'll have to go and find the ones who are lost Maud. We'll wait for Martha then we should all be here.'

Arabella stood and did a body count. 'Yes there's Martha and then we're all here.'

The ladies looked fed up to the teeth.

'Oh Dear! I think that's Martha's car. Is it Maud?' It was at that moment Martha's car pulled into the car park.

Margaret and Betty marched towards it like well drilled soldiers.

'What's that in Margaret's hand? Is it a stick Maud?'

'It does look like a stick, Arabella!'

'Surely she won't hit him with it? MARGARET!' cried Arabella. 'THROW THAT STICK DOWN!'

Arabella leapt up and ran across the car park. Maud tried to follow her, which in itself was a sight to see! Margaret and Betty turned round.

'What's up?' asked Margaret looking at her walking stick.

'Throw the stick down Margaret. You can't hit him. You'll get arrested if you do!'

Margaret burst out laughing. 'It's Bill's! I've been using it to push the bloody brambles out of my way! Mind you Arabella,' Margaret looked fondly at the hefty stick, 'It wouldn't be a bloody bad idea!'

'No need for that sort of talk, Dear,' she replied with a stern face. It didn't do to make Arabella look foolish.

'We all feel the same way as you do. Now Dear, would you leave this one to me? I know the president of the rugby club quite well. I doubt if the other two will show their faces! But we might be able to get some good out of this mess.'

Arabella didn't tap the side of her nose when she said this to Margaret, but she might just as well have done!

Richard Lee Wilson 2005

The Haunted Guesthouse

'This looks interesting, Cockroach!'

Wendy didn't appear to be listening. It was twenty-five-to-eight on a cold and wet Monday morning. She seemed to be daydreaming or still half-asleep. Strands of dark-brown hair covered one dark-brown eye, and the two-thirds, Grant could see of the other over her coffee cup, looked to be focussed halfway up the kitchen wall, not on her coffee cup, which was well tilted.

'I said, this looks in...'

'I heard what you said,' she brushed her hair to one side and yawned. 'I was thinking about tonight. Well? What looks interesting.'

She didn't sound that interested

'It's an advertisement for a weekend break in a haunted house.'

'Is it, where?' He had most of her attention now; Wendy was into things, paranormal!

'It's in the Drummer.'

'No, not the paper you nit, whereabouts is it?'

'It's not far from here; it's about a two-hour drive? It's near Flixby-on-Sea, and it's only a five minute walk, or so it says here, to a secluded sandy beach.'

'Hardly an inducement at this time of the year!'

She sipped at her coffee while her eye began to search somewhere above the pan rack.

'We might have an Indian summer.'

'Concorde might fly again.'

She put the cup down. 'If you're not interested, say so and I'll get back to the paper!'

'Get on with it.'

She pushed her hair to one side again. 'The place is called, Maudley Manor Guest House. It's set in seven acres of mature woodland; well that's what it says here!'

'Does it? Well they could have picked a better name for it, that's a horrible name for a house.'

'I don't see why.'

'Don't you. I think it sounds sad and mournful, sinister even.'

'It's not as sad and mournful as your hair. Are you going to run a comb through that haystack at some stage or what?'

'I'll comb my hair when I'm good and ready. I haven't had my toast yet, and you've a nerve, haven't you? Look at your own hair. Your head looks like a scorched hedgehog!'

'Thanks a lot, it was your idea to cover it in gel and have it sticking up all over. I hope Anty and Dickhead, or whatever they're called never have a flat-top. Because no doubt I'll have to have one if they do!'

She said, 'Rubbish' but didn't look up.

'At least I haven't a goose feather sticking out of mine!' replied Grant who yawned, stretched noisily and returned to the paper. Wendy searched half-heartedly for a feather that wasn't there!

Two minutes later he asked, 'Well, do you fancy a weekend by the sea? It's only seventy-five pounds, and that's all in. We could see if Rene and Steve fancy coming and make up a foursome.'

'I'll think about it while I'm combing my hair.'

'Ring me at work this afternoon then. I've lent the rake to the next-door neighbours!'

He laughed and poured himself another coffee; she muttered something about his doubtful parentage, then returned her eyes to the ceiling and thought about what she'd wear for tonight's hen party.

She strolled off into the lounge dragging her bare feet on the floor. But she was soon back.

'I've just spoken to Rene. She said they've nothing on this weekend and it sounds like a con to her but it could be mad. That's what she said. They're on for it if we are. I said we were. Rene said, "She'll Pencil it in." Can you believe it? Pass me a piece of toast. Thanks. She's been in one amateur production of the Mouse Trap or something and now she keeps an appointment diary. And the butter. Thanks. She must think she's Meryl Streep!'

'What did you say love? I was just checking the TV pages for the rugby.'

'I said there's a woman at the door. She says you are the father of her baby. Do you want to go and deal with it?'

'No, I don't!'

'Sit down you fool, I said it's on for the weekend!'

'What is?'

'The haunted hotel or whatever it is.'

'Brilliant, could be good. I'll give them a ring, later.'

'Ok. I'll be away in five. Kick or a kiss to get you moving?'

'Kiss and you've got toast crumbs on your lips.'

'So have you. See you later.'

Grant wiped his mouth with the back of his hand as he left the house.

'Well, what do you think?' Wendy did a twirl and Grant eyed her up and down.

'Are you going out or are we going to bed? If we're going to bed, it's perfect. If you're wearing that to go out on the town, don't hang about on any street corners!'

'Don't be a pain Grant, what do you really think?'

'I think you've a lovely grabbable bum!'

'You can't see my bum, can you?'

'No, well, not all of it!'

'I don't know why I bother.'

'You look lovely and you know it. If I hadn't just eaten, I'd eat you. Bones an' all.'

Wendy retreated from his outstretched hands and skipped into the kitchen. Grant followed her. 'I've booked the hotel for this weekend. It was a bit odd really; it was an answer phone. A ghostly voice said the booking will be confirmed by post. Tell Rene it's definitely on. She's going tonight isn't she?'

'Yes, the whole gang's going.'

'I pity the poor landlord then. Is Clara going?'

'Yes, of course she is!'

'I'll bail you out Wednesday morning then!'

'Very funny. Do you want a bit of Cheddar with that?'

'Yes please, just a couple of slices.'

'Do you want a top-up?'

'Why not?' Wendy did the cheese and Grant did the wine.

'Does she still burst into song every two minutes?'

'No, of course she doesn't. That was a one-off. She was doing the Mikado that week. She'd to keep exercising her voice, hadn't she.'

'I'd have said her chest muscles were big enough!'

'People pay good money to have boobs like Clara's.'

'The Montgolfiere brothers to name just two!' he laughed.

'Don't be a pig, and get those cheese crumbs off the floor!'

'Only kidding!'

'I know it! What time is it?'

'Time you were ready for off. It's already gone half-past. You said they were coming at half-past.'

'She's always late. I'll only be a few minutes.'

Wendy dashed upstairs as a car's horn tooted. She was down in a tick with, as far as Grant was concerned, a silk tablecloth thrown over her arm. She gave him a quick peck and said she'd be home before midnight. He told her if anybody fancied her, she'd to charge them the right price and not to come home with a purse full of loose change like she did last time. She called back, 'You'll be at the back of the queue from now on, Pig.'

She was in the car and half way up the hill when the phone rang. He closed the door and went to answer it.

'Mr Carlisle?' asked the deep melodious voice.

'It is,' replied Grant.

'Good, good. This is Mr Maudley of Maudley Manor. I am ringing to confirm your booking for the thirteenth. Two double rooms, Friday to Monday. Is that correct?'

'Em, yes it is,' replied Grant, whose thoughts had been elsewhere.

'Good, good,' replied the voice. 'I will send you all the relevant details through the post; they will be with you tomorrow. Wednesday at the latest. Are there any vegetarians in your party?'

'No, at least I don't think so,' replied Grant surprised at the question.

'Good, good. The reason I ask,' replied Mr Maudley as though reading Grant's mind, 'Is that at this time of year, you understand, it being so late in the season, we do not employ a full time chef. My wife does the meals and I'm afraid her knowledge of vegetarian dishes is, how can I put it? I would say limited. Yes, I would say at the very best, limited.'

'That's not a problem Mr Maudley; I'm ninety percent positive none of us are vegetarians.'

'Good, good. See you Friday evening. Have a safe journey. Goodbye Mr Carlisle.'

The line went dead before Grant had time to thank the man. It didn't register because the rugby quarter finals was on in two minutes and it was the Coq au Vins versus the Whatever-you-Knows, and his prayers and his money were on the Whatever-you-Knows! Grant loved it when the Welsh supporters started singing.

A very bright-eyed Wendy came romping in at twelve-thirty. She was greeted by a very dull-eyed Grant, whose prayers, and twenty pounds had fallen on stony ground.

'Didn't they sing those lovely hymns then, my poor darling?'

'Yes, they did sing, but they lost, and I lost twenty pounds. Am I still your darling?'

'No, you're not. Not if you've gone and lost twenty pounds. I should have listened to my Dear old mum before she was cruelly taken from me by the plague.'

'There isn't a plague lethal enough to take your mother to the doctors, never mind taken from you!'

Wendy giggled. 'Pig, she warned me about men like you. "He'll have you in rags before you know it," she said. "You'll be living on scraps," she said. "He only wants you for your body."'

'Shut up you idiot and either get a coffee or get to bed!'

'"He's a brute and a bully", she sa…'

Grant dived for her but missed by a mile as she ran laughing like a twonger up the stairs.

'Good morning, cockroach! Is there anybody there?'

'Clear off, I'm having a lie in.'

'It's eight o'clock, and I've brought your, breakfast.'

'Don't you dare draw the curtains, I've got a headache.'

'Oh my poor love, have you got a headache? Must be something you've eaten. I'll leave your runny-eyed egg and your fatty bacon on here.'

'Shut up, please.'

'I'm away in ten minutes. I'll give you a shout before I go, and don't forget you've an appointment at quarter-past-nine.'

Grant went back downstairs, picked up the post off the hall floor and went into the dining room.

There were only two letters, one from a credit card company that went in the waste bin, unopened, the other was from Mr Maudley which he opened. The only thing inside the envelope was a map showing directions to Maudley Manor Guest House. The map, although detailed, looked to be drawn by hand. There was no booking form or any other information given. Grant called out to his sleeping wife that he was off, and he'd see her around six.

Mr Maudley was busy setting the scene for his weekend visitors and his wife Gwendolyn was helping as best she could.

'How will you make a thing like that sound like footsteps walking across their room?'

'If you pass me that piece of stout cord, I will show you.'

Mrs Maudley, a heavy woman who looked to be in her sixties, took the end of the cord that was secured to a tightly wound spring and pulled it across the floor to her husband.

'Now Dear, just hold it there a moment while I check that the spring is perfectly secure.' He checked – it was fine. 'Good, good.' The long bolt that connected between two floor joists was more than adequate to carry the spring. The toothed rail that ran parallel to the joists and equidistant between them, was channelled and well greased and fixed firmly at three foot intervals across the length of the bedroom floor. He tested the rail for side-flap. There wasn't any movement.

He took the end of the cord from his wife and fastened it to an elongated O shaped bracket, which allowed a toothed wheel to sit on the toothed rail and move across the length of the room. Fastened to the wheel were two items that looked like dinner gongs. When the wheel moved forward the gongs, worked by centrifugal force, swung out and each one hit a stop fixed to the wheel. When the floorboard was replaced and as the wheel was pulled by the spring, the padded gongs gently hit the floorboard above it giving the impression that an unseen being was walking slowly across the bedroom and out through the wall.

'Help me replace the floorboards and we will test our apparatus.'

'These boards are too short. Look, there's a gap.'

'No, they're not My Dear. I have made a trap door at that end to enable me to wind the spring up each time our visitors go out.'

'But how will you release the spring, Archibald Dear?'

'I've already dealt with that, Gwendolyn Dear. I've led a cord-pull into the dining room and concealed it behind the dresser.' He gave her a beaming smile.

'You are terribly clever Dear.'

'Let's see shall we?'

The floorboards were fixed, the trap door was put in place and the carpet was re-laid. Mr Maudley went downstairs, pulled the cord and hurried back up to listen. They stood quiet as mice as the soft tread of an invisible being seemed to walk slowly across the bedroom floor. They both laughed like children when they found it worked perfectly. They went into the room next-door to assemble the other one. It took the rest of the day and part of the night but it was worth it, because thankfully that one also worked perfectly! If one of them pulled the cord in the next-door room first and then when the footsteps crossed that room, then the other one pulled the cord behind the dresser at the right time, it sounded as if the ghost was walking across one bedroom, through the wall, then across the other bedroom. The old couple were over the moon.

They started on Captain Boucher, the one-eyed pirate, the following day. They had difficulty keeping the maggots in the eye socket and had to resort to threading them along fuse wire till they got exactly the right effect. The rest of him was plain sailing. His pitiful moaning was achieved by using a piece of balloon rubber stretched loosely across two of Mrs Maudley's hair clips. The rotting flesh was nothing more than strips of silk cloth in various sizes dipped in flour and water then left to dry under the grill. They used green and yellow marker pens to give the rotting flesh that certain something. He looked terrifying when he was completely finished. He floated up passed the dining room window howling dreadfully with bits of flesh hanging from his face. Then as the return spring lost some of its tension and as Captain Boucher's ascension slowed, the dreadful howl became a pitiful moan. He then slowly disappeared over the roof into an alcove in the false chimney Mr Maudley had built. The wire he was fastened to went in there with him.

'Works a treat.'

'Good, good.'

Mrs Maudley applauded her husband with quick, short claps, rather like a child would. 'But how do you change the howl in his voice?'

'I don't change it, My Dear. As it loses velocity, less air is forced through the hole in his head so the balloon rubber doesn't vibrate as quickly. Therefore, the tone gradually becomes lower!'

'That's marvellous,' replied his Dear, laughing and laughing till she had to sit down.

The dreadful creaks and the rattling of chains in the cellars were a synch for Mr Maudley who'd been an engineer most of his life. He just hung two chains a yard apart on a knotted cable and wound it round an oval pulley. Fastened to the oval pulley was a circular pulley with a knotted cable that he wound from another pulley fixed in the shaft of the disused dumb-waiter. As he wound the pulley in the shaft, the cable in the cellar danced up and down, making the chains rattle and bang like mad, and as the knots were forced repeatedly part-way round the oval pulley and back again, the creaks and screeches they caused made the perfect sound.

The most difficult spectacle of all was the headless phantom. It took almost a day to get the mirrors exactly right and the ether from the old gas pipe still left buried in the wall to cling to the wax, and for the main mirror to swing silently back behind the panelling.

'Deary me, Archibald,' said Mrs Maudley when he'd finished fiddling with the angles, 'that is scary!'

'Indeed it is, Gwendolyn. Even though I say so myself?'

'I hope you don't give any of our guests a heart attack!'

'Perish the thought, Gwendolyn!'

'What else have you prepared for them? I saw you with some old newspaper when I was setting the table.'

'Ah, did you, My Dear? Well it was going to be a surprise for you so you would express real shock, but I might as well tell you. I've stuffed a small amount of that newspaper you saw me with up each of the cast-iron drainpipes at the front of the house. On Saturday night while you are serving their evening meal, I want you to send me to the kitchen for something – pepper I think. Instead of going to the kitchen for the pepper, which I will already have in my pocket, I will go and light a fuse attached to the paper. That will give me plenty of time to get back into the dining room with the pepper, to allay their suspicions as to where I am in the house. We need to be in their company when the haunting occurs.'

Mr Maudley smiled a quick little smile. 'Then when the fuse ignites the paper, the burning paper creates a rapid draw of air up the pipe and that rush of air makes a noise like a bull being slaughtered! It's really loud. I used to do it when I was a child. It makes a super noise! They'll never be able to guess what's going on.'

He laughed out loud this time and Mrs Maudley joined in. They slowly pulled themselves together and continued with their preparations!

They had a hard time getting the ghostly voice to sound exactly right from down the well because the well had dried up years ago when the new mains supply had finally been connected. The problem was, they were getting too many echoes. They seemed to go on and on.

'I must do something about this My Dear. Perhaps if I throw some straw down there, that might dull it. You wait here while I go and fetch some and we'll give it one last try!'

'Hurry up then, Archibald, it's very late!'

Mr Maudley was a good ten minutes before he came back with the straw. It was obvious to Mrs Maudley even in the darkness that he'd tried to carry too much because there was a trail of it on the ground behind him.

'Don't tut-tut, Dear; I will clear that up in the morning when I do the ghostly figure in the spinney thing. You'll love that one! I'll pop and switch the tape recorder on and we'll see what it sounds like with the straw down there.'

Mr Maudley went into the lounge and switched the machine on. He'd allowed a five minute time lapse before the moans and groans started so they could be in the company of the guests when a happening, happened! He hurried back out and stood beside his wife as the first dreadful moan filled the night.

'That sounds exactly as a ghost would sound, don't you think, Archibald?' She looked at her husband for confirmation.

He smiled. 'Superbly so, My Dear, in fact I'd say exactly like one!'

They went back into the house laughing again like silly children and he switched the tape recorder off while Mrs Maudley made the Horlicks.

'I shot the speaker wires up the old supply pipe with the crossbow in the dining room. I should have tied it to a rat's tail as we seem to have plenty!' They were still laughing when they opened their bedroom door. He whacked one off her pillow with a terrific blow from his tennis racket.

'Fifteen love, My Love,' he laughed. Then he threw the dead rat out of the window and fed the two caged rats in the wardrobe. He needed those! 'I'm beginning to think I might have overdone the rat thing My Dear.'

'Are you, Archibal...? She was asleep before she completed her sentence.

The crisp, early winter morning saw Mr Maudley raking the dropped straw and taking it back round to the stables. There was a stiff breeze that both hindered and helped. The wind had scattered the straw about but it was also covering the marks in the lawn made by the rake. Mrs Maudley brought her husband a huge pot of tea.

'How's it all going, Archibald?' She never ever called him Archie. That would have been unforgivable. For the same reason he never called her, Gwen. They were an old-fashioned couple.

'Thank you Dear,' he said, taking the pot of tea and cupping it in his hands. 'It is rather nippy. I should have waited until the sun came out, but I've got most of it up now and I've been able to finish the phantom.'

The steam from the tea misted his glasses but he didn't bother to wipe them.

'I think I'll use bouncing-Billy when the pump is running and use the Rotavator on that bit of garden over there.' He gestured to a bare patch of garden where the children's swing had once stood. 'The noise from the Rotavator will cover the noise of the pump and the valves in the cellar. You will have to turn it on while I am pretending to do the work. I'll show you where everything is.'

Gwendolyn nodded. 'I hope you don't strain yourself using that thing, it really does bounce about you know!'

'I will be very careful, you can be sure. Now let's see what happens. You've no need to stand out here, Dear, you can watch from the reading room. It's too cold to be standing out here. If you take my pot, I will come and watch from there with you. Then if the phantom is satisfactory, I will fill the blood-stain feeder on the stairs. Won't be long.'

He passed his wife his half full pot of tea. Mrs Maudley heard the pump start up, but it wasn't as loud as she expected. She went to the window and watched and Mr Maudley joined her.

'There do you see it?'

'Yes, yes!'

'Good, good.'

She turned to her husband. 'How on earth did you get it to look as good as that? Oh Dear it's gone.'

'I can't leave it dancing there too long, Gwendolyn. Can't have the guests spotting how it's done.'

'How on earth have you got it to do that?'

'With some rather clever return-valve arrangements.' Mr Maudley looked very proud of himself. 'When it slowly rears up from the ground the air supplies the body. Then when the body is fully inflated the air is delivered to the right arm, then the left arm, then the left leg then the right leg. That's what makes it appear to dance about from side to side. Then finally the air is sucked out very, very quickly and the whole thing is sucked into a niche under the bird table. The pump continues until the flap, which looks to be part of the base to the bird table, closes and the whole thing disappears! The pump switches off automatically and, hey-presto!'

'But how do you get it to move its head when it's tucked under its arm?'

He laughed with her.

'Stop it now. I saw its mouth move too. It is a phantom, isn't it?'

'Of course it's not. You are a silly thing. I don't think you would want a real phantom in your garden, would do you Dear?'

'I certainly would not.'

'Of course you wouldn't!

'When I made it, I fastened a piece of cord from its head to its right leg. I fastened another from its left leg to its bottom jaw. When its left leg inflates it tightens the string and the bottom jaw is pulled open. When the right leg is inflated, it tightens the cord attached to the head and pulls the head to the left. The whole thing is only made of mutton cloth sprayed with a fine coat of latex, so it's not very heavy and it fits perfectly into a cranny in the base of the bird table. My masterpiece, don't you think?'

'I do, Archibald, I do, I do!'

'Good, good. Let's see if it will pass close scrutiny. Perfectly, My Dear. The mosses round the base are barely scuffed. That will not be spotted by anyone! Now for the irremovable blood stain!'

They returned to the house where he went to the rats in the wardrobe. She, however, went for a small sherry and a shortbread biscuit. Everything was ready before teatime.

'Did I say a two-hour drive, or a two-day drive, Cockroach?'

'Keep your eyes on the road; we can't be far off now, surely? Have we passed Daleford?'

'I haven't seen a sign yet, have you Rene?'

'Only the one for Flixby-on-Sea. It said twenty-two miles. It was a long way back though. I thought we'd have been there by now.'

'How can we be there when we're here?'

Rene tut-tutted. Steve and Grant sniggered.

'You knew perfectly well what I meant, so don't be an arse, Steve.'

'Joke Chicken, joke.'

'What time is it?'

'The big hand's on…'

'Don't you start.'

Grant looked at the clock on the dashboard. 'Twenty-five-past-five or seventeen-twenty-five if you're metrificated Rene.'

'Can't say I've ever been metrificated Grant. Have I Steve?'

'Not by me, you haven't!'

'Something to look forward to then.'

'What did that sign say? I missed it.'

'Straight on, three miles.'

'Thanks, Cockroach.'

'Hell-fire what was that?'

'A bird of some sort. You missed it by a mile. You take the first on the left according to the map, and then the first, no, the second on the right. We should be able to see the sea from here.'

'I can't see the damned road for all this fog, never mind the sea!'

'Stop moaning, we're on holiday.'

'It's not fog, it's a sea mist.'

'Thanks for that, Rene. Didn't know you were a weather girl in your spare time.'

'Pay attention, Smarty-pants. You've gone past the turn!'

Grant stopped and reversed along the road. 'I can see it now. There's a sign on that tree. Yes, this is it.' He turned into the gateway. The scruffy-looking gates were wide open. They could see the lights of the hotel as they turned the last bend of the long, winding drive.

'Looks pretty welcoming to say it's ancient and haunted.'

'It won't be haunted, Cockroach, get a life!'

'It had better be slightly haunted or why have we come? If it isn't, I'll demand the money back!'

'We came because we needed a break, and so did you two. True or not?'

The pair in the back, who looked to be eating each other's tongue, nodded.

'Now come on, let's enjoy it. Whether it's haunted or not.'

They all piled out of the car and got their luggage out of the boot.

'Brr, it's hellish cold out here!'

'Hurry up then. I can hear the sea!'

'Yippee for you, Rene. Though it's probably Steve's teeth you can hear chattering!' They hurried into the guesthouse out of the cold.

'Good evening ladies. Good evening gentlemen. Welcome to Maudley Manor.' The man behind the desk looked more like a retired vicar, than a hotelier. They all said good evening in return.

'If you'd like to put your bags down for a moment. You are the Carlisle party, I take it?'

'Yes we are.'

'Good, Good.' Mr Maudley smiled warmly. 'I retained your booking form until you arrived in person, to save them being wasted, you understand? They didn't and he didn't enlighten them or wait for an answer.

'My wife will come though in a moment and show you to your rooms. Twelve and twelve, A. We don't have a room thirteen. My wife is very superstitious.' Mr Maudley smiled and so did the foursome. Then Mrs Maudley came into reception from the dining room. She looked like everyone's favourite Aunty.

'Hello, everybody, dreadful evening, isn't it?'

'Pretty grim,' replied Steve, rubbing his hands together.

'Were you held up by the fog?'

'Only as we got closer to the sea,' said Grant.

'Did you come along the cliff Road?'

'We didn't come through the town, or I don't think we did, did we Grant?'

'I've no idea, Cockroach. You were co-pilot.'

'They did come along Cliff Road, My Dear. I sent them directions through the post. I wasn't to know we would have a thick fog, was I?'

'No Dear, you weren't. But that's a terrible road to drive on even in the daytime, never mind at night in a pea-souper!'

'But it does take thirty minutes off the journey, Gwendolyn!'

'Yes, Archibald it does and well, you're all here, safe and sound so no point in making a fuss is there?'

Mr Maudley raised an elegant eyebrow and appealed to his guests for backing. They gave it saying there were no problems whatsoever with the route.

Mr Maudley and Mrs Maudley said, 'Good, good' but the guests would think differently in the morning when they went for a walk to the beach!

'Now if you've finished with everything, Archibald, I'll show them to their rooms?'

She turned to her guests and said, 'I've prepared you a seaside special for this evening's meal. I do hope you like fish and so ons?'

'Never eaten so ons,' said Grant. 'But if there's no gristle in 'em I'll have a go!' They all laughed.

'I'm glad you all have a sense of humour,' said Mrs Maudley still chuckling. 'You might need it before the end of your stay with us. Follow me then. Your rooms are up these stairs and on the left at the top.'

They wouldn't let her carry any of the bags.

'Here we are then. This is room twelve. Twelve A is that door there.'

She pointed to a pale blue door further on. Grant and Wendy took number twelve and Steve and Rene took the other.

'I will serve the meal at seven-thirty. You can take an aperitif at the bar, or if you prefer, at your table.'

She didn't show them into their rooms but said, 'I'm sure you don't need me to show you where things are.' Then she hurried off downstairs. The rooms although beautifully appointed, looked as old as the hills, felt as cold as the grave and had that faint musty smell of disuse!

The four of them were downstairs standing at the bar at six-forty-five. They ordered their drinks and took them to a small round table in the corner of the bar area and sat in the more comfortable chairs placed in perfect symmetry around it.

'It's a nice place,' said Grant to the others.

'Is it Elizabethan, do you think?'

'Some of it could be, if not all of it. Our room is.'

'I'm surprised it's so cheap!'

'It's not cheap, Rene, it's inexpensive.'

'Shut up, you pompous sod and drink your drink.'

'Wooo, it's a fight!'

'Shut up Cockroach, and stop mixing it.'

'Don't tell me to shut up, Pig, or you'll be having a sherry-rinse!'

The silly banter was interrupted by Mrs Maudley who suddenly appeared at the table.

'Dinner in five minutes, if that's fine with you?'

'Yes, that's ok with us. We're starving.'

'Well come on through, then.'

They followed her into the dining room; it was empty.

'Are we the only ones here?' asked Wendy seeing only one table prepared.

'Yes, out of season. We don't take more than four guests at the weekend. If you'd like to sit down, I'll bring your starter. I hope you like whitebait?'

She was off before anybody could answer but came back in no time with four medium-sized dinner plates overflowing with tiny fish, crispy lettuce and the rest of the trimmings. The starter on its own was enough for a meal, especially for the girls!

They ordered a bottle of white to help it down but she said she only had a medium dry Bergerac. They assured her it would be perfect and it certainly was good enough. She gave them a half hour to finish the first-course. At eight o'clock, Mr Maudley turned on the floodlights positioned directly against the front wall of the hotel. Their powerful beams shone halfway to Heaven. Mrs Maudley cleared the plates. The curtains had been deliberately left open. Mr Maudley entered the dining room two minutes before Mrs Maudley returned with a platter of seafood. There was enough to feed the Five Thousand. Rene was just finishing the dregs of her wine and was about to order a second bottle when she saw the effigy of Captain Boucher appear at the window straight across from where she and Wendy were sitting but didn't react immediately to what she was seeing.

The timing, the position of the Captain's appearance and the position of his face close to the window were perfect. He hung there momentarily and then slowly floated up past the window making dreadful moaning sounds. That was when Wendy saw him, and when it registered with Rene exactly what she was seeing they both, more or less at the same time, let out a piercing scream. The men leapt from their seats and yelled, 'What the hell was that for!?' Their screaming continued, as the ladies pointed at the window. It seemed to last forever. Rene's glass had flown out of her hand and shattered against the wall behind her. There was glass everywhere and their chairs had crashed to the floor. Wendy was white-faced and trembling. Steve passed Rene his napkin and told her bluntly to stop snivelling and pull herself together. She began to get angry. The men with their backs to the window hadn't a clue what was going on. Finally they looked where the two terrified ladies were pointing but it was too late! The terrifying corpse of Captain Boucher, magnificently under-lit by the floodlights, had vanished. It was at this point Mr Maudley stepped forward.

Mrs Maudley had left the room to stop herself from bursting out laughing and had got as far as the laundry before she had to let herself go! Mr Maudley had, with superhuman effort managed to control himself.

'Young ladies. I'm terribly sorry. I had no idea he would appear tonight. Let me get you a double brandy – on the house of course. Just to settle your nerves. I won't be a moment!'

He was away and back in no time. Grant was asking Wendy what had happened but she could only shake her head in disbelief and confusion. Rene was glaring at Steve. She'd already called him an S-H-I-T, which because she never used such a word, told him she was very angry. He was apologising by explaining she'd made him jump out of his sodding wits! Her face told him he wasn't getting off that easy.

'Please. Take these and I will explain.' He gave the brandy to the ladies and re-organised their chairs for them. 'Please sit down he won't harm you! I had no idea he would appear tonight. I think my wife has gone for a dustpan and brush. Do try to eat something while I explain to the gentlemen what you saw.'

They took their seats but didn't touch the food. The two men did.

'I think the young ladies saw the ghost of Captain Boucher. It gave me quite a shock when I first saw it, but he's never harmed anyone. Never! He's a pirate or a smuggler who was caught and hanged near here. He used the cellars and the secret passageways of the old Manor House to hide his contraband, or at least that's what the locals say. Perhaps that's why he keeps on coming back. But do believe me, he won't harm you!'

'Scaring people half to death is harming someone, I'd say,' snapped Grant.

'I did warn you, sir that the Manor is haunted. And I did think that was the reason for your visit. There are other ghosts here so if you are concerned for your wives' safety, I would suggest you leave! I will say this, they might frighten you but they will not harm you!'

It was then that Mrs Maudley returned with the dustpan and brush and a complimentary bottle of Moet. She left it unopened, sitting in its silver ice bucket on the table. As she turned to go, the sounds of rattling of chains and dreadful shrieks erupted from below their feet. 'He's got into the cellars. I will go and sort it out. He's frightened of me!'

The girls were sitting bolt upright and staring at each other when Mr Maudley hurried from the dining room with his crucifix held high and muttering a prayer just to lay it on a bit. He went to their private sitting room, had a chuckle, put his feet up for ten minutes then he switched off the machine. He returned to the dining room and apologised for the amount of time it had taken to get rid of Captain Boucher. He then said, 'If you are staying tonight, it might be a good idea to lock the doors to your rooms. Just in case he comes back. I will keep the bar open until eleven-thirty. After that you must serve yourselves. There's a pad and pen to mark down what you have at the side of the till. Bon appetite!'

He walked straight-backed, to the bar and had a cup of tea. Mrs Maudley joined him a few minutes later. She also had a cup of tea.

There wasn't much banter during the meal. There were however dozens of reasons provided by Grant and Steve to explain why there were no such things as ghosts and what the girls saw was a trick of the light, or a reflection of the swaying bushes at the side of the window. None of them, as far as the girls were concerned, were worth listening to, never mind considering. We saw it, you didn't! Was all they got in reply. Steve's suggestion that it was alcohol-induced didn't go down well. He was told where to go and which bus to catch! At least the conversation got the girls over their initial shock and they were eating now. They didn't even listen when their husbands started on about the din from the cellar.

'Who's having a nightcap then? We could all have a glass of rum or a large brandy. Duty paid of course,' he grinned. 'Come on.'

He stood, the others followed suit and they all went into the bar.

'I hope you enjoyed your meal after all that nonsense with Captain Boucher,' said Mr Maudley.

'It was delicious,' replied Rene.

'Good, good.'

'It really was. Your wife is a fabulous cook, Mr Maudley.'

'Thank you, and yes, she certainly is. Now, what can I get you all?'

They all had double brandies and took their time over them. Then they went up to their rooms when Mr Maudley closed the bar.

They were in bed by midnight and half asleep when Mr Maudley pulled the cord for the invisible ghost to cross their bedroom floors. Grant heard it first. It was a bit louder in the still of the night than Mr Maudley had intended.

'Can you hear that?' he whispered.

'What?' whispered Cockroach.

'That, there's somebody in the damned room. Can't you hear it?'

The whisper had become a hiss. He switched the bedside light on as the invisible ghost passed the middle of the room and walked on towards the bedroom wall.

Grant, with his head swivelling left to right, said, 'There's nothing here!'

'I can hear it,' hissed Wendy looking everywhere. 'It's walking towards the wall over there!'

Grant jumped out of bed, ran to the centre light switch by the door and turned it on. As far as he was concerned whatever, or whoever it was, had just walked through the wall. This was confirmed by a loud scream and a loud knocking on their door.

'Are you all right in there?' called Mr Maudley.

'Is there anything wrong?' shouted Mrs Maudley.

Their timing was perfect. Steve opened the door as Grant opened his.

'There was somebody in our room!'

'It's in here!' shouted Steve, 'It's just walked through the wardrobe. It must still be in there.'

Mr Maudley looked at his wife, she looked at him and then they both nodded their heads.

'It must be Mad Harry; he died in number twelve and thirteen.'

'Who the hell's Mad Harry and how the hell could he die in two places at once, for God's sake?'

'Please Mr Carlisle, pull yourself together. He's perfectly harmless. I'm beginning to wonder why you came on this weekend break at all!'

'I'm not apart, Mr Maudley and the truth is, I never thought for a minute your Hotel would be haunted!'

'Well, there's a thing!' snapped Mrs Maudley, crossly. They were standing in front of the wardrobe by this time and ready to open it. Rene, who was still in bed, had the duvet tight round her face with her eyes peering over the edge; ready if need be, to pull it as fast as she could over her head.

Mr Maudley yanked both wardrobe doors open in one theatrical movement and stood back. Grant peered into the wardrobe from six feet away and said nothing. The wardrobe contained nothing but their clothes. 'You see! Nothing. I told you he wouldn't harm you. And you asked how he died in both rooms. I will tell you. Poor Mad Old-Harry committed suicide by running head first into that wall over there. They said at the time he was trying to knock his head off to get rid of the demons inside. These walls are lath and plaster as they were then. Unfortunately, as he crashed into the wall instead of coming up hard against a brick wall, as he no doubt intended, he went halfway through the wall and he impaled himself on a rather strong, sharp lath. They found him there a week later. That is how he died in both rooms, Mr Carlisle!'

Grant and Steve stood and looked at Mr Maudley as if they thought he was Mad Harry; Rene had her head under the duvet; Wendy was holding on tight to Grant's arm and Mrs Maudley was nodding her head and saying, 'That's the truth, indeed it is!'

'Now might I suggest we all go back to our beds? If you need to know more, I'm sure it will wait until morning. Goodnight all,' said Mr Maudley.

'Goodnight,' said Mrs Maudley then they went back downstairs. The guests, after reassuring each other, returned to their beds.

After a full English breakfast the four were persuaded by Mr Maudley to take a stroll down to the beach, and if they decided to go by way of Cliff Road to keep away from the cliff edge.

'It isn't safe, near the edge. There's a very deep drop there and a great deal of erosion along this part of the coast, which the government, I'm afraid, chooses to ignore!'

They went via Cliff Road. The drop to the beach from one place along the road, had to be at least fifty meters down and in places the road was less than two meters from the cliff edge. Rene, who was terrified of heights, refused point blank to go anywhere near the left-hand side of the road, never mind, look over the edge of the cliff like Steve was doing. She told him, 'If you don't get back over that stupid, useless barbed wire fence, NOW, I'm going home!'

Steve kicked a stone over the edge and watched it go then he turned his back on the view and went over to Rene. She wasn't hysterical, but she was pretty close. They heard a slight rumbling sound then the crashing of rocks and watched in disbelief as a piece of the cliff edge collapsed. It was three metres long and a metre wide and it was where Steve had just been standing. Rene screamed and grabbed hold of Steve as if she thought he would be sucked out of her hands and over the edge, then still holding him, she burst into tears. He held her now and showed his love without hurting her too much. Grant was as cross as hell, couldn't believe anyone who was right in the head, would suggest a route like this, fog or no fog. He was going to have a word with Mr Maudley when they got back and a word with Steve for acting like a moron!

He didn't because they had drinks in the garden and Mr Maudley was nowhere to be found. He didn't have a go at Steve because he hadn't stopped apologising all the way back to Maudley Manor.

'I think he's raking up the leaves. The wind blows them everywhere. Or perhaps he's gone for Bouncing-Billy so he can use the Rotavator on that bare patch over there.'

She pointed to where the swing used to be, then smiling; Mrs Maudley went off with their order for drinks.

The spectre of the well appeared as Mr Maudley turned the far-corner of the Manor. He was being led by a noisy, self-willed Rotavator. It didn't help his control as he raised one hand to wave to the group sitting on the bench facing the well. He had to grab it quickly or it would have pulled him over. Rene's empty glass had already shot over her shoulder and the bench had gone over backwards as she leaped up.

'Did you see that horrible thing?'

'Where?' one of them shouted.

'There! There! Under those bloody trees!'

She'd completely lost it. She was pointing at the trees and heading for the Hotel entrance when at the same time there was an almighty bang and the spectre exploded. Bits of latex-covered muslin flew everywhere. The moans and groans from the well went off the scale. They had to clap their hands over their ears it was so loud. The din easily drowned-out the phut, phut, phut, from Bouncing-Billy's exhaust. Grant, hands over ears ran across to the trees and saw the fake spectre scattered far and wide. When he turned back, there was no sign of Mr Maudley, or Mrs Maudley. They were having hysterics in the cellar, where he was manually turning off the compressor because unfortunately, the delay-timer upstairs had blown!

'Mu... Must...Must, have been, have been.' He burst out laughing again.

She was just as bad. 'Di... Did you see their fa...?' She couldn't spit it out either.

Mr Maudley removed his glasses, wiped his eyes and controlled himself. 'I did. It must have been...' He burst out laughing. 'It must have been the back-blast from the dummy!' He could still barely spit it out.

Mrs Maudley suddenly stopped laughing and became very serious.

'They are bound to put two and two together, Archibald. They'll know we tricked them.'

'Does it matter, Gwendolyn Dear? I haven't enjoyed myself so much since last year, and at least some of them worked very well, I think? And I haven't seen you laugh so much in years!' He gave his wife a kiss on the cheek. Her cheeks were cold as ice. She gave him a hug.

'Come on Dear let's go upstairs where it's warm and face the music.'

'I'll have to remodel the spectre for next year My Dear. Can't think there'll be much left of it,' he giggled!

There was some music to face and it was all cacophonous, as long as a symphony at the Albert Hall and twice as loud. Grant, demanding a refund, and being politely refused one, left the hotel in a foul mood. His parting words were, 'You will be hearing from our solicitors!'

Mr Maudley replied, 'I very much doubt it, young man.'

Then Mr and Mrs Maudley, both with a big smile on their faces, waved them off. The departing foursome didn't wave back although they'd got what they'd paid for! Well at least in the Maudley's eyes they most certainly had.

'Don't go on the coast road into the village!' demanded Rene. 'I'll be sick if you do.'

'I'm going into the town for a good-old pint of bitter,' grunted Grant selfishly. 'And this is the quickest way. So shut your eyes and pretend you're somewhere else!'

'Stop the car. I'm getting out. I'll find my own way there!'

Grant took no notice.

'STOP THE CAR, NOW! Or I swear I will strangle you!' Rene removed her scarf and was about to throw it round Grant's neck when they caught sight of the sea. Rene was near to passing out.

Steve shouted, 'DO AS SHE SAYS, Grant. You know she's terrified of heights. Now stop the BLOODY car!'

'The brakes won't work!' yelled Grant!

Steve leaned across and yanked the wheel, hard over to one side. The car came to rest in the middle of the field on the right of the road, well away from the cliff edge. Rene almost fell out of the door. She staggered into the bushes at the side of the field and threw-up.

Steve jumped out and dashed to help his wife. He'd seen Grant press the brakes and they'd worked perfectly.

'Grant, you sick bastard,' snarled Steve over his shoulder as he ran to the bushes. 'Come on treasure, we'll walk down to the town.' He carefully dabbed her mouth.

'Not on that road, no way!'

'No Love, we'll follow the bridle path over there.' He pointed to a path that ran parallel to a long line of bushes which were well away from the cliff edge. 'It's only half a mile to the town.'

'I was only joking. It's supposed to be a scary weekend isn't it?'

Steve told him to clear off. Grant reversed the car out of the field and returned the way they'd come. Not because he wanted to, no, Wendy had given him an absolute roasting for playing such a sicko's trick.

The foursome met at the pub within minutes of each other.

'Look, I'm sorry; I didn't mean to terrify you. It was supposed to be a joke. Let me get them in and I'll say sorry again when we get inside.'

None of them noticed the sign hanging over the open door.

'What will it be then?' asked the red-faced landlord. Everybody in the pub had the same ruddy outdoor complexion.

'Two pints of Mad Old Harr…' Grant wasn't allowed to finish.

'That ain't a beer Sir; it's the name of the pub,' said the landlord grinning widely.

Grant, slightly flummoxed, re-ordered. 'Two pints of bitter then, and two gins and bitter lemons, please!

'Coming up. Do you want ice in your drinks, ladies?' asked the landlord filling two pint glasses at once. The ladies declined. He served the beer first and to Grant it looked perfect.

'Is this Mad Old Harry anything to do with the Mad Old Harry up at the Guest House?' asked Steve, licking the froth off his lips.

'Aye, he's the same one,' replied the landlord with his back to them.

'Is this a haunted pub, then?'

'Aye, it is.'

Steve smirked and Grant nearly spit out his beer.

'There's Captain Boucher, he comes and visits us now and again. There's the headless spectre, he lives down the well at the back. It's dried up now lucky for him, 'eh lads?'

The locals burst out laughing.

'There's the blood stain that won't wash off, and of course Mad Old Harry walks the bedrooms some nights and then there's the ghost who lives in yond mirror.'

The landlord nodded to the far right of the room. 'That's about it, ain't it lads? I reckon.'

'Aye,' they chorused. 'That's it.'

'That's a strange coincidence,' said Wendy sarcastically. 'They're exactly the same spooks they had up at the Manor.'

'I don't know why you should know ought about the manor, you ain't from round here, but it ain't no coincidence, young Madam!' replied the landlord not liking her tone. He turned with their drinks and stood them on the bar.

'They all came down here when the Manor burned down. They'd nowhere else to go. The place was completely gutted. Only the old gates are left, and they've all about had it.'

'Burned down, you say! Where then are Mr and Mrs Maudley this afternoon?' asked Rene, determined not to smirk.

'Where they are every afternoon, young lady! They're over there, have been for the last fifty or sixty years to my knowledge.' The landlord pointed towards the door. 'They've been there ever since the fire.'

The foursome turned and glanced through the open door.

'But that's a cemetery,' said Grant and burst out laughing.

'Aye that's very observant of you lad, it is a cemetery! Mind you I don't know what you find so funny! Where do you expect dead folk to be buried, Tesco's car park?' The regulars all laughed at that. 'There were no Tesco's in them days, were there lads?'

'Nay, not round here there wasn't!'

Richard Lee Wilson 2003

The Inheritance

It all began on Monday, March the third. I say it all began on the third because that's when the letter came. It had snowed during the night; not the huge flakes of snow which disappear at the first rise in temperature, but the fine powdery stuff that lies on every surface like icing sugar and seems to hang about for days. I threw my housecoat round my shoulders and went to get the milk off the step. The postman was coming up the path waving a big brown envelope.

'This won't go through your letterbox, lady.' He was right it wouldn't. I waited on the step, icy cold milk bottle in one hand icy cold door handle in the other. 'Nasty stuff this.' He handed me the envelope. 'It will still be here in a month.'

'True,' I replied letting go of the door handle and taking the envelope. 'See you.'

'Yes. See you,' I replied and went inside. I pushed the door shut with my foot and put the bottle of milk in the fridge, then I looked at the envelope. It was from a firm of solicitors I'd never heard of so I put it on the worktop. Coffee first, letter second. I half-filled the kettle and switched it on.

I sat at the worktop and looked again at the envelope. My name and address were beautifully handwritten in a delicate forward-sloping script. It was a joy to see such writing. Everything nowadays was either electronic or scribbled. I turned the envelope over. The solicitor's address on the reverse was in the same delicate hand. The kettle boiled so I put the envelope down and made my coffee. I couldn't think why a solicitor would want to get in touch with me. This house was leased annually and I had always paid in advance. None of my relatives had died recently or at least not to my knowledge.

I slit the envelope with a Kitchen Devil being careful not to spoil the writing. Silly really but I'm like that. Great Aunt Blanche had left me a house in Mulham –on-the-Hill. I didn't have a Great Aunt Blanche and I'd no idea where Mulham-on-the-Hill was. Obviously somebody had made a mistake. The house and gardens, according to Mr Shawcross (the senior partner) were in poor condition and would need much restoration. This being due to the fact that Miss Blanche Agatha Mulberry had spent most of her life overseas. There were a number of other things mentioned but the one that made me smile was item seven that stated: 'The east wing of the aforementioned property is haunted and must be left uninhabited and completely undisturbed. If item seven of the bundle is unacceptable to the above mentioned Miss Lydia Moran, the property will be sold at auction and the proceeds distributed equally and without preference to Mulham-on-the-Marsh Donkey Sanctuary and Mulham-on-the-Marsh Cats' Home.'

I decided to give mother a ring then I'd ring Mr Shawcross and give him the bad news. Shame really, I thought to myself. Must be a big house if it's got a wing or two.

Mother had never heard of a Great Aunt whatever or wherever it was on the hill. She swore blind she'd been listening to me but she had to dash because she'd a ten o'clock appointment and her hair had suddenly decided it was going to stick out sideways and upwards. She'd need at least an hour to sort it but why not ring Uncle Alistair – he knew all about lineage and things ancestral. 'He's not your real uncle and I haven't seen him in ages but you know who I mean, Liddy. His number should be somewhere in the book.'

I said, 'I do know who you mean Mother, and I'd give him a try.' Then I said, 'bye' to an already dead phone. I trawled through mother's old phonebook-come-diary and after finding it scrawled on the back of the book, I rang Uncle Alistair. I told him who I was and about the solicitor's letter.

Alistair remembered me well and he knew all about Great Aunt Blanche. He congratulated me on my windfall before saying, 'So long as it's not the old pile at Mulham!' I told him it was that old pile.

He laughed and said, 'Poisoned chalice, Liddy. You might get a few pounds for the land. Bit of a ruin. Indeed quite a lot of a ruin. She was my mother's eldest sister. But I didn't see much of her, all a bit before my time Liddy! Reputedly terribly-wilful. Considered to be a bit of a girl-girl in those days. If you know what I mean. Totally unwarranted. Married a German you know. Said he was a Count. Count Von Schloss or something. Silly arse wore a monocle and strutted about like a Peacock. Of course the only claim he had to being a Count was he could count other people's money. Took her for a small fortune. Absolute waster. Came from somewhere in France or Poland it turned out. Can't say what happened to him. Disappeared in mysterious circumstances or so I heard. Great Aunt Blanche probably slit the thieving bugger's throat or pushed him overboard while they were on one of their many cruises. Actually Liddy, she wasn't related to you at all, well not a blood relative if you know what I mean. Died three or four years ago. Could be six. Of course I went to the funeral.

Sad affair. Not a lot there. Well must dash going-to a séance at nine. Real fun! Pop round to Mulham-on-the-Hill at some stage and I'll meet you there if you like. Haven't seen you or that gorgeous mother of yours for ages. Sorry about your father, Liddy. Did my best to get back. Got stuck with a foul ailment in a Bombay hospital en route from Nagpur.'

I thanked him for the sentiment and said I'd love to call round. Even though it's been years since I last saw him, I liked Uncle Alistair very much. I put the phone down. I'd ring Mr Shawcross about the 'old pile' during my lunch hour. There was another light fall of snow as I ran for my bus. I hated the horrible stuff. Roll on summer, I muttered between shivers.

At the third attempt I got through to a Mrs Wainright and was given an appointment to see Mr Shawcross on Wednesday the fifth at three-thirty. Even though Uncle Alistair had given me some information about the condition of the house I had no idea what to expect but I was still quite excited about it and could hardly wait for Wednesday. Mother couldn't come with me because she had a prior engagement at Marco's in the High Street! The fitting couldn't be postponed because it was the last one and the outfit had already taken forever and a day! I dreaded to think what this latest effort would look like. I thanked her anyway. She said it was 'nothing darling'. And that's exactly what it was, nothing! So no change there.

After going through the formalities of identification Mr Shawcross read out the details of the Will. I was peered at every so often by him as if he was making sure I was still there or to check that I understood the first party of the second party etc. I didn't but he couldn't have known from my expression.

The house was built in eighteen-sixty. It had ten rooms and stood in one-point-three acres of ornamental gardens. The property was freehold and it was within six miles of the M1. The house had all the usual amenities. I wondered if he meant water and electricity.

I was in there less than an hour at a cost of one-hundred-and-forty-five pounds. The transfer would cost me all my savings and two-hundred pounds, which I borrowed from my half-interested mother. She was not short of money – time to bother with me is what she was short of! Had I asked for two-thousand it would have been handed over to me on our way to her front door.

I drove down to Mulham-on-the-Hill leaving home at four on the Friday. I'd packed everything I thought I might need in two collapsible boxes that I stowed on the back seat of my Escort estate car. There were piles of room in the back if I decided to sleep in the car. It was quiet on the roads and the countryside was pretty but by the time I found the house it was well dark, and it was eerie, and it was cold, bitter cold. I half-expected the screech of an owl or the howl of a wolf. If there'd been a gate at the bottom of the drive it was gone. I turned in. I heard and felt the tyres crunch and crack like gun shots as I bounced over dead branches littering the drive. I held my breath hoping against hope that I wouldn't get a puncture and I wouldn't see a ghost!

I got out of the car and left the headlights on so I kept close to it. Ivy clung like ragged blankets to the front of the house and most of the trees closest to it. The uncovered windows stared back at me with a loneliness I found hard to shake off. There were rustlings and night noises. I shone my torch all over the garden to see where they came from but it was a waste of time. I scrapped the sleeping in the car idea as totally illogical and drove back to the village. The need perhaps of going to the toilet in the middle of the night swung it and the haunted bit had got inside my head. I don't think I'm a coward but to sleep on my own in the car up there I decided would have been a pretty stupid thing to do – my sleeping bag was well past its best too.

I was given directions to the Cow and Calf from the landlord of the Old New Inn which didn't do bed and breakfast. I had half a lager with blackcurrant as a thank you and left. I was made welcome at the Cow and Calf and offered a well-above average single room with en-suite facilities. I decided to have my evening meal there and finish my sandwiches tomorrow. I had homemade steak and ale pie with delicious creamy gravel-free gravy and two veg (both of which were not raw). The meal would have shamed grandma let alone mother whose responsibility for feeding her one-and-only brat had been delegated to Captain Bird's Eye or the ever-changing staff at Mac Donald's. I was in my room by ten-thirty and asleep before I knew it. Breakfast was as good as supper and the pot of tea for one was a far-distant cousin to those things with string on, at fifty pence per box. There was enough in the pot for three cups and I sat for a while over the last one before settling up and going back to Mulham-on-the-Hill.

I drove past the Donkey Sanctuary on the way back and had a slight twinge of conscience. The farm looked as if a cash injection wouldn't do it any harm and I felt for a moment as I saw some of the residents standing forlornly by the barbed wire fence as though I was stealing food from them. When I stopped for a second at the bottom of the drive and saw the house in daylight, these slight pangs faded in a tick. I felt now like I'd relieved them of a dreadful burden! I drove slowly up the litter-strewn drive.

The house was a mess from its sagging roof to its wilderness of the so-called ornamental gardens. Whatever statues or ornaments had adorned this half-derelict pile had either crept away in disgust or had been stolen or smashed by vandals. I felt terribly sad. I didn't cry but I felt as if I should, not for me but for the terrible waste and neglect of it all. It must have been a beautiful house at one time. I got out of the car and as I shut the door I heard a hissing noise. I soon realised I hadn't been so lucky this time. Sticking into the side of the front tyre was a sharp piece of forked wood. I pulled it out and threw it as far as I could. The hiss got louder and the tyre was flat in seconds. Rubbing my elbow I told myself I'd see to it in a minute. First I'd have a walk round the outside of the house or at least as far as the evil-looking tangles of brambles would let me. I'd got my jeans on but the thorns on some of the dead ones looked lethal.

Every wall of the house was either covered in ivy or covered in moss. The roof at the back wasn't much better than that at the front. There were two wings to the house; the east wing was in much better condition than the west wing, perhaps that's because the east wing was only two floors. The west wing (I was only working from the number of windows) was three floors high. The top floor looked low because the windows extended up from the roof. The roof slates over the west wing were in a very poor state. Fifty percent of them looked to be cracked or had slipped. The only person I knew who could give me some advice on the cost of repairing the building was on holiday in Egypt. A sort of coal to Newcastle holiday really. Harry worked at the Foulton Museum of Antiquities. He lived and breathed anything old but he also dealt in property. He'd a few houses and flats that he let to students and he'd done very well out of it. I know he fancied me and I sort of fancied him but that's as close as it got. He was a scholar-come-property tycoon and I taught geography to Neanderthals. We were poles apart and like I said, he was in Egypt for another week as far as I remembered. I decided to go home and see him when he came back. Another week or so wouldn't make a difference to the state of the house.

I went back to my car and got out the spare wheel. It was flat and I was as cross as hell. I'd told Brian to see to it when he tested the car; he'd either forgotten or there was a fault with it. I hadn't checked the mileage from Mulham-on-the-Marsh to the house but it had to be more than three miles and I didn't fancy carrying or rolling a wheel back there. It was then that Uncle Alistair came round the corner of the house and shouted hello. I nearly jumped over the car and I very nearly stooped to a string of Anglo Saxon expletives!

I was speechless for a moment. 'You scared me half to death. You are Uncle Alistair?'

'Of course! Didn't you recognise me?'

'Well yes, but not straight away. I'd no idea you were here. It was the shock of suddenly seeing you.'

It was a poor excuse but I couldn't have said you look like a very old man! I wondered what I looked like to him.

'Sorry Liddy. I thought you'd seen me. You appeared to be looking my way and you haven't changed much, I recognised you immediately.' I felt awful.

'Well, what do you think of it then? Pretty well neglected don't you think?'

'Pretty well,' I replied trying to smile and control my racing heart beat at the same time.

'Have you had a look inside?'

'No not yet. I didn't think the door would open. It's half-covered in weeds and stuff.' I pointed to the door.

'The door opens quite easily and it's a lot better inside. Why not go in and have a look?'

'I've got a puncture and the spare wheel's flat. I need to see to that.'

'Oh dear. But you can sort that out later. There's a garage at Mulham-on-the-Marsh. You can ring them on your mobile.'

'I didn't bring it. It's out of credit.'

'That's awkward.' Uncle Alistair looked a little confused. In fact he looked a lot confused.

'Couldn't you give me a lift in your car? It's not far so it won't take long!'

'I don't have a car Liddy, but you can use my phone.'

'You've got a mobile?'

'No, I haven't a mobile silly girl. You can use the house phone!'

'There's a phone in there?'

'Of course there's a phone in there. I live here. In the east wing!'

He smiled and pointed. I didn't remember Uncle Alistair ever smiling like that!

Richard Lee Wilson 2006

The rainbow Twins

The old man with the badly knotted tie and stained waistcoat sat alone on the park bench. He always picked the same bench, his favourite. He used to sit on this bench every Saturday morning with Marie. He'd forgotten his hat for some reason and now as the wind picked up it wafted what bit of hair he had up and down like tufts of very fine dry grass. He didn't seem too bothered. The lonely old man was only watching the world go by. His Saturday visits to the park had become a ritual since Marie died. It was at least five years ago but coming to the park brought her closer to him. He never told anyone how lonely he felt or how much he missed her but God he did miss her. In their later years, they always came to the park on a Saturday mornings. They'd leave the car at home and catch the ten o'clock bus to the stop at the bottom of the park. Then they'd walk up the middle avenue loving old hands clasped together like they were a couple of young teenagers. They always made for this bench, they liked to sit here for a while opposite the pond to feed the ducks and watch the kids running round.

They hadn't had kids of their own; they'd tried often enough. According to the specialist they'd consulted and after numerous invasive examinations he'd told them it would be impossible for Mrs Porter to conceive. Mr Porter was working fine. The doctor smiled briefly, he was doing his best to lighten the blow, but the blow fell. He did explain what it was but neither of them could take it in. Something to do with the lining of the womb was all that registered. The shock of the revelation numbed her; it was as if he'd smacked her across the mouth. The old man remembered the look on his wife's face as her hands flew to her sweet little mouth to stop the cry of anguish. The effort was a waste of time; the sobs were already free. He remembered how she looked at him, a look of fear and indecision. She had desperately searched his face for reassurance. It was as if she felt inadequate. It was as if she expected him to walk out of the clinic and her life. She'd no need to worry not for one second. Even though he was deeply hurt, he held on to her so long and crushed her body into his. All the while his eyes had promised his love and protection. The specialist had suggested they think about adoption in the future. Don't concern yourselves now but perhaps in the future. They never did, it wasn't what they wanted, it wouldn't have been right.

There were other places that brought her memory closer but most of them had shut down or had been demolished and the site put to better use. There was Hobbies where she used to get her paints. Hobbies was an Oxfam shop now or was it Help the aged? He couldn't remember. Sometimes just before he fell asleep he could smell the odour of linseed oil. It used to be everywhere; she seemed to carry the smell round with her as she collected bits of twigs and clusters of leaves from the garden for her latest effort as she called them. She'd rummage in his workshop to borrow chisels or his smoothing plane. There were times often when she'd steal bits of wood shavings as if they were gold snow flakes.

'I desperately need all these things,' she used to say when he grabbed her coming out with a handful. She'd have red paint on her lovely little chin. She'd have dark blue on the side of her beautiful smiling face, that same violet blue of her eyes. She did get herself into an awful mess sometimes! The lonely old man smiled at the thought of the forfeits she volunteered to pay and the memory lay soft on his lips. Then he thought of the last five years without Marie. The old man slowly shook his head in disbelief

The searing pain he'd been getting recently across his chest came suddenly and without warning. The pain made the old man gasp for breath as a fierce shudder racked every part of his fragile old frame. The pain was a lot worse than the last time it hit him, even though the weather was a lot milder than a fortnight ago. He took one of the pink tablets and forced it with trebling fingers under his tongue. He did it exactly as the doctor told him he must. Odd really thought the old man as the pain lessened and then went completely, I thought I'd run out of the pink ones. Memory going like the rest of me, he muttered to himself.

It was nice in the park even though a gang of teenagers playing football further down the avenue were making a racket. He looked up the tree lined avenue which meandered into the distance and sighed with some pleasure. The warm gentle breeze danced slowly through the sycamores and caused little sparkles of leaf-shimmer when the clusters of leaves swayed out of the shadow and in to the sunlight. The gentle breeze made each tree sound to sigh with pleasure and to tremble with delight as it passed from tree to tree. It looked to the old man as he glanced up like the breeze was stealing intimate caresses in its journey up and down the avenue.

The tall blond haired man with the daft Labrador dog said hello as he passed but the old man didn't acknowledge him. The old man's eyes were closed. He was far away under some other trees by the river. He was with Marie. She was lying in his strong arms with her firm breasts pressed hard against his chest.

'Come and ravish me,' she used to say with a face flushed full of mischief and excitement. Then she'd strip naked throw her panties at him and run unashamedly into the river splashing like a child and daring her big strong man to follow her in. Her big strong man never disappointed her.

The lonely old man was brought back to the present and some confusion by a green tennis ball. The ball had bounced off the front curve of the bench, rolled into and out of the old man's lap. The ball finally finished up between the back two lathes of the bench. It had been thrown by a father to his five year old butter-fingered daughter in ragged play jeans, who had, after a mad rubber-legged dash across the avenue retrieved it before the old man was fully aware of what had woken him. She was halfway back to her daddy and squealing 'got it daddy' while the old man's fingers were still fumbling to find the ball. Her daddy looked at his child as if he'd found the Holy Grail!

The old man rubbed his eyes but felt little sensation. He wondered what time it was and if the chap with the yellow Labrador had come past yet. He looked up the avenue and he saw the man with the dog.

'Must be nearing eleven o'clock,' he muttered. 'Time for a cup of tea and a cake up at the refreshment rooms,' as Marie called the café. She loved to go up there and yap with the students. Her arms went everywhere and she sketched things on the white paper tablecloths. 'I suppose they'd call it graffiti nowadays.' The breeze took the quietly mumbled words off down the avenue. It didn't take them very far, they were barely audible when they were first uttered. He used to watch her eating endless pieces of sticky-bread as she used to call it and drink endless cups of tea, but she never got fat. Nervous energy used to burn it off; well that's what the old man thought. He could picture her now, sitting there with her grey hair tied in a bun. All that stuff she used to go on about. Topic after topic. She'd resolutely stick to her guns and she would never raise her voice regardless of the provocation. What a treasure she was. A terrible sadness filled the old man's eyes as the memories of her lingered in his thoughts. The old man sighed and with the aid of his walking stick and patience, he got to his feet. He stood for a few moments to steady his legs before setting off for the café. Memory is a tainted gift he decided.

Slowly and with care he made his way up the avenue. He didn't want to risk falling again. He remembered what happened the last time he fell and that happened while he was at home, blooming hearth. He remembered he finished up coming out of hospital with a new hip. He doubted they'd fit him another, not at his age. Once you're over eighty they don't seem to bother with you. He decided to stay on the right hand side of the avenue, well out of the way of a bunch of hooligans making a nuisance of themselves with a football. They were supposed to be kicking it to each other but they didn't care where it went or how hard they kicked it. The biggest lad had already kicked it across the grass where a young couple were sitting. The ball had been passed to the lad but he didn't make any attempt to control it, he just kicked it as hard as he could. The thing had shot across the grass and knocked a bottle of orange juice all over a blanket the young couple had spread out on the ground. The chap who was six feet tall leapt off the blanket and told them that if they didn't clear off he'd come over there and give him a bloody good hiding. The chap was furious. The old man hadn't seen the carry-cot with the three month old baby in it sat at the far end of the blanket but he could hear it crying. He was sure the big chap was going to go over to them and he would have done but his wife restrained him saying, 'don't bother with them Mike, they're not worth the hassle.'

The old man turned away shaking his head and wondered why God had taken Marie first and not him. Probably because she'd make a good angel. As if God hadn't enough angels already? The old man wasn't smiling. The hooligans ran away down the avenue using bad language and still being stupid with the football.

The old man stopped for a breather, but instead of sitting down he just rested on his walking stick. Further down the avenue a couple of girls were walking towards him, they were twins and they were dressed exactly the same in old fashioned blazers and skirts but to the old man they looked as smart as he'd seen in ages. The thing that caught the old man's attention was the colour of their clothes. Their blazers and their skirts were the same colours as a rainbow. From the top going down the colours were shaded perfectly from red to purple. To the old man the girls looked marvellous and they were smiling at his as if they'd known him all his life. He wondered what was going on. Then the louts with the football came chasing back up!

The lad that had kicked the ball like a lunatic shouted some remark at the rainbow twins, fortunately the old man didn't hear exactly what he'd shouted or he might have attempted to thrash him with his stick. The next thing the lad did was to kick the ball at them. His friends thought this was hysterical. Then as the louts were jeering a couple of weird things happened! The ball hit the twin on the left at the side of her face and it hit her hard. But instead of the girl crying out in pain she smiled at the lout instead. The other weird thing that happened was, instead of the football bouncing off the girl's face and rolling down to the tennis courts behind her, the ball appeared to twist in mid-air and fall at the feet of the other twin who had already bent down to pick it up. She picked it up and smiling a beaming smile she passed it to her sister who smiling exactly the same tossed it gently to the lad who'd kicked it at her. It was already on its way to him when he snarled, 'give me my ball back you stuck up git!' The girl didn't stop smiling. Two men walking past did. They'd heard what the lad had called her, but before they could do anything about him, the lad had caught the ball. As soon as it was in his hands his body buckled and he staggered back as if the ball was made of lead. The next thing he did was stumble over the small railings and into the duck pond. He was still trying to let go of the football when he went under the water.

A small group had gathered by this time, and it was their turn to laugh, but he seemed to stay under for quite a while. A middle aged woman started to panic. She rushed to the edge of the pond and shouted. 'Can't one of you men get him out, he's drowning!'

Some of the others joined in. A tall man whipped his coat off and threw it on the ground. Then just as fast he kicked his shoes off. He was just going to jump in when the lad, spluttering and spitting filthy water out of his mouth suddenly reappeared. Water poured off him and he was covered in black slime. He grabbed for the side of the pond and tried to clamber out but he couldn't get a grip on the smooth stones lining the pond; he was swearing his head off when he slipped back in.

His mates didn't offer to help him because they were all too busy taking the mickey! 'First bath this month Dogga.'

After watching him struggle to get out, one of the twins went to give him a hand, the rest of the crowd had moved away because of the bad language. They'd left him to his just deserts as one of them said.

Another one of his mates said, 'Let the girlies help you Dogga.' The other twin went over and between them the pulled him out. The filthy mud clung to him like a thick coat of stinking black paint and he was raving. He roughly pushed the twins out of his way and threatened to kick the crap out of his mates if they didn't find something to get this f.....g shit off him. The old man heard none of this. He was walking slowly up the sun-dappled avenue with the twins. Mally, the smallest of the gang had seen how the twins had caught up with the old man and he'd seen what happened with the football and he knew it was impossible! The rest of them hadn't seen the twins disappear into sparkling golden dust and then reappear; they were running round trying to find something to get the slime off Dogga and to find a long stick to fish the ball out of the pond.

The old man was astonished by the kindness of the twins. He couldn't understand why they were bothering with him or why they should go to the trouble of walking up to the café with him. He didn't ask them, he was as pleased as Punch.

'Get the ball one of you. Come on you dick heads, I only got the thing yesterday. Get your fingers out or I'll throw the lot of you in the f.....g pond!'

'It's not in the pond, Dogga.'

'Course it's in the F.....g pond get it found or I'll have you!'

'It's not there Dogga, trust me?'

Eboe, the only black lad amongst them was looking out over the pond as if he expected the ball to suddenly shoot up in the air on the end of a magical fountain.

'Well? Can you see the f.....g thing?'

'I only see sadness and sorrow on the water, I see pain and hunger.' Eboe hung his head in mock dejection. 'I see nothing else.'

'You mad bastard!' Dogga laughed, but only for a second. 'I'm off home to get cleaned up. Are you coming?'

'Sure brother, like the end of the world is coming!'

'What are you gawking at Mally? You little turd, the ball's not up there, you stupid cluck.'

'I was eyeing them birds up, them dressed like fireworks. There's something weird about 'em!'

'There might be to you? It's probably because they've got knockers, no girl you've ever been with had knockers. Come on Oboe I stink, I'm off home.'

Mally was glad; he wanted to be well out of there. He was sure the girlies were witches. Bril' looking witches, but definitely witches. Mally didn't pay much attention to religious studies at school!

It was nice in the café. The old man and the rainbow twins sat at a table by the window which overlooked the tennis courts. The old man watched with some envy as the players leaped about the court. They appeared to have all the energy in the world. Marie used to play tennis and she used to bounce about as much as the ball but the old man never played, he often went with her to cheer her on but he preferred rugby. Now as he watched them he wished he'd played both.

'Sir, would you like your usual?'

'I'm sorry Alice, I was watching the tennis but yes please.'

Alice smiled and said, 'no matter. What would you two young ladies like?'

The twins ordered a bottle of water. Saying 'they were not hungry and that they didn't drink anything other than water.'

Five minutes later a toasted crumpet and a pot of tea for one was brought to the table, with it was a bottle of water and two glasses but the twins didn't drink any of the water, they did however pour it into the glasses. The old man watched them and watched them and wondered why on earth they should want to be in his company, but whenever he approached the subject they smiled, shook or nodded their heads then entirely changed the subject. The old man after a while didn't bother asking. It was relaxing for him and he did take delight in their presence, it made him feel twenty years younger and the pain hadn't returned. He touched the wooden table top and gave a little whistle. The two girls smiled sweetly.

When Dogga got home and after he'd cleaned himself up he decided to go back to the park and if the girls were around he'd chat 'em up. They were definitely worth a go at he sneered to himself in the mirror as he combed his soaking wet hair. He told Eboe who had tagged along with him and he told the television in particular that everything on it was crap and only fit for four year olds or morons. He shot the television with the remote control and threw the slender pistol on the settee.

'Come on Eboe, I'm off to find them two birds.'

Eboe followed him out of the house and up to the bus stop. They both had bikes but they didn't bother with them. They thought they'd outgrown their bikes.

Ten minutes later they were having a fag and posing against the ornate stone gateposts at the parks main entrance. They might just have carried it off if Dogga, after taking a good long pull at his cigarette hadn't nearly coughed his head off.

'Come on let's go and find 'em,' snapped Dogga, whose eyes were still watering like mad and who felt and looked stupid. They chased off up the avenue. Dogga flicked his cigarette into the flowerbeds by the fountain as they ran past.

'Can you see 'em anywhere?'

'I see only tribulations brother.'

'I'm not your freaking brother you daft bastard! Come on they're not round here, let's look up by the pond.'

Dogga strolled off looking all over for the twins. Eboe, acting the fool danced round him but only because he knew it got up Dogga's nose. Dogga ignored him, his mind was on other things and it had nothing to do with dancing. They reached the fork in the avenue. The road to the right led down to the tennis courts. They continued up the avenue which led to the café and the top entrance to the park.

'I can't see 'em anywhere!'

'They've departed for paradise man, right on the end of a rainbow,' chanted Eboe and spread his long arms to encompass the whole sky.

'So will you if you don't shut your grinning face?'

'They isn't here man," taunted Eboe. 'We might as well go back home.'

'I aren't going anywhere till we find 'em, so come on! We'll try up by the swings, they could be up there.' He didn't wait for an argument from Eboe because he knew he wouldn't get one. 'If they aren't there we'll get a beer in the café.'

'They won't sell beer to minors and that's us big man!'

'Then we'll have a freaking coke instead.'

'That's bad for our street cred boss!'

'Ef the street cred! I'm going for a coke!'

Ebo shrugged his shoulders like they weren't fastened to his body and slouched after his mate.

Dogga stopped dead; Ebo slammed into him and knocked him off balance by treading on the heel of his trainer just as Dogga said, 'They're in the café Ebo, look, both of 'em. And watch where you put your size elevens or my size tens will be wedged up your bullet hole. And why do you have to walk about like a freaking octopus? Aren't your freaking bones joined together? Get my trainer and watch where you're going!'

Eboe got the trainer. Dogga went down on one knee and slipped it back on.

'You ought to fasten them man, they could cause an accident!'

'Freaking hell! Are you my mother now? Shut it and come on!'

Dogga got a coke out of the machine and threw another to Eboe. Alice hurried past and asked them if they wanted anything else. Eboe replied no thanks Dogga grunted an indiscernible reply and swaggered across the packed café to where the old man and the twins were sitting.

'Hi you two, remember me?' he leered. He ignored the old man. The twins gave him the briefest smile and turned their backs to him. Eboe decided to play it safe, he took his can of coke outside this could be bad news.

'I'm talking to you!'

The rainbow twins paid no attention to him. Dogga took a swig of coke and pursing his lips he casually spat a stream of it at the head the nearest twin. Unfortunately for Dogga it appeared a gust of wind from somewhere diverted the spray into the face of the big guy sat at the next table. What seemed weird to Dogga in the short time he had before the man got hold of him by the scruff of the neck called him a dirty young bugger and threw him out of the café, was the amount of coke which drenched the guy. Dogga couldn't believe it. He'd only sprayed an eyeful; the guy looked to be drenched in it.

'Next time you try anything like that sonny, I'll knock your silly head off!'

Eboe saw Dogga stagger then roll down the steps and land hard at the bottom. 'Hey man, what happened in there?'

Dogga was raving. Eboe went to help him onto his feet.

Dogga didn't want his help. 'I don't want any effers help.' He snarled and pushed Ebo out of his way. 'I'm gonna have that bastard'

'Forget it man, he's a big mother, he could hurt you man.'

'Piss off, I'm going back in. Get away!' Dogga was losing it.

'Don't Dogga, he'll hurt you! Let's get away from here I don't like the vibes man. It's not right. This park's no good! I'm away from here, got a bad feeling man!'

Dogga told him to do what he effing liked. He wasn't going anywhere till he'd sorted the bastard who threw him down the steps. Eboe stayed.

'Them effing dips will be out of there soon with that old geezer. Nobody takes the piss out of me!' Dogga had lost it; there was no way he was going to walk away from there.

The big guy and his friends came out of the café, Dogga gave them the finger. The big man shook his head at the idiot. His friends took no notice of him. Dogga lit a cigarette and waited. They'd be out soon he told himself. He waited. He finished his cigarette and ground it into the tarmac.

'I'm going in Eboe, are you coming?'

'No man,' called Eboe who was dancing with the railings.

'I'm staying here with these skinny chicks,' Dogga shouted.

'You're mental!'

Dogga climbed the steps and went into the café. The place was empty. Angry as hell he turned to go thinking they all must have left by the emergency exit at the back. He kicked a chair and crashed his fist on a table top. 'Bastards!' he shouted at the top of his voice. 'You crafty bastards.'

There was the sound of a door closing somewhere. He ran to the service door leading into the kitchen, the door was open but there wasn't a soul in there. Then from behind him he heard the noise of a chair leg scraping across the floor. The sudden noise made him jump.

He spun round fists balled and shouted again. 'Who's in there?'

He darted back into the café, it was empty. 'Ef this, I'm out of here.'

His voice echoed through the empty rooms. He went to the main door, it was locked. He felt a chill on his back. He shivered as he yanked at the door handle. It snapped off and fell to the floor. He could see Eboe dancing with the railings and shouted him to come and open the effing door.

'It's freezing in here you crazy bastard. Come and open the door!'

He punched his balled fist on the glass as the place got colder and colder. He couldn't stop shivering.

'Eboe, are you effing deaf, it's freezing in here get this effing door open.'

'He can't hear you,' whispered a voice that seemed to come from every part of the room. 'No one can hear you.'

Dogga spun left to right, right to left like a clockwork monkey. The hairs on the back of his neck stood out like pig bristles as a dread chill numbed his body.

'Come out here and you'll hear me,' snarled Dogga ready to give whoever was in the cafe a good kicking. 'Come on, I'll have you, you bastard!'

'I don't think so!' whispered the voice, which seemed to echo from across the café and come from inside his head at the same time.

The café began to darken. Then it went as black as night, now he couldn't see a thing. Dogga kicked the door as hard as he could but it didn't budge. He tried to smash the glass but his kicks didn't even crack it. The glass was stronger than tool-steel.

'Eboe!' He shouted again and again at the top of his voice when something icy cold brushed against his face and the voice said, 'He can't help you, he can't hear you, and he's gone.'

He collapsed when its icy fingers caressed his throat and lingered there, and the thing's fetid breath made him vomit.

'Eboe's gone,' hissed the voice screaming for him is a waste of breath. He twitched in terror where he lay. His hands covered his face as he slobbered for Eboe.

'Perhaps you won't be so clever after this? If there is an after this for you boy?'

'What's wrong with you man?' asked Eboe shaking Dogga like mad.

'He's had some sort of fit,' replied the waitress. 'He started swearing and carrying on something awful. He tried to break the door down didn't he Shirley?'

The other woman nodded. 'It's a wonder he didn't smash the glass, kicking at it like he did. Do you think we ought to call the police or an ambulance? Look out he's trying to get up.'

Eboe said there was no need he'd be okay soon man. The waitress didn't like being called a man. 'Well if he starts again I will have to call the police, he could have hurt somebody?'

Dogga shaking his head and muttering got to his feet.

'Man you look like shit!'

'What's happening? Where's that thing?'

'Cool it man, there isn't no that thing. You must have drunk some of that pond water, it must have done something to you.'

Dogga looked round trying to take it all in. The café was full of people; he couldn't understand what was happening. Then his brain started to function. He began to realise where he was and suddenly it clicked.

'Get out of here!' He yelled and shot past Eboe and tore off down the avenue like somebody demented. He kept glancing over his shoulder to see if the thing in the café was coming after him, and it didn't slow him down! Eboe didn't catch up with him till he reached the park gates. Dogga was bent double he could hardly breathe, but he told Eboe to mind his own effing when Eboe asked what had happened in the café.

The old man drank his third cup of tea, it was a bit weak but the third one always was. The twins hadn't drunk or eaten anything and the old man had noticed. He also noticed that they kept looking at their wrist watches. The old man asked them if they had somewhere else to go and if so he had no objections to their going because he would be going very soon? They answered with gentle smiles saying the time wasn't quite right at the moment. He'd never seen smiles like them. He had never felt as relaxed for a long time. He thought of Marie. The twins looked at him and smiled and looked again at the time. There was a commotion on the tennis courts. One of the players had suffered a massive heart attack and collapsed; the waitress said there was an ambulance on the way. The twins stood up.

'We must go now Edward it's time. Marie is very happy and she's looking forward to the day you join her so please don't worry about her.'

They smiled their beautiful smile. We must go now we are wanted immediately on the tennis court. Goodbye Edward we will see you again. There was a golden shimmer of what could only be angel dust and the rainbow twins were on the tennis court. They were smiling and holding the hands of a pale faced man who was looking down on himself.

Richard Lee Wilson. 14 4 05

The Rookery

The wings of the Phoenix weren't right; they were too rigid and lifeless. When April looked at it from the left and slightly below the level plane she decided it looked contrived.

'Perhaps I ought to leave you alone and concentrate on the enchanted forest?' It didn't answer.

She turned her attention to the work on the easel. The forest looked like it had been hit by lightning! She considered the perspective and was sure she couldn't improve it. She was enveloped in it. It was the perspective she'd strived for. The background was perfect and the middle ground secretive, but if the viewer looked hard enough he or she would see the elves cavorting in the sunlit glade. It was off-centre just enough not to draw the eye.

'Yes', she muttered, 'dead on.'

It was the three oak trees; their leaves looked scorched. She'd have to do something about them because they spoiled the whole affect.

She took a shaved-down lollipop stick and a fine brush, dabbed the brush in the white and was about to load the stick with a mix of ultramarine and chrome-green when the phone rang. April, putting the lollipop stick down but keeping the brush in her hand, said, 'Damn the thing,' then decided she'd answer it.

She didn't hurry because she had a thing about answering the phone and always went to pick it up in her own good time. If she was creating (which at this moment she certainly was) she sometimes didn't answer it at all; she just left it to William (if he was there) to answer the damned thing. He wished she wouldn't. He wished she'd answer it no matter what she was doing, especially when it was him who was trying to get hold of her.

William, on the other hand, stopped whatever he was doing at the first bleeps and tried to get there before the second bleeps ended. It was as though every call was a deadly emergency. His reasons for getting to the phone were rubbish!

He'd say, as convincingly as possible, 'It could be a client Angel, can't ignore them, can I?' Or, 'I could have broken down on the motorway.'

Why he always came out with the same nonsense was beyond April, because neither he nor she gave their phone number to his clients; hers yes on the odd occasion, his never! And what could she do if he had broken down? She wasn't a mechanic. She was a struggling artist and sculptor.

It was bad enough his work colleagues having their home number, never mind his clients. They were an over-the-top lot, and in her opinion, as useful as a vote in China. 'Advertising guys', they called themselves. Soppy sods! Since when has a woman been a guy. If anyone called April a guy, she'd give them a good slapping! April's character had the complexities of a Rubik's cube, but once a person has found and learnt how to use the formula, she was a darling. William, luckily, had found the formula early on in their relationship.

She wiped her hands and moved her wavy chestnut coloured hair to one side, but still managed to dab a smear off flake-white into it as she slid the paintbrush behind her right ear, then she picked up the phone. It was the estate agent, Mr Pickles of Amberley's. She waited while he made this formal and unnecessary introduction. April knew the voice well.

'Good morning Mrs Ward.'

April said, 'Hello Mr Pickles.'

She never said, 'Yes it is', or, 'speaking' even if the caller asked, 'Is that Mrs Ward?' Nor did she demand, 'Who's that?' like her father used to bellow down the phone, as if the caller was stone deaf. All she said was hello and her name if she recognised the caller's voice. She didn't waste time on the phone.

'I think I've found you a place,' fibbed Mr Pickles. He hadn't found her a place.

Had he been perfectly honest, he would have said, 'We've had it on the books for ages and I'm sick of showing it to people. It's called The Rookery. It's on the old Devon Road. It hasn't got a number. The Parish church is on the left of the road. The house is about a hundred yards up on the right (that's if you come from the town end). It's the opposite if you come the other way.' It would be, thought April!

'The house is old, built in the eighteen-nineties and fairly dilapidated, but it has five rooms plus a cloakroom and so on, on the ground floor. On the first floor there are six bedrooms, and two bathrooms. You did say you wanted lots of rooms, didn't you?'

'Yes, we did,' confirmed April, 'but the rooms need to be fairly big.'

'They are. They're far more spacious than those in the chapel conversion you and your husband looked at.'

'Excellent that sounds good.'

317

'That's fine then, and goodness knows how many attic rooms there are. It's all very higgledy-piggledy up there, with stairs going in every direction. It does need some work but that's reflected in the price. There are a number of cellars that seem to go on forever and what was a double garage or at one time perhaps, a stable or coach house. It's well worth a look at, and its well within your price range. I can arrange a viewing for this afternoon, if you're at all interested?'

As soon as he'd said, 'Higgledy-piggledy', April had been interested; in fact she'd been more than interested. She'd been, as William called it, 'dangling on the golden hook'.

Instead she ignored the eager butterflies swarming in her stomach, got a grip and said, 'Sounds fine. What time?'

'Half-past-three. Is that convenient?'

Now, this very minute would have been convenient for April. The place sounded perfect and the name of the house was lovely.

'Yes, that's ok with me.'

'I'll see you at three-thirty then.' He hesitated for a moment.

'Is there something else?' she asked looking across at the waiting clay and canvas and curled her toes.

Again, Mr Pickles didn't answer her immediately; then he said as casually as he could, 'Do you believe in ghosts, Mrs Ward?'

April laughed and said, 'Of course not, why?'

Again the hesitation.

'Don't tell me the house is haunted, Mr Pickles?'

'It does have that reputation.'

She heard a very slight sigh as he continued. 'The previous occupier disappeared in mysterious circumstances, presumed dead by the authorities. There have been sightings of someone, an old lady actually, in and around the house but they were never witnessed by a third party and she's never been found, but they were all adamant that they'd seen something odd. So it could well be haunted, I'm afraid.'

'Well I'm not afraid, Mr Pickles. As I said, I don't believe in ghosts. See you there at three-thirty. I'll let my husband know; he might be able to come. Bye'.

'Goodbye Mrs Ward.'

April put the phone down, had a quick think and picked it back up. She rang William! The brush from behind her ear dropped to the floor leaving a streak of white paint in her hair and she picked it back up rolling it between her fingers. She was told after one minute and twenty-four seconds, by the girl at the other end of the phone that, 'Double u, Double u, is with a client and is not available at the moment, Mrs Ward. But you can leave a message if you wish.'

She did wish. She gave Allison the details about the house and the time she would be there. The phone was put down after a quick thank-you! She would look at the Rookery on her own and could tell William about it later. She loaded the lollipop stick and got to work on the leaves telling herself not to go mad with them, or she might interfere with the long, sinister faces gazing out at her from the tree trunks.

She met Mr Pickles outside a large stone-built house that had seen better days – much better days. It was set back from the road behind a high and very scraggly privet hedge. April counted five attic windows at varying heights along the roof at the front and could see two more attic windows by standing on her tiptoes. These were on the left-hand side roof as it sloped away behind a magnificent Sycamore tree, which, in her estimation, towered at least twenty feet above the house.

'Rather run-down I'm afraid,' Mr Pickles said, answering a question April hadn't asked, but like a few other questions, it was lodged firmly on her 'ask him' list in her head.

'It's not a problem,' replied April trying to peer through another hole in the hedge at an odd-shaped building at least three stories high. It was attached like a sentry to the front right-hand corner of the house!

'Is that a tower over there on the right?'

'Yes, it is, but I don't know why we are standing here. If you come with me, the entrance is round that side there. We don't have to stand here peeping through the hedge!'

April returned his smile and followed him round the corner to a side lane that ran between The Rookery and a much grander house, which looked immaculate.

The rustic wooden gates that were no more than ten yards along, were hanging open. Tied to the gate was a rather smart sign and on it in gold letters was the house name – The Rookery. – April noticed as she followed Mr Pickles through the open gate that the garden was in better condition than the building. The two rectangular front lawns looked to have been mown recently, and the tulips under the sycamores were in full-flower. She noticed with surprise a bird table and a bird bath in the centre of the larger of the two lawns. The bird table was full of bird seed and nuts that a grey squirrel was making the best of. A magpie swooped down and grabbed its

319

share then flew back chattering into the nearest tree. The squirrel ignored it but then scurried off when the visitors walked towards the front of the house. It was obvious someone was looking after the gardens. She asked Mr Pickles about it as they walked towards the door.

He told her he knew nothing about it, but perhaps Mrs Gliss's son who owned the house was looking after it. Just at that point, April spotted a face looking out of the top window of the tower. She waved and shouted hello.

Mr Pickles turned sharply. 'Who on earth are you saying hello to?'

'The old lady, there at that window, up there!'

He looked up and laughed with embarrassment because she'd made him jump, and said, 'Must have been a reflection or something. There's nobody in there Mrs Ward. The house is empty. It's sold with vacant possession!'

He knew it was empty because he'd been here four times and hadn't seen a soul! And anyway, who could live here? It was a real mess inside.

'There was someone there. I saw her! She had pure white hair. You could see it a mile away!'

Mr Pickles shook his head and after a moment he said, 'Well, it's supposed to be empty. We were told by the owner that it was. Perhaps it's the ghost you saw, or a trick of the light?' He laughed.

'Well we'll soon find out.' April knew what she'd seen, and it was no trick of the light. She dropped the subject and led the way to the front door as a drill Sergeant would.

'There are no such things as ghosts, Mr Pickles!'

Mr Pickles found the right key from the small bunch in his hand, and unlocked the door. He didn't argue the point. If a prospective buyer said there were no such things as ghosts, then there were no such things as ghosts! He thought it could be a squatter who'd got in. Then after a moment's thought he dismissed the idea as ridiculous but he didn't suggest this to Mrs Ward. He wanted this place off the books and if he could sell it to the Wards, he'd be cock-a-hoop and so would his partners. It wasn't the case that the property was expensive; they weren't trying to screw every penny out of the deal. In real terms it was an absolute bargain. Some property developer would make a fortune by turning it into upmarket apartments. It was as if for some reason, it just wouldn't sell.

As he pushed open the door, they were met by the usual musty smell of a house that had been empty for a very long time.

'Wow, it pongs a bit,' said April as she stepped inside. 'How long had it been empty?'

'According to the vendor and partly because the last people gave back-word, well over two years, I'm afraid.'

'Who on earth has allowed it to get into this state?'

Mr Pickles shook his head. 'I don't really know. It's all a bit odd. The previous owner was a widow. Her late husband was a Royal Navy man. He was killed in the war. She was in her late seventies or early eighties. The son owns the house; I don't know why it went to him. Perhaps he left it to get like this. He hasn't lived here for years. It's a shame. It must have been a fine property at one time.'

April led the way to the door of the tower or where she thought the door to the tower ought to be, but as they entered the end room at the front of the house there wasn't a door to be found.

'That's odd,' said April and went to look in the room next door. A moment later Mr Pickles followed her in.

'No door here, either. Perhaps you can only get in from the outside?'

'Maybe,' replied Mr Pickles. 'I've never been in the tower. The last people, the ones who gave back-word, were going to have it demolished. They said it overpowered the house.'

'I'll go and see if there is an outside door.' April liked the tower. She liked it very much.

He left the room and she followed him back along the corridor into the large entrance hall glancing round at the neglect of it all. The paper was hanging from the ceiling in the corner and the walls were stained with damp. The woodwork and especially the banister spindles had shed most of their varnish. April thought it a crying shame. It must have been beautiful at one time. The chandelier was elegant but filthy with dust. The stair carpet was filthy, and on the treads at the bottom of the stairs they were badly spotted with mould. It would take time and more than a few buckets full of elbow-grease to sort this lot out. They'd have to watch the pennies, but she would sort it out. April loved it and she was having it. And if the tower was self-contained they could maybe let the rooms. The money would be very useful.

She would discuss her idea with William, and tell him all the place needed was some tender loving care. She was brought back to the present by Mr Pickles saying the door to the tower is on the far side but it's locked and he didn't have the key!

April suggested they force the lock. Mr Pickles said it would be impossible. It was a very sturdy lock but he would telephone Mr Gliss and ask for the key. She told him to go ahead. He said he hadn't meant he would do it then and there. She asked why not and explained she'd every intention of negotiating for the house. He was surprised and delighted but he didn't let it show.

Instead he said, 'Perhaps we should have a good look round first.'

She replied, 'There's no need, I think it's perfect! Obviously we'll get a surveyor's report and if there are no serious problems, voila!'

She was more than keen to have it but she wasn't stupid!

'We do have a surveyor's report, Mrs Ward. The last couple had one done before they gave back-word. I'll post you a copy. As far as I remember there was only one thing that required attention and that was woodworm in some of the timbers in the tower roof. The vendor had it dealt with by Rentokil. But you can check the report yourself when you get it.'

She thanked him. Said, I will, and went upstairs. They spent nearly two hours exploring the bedrooms and three of the attic rooms. All the rooms they looked at upstairs were in better condition than those downstairs. They didn't go into every room. April had seen enough and it was exactly as he said it was, 'Higgledy-piggledy', and there were loads of little flights of stairs going all over the place. April loved it. All she had to do now was convince William. She'd do a candlelight dinner with all the trimmings. After that she'd wear those slinky midnight-blue silk pyjamas. They would divert his attention!

'Do you want to see the gardens at the back? Then you'll see why it was called, "Bracken Hollow".' He locked the door.

April looked up at the tower window, and then she followed Mr Pickles down the path that led toward the back gardens.

'I thought it was called "The Rookery!"'

'It is now. The name was changed three or so years ago. Not long before Mrs Gliss disappeared.'

They were round the back of the house now and sure enough April could see why it had been called Bracken Hollow. The ground fell steeply from the house then rose just as steeply towards a dense wood about fifty yards away. But there in the dip, halfway between the wood and the house, was a circular hollow of at least thirty feet in diameter. The hollow was packed with an amazing variety of coloured ferns.

'Wow, they're lovely. Look at all the different shades of green and gold and the red ones in the middle are glorious! I've never seen as many ferns.'

Mr Pickles nodded enthusiastically in agreement even though he wasn't keen on ferns.

'Have they always been here?'

'To the best of my knowledge they have. Or at least I assume they have. They certainly look as if they have. Don't you think?'

April agreed that they had.

'I wonder why she changed it. You know, the name of the house?'

'I'm afraid I haven't a clue. But according to Susan, who works in our office, Mrs Gliss's son Alec was doing his best to get his mother a place up at Haven Park. He inferred she was going a bit strange. You probably know of the place. It's a nursing home, but they give them a posher title these days.'

April, being only thirty-two, didn't know of it.

'Well it's a very select residential home not a mile away from here. He said the house was too big for her to keep. But Susan who was one of her part-time carers said she was having none of it and seemingly there were quite a few rows about it. Susan, who I'm afraid is a bit of a gossip, said that on the last occasion Mrs Gliss banged her stick on the floor and stormed out of the room saying, "I should never have agreed to your father leaving the house to you. All you want is to be rid of me so you can sell my home." He went after her trying to explain it was for her sake not his and he'd give her the house. She was welcome to the place. She ignored him then banging her stick down even harder she said, "I would rather die and be buried amongst the ferns than go and live in an old folks home." Then she began to sob, but she wouldn't let her son near her when he tried to comfort her. He was deeply upset and totally at a loss. And Susan really was out of her depth. She wasn't a psychiatric nurse, or as far as I'm aware even a trained nurse. She and the other two part-time carers were employed privately by Alec; the son that is. He rang the Doctor, which infuriated Mrs Gliss even more. Susan said it was terrible. When her Doctor arrived he gave her something to calm her down then he rang for an ambulance. Susan stayed with her till the ambulance came and took her to the local hospital for observation. That was the last time Susan saw her.

'The following week Mrs Gliss was allowed to come home. She changed the name of the house and disappeared. Alec reported his mother's disappearance to the police and she was recorded as a missing person. But she wasn't the only one to go missing. I'm surprised you don't know about it. It was in all the local papers and a couple of the nationals.'

'I did hear something about missing ladies, but I'd no idea who they were.'

'I think there were three altogether. They vanished in the same week or the week after, as far as I remember. I don't know all the details but it's still going on. I'm not sure if there aren't four missing now. Yes it's four. One went missing last week. She's in her late seventies. She was a resident at Haven Park according to Susan. She's keeping her eyes on it because her mother's at Haven Park and she's worried sick in case she goes missing like the others. The police are still investigating. Those were the headlines in yesterday's Wakeford Express. Getting nowhere I suspect. But they're making and have made extensive enquiries! Or so they say. Which means absolutely nothing!'

All the time Mr Pickles had been talking, April had to all appearances been watching the ferns sway gently in the breeze. But she had at times taken a few furtive glances up at the windows. They'd walked down to the hollow and she was far enough away from the house now to see if they were being watched. She'd had a strange feeling that they were but she'd seen nothing. They walked back round to the front of the house.

'It must be terrible for the families,' said April going through the gate, 'not knowing what's happened to them. Surely the police could be doing more?'

'They are doing everything they can. That's the last thing the Chief Constable put out. But he said that more than a week ago. Like I said before, they're getting nowhere!' He followed her to her car.

'I must be going, Mr Pickles. I've a lot to do. Can you get the tower key for tomorrow morning? I can't come back today; I'm up to my neck in it all afternoon!'

Mr Pickles promised he would try his best and that he would ring her first thing. She asked him to make it second thing as she might have a lie in!

'Around ten would be best for me.'

He nodded then she got in her car, waved, smiled and said, 'I really do hope they find them.'

Mr Pickles stood there, watched her go and looked back at the house for a few minutes. He wondered where its attraction was, and shook his head. The house, although mock Jacobean, and expertly done, did not appeal to him. He had one last look up at the tower before going on to his next appointment. The empty windows stared back!

April loved the house and wondered about the old ladies. Then her thoughts turned to William and how she could get him to want the house as much as she did. First, she'd open that fruity Hardy's. Second, she'd see if she had any of that Armagnac William liked! If not, she'd get some! Then a great meal. Then...!

William was late. He got in at eight o'clock. April had made absolutely sure everything was ready for eight-thirty. The half-formed Phoenix and the enchanted forest had been swept from her thoughts, very reluctantly but almost definitely. She had popped back in once when she thought perhaps the wings were too far back from the head but she didn't fiddle with them.

He was already in jeans and sweat shirt by twenty-past-eight. The starter, Gesier du Oi, melted in the mouth. The fillets were perfect-pink. The blue Stilton sauce poured lump-free like double Devon cream over the delicately-peppered crêpes. It was tantalizingly different. Between mouthfuls April, who'd decided the pyjamas might be too much of a distraction, had settled on her smart, unassuming little red frock, told him all about the house. Where it was, how beautiful it was and how stunning it could be. What character it had. What a super tower it had. What potential! William, knowing now what the meal was all about kept looking at her through the flame of the candle. He didn't tell April he'd come home that way, or that he'd stopped and had a close look at the outside of the place. He let her get on with it. No man in his right mind would waste an opportunity like this, besides he'd loved what he'd seen of the old house and the nice old lady who was having a wander round! William did believe in ghosts but he knew nothing about the rumours surrounding the house or the missing old ladies. He rarely read anything but the Times.

He finished his Armagnac, topped it up and smiled at his lovely April who hadn't a grain of marble dust, blob of clay, or spot of paint anywhere to be seen. He'd smiled this odd smile throughout the meal. April had smiled back at the handsome devil, thinking he must have claimed a client's scalp and a wealthy one at that! William made no mention of his visit to Amberleys or The Rookery. He did promise, as he cradled her head in the sleepy, soft warmth of the night to go with her to see the house in the morning. He nearly said to see it again but somehow, even though his thoughts were concentrated elsewhere, he didn't!

Mr Pickles rang as promised and he had the key for the tower. April said they would meet in an hour if that was ok with him. It wasn't but he assured her it was. Priorities, priorities, he told himself pocketing his mobile. He would put back his next appointment. It was no big deal. A three bedroom semi can be sold anytime. He'd a queue of buyers for those. He rang his office and asked his secretary to sort it out and so she did!

William parked behind Mr Pickles' Audi, who was standing by the gate talking to someone on the phone. He put it away as April drew up in hers. The couple approached him and April introduced him to William. They followed Mr Pickles to the tower. The door opened without a problem and the smell was exactly the same as the main house – so was the condition of the rooms. They didn't waste any time in their exploration of the tower. All three floors badly needed work, perhaps more so than the rest of the place. William didn't have much time but he did have a look at the layout and condition of the main house and asked if the upstairs rooms were in the same condition as the ones on the ground floor. Both Mr Pickles and April said they were in better condition than the downstairs rooms.

'It's a shame it's been allowed to get into a state like this, but we'll make an offer for it Mr Pickles, subject to the usual things.'

April was astonished. He just grinned that rather odd smile at her he'd used at the table last night when he saw the surprise on her face.

'It's like I've seen it before somewhere April, I love it!' They would sort out the formalities later.

He had to dash. 'I've got a meeting in twenty minutes, Treasure.'

He offered his hand to Mr Pickles and thanked him for his time. William went off to his office and April went home to sort out her forest!

They received the surveyor's report on the Wednesday of the following week. The surveyors were Blake and Cawfield, the same people who had done the survey on their present home, and there hadn't been a single problem in the eight years they'd lived there. Mr Pickles had been right about the woodworm infestation in two of the beams in the tower roof. A later inspection by Blake and Cawfield confirmed Rentokil's operatives had done their usual thorough job.

Mr Pickles hadn't mentioned the damp in the front wall of the dining room caused by a six-foot long raised flowerbed, which had been built against it. The report concluded that if the flowerbed was removed, the problem would be solved! William didn't remember seeing a raised flowerbed at the front of the house and when he asked April she said she was positive there wasn't one there. He rang Mr Pickles who told him it had been removed by Alec and a new air vent had been fitted. The old one had been blocked and badly corroded. There was no mention of this on the later report. William rang Blake and Cawfield's and asked if they knew anything about it. They confirmed that it had been removed but they hadn't been involved with the removal. That was why it wasn't on the later report. William thanked them and made a mental note to check the dining room wall.

He rang Mr Pickles and made him an offer of eight-thousand pounds below the asking price. Mr Pickles made a pretence at haggling but would put their offer to Mr Gliss. Their offer was accepted and yes they would gladly handle the sale of their present house, subject to their staying here until they could move into The Rookery. That was fine. The valuers would be round in the morning at approximately ten o'clock. Yes, April would be there to show them round. From then on April dealt with the details. By the end of July the first and second floors of The Rookery were finished. So was the Griffin, and the enchanted forest was well on its way too.

The Wards moved out and into their new home on the first of August. The tower, the attics and the cellars would have to wait. The couple who had bought their present house had to move in on or before the third, otherwise the chain would collapse and they wouldn't be able to complete. Their offer had been so good the Wards had agreed to the conditions of sale. It had been hard graft but what setbacks there were, had been mostly minor and had been dealt with by April, her mother, or her mother-in-law or sometimes all three of them. The plasterers, joiners and plumbers didn't stand a chance! The only hiccup for the contractor had been when one of his plasterers came storming down the stairs from one of the attic rooms and told him, 'He'd had enough of being told by some bugger's starving grandma how to bloody well plaster! And he could stick his job.'

His boss hadn't a clue what he was on about but he didn't bother persuading him to change his mind as he didn't think his work was up to much. There were plenty more plasterers where he came from and better at it! His replacement arrived the following morning.

The house-warming had gone down brilliantly. Everybody, as instructed, had brought a feather with their name-tag on. April had supplied the little silver-coloured tags to tie to their feather, but each guest had to supply their own feather. The feather that April thought was the most unique would win a bottle of twenty-year-old malt.

When her mother had asked, as she offered hers, 'Why a feather of all things, Dear?' April had looked at her as if she was simple and said, 'Rookery mum, feathers, you know! Where Rooks live.'

Her mother had returned the same look, shook her head, said there were no rooks here, kept her feather and gone to chat with William's mother. April had to get the feather from her later. She wanted them all pinned to a board that she'd hung on the wall of her new studio, which was at the back of the house and overlooked the ferns. Superb thought April. Stunning! William said the place was magic.

The first happening (as April subsequently called them) was when she and William were in bed on the night after the house-warming. It was just after midnight as April was reading. William was trying to get to sleep even though April's bedside lamp was on. They heard a sudden thump, a bang, a howl of pain (swore April), (howl of wind in William's opinion), a sort of rattling noise then utter silence.

William got out of bed and said, 'I'll go and check the windows downstairs to see if one had been left open and the wind, which had been gusting on and off all day had blown it off its catch.'

'Be careful William, it might be a burglar!'

William played rugby in the amateur league, he was six-three and very good at his sport. If there was a burglar it would be the burglar that would have to be careful, very careful. But William promised he would, just the same.

April decided to go after him. She got out of bed and followed him as he went out of the bedroom, but she stopped on the open landing where she could see him. He checked the front door and the small window beside it; then he disappeared in the direction of the sitting room. None of the windows were open in there. Methodically, he checked the rest of the ground floor rooms but found nothing untoward. April followed him round and wondered (as she stifled a giggle at his white bum) if he realised he was starkers! She'd picked up the poker from the fireplace in the sitting room but she needn't have bothered. Then just as he was about to give the all clear he realised he hadn't checked the pantry. He returned to the kitchen and April followed. He opened the door to the pantry and noticed that the window was open. It was off its catch and there were bits of cheese and boiled ham scattered about on the pantry floor. When he turned the light on he saw there were signs of the same stuff on the window ledge.

'A cat must have got in. The window's too small for anything bigger.'

April put the poker on the work top got his raincoat off the back door, handed it to him and said, 'Don't you think you ought to put that on?'

He laughed and said, 'It's a bit late now but I will.' Then he took it from her and put it on.

'Lucky it wasn't a hungry squirrel!' April smiled nicely.

'Good one Angel. We've a game this Saturday. I'll tell the lads what you said.'

'You'd better not!'

He closed the window, shut the pantry door and left the scraps of food where they were. April said she'd deal with it in the morning. She returned the poker to the sitting room and led the way upstairs to bed. It was twelve-thirty.

The second happening, occurred a week later, although according to April, there had been lots of semi-happenings as she called them.

William had told her, 'They were nothing more than the usual noises that all old houses make. All old houses creak and make weird noises. It's caused by temperature changes. It's nothing ghostly or paranormal. Now go back to sleep, Angel.'

When she heard the noise of the second real happening, the time by April's studio clock was nine-fifteen. She rushed into the corridor that ran between the rooms at the back of the house and the sitting room and the dining rooms facing the lawns in front of the house. She rushed out as William dashed out of his study come glory-hole.

'Did you hear that?' asked April, not sure where the bang had come from. 'That wasn't a change of temperature.'

William pushed past her and ran down the corridor. 'Yes I heard it, hell of a bang. Didn't you see her?'

'Who?'

'The old woman with the white hair. She went in there!'

April caught up with him as he ran through the door into the sitting room. He was trying the windows when April got there. The room was empty other than for William who was looking behind the curtains by suddenly snatching them away from the wall then sticking his head behind the curtains as fast as he could to see if she was hiding there. Next minute he was leaning over the back of the settee standing in the corner by the lamp.

'That's impossible!' he said as he checked behind the easy chair against the panelling.

'A stick insect couldn't get behind there, you nit.' But regardless of what she'd just called him she had a look.

'Welcome to the nitwit's club.'

'I only looked because you'd moved the chair.'

'Of course you did, Treasure. Well she's somewhere in here! I saw her come in. She was all in black and her face and hair were as white as a sheet.' He brushed his hair back like he always did when he was confused or annoyed but it instantly flopped forwards.

'I might as well tell you before you pull the room apart.'

'Tell me what?'

'Before I tell you I'll just say this; I don't believe it, and I don't care what you say, or if you think I'm crazy but this place is supposed to be haunted!'

'Haunted!' he burst out laughing. 'Haunted by whom? What?'

'He didn't actually say who by, but he inferred it was the old lady who used to live here.'

'Who inferred?'

'The estate agent, Mr Pickles. He said one or two people had seen an old lady. Sometimes she was seen at a window, sometimes walking in the gardens but they were always on their own. Nobody could confirm what they said was true, so nobody really believed them.'

April didn't say anything for a while, and then as if she was throwing down a challenge she said, 'I've seen her. I saw her the first time I came here. She was in the tower. I made Mr Pickles jump when I shouted hello to her. He looked up at the tower and said he couldn't see anything. He supposed it was only a reflection or something but at the time I thought he'd said that so we wouldn't be put off buying the house.'

'Why are you looking at me like that?'

'Because now I feel guilty because I didn't tell you before.'

'Don't feel guilty Sweet-thing. You remember the superb candlelight supper you did. You came here in the afternoon to have a look at the place and then the same night you...?'

'Of course I remember. How could I forget?' She kissed him lightly on his cheek.

'I called here the same day. I must have only missed you by minutes. Thought I might as well have a quick look on my way back to the office. I knew you'd want it as soon as I saw it. Funny enough I loved it at first sight. It's a stupid thing to say about a run-down old house. But when I saw the old lady walking round the garden I thought I was at the wrong place. They'd told me at Amberleys that the house had been empty for two or three years. There was no point going in, so I waved to the old lady and left. She'd...'

'You sly rat!'

William grinned, 'Fox, precious, sly as a fox, crafty as a fox. Foxes are crafty; in fact they're nearly as crafty as vixens!' William prodded the end of April's nose. 'There stands the accused.'

'You sat through that dinner knowing all the time what I was up to!'

'Hey, wait a minute, Buggerlugs. You're the one who prepared that lovely meal and set the scene. You know me Sweet-thing. I didn't want to spoil the moment or throw a chance like that away.'

'You...Just a minute. You said you saw the old lady! And you waved to her! How far ... where in the garden? Did she...'

'Steady on Precious. I don't want you to burst and cover our magnificent carpet in mush. Yes I waved to her. She was over by the tower. She was twenty or so metres away. And no, she didn't wave back because she'd gone when I turned back.' He was marking each reply on his fingers.

'Stop that or I'll bite the next one off. Did you see her go?'

'No, I did not see her go. The privets were in the way.'

'Don't you dare humour me! She's supposed to be the ghost.'

'Is she? Well she looked solid enough to me, and she wasn't floating. Ghosts float about, don't they?'

April gritted her teeth and shook her head. 'How should I know?'

William sat on the chair arm. 'Maybe she's disappeared through one of the walls?' laughed William. 'She certainly isn't in here! But I'm absolutely sure I saw her come in here. And that my love is a fact! So if she came in, and she isn't a ghost, there must be a way out of here, other than the door and the windows. All we have to do is find it. Agreed?'

'Of course I agree,' said April and began tapping the panel she'd been leaning against with her knuckles.

They spent over an hour searching for a concealed exit. They didn't find one. William was beginning to have doubts. The last place they checked was a store cupboard set in the wall at the far right-hand corner nearest the window. They'd had it made into a walk-in media centre. Neither William nor April wanted the hi-fi equipment, or the rest of it on show. It was all silver and black and it had more stand-by lights than Concorde. There was no sign of the old lady in there. But, argued William, there would be room for a little old lady to stand behind the doors then shut them behind her and hide. April wasn't convinced but said it didn't matter because there was nobody in there and he'd been seeing things, or he was taking the Mick! He told her in the nicest possible way, to sod off.

They closed the door and returned to what they were doing before the happening. She said she'd a lot to do and they'd wasted enough time looking for an imaginary ghost that doesn't walk through walls. It was later that night, just before William fell asleep that he suddenly thought he'd heard two doors slam. He didn't waken April; she was sound asleep and snoring like a hippo. He'd tell her in the morning but fell asleep wondering where the other door could be. Had he given more thought to it when they'd checked the old store cupboard, he would have realised where the other door might be!

A bad happening occurred a week later. April was working in her studio at the back of the house and William was on the phone. April was sorting her colours and preparing her palette. She was excited because she'd been invited to show some of her work at the Cornstalk Gallery in Birmingham. It was her first real major showing. She saw the old lady as she turned to put the turps on the windowsill for a minute while she made room in the cupboard. The bottle dropped to the floor. It was as she swore and started to bend down to pick it up that she saw the old lady fall, then tumble head over heels down the steep banking leading down to the ferns.

She yelled, 'Oh hell William,' who heard her shout and said, 'Call you back.'

He slammed the phone down and ran to April's studio. April was outside and running down the garden when William caught up with her. They knelt down and carefully eased her into a comfortable position.

'Are you hurt?' gasped April. The old lady didn't or couldn't answer. She'd been clutching a plastic bag when she was hurrying from the house. When she'd fallen she'd let go of it. The bag and its contents were scattered across the grass. William was astonished to see bits of food and tins of fruit scattered everywhere. He pointed them out to April.

She barely gave them a glance as William said, 'I'll call an ambulance.' April asked him to hurry.

The old lady gasped as best she could. 'No, I don't want an ambulance!' But William ignored her and ran back to the house. It was obvious to him she'd broken her arm. He'd seen plenty on the rugby field.

He returned with a small glass of brandy and told her to take a sip. April held it to the old lady's trembling lips. She managed with difficulty to get some of it down.

'We should get you into the house.' She looked up at William.

'Don't worry April, she's going to be all right.' He smiled at the frail old lady; then he carefully lifted her off the grass as though she was weightless. April had very gently eased the broken arm across the old lady's waist but she winced as William made towards the house. April ran ahead and opened the door.

'Put her on the settee in the sitting room till the ambulance comes.'

The old lady ignored all their questions, and had already closed her eyes. They made her as comfortable as possible under the circumstances and waited for the ambulance. They didn't have to wait long because within minutes she was in the care of the ambulance crew and on her way to hospital.

April sighed and dropped onto the settee while William poured them both a brandy. He knocked his back. April sipped hers then put it down on the coffee table.

'Phew, so much for the ghost then!'

'What do you mean, April?'

'She wasn't a ghost, was she?'

'No, she wasn't, and she wasn't the lady I saw when I was looking at the house either. She was taller and she wore glasses, the ones with very thick lenses.'

'Well who is she then?'

'I've no idea. Maybe she's Mrs Gliss? I'll ring Mr Pickles and get her son's phone number.'

William was back in no time. 'Here.' He passed her the scrap pad. 'The top one's his home number.'

April went to the phone wondering why the task had been delegated to her! William went and cleared the stuff of the grass at the back. He'd cleared most of it when April called him from the doorway.

'He's going to the hospital. He couldn't stop thanking us and said he'd let us know how she's getting on, as soon as possible. Are you bringing that in?'

William held the bag up and laughed. 'Yes, I'm bringing it in. I want to know if it's out of our pantry!' She had a look in the bag. It wasn't. April didn't need to look in the pantry as she didn't buy tinned rhubarb (she thought it was horrible stuff) or the tinned gooseberries, which she thought tasted even worse.

'I wonder what she was doing here, and why she wouldn't tell us?'

William shook his head. 'Maybe she thinks it's still her house? Can't think of any other reason.'

The phone rang and William picked it up. And after a few minutes he said, 'Oh, well I'm sorry about that. We thought… Yes, I'll tell my wife. Goodbye Mr Gliss. Hell, he was a bit abrupt. She isn't his mother, she's a Mrs Hirst. She's one of the missing ladies. The police are with her now, but she won't say where she's been or why she was in our garden! Mr Gliss told me they want to talk to us.'

'When?'

'He didn't say. They told him they'd need to have a word with us. That's all he said. He wasn't well pleased when he found a stranger at the hospital instead of his mother.'

The police called Thursday morning at ten-thirty but William wasn't there; no he had a very important meeting. Nothing would keep him away from that as it involved big money. He could be there Wednesday or Friday. Thursday was impossible. The police decided Thursday was best for them! April invited them in and made them tea. They were there two-and-a-half hours. April somehow managed to keep her cool, even when they went over every little detail for the umpteenth time. The inspectors parting words were, 'If you find any more old ladies wandering round your garden give us a ring immediately!'

April's final words were, 'I hardly think that's likely, Inspector.' But she smiled nicely and said, 'I will get in touch the moment I do,' and sadly she did have to get in touch.

She found the body of Mrs Gliss and two very distressed old ladies standing beside the body by the bird table. She'd only been away from the house for an hour as she'd gone to the local art shop to get a couple of colours. Mrs Gliss had been putting food out for the birds when she'd had a severe heart attack. April didn't know that at the time and William was away for three days in Portsmouth.

The ambulance arrived before the police and took Mrs Gliss away. April took the two grieving old ladies into the house, showed them into the sitting room and went to make them a cup of tea. When she returned, one of the ladies had gone. Surprised, April put the tray on the coffee table and asked the old lady where her friend had gone.

'Clara's gone downstairs for her things.'

'Where downstairs? What things? Do you mean the cellars? It's filthy down there.' April wondered if the old lady was ga-ga.

'It isn't where we live.'

'Live! You can't mean you live in the cellars?'

The old lady looked at April and nodded very slowly saying, 'Yes we do. Poor Dorothy, going like that after all she's done for us!'

The old lady began to sob quietly. April's thoughts went everywhere. They can't live in the cellars. Why would they want to live in the cellars? Could these be the ladies who went missing? Can't be? Why would they come here? She wished the police would hurry up!

She sat down beside the old lady who had stopped crying, and tried her best to console her, even though (by the look on her face) it was the last thing she needed.

'I don't know your name. Mine is April, and we live here!'

'Mine is Fiona and you don't need to talk to me as if I'm a simpleton!' Fiona sipped her tea.

Clara, sombre-faced, suddenly reappeared with a small brown suitcase in one hand, and two plastic bags in the other.

'You may as well get your things, Fiona Dear. No doubt we'll be going back to that place!'

April gasped. As far as she was concerned Clara had just walked through a closed door! April was sitting facing the sitting room door and she hadn't seen it open, yet there was Clara, standing there, large as life! Clara put her things down and looked at April whose mouth was still open and whose eyes were nearly as big as saucers.

'You look as if you've seen a ghost, young lady!'

April was sure she had till she realised plastic bags and suitcases don't pass through solid oak doors.

'Where…? How…? How did you do that?'

Clara didn't get chance to reply as the doorbell rang. April (still slightly flustered) went to answer it. It was the police. They followed her to the sitting room but both the old ladies had gone! The police looked at her and she looked back at them.

'She was sitting on the settee drinking tea, not two minutes ago,' insisted April, feeling stupid again. The Inspector nodded at her as if she was stupid! Then within seconds (or so it seemed to April) they were both standing in the doorway. Both had bags and suitcases. They came into the room and put the things on the floor.

335

'We're ready, Officer!'

The Inspector gave them a little smile and shook his head.

'You're not under arrest ladies, but if you are the ones who disappeared in nineteen-eighty-nine, I think we and Mrs Ward deserve an explanation, and there's a case of breaking and entering to be considered!' His smile had gone.

'We do have a key Officer, and we were invited here by Dorothy Gliss. We are not common criminals!' The old lady was obviously angry.

The Inspector patiently assured her he'd never thought for one minute that they were. All the police wanted was a brief statement from them. All April wanted to know was how they got into the cellars. For the moment, April's want had to take second place.

Slowly, and with a fair amount of cajoling, the Inspector got their statements. They'd been invited to stay here. It was Dorothy's idea. She was a very independent woman and the only way they would be able to get her out of her home of over fifty years, was to carry her out in a coffin! The Inspector stopped himself from telling them it wasn't her house now. They lived in the cellars that were spotless, at least the ones they used were spotless and they sometimes lived in the attics. They had everything they needed and only came out when there was no one in the house. They had a key and used the hidden panel just behind them. It's there, on the left-hand side of the door where the wall is recessed. You have to press those two pieces of ornamental carving; those that look like bunches of grapes. There's a narrow flight of stairs behind there. We use those! There's one that leads to the tower from the cellars. She used to go and look at the garden from up there. We all did. We were better off here than that place over there, treating people as though they were babies. I've never knitted in my life, or played silly bingo.

The old lady tut-tutted and looked disgusted. 'Dorothy told us it was only a matter of time before the house was sold and someone would find us. We said we should find somewhere else, but she said The Rookery was perfect. That's why she called it The Rookery. Dorothy said it's where we would have a safe nest. And it would grow and grow as more joined us. Just like a rookery does. If our families don't want us, we don't want them!' April had to clear her throat.

Their families did want them! They whisked them away with endless thanks and apologies and the police didn't bring any charges against the old ladies. April didn't look for the hidden entrance to the cellar till William came home and she'd told him everything that had happened. She said she would have felt like an intruder. He understood exactly what she meant. After checking where the ladies lived, they had the panels made into doors so they could take a shortcut to the tower. They went up there as often as they could after they'd decided to renovate the tower before the attics and cellars.

William was the first to spot the nest. It was built high in the topmost fork of the sycamore tree. He was putting a coat of white paint on the middle window on the second floor and pointed it out to April. She swore she hadn't seen it before, or the two rooks fussing round it. William said he hadn't noticed it either but it was great to see them! She nodded as she turned to him with a look of contentment on her face and a smear of white paint on her cheek. He took her hand and kissed it. Neither of them saw the beautiful young woman with long, black hair staring lovingly from the end window of the room on the floor above or the dashing young naval officer holding her hand in his and pointing at the rooks! But then, nobody could have seen them. The youngsters had already flown the nest!

Richard Lee Wilson March 4th 2004

The twelfth man

It wouldn't take long to get down the cellar. There were only nine steps down. He'd often counted them. When he was a child he'd played down there with the other boy, a very pale, sickly young boy with big staring eyes. The pale young boy with the funny eyes had counted them along with him.

There were thirteen steps up to the first floor landing and twelve up to the attic, where the old man was positive the pale young boy slept. He knew there were twelve without a shadow of doubt, because they'd counted those as well, but he could barely remember the pale boy's name.

'Wasn't it Josiah?' he mumbled to himself. 'No', he answered. 'Was it Don Bradman? He was as good as him,' the old man chortled. 'It was Joshua. Joshua fought the battle of Jericho.'

The old man grimaced and bit at the edges of his droopy moustache trying hard to remember what had made him think of the battle of Jericho, and with even deeper concentration he tried to remember what had become of his pale-faced friend and his cricket bat. In the darkness, he carefully held onto the hand rail and slowly (in a breathless whisper) counted the steps. It wouldn't be wise to be heard. A tiny smile flickered briefly in the darkness.

'Eight, nine, ten! Impossible! Have I miscounted?' He whispered, 'Must have done?' Now without the effort of a whisper, he continued down. Nine, ten, eleven! Impossible, because he could feel yet another one. He scraped his heel down the slippery face of the next riser, feeling tentatively for the level surface of the next step. He cursed in anger and frustration at the faulty light bulb and damned the stupid candle. As he cursed, he wondered why his friend had gone away. He had thought his friend liked him. Perhaps he didn't thought the bewildered old man, as yet another step presented itself.

Had that horrid Doctor or the vicar anything to do with it? He felt, but he wasn't absolutely sure, it was after one of the vicar's visits that his friend had gone away. The old man remembered being sent to bed early on the day the vicar came that time. The Reverend Pugh was always calling in; the nosy old soddy with the purple nose! Sent to bed again, even though he'd done nothing wrong. It was his friend who'd been naughty. His friend had heard the vicar whispering to mother like he always did when he just

338

popped in. Good day to you! Chortle, chortle. Rubbing his big fat purple nose. Saying all those nasty things about his friend. His friend could have kicked old soddy's shin. The old man knew his friend could have, and should have for the lies he told to mother. His friend always told him everything. That's how he knew about the lies!

His elder brother was allowed to stay up. He remembered the strange noises he'd heard late into the night. He remembered (while stamping up the stairs) the injustice of it all. He remembered his mother's terrified face staring up after him. He remembered his father's agitation and odd behaviour, stamping up and down like that; most unlike his father. He remembered his sister weeping and clutching his mother's hand. But most of all, he remembered the terrified look on his brother's face, who stood silently in the shadows of the cellar doorway. Perhaps I'd been sent to bed early on the recommendation of Doctor Horrid-Hindle. He was there as well, concluded the old man!

He had felt a lot better the next morning and his illness had gone completely within the week. He remembered running round the garden with his cricket bat and Rover; he hadn't done that for ages. He'd love to play for the school with his very own bat, but his brother, captain of the first eleven, would only ever pick him as twelfth man. His pale-faced friend promised he would get him in the team. But he couldn't remember why he had to go down the cellar today, of all days. He knew it was important, but he'd forgotten why. Was it because it was his birthday? Or was he looking for his bat? The old man couldn't remember.

There was another step down. The old man cursed his failing strength and he cursed his failing memory. Perhaps there are nine stairs up to the attic and twelve down to the cellar. He tried very hard to convince himself.

There was some sort of faint glow, or was it a flicker of light? It seemed so far away and, it was so deep down. Were his eyes playing tricks? Obviously, they were. There was another light switch at the bottom of the stairs that illuminated the far cellar; it should still be there, shouldn't it? As far as he knew, nobody had been down the cellar since that night. He would soon be at the bottom. He would soon find it, and then his anxieties would soon disappear, wouldn't they? There was a horrible foisty smell of damp clothes that he didn't like. He began to feel the cold handrail slipping through his fingers. His grip tightened, but not quite enough. He slipped sideways but grasped the handrail firmly with his left hand as his right gained good purchase. After regaining his balance, he stood still and took a few deep breaths to steady the rapid beating of his heart. His thoughts turned momentarily, to his brother and sister, who in the same week had gone away, both in a big black limousine. They had one each. His brother was in the front one and his sister was in the back one. The old man never found out why. He was forbidden to mention the subject. He knew his parents were sad because mother never stopped crying, and father never smiled. They should have let them stay at home! He could have told his brother how well he was playing; now he'd got into the team

The faint glimmer emanating from deep below him became a shade of a shade brighter. He risked taking his right hand from the handrail to rub his eyes. He peered, straining his eyes. He did his utmost to focus in the darkness. Whatever it was, it was definitely beginning to take shape and substance. What on earth is it? pondered the anxious old man. It looked (in the blackness of the cellar) to be a bundle of some sort, but it was too dark to make out. Perhaps it was a bundle of old rags? Perhaps it was a dead dog that had got trapped down there? He asked himself questions that his mind couldn't answer.

'Must have been in the cellar for years, mustn't it?' He didn't give himself a reply. He tried to remember when he had last come down here. Sixty years ago, must be at least that, if not more? He was beginning to wish he hadn't found the damned key. He wasn't allowed to play in the cellar or the attic, not after the vicar had been, or was it the Doctor? Then his brother and sister had gone away with the old man's pale-faced friend. Must be seventy years? God where have the years all gone, and where has the key gone? He didn't remember leaving it in the door.

Another step and another. That must be fourteen, if not fifteen? He swore and must have lost count. He didn't think he had. He took another breather, which lasted far longer than the first. He tried to hold back a shiver when the creeping damp air penetrated his lungs. A pointless exercise he concluded then he shivered all the more. He took both hands off the rail and rubbed them hard together. Yet another pointless exercise; it would take more than a feeble massage to get the thin blood flowing properly. But he persevered.

What was that? He cringed and shuddered involuntarily. He'd felt something brush past him and now he could hear a faint scurrying as something, maybe a rat, or a cat. Had it gone up the stairs? He couldn't be sure. It felt a bit big for a rat – must have been a cat. Was that yet another step? God in heaven, where on earth does it end? The old man began to panic. He turned sharply, hearing a noise from behind him, then looked back up towards the cellar door. The damned thing had banged shut. The faint, grey rectangular patch of light behind him disappeared. He searched his pockets for the umpteenth time but there were no matches to be found, not even in his waistcoat pocket. He usually had one in there as he used them as toothpicks, but not today. He must have cleared his pockets out but didn't remember doing so.

He turned and glanced back up again into the silent, heavy darkness, wondering (undecided) whether or not to go back up. He could not for the life of him think why he'd decided to visit the cellar. Why after all these years, he uttered silently to himself. I must be going insane, and at my age. If I didn't remember what happened then, why the hell should I remember now? His thoughts were everywhere. His hands began to tremble, then his wrists and arms. Then his whole body began to shake so he took one of his tablets, one of the blue ones. At least he hoped it was the larger of the two! The little blue and white containers were very nearly the same size. It hadn't been easy, he'd spilled one or two on the stairs, what with the shaking and the darkness and their damned stupid lids. The trembling and shaking subsided then finally it ceased. It had taken at least five minutes for them to take effect, and now he was even colder.

He took another step down the stairs.

'Was that a bundle of old rags in the corner?' he asked the darkness as he tried hard to focus.

There was no answer from the darkness to his trembling voice. He decided if he wasn't at the bottom after this last step, he would go back upstairs and never come down here again. The decision was made. Tentatively, he took one more step. Was he at the bottom? Yes he was! He could feel it. Now perhaps he could find what he was looking for. He'd put his right foot forward, and felt the smooth level surface of the well-worn stone flags. They were a lot smoother than he remembered. The old man shuddered and sighed heavily as he was more than relieved! But where had the damned light switch gone? It used to be here, on the left, by the start of the long passage to the far cellar. That's where his pale-faced friend got his brother to pick him for the cricket team. It must have been in the daytime because he never saw his friend at night and never when it was as dark as hell like it was in his bedroom. His midnight-blue curtains were invisible without a light on. His cold fingers scratted and scrabbled uselessly along the face of the wall where the switch should have been. Where in heaven's name was it? His fingers fumbled in vain along the damp, cold wall.

'Ugh,' he mouthed in the darkness. He'd snagged his hand in a huge cobweb. 'Ugh.' He nearly retched. He hated the filthy things, and the even filthier things that made them. He'd had this dread of spiders since the time his brother pushed him into a wodge of old underfelt stored in the wood shed. It was packed with the filthy things. They were everywhere. He tried desperately to brush it from between his fingers, but only succeeded in getting the clinging stuff further up his arms and then on his neck and face.

'Ugh, you foul thing,' he gasped again as he desperately pulled and brushed to get it off. Some clung to the corner of his mouth. He nearly choked as he swallowed the bile that had invaded the back of his throat. He dragged at the filthy strands. Sweat stood out on his forehead like glass beads. Would he collapse like he did in the wood shed? His legs turned to jelly and he sagged against the wall. He nearly bit through his bottom lip as he struggled to pull himself together. He grabbed for another pill but it was difficult from the position he was in. His shaking fingers succeeded as he gulped down more bile along with the tablet that burned his throat. The sensation seemed to help him and he very, very slowly, pulled himself together. The old man wheezed and took more deep breaths, something his new Doctor had ordered him to do whenever he had an attack such as this.

He searched his memory but it was too long ago. He should have come and looked for them before, when he was younger, but he always came up with a good reason not to, such as always blaming the lost key, or the strength of the door, or his illness. When the urge to search for them got really strong, he always pretended he couldn't hear any noises at all and left the house.

He found the light switch; it wasn't where it should have been and the damned thing wouldn't work or maybe the blasted bulbs had gone. It was a bit lighter, but he couldn't see much at all. He could hear the noises, but that was nothing new. He began to think he could hear someone breathing. Then he began to think he could hear quite a few people breathing but that was nothing new either! If his brother and sister were playing their rotten tricks on him once more, he would get his pale-faced friend to punish them again but even harder this time! He wondered what had happened to his cricket bat and he remembered his friend loved that bat.

He never hit the pale young boy with the big sad eyes as he never played rotten tricks on him. Instead, he kept him company and spoke to him all the time. He could remember his father telling him to be quiet but he wouldn't. Why should he keep quiet? He was his friend so he'd told his father to leave his friend alone or it would be the worse for him! He remembered his father taking his glasses off and getting really cross. Then his father shouted at mother, pointing at her with his glasses. Mother didn't shout back and he remembered how really worried she looked and how she quietly but firmly suggested to father that she should telephone the vicar. Then he and his friend had counted the steps as they both went slowly to their beds

The old man found another switch, a switch that somehow registered, but only elusively in some dark corner of his memory. 'I do know about this switch,' muttered the old man. 'I know I do,' but the why of it wouldn't come to him. He debated with himself whether or not to use the switch again. He had used it before, many a time. 'Of course!' he shouted out. The answer came like a bright shining light. He'd used it when his friend had come back to see him! He'd used it often. His friend always came back when he came down here! He smiled and pressed the switch and his pale-faced friend smiled back from the dust-smeared mirror as all hell broke loose on the floors above. The orderlies in the secure unit ran up and down and round and round exactly like the patients they were supposed to control. They finally found him this time in the hospital laundry telling his pale-faced friend over and over again to always keep a straight bat, even when thrashing the life out of one's elder brother!

Richard Lee Wilson January 2003

Time to die

'Where's Adam?' called Foxy as he leaned out of the doorway of his office. He hung there one handed for a second on the door jamb in this sort of semi-dance pose. It appeared as if Detective Chief Inspector Fox was looking into the incident room to see if his people were hard at it; he wasn't, and they were. He was a tall, slim-built man, and with his longish nose and not quite devil's eyebrows he looked more like an academic than an ex-army captain. He had a thin-lipped mouth and narrow chin which, to those who didn't know him, obscured his generous nature. His once black hair with its parting as straight as the flight of an arrow, and exactly like his maternal grandfather's, showed the inevitable slow creep of grey round the temples and up behind his ears. His eyes were grey and were very rarely flinty. When they were, it was best to head for the hills or go for a smoke in number four cell that had a duff light switch.

He didn't call loudly or impatiently. He never did as it wasn't in his nature. He was from Durham but the accent was almost, but not quite gone. He was a quiet-spoken man and not one for excessive ranting and raving if something went wrong, or even badly wrong. Some considered him to be too much of a gentleman. Others said he was a nice guy. In most ways he was. It wasn't exactly a facade, but he did encourage people to think he was what they thought he was. It put people (and suspects in particular) at their ease. It made them more open to his peculiar style of questioning. When he interviewed these people (as he called them) he'd let them relax, so much so, they thought they were in conversation with an old friend! It would dawn on them as the Chief Inspectors face turned to stone, that it most certainly wasn't! Detective Chief Inspector Fox was nobody's fool and you could count his good friends on one hand.

He called out again as tired faces turned his way and he was asking a question, nothing more than that. At this moment he didn't need Adam but he did want to know where he was. He'd just had a thought on the Paulter case and he wanted to kick it about a bit with him. He often had these random thoughts and usually they had nothing to do with the case he was working on but they were invariably significant!

Nobody knew where Adam was. He'd taken a call and gone out at around about nine fifteen. Constable Peen returned to her processor and Fox went back into his office after a hand wave of thanks to his lads and lasses (he couldn't break from the habit of calling people younger than himself lads and lasses); he'd no need to bother trying really, none of them took offence. There was no immediate rush, he'd made a careful note and they could go over it later. These unspoken thoughts went through his mind as he sat back down at his desk and closed the file marked, Paulter. He drummed his fingers for a moment on the blotter then leaned back in his chair and closed his eyes, then steepled his fingers and reconsidered his earlier thoughts. If the taxi driver who dropped the two blondes outside the bank had told the truth (and there was no reason why he shouldn't) those two women had gone into the bank only minutes before the robbery at the chemist's shop next door. Or what if the taxi driver was lying and was in on the robbery? It wouldn't be difficult to prove but it just wasn't feasible. The Inspector couldn't think of any good reason why the taxi driver would draw attention to himself by coming forward with information about his two passengers. 'Service' taxis were a one-man-band; if he was lying he had to be stupid to volunteer the information and put himself bang in the middle of the frame. No, decided Fox, it would be more than stupid. He'd absolutely nothing to gain! There had to be another taxi involved! Fake or real?

His phone buzzed breaking his train of thought like the bursting of a soft balloon and he bounced forward in his chair and picked it up. It was Adam. He told Detective Chief Inspector Fox he'd been called to a house where the occupant had heard gunshots. She thinks it came from a, Mr. Pilling's house across the field but she's not certain.

She said, 'This sort of thing happens all the time. If it isn't a farmer shooting rats, it's a farmer shooting crows or rabbits. But this sound wasn't the same or I wouldn't have bothered the police.' Mrs. Malcolm also said, 'These shots I heard were more like muffled cracks than the loud blast of a shotgun.'

'Give me Mr. Pilling's address, Adam and I'll meet you there.' The Inspector jotted it down, then called for a car and a driver. Inspector Fox didn't drive, he had a driving licence but he didn't have a car. His wife Isobel did but he wouldn't drive it. Cars to him were small buses and he never wanted to be a bus driver ergo, he didn't want to drive a small bus. He liked to sit back into the leather of the seat and relax, be it in a taxi or whatever; it gave him more time to think.

His car and driver arrived promptly (unpunctuality to Inspector Fox was as bad as a soldier being on dress parade in odd slippers). The driver was Constable Churchman! Detective Inspector Fox knew him well as he did most of the drivers.

He got in, gave Churchman the address, settled back and said, 'If you go more than forty miles an hour, Constable, I will poke you in the eye with my stick!'

Constable Churchman smiled wryly, nodded and said, 'Yes Sir,' because he knew Foxy would be true to his word even though there was no sign of the Chief Inspector's walking stick. On the one and only occasion the Chief Inspector and Constable Churchman had been inadvertently involved in a car chase at speeds in excess of seventy miles an hour, the Inspector had been as sick as a dog! Constable Churchman was left to sort out the mess! On this occasion, the needle never passed thirty-nine miles an hour while on the way to Hagg Wood Cottage, Elderberry Lane, Lower Pagley.

When Chief Inspector Fox arrived at the house, Detective Sergeant Adam Heaves was waiting on the top step outside the open front door, having arrived there no more than five minutes before the Inspector. Adam was drawing hard on a cigarette. There was pallor on his normally tanned face and he was rubbing unknowingly at the back of his neck where his fair hair almost reached his coat collar. Detective Inspector Fox made a mental note of this as he quickly took in the surroundings. To call a house this size a cottage was obviously someone's idea of a joke or a bad attack of inverse snobbery. To the Inspector's eyes a more suitable name would have been Hagg Wood Mansion! The house screamed Georgian elegance at its absolute best. The gardens surrounding the paved drive were (in the Inspector's opinion – and he knew a fair old bit about gardening) perfect in every detail other than a multi-coloured bed of crushed lupins under the open front window. On the drive just in front of the police car, were two long, black skid marks giving the impression somebody had driven off in a big hurry. All this was noted by the Inspector.

'Keep away from those would you Harry when you go?' Fox pointed to the skid marks.

'Yes Sir, I saw them when we came. Looks like the starting grid at Brands Hatch,' grinned Harry, who was standing behind Fox.

Adam finished his cigarette; Foxy, was a non-smoker, but by no means a fitness freak. He had a thing about people who smoked and thought it tragic (even before the risks were known) to see people still finding need of a dummy. The Constable approached his Inspector.

'She was right Sir, and it's bad! Shot through the back of the head. The entry wound is just below the crown. Killed instantly by the look of it!

I've rung for an ambulance and Doctor Mayhew and the team are on the way. There doesn't seem to be anybody in the house. I've checked the ground floor, but I didn't go wandering about upstairs. I thought it would be best to wait till you got here Sir.'

Chief Inspector Fox nodded.

'The body's through here Sir.' Adam led the way.

'Check upstairs Harry, but be careful!'

'Right Sir.' Constable Churchman climbed the stairs.

Fox and Heaves watched him go up. He called out, 'Police, hello,' then turned left onto the landing.

'Be canny, Harry.'

'I don't think there's anybody here Sir,' offered Adam with a shake of the head. 'The killer would have to be crazy to hang round here. You'll see why Sir, when you look in there! And there's the tyre marks outside!'

Fox followed Heaves into what was obviously a study. The body of an elderly man was slumped forward in an old but immaculate wooden swivel chair. The back of the man's head was covered in blood where the skull was shattered. There was blood on the floor and more on the back and arms of the chair. There was also a pool of blood on the desk where the man's head had come to rest at an unnatural angle. The features on the right-hand side of his face were difficult to make out, most likely, thought the Inspector, by the exit of the bullet.

'Awful Adam.'

'Yes it is Sir.'

'Are you feeling all right now?'

'Yes Sir, I'm fine.' Adam smiled a quick self-conscious smile. 'It caught me out Sir, I must admit!'

Fox smiled as he remembered what happened on his first murder case.

The room was lined on three sides with bookcases and open bookshelves and the window wall was the only wall without some sort of shelves. The elderly man had been sitting at his desk facing into the room, with his back to the window-wall but not exactly central to it. His desk was positioned slightly to the right of the window. Directly behind him was a long-case clock, standing against the wall on the right-hand side of the window. Hung on the left-hand facing wall beside another long-case clock, was a portrait at least a yard square of some stern-faced middle-aged man with side-whiskers and a white, neatly trimmed beard. The picture looked as if it hadn't been dusted for months. Inspector Fox counted twenty-one clocks of all shapes and sizes in this room alone and they'd passed two more long-case clocks on the way through. Some were on shelves in the cases between the books some were on side tables and three (in pride of place) were on a flip-top table beneath the window. The skeleton clock on the windowsill was on its face to the right of a couple of scuff marks. One of the bookcases had been pried open. The lock was destroyed and the wood splintered on both the door and the frame. The sturdy-looking door of a steel wall safe was hanging open. There were deep gouge-marks in either side of its shattered lock. Inspector Fox and Adam jotted everything down and they would compare notes later. It was a system the Chief Inspector demanded must be followed at all times.

'Looks like whoever did it came through there, Sir.' Adam pointed to the open window.

'It certainly looks that way Adam! Was the front door open when you arrived?'

'No Sir, it wasn't. It was closed but not locked. I saw the body through the window and I thought he was asleep from what I could see of him when I first looked in Sir, so I called out to see if he was. He didn't answer and I called again, but still no answer so I came round to try the front door. I didn't want to get too near the window in case I disturbed anything. The lupins under the window were already trampled. I stood well away – I stood there on the edge of the grass and I marked where I stood with a small stone.'

Adam pointed through the open window to a spot on the lawn at least four feet from the window.

'Good thinking.'

The Inspector then frowned and gazed round the room.

'I can think of no reason why the person who did this didn't take the time to wipe the marks off the windowsill, stand that clock back up, shut the window, draw the curtains and walk out of the front door, can you?'

'Whoever it was was in a hurry to clear off, Sir! And perhaps the marks weren't noticed. It's more than likely he did go out through the front door, Sir. No point climbing back out through the window.'

Fox frowned again. Then as his eyes wandered round the room he said, 'Yet he had time enough to find the safe behind the bookcase, find something to force it and take whatever was in there. Unless of course the murderer knew where it was!'

Fox looked pointedly at Adam who nodded.

'And I agree, Adam, he probably did leave the house by the front door. But if I'd been in the murderer's shoes, I would have removed the marks from the windowsill, closed and fastened the window, drawn the curtains like rest of them in the house and then left through the front door. I would also have locked the door and kept the key until it could be safely thrown where it could never be found. Then if by some chance someone heard the shots and thought it wise to call the police, and the police come round here, the door would be locked the house would be secure! Consequently, the police would think nothing was wrong and leave, having decided from the appearance of the house that the occupants were out. The killer by doing that would have had as much time as he wanted to get away from here!'

Again, but this time with a couple of shakes of his head Inspector Fox glanced round the room.

'I take it you noticed the tyre marks on the drive?'

'Yes Sir, I did. The murderer must have been in a mad rush to get away.'

'You think so do you? Why do you think the killer would draw attention to himself or herself by driving off like a maniac? Could have been a woman? Did the lady across the field mention the squealing of tyres?'

'No sir she didn't. All she said was she'd heard two gunshots in quick succession. Actually, she said she'd heard one shot then she'd heard another minutes after the first.'

'Minutes you say? I wonder if she heard the echo of the first shot. Although minutes could mean any length of time. I would have thought though, with the house surrounded by thick woodland, there wouldn't be much of an echo. The sound would be absorbed by the trees. I must ask her. But first let's hear what Doctor Mayhew has to say. Just one little thought, Adam. If that's the house over there...' Inspector Fox pointed through the window to a white-painted cottage fifty or sixty yards away across the open field '...and if her attention was immediately drawn by the shots, wouldn't she have seen a car tear away from here?'

'She never mentioned anything about a vehicle at all, Sir.'

'Do you have the lady's telephone number?'

'Yes Sir, I have it here.'

'Give her a ring would you and ask her if she can see me over her garden hedge waving from this window. No don't use that, use the phone in the hall or your mobile.'

349

'Sorry, I wasn't thinking Sir.'

'Forget it, it's no big thing – I've often done it.'

Adam left the study and Fox leaned over the flip-top table and began waving out of the window. It was a few moments before the lady answered.

'She says she can see you clearly,' called Adam from the hall.

'Ask her if she saw a car here at all today.'

'She says, no, only the ones here now Sir.'

'Thank her Adam and ask her if it would be convenient if we call over there in half-an-hour or so.'

'She says that's fine, Sir." Adam replaced the telephone and returned to the crime scene.

The Inspector, standing quite still with his hands on his head and looking as though he'd been sent to the naughty corner, was peering at the portrait of the white-haired man.

'Have you made a note of the dust on this, Adam? Odd when everything else in here looks as though it was cleaned five minutes ago.'

Adam hadn't made a note but he did so now, while the Inspector was still facing the picture. Fox heard the faint rustle of paper and smiled to himself. Adam was a good detective, and was improving in leaps and bounds, but he was young. He had a few rough edges to round off and he still had plenty to learn, even if he didn't think so himself.

'Have you finished making a note yet? I'm sick of looking at it! He's got cruel eyes!'

Adam stuffed his notebook back in his pocket. Harry came in saying there was nobody in the house.

'Thanks Harry, you can go. I'll come back to the station with Adam.'

'Right Sir.' Harry left the house.

'Check the safe Adam, it's probably empty but have a look just the same.'

Adam went to the wall safe. 'There is an envelope in here Sir.'

'Is there by God?'

'Do you want me to get it?'

'Yes, yes bring it over.'

Chief Inspector Fox was bent over the desk trying to inspect the left side of Mr. Pilling's face. Adam waited with the envelope hanging from his finger tips.

'Pop it on the table over there please; we'll let the team have a go at it first.'

Adam placed it carefully on one of the centre tables as Doctor Mayhew called out from the hall, 'Show them through Adam; I want a closer look at that safe.'

Fox went over to the wall safe. He looked closely at the damage round the lock, then as he came away he said, 'Now there's a thing! I wonder if they'll spot it!'

Three detectives in white, paper boiler suits and two ambulance men followed Doctor Mayhew into the room.

'Hello Paul, we've got a nasty one for you this time. If you two wouldn't mind waiting outside please, he's well beyond your help. I'll call you when we're ready for you.'

The two ambulance men glanced at the body, nodded and left the room. The scene of crime team greeted the Inspector and Adam then they went efficiently about their business. Dozens of photographs and samples were taken; fingerprints were methodically searched for; questions were asked and answers were given. They found a clear print on the frame of the damaged bookcase and three clear prints on the handle of the safe.

'I've got something here Sir. These three are clear as crystal!'

Doctor Mayhew, who was the Regional Home Office pathologist, carefully examined the victim.

'If you've done here chaps, I need to move him.'

'Yes, Doctor, we've got all we need from there.'

'Thank you Sergeant.' The Doctor gently raised the victim's head.

Inspector Fox had returned to the wall safe and was now inspecting the prints on the handle.

'Odd, very odd, don't you think so Adam?'

Adam wondered what was odd. 'Why odd Sir? If they're the murderer's prints, it confirms what I said before. He must have been in a big hurry to clear off!' Fox looked disappointed. Adam noticed the look and wondered why. No point hanging about once the job's done, thought Adam.

'You think there's more to it Sir?'

'I do that, have you noticed the direction of the damage to the dead-latch Adam?'

'Yes Sir, it's a mess!'

'The direction of the bend in the dead-latch Adam, not the state of the damage. Go and have another look, now! Have you seen it, Patrick?'

The Inspector turned to Sergeant Mahone.

'Yes Sir, I've seen it. If it was pried open it should be bent the other way. I've made a note.'

'Good man. Any prints on the window, or the sill, or that clock?'

'No, but there's a few smudges on the bottom edge of the window frame both inside and out. The window's obviously been forced open. The fastener's been shafted Sir, but what prints there are, are useless, there's nothing else for me over there.'

The Inspector thanked him and turned to Adam.

'Well?'

'I see what you're saying about the lock Sir. Maybe the murderer tried to slam it shut. The latch doesn't look to be that strong, It's only thin steel Sir. But there are clear prints on the handle of the safe and the bookcase but nowhere else.'

'That's exactly what I'm saying. It looks as if he deliberately signed his name to it, doesn't it?'

'It does Sir, but once the murderer had emptied the safe, why would he hang around? He'd want to be out of here. There's no other explanation, Sir.'

'Yet he had time to do the dusting before he dashed off, kind of him hey Adam?'

Adam thought a minute, and then said, 'It could have been done before the murder Sir. He must have a cleaner for a house this size!'

'He could have, but let's wait and see, eh?'

'Single shot to the back of the head. The bullet entered in a downward projection from left to right. It's still wedged in the lower right cheek bone. Impact must have spun the victim's chair approximately nine or ten inches in a clockwise direction. Victim's right foot is pushed hard against right-hand side of the knee hole. Scuff marks clearly shown on carpet.' Doctor Mayhew was dictating to a small tape machine as he went about the examination. 'Dead no more than an hour. Bullet will be diffi…'

'Sorry to interrupt Paul, but you said bullet singular!'

The Doctor switched the machine off as Inspector Fox joined him by the desk.

'Yes Peter, single shot from somewhere near the right of the window. The shot was fired from above. Why? Do you have a problem with that?'

'No, not a problem as such, just another oddity. We have a witness who said she heard two shots!'

'Have you? Well as yet I've found only one entry wound Peter, so I can only think she must have thought she heard two shots. Perhaps she heard the echo, is it possible?'

'Perhaps,' replied the Inspector but he very much doubted it. 'Too many oddities for my liking, Paul!'

Paul sniffed but didn't reply as he knew what Foxy was like.

'There looks to be a lot of blood around to say it's a head wound.'

'Yes, that's true, but bone splinters will have caused secondary trauma. I'll know more after the autopsy.'

'Hardly think the sound would echo!' said Inspector Fox more to himself than to anybody in particular. 'In fact, even if the second sound she heard was an echo of the first, it doesn't make much difference; nothing here feels right to me. Think about it, someone forces that window to gain entry, then knocks that big brass clock over. The victim doesn't even look round to see what the noise is all about.'

'Are you talking to me?' asked the Doctor breaking the Inspector's train of thought.

'Not in particular, I'm listing the oddities.'

The Doctor sniffed again and went back to what he was doing.

The Inspector continued. 'He sits there while the murderer shoots him. Then whoever shot him breaks into the safe, leaves a couple of sets of prints, then races away! I don't think so!'

Foxy was off on one, thought Adam making himself busy.

'He could have been having a nap, Peter, or not in the room at all when the widow was forced. Could be he heard noises and came to see what the hell was going on. The killer could have left the window down and the curtains closed, then just waited outside till things settled down. Perhaps the victim, finding nothing disturbed, sat at his desk for a while to do some work and nodded off; the elderly often do. And the prints could be his?'

'Patrick has already said they're not, but yes he could have dropped off; however, I don't think he did. Let's see what's on the desk when we move him. I'll give you odds of a hundred-to-one he wasn't asleep! And I bet when we go poking round the garden we'll find the gun, but not with the same prints on it as those on the safe door!'

The Inspector would have been wrong about the gun! They did find a small crowbar in the lupins under the window but there were no prints on it. They also found a screwed up duster.

There was a commotion outside and voices were raised. Then a well-dressed woman of about fifty-five stormed into the room and called back. 'Nobody would dare to murder Father!'

She looked like thunder and stopped dead in her tracks when she saw the man sprawled across the desk, staggering backwards as if she'd been smacked full in the face. Adam, being the nearest one to her, went to her thinking she was going to pass out. Instead her hand went to her mouth and she looked at everybody in the room as if she was lost. Then as she gnawed at her fist, she screamed. Doctor Mayhew and Chief Inspector Fox gave her what comfort they could. They helped her into a chair making sure as they did that her back was towards her father's body. She declined the offer of a brandy and no, she didn't want a sedative. She didn't want anything. 'I will be perfectly all right in a moment,' she said but she wasn't. She sobbed quietly with her face hidden behind her hands. The Doctor indicated to Fox that he would take her outside and the Inspector nodded in agreement. Despite her obvious reluctance, the Doctor led her out of the room and into the garden. Between sobs she flatly refused to sit in his car with or without the door open. She wanted to call Nat, her husband. She would have to tell her brothers.

'What on earth is going to happen at the office? Leave me please Doctor; I must get to the phone!'

She rushed to the telephone in the hall and dialled a number. Doctor Mayhew passed her as he returned to the scene of the crime.

'She's contacting her brother and seems to have pulled herself together a bit. Terrible shock for her seeing her father like that!'

'It's bound to be, she shouldn't have got past the men outside!' replied Fox, biting at his top lip.

He then asked quietly, 'Have you finished with him? Can we move him, Paul?'

'I've finished, what about you, Malone?'

'Yes, all done and dusted in here, Doctor. Oh, and Sir, that envelope, two beauties on it, and it's his Will!'

Mahoney offered a smile and waved his little brush. He was trying to lighten the atmosphere.

'Thanks,' replied Chief Inspector Fox carefully picking up the envelope and putting it in his pocket. He offered a smile to Mahoney in return.

The woman came back into the room but didn't go near her father's body. Inspector Fox made a mental note of her reluctance and escorted her out into the hall.

'Do you...'

'No,' she interrupted. 'I'm fine. I'm quite all right now. It was the shock of seeing...' She didn't finish. 'Look, you must excuse me. I must go to the office as I haven't been able to contact my brothers. There are things I must do! Where will you take him?'

'To the mortuary.' He left the rest unsaid. 'Procedures must be followed. I'm very sorry. And I'll need to speak to you at some stage; now's not the time, but sooner rather than later if you don't mind.' She pushed a renegade tussle of greying hair firmly back behind her ear and tears welled unheeded into her eyes. She looked at him but didn't speak, just staring right through him as though she hadn't heard a word he'd said!

She left the Inspector standing in the hall and he didn't stop her leaving. She would be questioned at a later date – now definitely wasn't the time!

'I couldn't get anything from under the window outside Inspector, too much trampling.' Harper one of the crime scene investigators strode through the front door as if he owned the place.

'That's something in itself, James, don't you think?' replied Fox as he followed the man's massive frame into the study.

'If it is Sir, I don't know what it is!'

Inspector Fox smiled. He liked Detective Sergeant Harper. With Jimmy Harper, you got exactly what it said on the tin.

The Doctor was examining the body that they'd managed to get in an upright position. The wound to the face was dreadful.

'Looks like you were right Peter. He wasn't asleep, he was writing something on this pad. He didn't get very far with it. Come and have a look. There are only half a dozen words. I can't make much sense of it, perhaps forensics can; they'll clean up the paper.'

Adam had joined the Inspector as he came into the study and they were both over by the desk. The paper was badly stained but the address of the cottage at the top of the sheet was clear. Inspector Fox carefully lifted the sheet of paper off the desk only to find the few words left were illegible. There was a hole through the top of the desk. 'Ha, what's this? Is that where the missing bullet finished up? The desk top is solid oak by the look of it. Get it out Sergeant would you?'

Sergeant Mahoney nodded, took a probe from his case and replied, 'I'll get it out Sir, no trouble at all.'

'It looks to have gone in at a very similar angle to the one that killed our man here.'

'Yes, it looks it!' replied Fox.

'There's a nasty gash across the right side of the victim's neck, there,' said the Doctor as he carefully angled the victim's head sideways.

Fox leaned over and had a closer look. 'Nasty, it certainly is!'

The Inspector was silent but only for a split second. 'Gets odder by the minute Adam!'

Adam didn't think it was odd. 'Sir, I think the murderer missed with the first shot and killed Mr. Pilling with the second shot. That's why Mrs. Malcolm heard two shots close together.'

'Didn't Mrs. Malcolm say, "Within minutes of each other"?'

'Well yes sir she did, but that could have been a manner of speaking, couldn't it?'

'It could Adam. We'll find out exactly what she meant when we go over there!' It darkened outside as it started to rain.

'Got it Inspector, or what's left of it. I don't think we'll get much from it, but at least we know now there were two shots fired.'

'Yes we do.' Inspector Fox rubbed his chin. 'We certainly do! And I wonder if the murderer had a brass band play the March of the Valkyrie as he or she climbed in through the window!'

There it is, thought the Sergeant; Foxy's got that look on his face. Adam had heard of the march but wasn't aware of its significance to his Inspector.

'Do you mind finishing off here? I've got all I need for now. When you leave, you know to secure the building and seal this room. And…' said the Inspector with an ambiguous grin, 'check the garden on both sides of the drive for the weapon. We shouldn't be more than twenty minutes and I think you'll have found it by then.'

Sergeant Malone wasn't convinced but you couldn't tell that from his confident reply.

'Come on Adam, let's go and have a chat with Mrs. Malcolm.'

The rain came down in sheets and they dashed to the car. It was ten minutes before it eased off. The puddles in the lane leading to Mrs. Malcolm's house were expertly skirted by Adam.

Chief Inspector Fox stood at the window and watched the white-clad policemen search the garden from the warmth of Mrs. Malcolm's front room. He held a cup of delicious tea in one hand, and a very average piece of fruit cake in the other – his second piece. He'd managed (as dry as the cake was) to get the first one down! Mrs. Malcolm took great delight in the fact that both policemen loved her cake and warmed to the Chief Inspector. What a gentleman he was, Just like her brother Simon. Yes, the shots she heard were within a minute of each other. Maybe two? Yes she knew lots about the Pilling Family.

'Mr. Pilling,' confided Mrs. Malcolm to the two policemen, 'is a widower and he's a real nasty piece of work. His wife had died nearly ten years ago. They have three children, two middle-aged sons and a daughter. The daughter was the middle one. Andrew was the youngest; Steven, a creepy devil was the eldest. He was as bad as his father if not worse. Andrew wasn't much better and Geraldine was the best of a bad lot. She was happily married. Both Andy and Steve (as they liked to be called) were divorced. My late husband did a lot of work for Pilling over the years and he always made him wait for his money. I don't know why he bothered. We were comfortably off so he didn't need to work at all. Damned clocks. Sorry, but it makes me cross to think about it.' Mrs. Malcolm had sighed as she'd recalled the wasted days. 'We could have spent more time, lots more time together, Inspector, but you don't think of that till it's too late. And you know, you can't get it back!' Her wagging finger emphasized the point. 'Morris, my late husband, loved clocks. I used to think he thought more of them than he did of me. But he used to laugh like a goat when I told him so.' She forced a little laugh. 'Not like that nasty creature over there.' She made the word creature sound like scum. 'I know one shouldn't speak ill of the dead, but he was an evil man. He didn't love his clocks. He only worked on them. It was all money with him. Morris use to say, "The miserable s-o-d was brilliantly clever with the works and things, and he could work wonders with them." He said they were worthless if they weren't perfect. Couldn't sell them for top money was one of the things he used to say to Morris. 'Pilling made that Jack-in-the-box there. I don't know why it's still here really. Thing scares me to death every time the grandchildren come. Ugly red-faced thing leaps out, then it twists and turns, croaks hello then pulls itself back in and the lid shuts. I haven't wound it up since it nearly had Emma's eye out. I've told them the spring's broken. That's only a white lie, but better to be safe than sorry. Anyway, oh yes, I was telling you about him and his clocks. Well it was all money and possessions with him and those selfish sons of his. He still owes Morris over three-hundred pounds. I never expected him to pay. Morris said he would one day. Well he has!'

She pulled a face then sighed and dabbed her eyes.

'I'm all right Inspector; it's the memories, sad and happy ones alike. You know what I mean. It all makes life seem like a waste of time! Anyway, Geraldine, or Jerry as she prefers, I don't know why they bother christening them these days, do you Inspector?'

He shook his head.

'Well as I was saying, Jerry was the only one worth bothering with according to Morris. I don't know them that well,' she sniffed. 'That's because Morris said, she got out of her father's clutches early, or he would have tainted her like he did the other two. He didn't like the idea of her getting married. He said her future husband was a nobody and always would be. But she's strong willed. Well seemingly, her husband proved him wrong. She takes after both her parents. He liked him even less when Nathaniel, Mr. Porter… that's what they call her husband – I think that's his name – became a somebody! But all that's bye the bye now isn't it?'

It wasn't but Inspector Fox nodded in agreement. Nothing to him was bye the bye.

'Anyway, whoever it was who killed him probably did him a favour!'

There was no reaction from Inspector Fox at this bolt from the blue.

'Whether they knew it or not though, is another thing. More tea or cake?'

Both the men accepted her offer. Adam was learning, noted Chief Inspector Fox as Adam took another piece of cake. Actually, Adam liked the cake and he hadn't eaten till now. Mrs. Malcolm's rotund body folded neatly over her broad green belt as she leaned over to pick up the teapot.

Inspector Fox gave Adam a nod and turned once more to the window.

'What did you mean when you said, "They did him a favour", Mrs. Malcolm?' asked Adam, now he'd emptied his mouth and before he filled it again. 'Was he in trouble or something? Maybe with the police?'

Adam took another bite and turned to the Chief Inspector. Foxy quietly sipped his tea and said nothing. This information neither hindered nor helped one of the theories he'd been slowly but methodically working on. He was glad of the distraction. Now she was facing Adam, he could slip the third piece of cake into his pocket.

'No, nothing like that, well not that I know of. He was dying; he'd only a short time to live. Maureen told me. She's the district nurse and also a friend.' She smiled warmly. 'A good friend, who helped me with Morris towards the end. She told me Pilling had a terminal illness and said it could kill him off at anytime. She didn't tell me what it was; I assumed it was a cancer of some sort.' She turned back to the Inspector. 'Has it gone already? Here take another slice. I'll cut you a bigger piece this time.'

'No, please don't. As delicious as it is, I couldn't be so greedy, Mrs. Malcolm. I think you should save the rest for the next time we come, don't you?'

He tried his best to raise one eyebrow, but had to settle for a smile instead. Even Adam believed him. Had the Chief Inspector chosen a stage career he would have rivalled Lawton!

She laughed and said, "She would" and put the plate back on the table.

The Inspector turned to the window again. 'Was there a car at the house last night, Mrs. Malcolm?'

'Yes there was Inspector. A bright red one.'

'Did you notice what time it left? You might have heard a squeal of tyres, sometime around ten o'clock, perhaps? Before the storm?'

'Well I never.' She made a slight snorting sound. 'How extraordinary of you to know that!'

'I wasn't certain, Mrs. Malcolm. But I'm glad you confirmed it for me.'

'Well let me see. It was definitely after half-past-nine. Because it's then when I drew the curtains. I left the top window open two notches like I always do even though it was threatening another thunderstorm last night. You wouldn't think it was June, would you?'

Three heads shook as one.

'I like a bit of air in the house. It gets a bit heavy in here during the summer months, what with the low ceilings and the trees in the front garden. Morris always had the windows open, even the ones upstairs. Even in winter.' Her eyebrows rose. 'Said he liked to fall asleep to the night noises. He wanted them open on the night he died.' The sadness of a lonely woman returned to her soft brown eyes. 'It was the first of February six years ago. It was a bitter night. Well that's all bye the bye. I'm sorry, I do go on sometimes.'

'There's no need to apologise Mrs. Malcolm.' The Inspector gave her his warmest smile.

'Life is no less cruel to the angelic than it is to the devilish! That's what my mother used to tell me at every opportunity.'

'I'm sure you're not a devil, so please don't apologise.'

'I was a devil when I was younger, Inspector!'

They both laughed together. Adam, born two generations later, offered a polite flicker of a smile.

'Now let me be sure.' She tapped her bottom lip, then after she'd formed a picture in her mind, she said, 'It was before that silly programme on the other side. They put it on because the BBC news comes on now at ten o'clock. I've stopped watching the news. I can't be bothered with it anymore. If it's not some poor souls being blown to bits, it's doom and gloom or even worse it's politicians going on about how much good they do. Good for nothing, I say, every last one of them. All they do is line their own pockets or their cronies' pockets. They must think the public were all born yesterday. It's not the deceit that bothers me; I know what they're like, it's the insult to our intelligence when they expect us to believe what they say! There was something or other celebrity rubbish on last night so I turned it off. I've taken up reading again Inspector,' she said smiling. 'I can't think for the life of me why I ever stopped. Oh I'm sorry I'm doing it again.'

'Relax Mrs. Malcolm; we all go on as you call it.' She returned Adam's grin.

'Well it was while I was reading and before the heavens opened, which I think was just after ten o'clock. I do hope that helps?'

'Perfectly, Mrs. Malcolm and thank you very much. We'll need you to stop by at the station when you're in town. It's the main one, on Blackley Road. We'll need a formal statement. Do you know Blackley Road?'

'Yes, it runs behind the market hall, doesn't it?'

'That's the one.'

'I usually go into town on Fridays. Is that soon enough?'

'Yes, that's fine. Right Adam are you ready?'

'Yes Sir.'

He placed his cup on the coffee table next to the Inspector's and thanked Mrs. Malcolm for everything. The Inspector offered his hand, which she shook firmly. He wished her a goodbye and the two policemen left.

'Dreadful lane this, where does it finish up, Adam?'

'At a gate into those fields back there Sir.'

'What's over that side behind that hedge?' The Inspector pointed.

'More fields Sir, why?'

'Just making sure the screech of tyres couldn't have come from anywhere else.'

'They couldn't have come from the main road Sir, it's too far away.'

'You're right Adam they couldn't!'

They drove back to Hagg Wood Cottage making no conversation; the Inspector, sitting back in his seat, was deep in thought.

Adam stopped the car well clear of the tyre marks and they got out. Sergeant Malone and Doctor Mayhew came out to meet them. The ambulance had gone. 'Nothing for us upstairs Sir. I've checked all the obvious places for prints. The ones I did get from upstairs are all his and by the way, we didn't find the weapon. We found a crowbar in the lupins and a duster and the crowbar was clean as a whistle. Who ever shot him, must have taken the gun with him. Did you have better luck over there with the neighbour?'

'Yes, quite a lot. Those are from last night between half-nine and ten o'clock.'

Fox pointed to the tyre marks. 'And here's a twist. According to Mrs. Malcolm, our Mr. Pilling didn't have long to live, and Pilling and his sons were nasty pieces of work. He certainly wouldn't be missed.'

'That isn't the impression I got from his daughter!'

'No, me neither, Sergeant, but Mrs. Malcolm also said, she, the daughter, is the only one worth bothering with. She knows a lot about Mr. Pilling wouldn't you say Adam!'

'Yes Sir.'

'Why's that? Has she bugged his house?'

'No Sergeant she hasn't.'

Inspector Fox grinned with his Sergeant. 'Her husband did a lot of work for him, seems they were both keen horologists.'

Adam smiled and said, 'They collected clocks!'

'Thank you for that, Adam.' There wasn't the slightest hint of mockery in the Inspector's remark. 'No need to tell you all I would like your reports yesterday! And you Adam, I want you to get me some addresses. We need statements from the sons, the daughter, his solicitor and his Doctor. Post haste.' Fox counted each one off on his fingers. 'Seal this place before you go. Catch up with you all later. Right Adam!' Chief Inspector Fox got into Adam's car, nodded to his team then settled back.

They got back to the station at five-past-two; five minutes too late for the full lunch so Fox settled for the last of the ploughman's lunches. (Molly had only done four because nobody seemed to like them) or that's what she told Heaves. The truth was she'd told her friend Carol they were a fiddle-faddle to prepare and took up too much of her time. If he wanted to order one for tomorrow she would put one to one side. Adam settled for a bacon and egg sandwich. Neither of them had a pudding. As soon as the two left the counter Molly wrote out a sign and stuck it on the wall by the till. It read, 'To avoid disappointment, Ploughman's lunches must be ordered the day before they're wanted.'

Inspector Fox read it and smiled so he knew full well why she'd put up the sign. Adam went to order one for Wednesday and Thursday not because he liked them but just to see what she said! She threatened him with a ladle so he took a sachet of brown sauce and said menacingly, 'If you hit me with that, you're nicked. Assault and maybe a bit of battery and look, look at all these witnesses. I'll have you away in no time; you'll have to cook in the cells downstairs.' He flashed his handcuffs and Molly and the others in the canteen who had taken any notice got a laugh out of it. They finished eating and went upstairs. Fox sat at his desk and Adam sat facing him.

'Adam, I want you to get me the address of Mr. Pilling's firm. I'd like you to speak to the sons today. The daughter more or less confirmed they'd be there at some stage today. If they're not, find out where they are, will you? I want you to see them today!'

'Right Sir.'

Adam left the Inspector's office and the Inspector followed him out. He announced to the lads and lasses as he walked through ops that he'd be in the mortuary for a while. If not, he'd be in the lab. His announcement was acknowledged by most of them in the room then the Inspector went downstairs.

To Inspector Fox the mortuary, even with the staff bustling about always felt a lonely, sad, impersonal place. It wasn't the sight of the dead bodies that bothered him; he'd seen hundreds a lot worse in his army days, and many more since for that matter. It seemed to him that the bodies in here were abandoned. No mates there, no devoted wife, no family to help share this last indignity. Perhaps it was the glaring reflections of tube-lights on the white painted walls and the shadows beneath the stainless steel equipment that put him in this mood. It didn't help to have a two inch wide band of red paint forming a frontier between the upper and lower halves of the room!

'Why red in a place like this?' He muttered and shook his head. 'It's all too clinical.' Would it be less impersonal if the walls were painted in peach or lemon and the bisecting line in bright orange? He thought not. He pushed these thoughts to the back of his mind and greeted Doctor Mayhew.

'Anything to add to what we already know, Paul?'

Doctor Mayhew put down a rather grim-looking surgical tool and stood back from the table.

'I haven't done with him yet, Peter. But I'm ninety-five percent sure now that the laceration on the side of his neck was caused by a bullet; the one embedded in the desktop I should think. There was no sign of another bullet in the room. Patrick Malone might be a comic but he doesn't miss a thing. If you look closely you'll see the wound is much too wide and irregular for a blade. And I can confirm what the neighbour said. He hadn't got long. The tumour is massive; it could have killed him any time within the next fortnight or three weeks at the most. It's a miracle he got about at all! But there's something that puzzles me. Come into my office and I'll show you!'

Doctor Mayhew took the Inspector into his office and picked up a photograph off his desk and gave it to the Inspector.

'Look there.' The Doctor pointed out some spots of blood just in front of the clock.

'What's wrong about them? They look like all the others to me. There's bound to be blood spatters going in every direction after an impact like that in the back of his head!'

'Perfectly true Chief Inspector and who would know that better than you or I?'

The doctor's blue eyes twinkled. 'But look again; these don't go in any direction. These are from above. They're circular, all the others on the desk (other than the pool of blood there) are elongated away from the source of the wound!'

'Another anomaly Paul, so what are your conclusions?'

'I would say Peter, that the victim having received the wound in his neck, got up from his chair and went for his assailant, who (if you look where the blood spots are) must have been standing somewhere near the window or the clock. Then the victim was forced to sit at his desk again and shot in the head.'

'You're absolutely sure about this, Paul?'

'Absolutely, and in his physical condition he wouldn't have been able to put up much of a fight. I'm astonished he was allowed out of hospital.'

The Doctor frowned. Something else was nagging at him but he couldn't quite put his finger on it what it was. Then it suddenly came to him.

'The only problem I have with it is why aren't there more powder burns on the scalp?'

'The killer could have stepped back a couple of paces before he fired.'

'To stop getting covered in blood, do you mean?'

'Can't think of any other reason!'

'He could have been standing or leaning on his desk when the first shot was fired. Then while still in shock, staggered against the desk and slumped into the chair. Then the assailant comes up behind him and shoots again. Is that a possibility?'

'No, not a chance.'

Inspector Fox didn't for a minute think there was.

The Doctor removed his glasses and shook his head. 'The laceration is diagonal. Look.' The Doctor offered the Inspector another photograph. 'See? It's higher just below the ear than it is towards the throat; see there, its trajectory is in a downward direction.'

Chief Inspector Fox nodded. 'I think he had to be sitting more or less upright when the first shot was fired. When he missed with the first shot, the assailant had another go and killed him with the second bullet! Both bullets have the same trajectory pattern!'

'Hem,' replied the Inspector nodding and gnawing on the inside of his cheek. 'Do you have a copy yet of Sergeant Malone's measurements from the scene? They could give us some idea of the assailant's height.'

'No, not as yet. I should have them shortly and I have asked him for copies. He did say they were on the way down.'

The Doctor looked at the clock. 'But that was only ten minutes ago. I'll chase them up if you like?'

'No need, I'm going up there. I'll get my copies and chase yours at the same time. Anything else for me?'

'Nothing that won't be in my report.'

'Cheers then.'

'Bye,' replied Doctor Mayhew already turning back to the body. The reason Inspector Fox wanted to get upstairs wasn't only to get the measurements, he needed to think and he thought best when sitting in his own office, in his own comfortable chair with his eyes closed. Standing under the glaring white lights of the mortuary was not productive for his complex thought processes. There were so many anomalies about this murder he wasn't sure from which direction to start. He sat in his chair and closed his eyes assembling each oddity in the form of a list, then he arranged the list in alphabetical order. It would be noted down as soon as he was satisfied he'd covered everything. Blood spots; bookcase; bullets; clocks? He wondered for a second if they were pertinent. Desk top; fingerprints; safe; skeleton clock. Victim! He gave a few moments thought to Mr. Pilling, before once more rebuilding the scene in his minds eye. Weapon; Will; window; daughter's reaction. He squeezed this into its proper place. Flowerbed. He wrote that where it belonged. Then he went through them all, one by one. He sat quietly and without disturbance for nearly an hour. His people knew not to bother him. This almost ritual was sacrosanct. He suddenly sat forward, took a pad and made a list then he underlined in red the three most important elements of the case!

He left his office and went into the operations room.

'Would somebody get me a cup of tea? Plenty of sugar please.'

Detective Constable Wendy Thorpe, a very feminine and tenacious young officer got up from the computer she was using.

'No, not you Wendy. I want you to do something else for me. I want you to call Adam for me and ask him to find out who the victim's solicitors are. He should have that information by now. Then I want you to get round there, explain the situation to them and see if they know about the Will we recovered from the safe. If they do, tell them we're holding it as evidence. I want you to see them today. Right?'

'Yes Sir.'

Wendy picked up the phone and called Adam's mobile.

'I'll have my tea in my office,' he said leaving the hive as he called the incident room. He didn't ask anyone in particular to get his tea, but he knew he wouldn't have to wait long for it and it wouldn't be the rubbish that spewed out of the vending machine!

He'd finished his tea when the phone rang. DC Thorpe was on the other end. He smiled when she told him the stuck up so-and-so's had a Will there but they couldn't let me have a copy at this time. 'Mr. Brockley, the senior partner said, "We would have to apply through the proper channels." But after a bit of wheedling, he did say if certain conditions of the Will were met, who the main beneficiaries were, it's more or less equal shares. Geraldine gets a little extra by way of her mother's jewellery. He also told me they had no knowledge of any other Wills!'

'Indeed,' said the Inspector. 'So the eldest son gets a third! Well, Wendy, not according to the Will I have here! He gets it all according to this. Did he mention any other beneficiaries, or what these certain conditions were?'

'No Sir,' came the prompt reply.

'Did they give you the date when the Will they hold was drawn up?'

'No Sir!'

'Are you still at the solicitors?'

'No Sir, they more or less kicked me out. He took a call from one of the Pilling brothers just before I left. I don't know which brother, but a Will was mentioned. He wasn't on the phone long. He said they close at four-forty-five. He more or less followed me down the stairs, Sir!'

'Where's Adam now?' asked Inspector Fox, looking at the clock.

'He's still at the Pilling office as far as I know. Said he was with Steven Pilling.'

'Did he mention the Will we found in the safe?'

'Yes, but I don't know what went on after. The sister's there. I think he's already had a word with her. Sound's a right family, Sir!'

'Yes that's the impression I got from Mrs. Malcolm. She's the lady across the way who reported the gun shots.'

'Yes, Adam mentioned her, and her cake.'

The Inspector could almost hear the smile in her voice. 'Did she tell you the sons were adopted, Sir?'

'No, Wendy, she did not! Now there's a thing.'

The Inspector gave that little gem some thought. 'What about the daughter? Did Brockley say anything about her?'

'Yes Sir, he said, "She was their only issue!" He made her sound like a one-off monthly magazine.'

The Inspector smiled then said, 'I suppose he would. Anything else?'

'No sir that's it more or less.'

'Ok, oh and are you seeing Adam tonight?' There was a short silence while Detective Constable Thorpe said in her head, damn it, how did old Foxy get on to that.

'Are you still there, Wendy?' asked Inspector Fox, flicking his tongue across his teeth. He knew exactly what she was thinking, and he knew what his nickname was!

'Nothing's arranged Sir,' lied Wendy, much too late.

'Well if by some slight chance you do see him tell him I want a word with him about the Paulter case.'

'Will do. Do you want me back at the nick, Sir?'

The Inspector looked at his watch. 'Your shift ended twenty minutes ago, so no. But if you do bump into Adam, don't forget what I said. I'm away myself now. I'll be in after one o'clock tomorrow.'

'Right Sir, cheers.'

'Yes, bye.'

He put the phone down, picked it back up and rang for a car. Then he popped the Will into his desk! He'd sort Mr. Brockley, and his proper channels out tomorrow! If the Will lodged with Brockley pre-dated the one in his desk, it would mean the daughter and the other son would get nothing. He was on his way home within six minutes.

Traffic was end-to-end right up to the third lot of lights at Benbow Junction. The Inspector sat back in his seat and closed his eyes to the queues and his ears to the blaring horns and the annoying thud of diesel engines. He gave a lot of thought to the eldest son. Why would the father leave nothing to the other two? If the Will in his desk had been drawn up after the other one, that would be motive enough for one of the sons to kill. The house alone had to be worth over seven-hundred-thousand. He wondered about the business. The daughter appeared worried about that. Didn't she say what's going to happen at the office? Or something about the business? I'm sure that was the first thing she said when she saw her father's body. Then he thought about the silly nonsense of the trampled lupins and the skeleton clock lying on its side on the windowsill. Impossible, he told himself. And he gave a lot of thought to the two bullets!

'Are you going back to the nick later Sir?'

'What? Are we here? Sorry Constable, I was miles away.'

'I asked if you were going back to the nick, Sir?'

'No, not tonight.'

'How's the case going?'

'Which one, Constable?'

'The murder case Sir, it's all round the nick.'

'If you're asking about the Pilling case, I'd say it's very early days but it's going well.'

The Constable looked surprised as the Chief Inspector smiled. 'See you tomorrow.'

'Ten o'clock Sir, as usual?'

'No, I'll ring for a car when I'm ready.'

'Right Sir.' The car pulled away.

Isobel greeted him at the door; she was in what she called her scruffs.

'Been in the garden, Bel? Looks like you've brought most of it in here!' The Inspector grinned and shook his head as he pointed to a massive bunch of flowers on the hall table. She kissed him.

'Have you left any for the bees?'

'Of course I have. These are not for me; they're to be auctioned off tonight. I hope you haven't forgotten where we're going!'

'No, I'm looking forward to it.'

'Let's have a drink and I'll come out and help you clear up.'

'I've done most of it, there are just some dead branches I've lopped off the copper beech. You can stick them in the shredder if you want.'

'Let's have that drink first, and then I'll go and change. There's plenty of time. It's nothing formal tonight, is it?'

'No, I'm going in jeans and sweatshirt. You can if you want?'

'I don't wear jeans to go out in, and you know it. Jeans are for cowboys.'

He did a poor imitation of John Wayne. 'Not men of my standing.'

'Get lost, you wore some last Saturday!'

'Don't remember! Are you having one?'

'Yes, I'll have the same as you.'

'What's for dinner?'

'Nothings for dinner! We're going to a barbeque. Every body's taking something along.'

'Damn it, I'd forgotten it was a bloody barbeque. Can't we have something before we go?'

'Don't panic Peter; I've done yours in the oven. You've got chicken legs and a couple of slices of pork steak.

'Insult me if you like but my legs are the same as everybody else's legs. I'll go and put my jeans on and feed the shredder.'

'I'm going in the bath, I won't be too long and you can come and wash my back!'

'Ok, but it might make us late!'

'Get on with your work you; I'll wash my own back!' She laughed, took her whisky and disappeared through the door.

Inspector Fox sat for a moment on the settee arm and sipped his drink trying his best to ignore his work. He cleared his head and went to get his one and only pair of jeans.

The Barbie, as everybody called it, was a runaway success as far as fund raising was concerned. To Fox it was a nightmare. The smoke and the stench of overdone beefburgers, onions, pork chops and the like seemed to follow him everywhere he went. Isobel told him he's to go and see someone and to stop mewling and enjoy himself. His answer was to take hold of her and lead her to the marquee.

'I don't care who you want to see! You're my wife not the bloody mayor's!'

They danced till just before midnight and had a great time. Inspector Fox didn't get ratted as Mandy (Isobel's friend) said he did, but his eyes shone. Mandy, whose marriage had been a sham from the beginning, never considered that anybody could be happy dancing with his own wife.

It was when they were in the taxi on their way home that another thought struck him about the robbery. Did both taxis have two female passengers in them? Two went into the chemist shop as two went into the bank! That would work. They were attractive blondes. If they were made up to look similar, the witnesses in both the bank and the shop would see a taxi and two females. Maybe they were talking about different taxis?

'What are you muttering on about, Peter?'

'Nothing Bel, just thinking.'

Inspector Fox rang for a car at eight-thirty. He'd decided to cancel his eleven o'clock appointment with his osteopath so he would ring her and get an appointment for Friday because his back felt fine at the moment. He was at his desk by nine-fifteen and on the phone to Mr. Brockley. He'd got past Mr. Brockley's secretary by putting his Chief Inspector's head on. The Will on Fox's desk did postdate the Will held by the solicitors and by over two months. Mr. Brockley couldn't understand why Mr. Pilling had approached another solicitor. He was most perturbed! Inspector Fox couldn't help him.

'No, I have not had sight of the other Will. I explained so at length to your officer only yesterday. I am more than astounded. Mr. Pilling has been with us for more than thirty years.'

'Would you give me the date of that Will, Mr. Brockley?'

'This one was drawn up a little over two months ago. April the twelfth. I saw to the details and advised him on certain matters concerning the Will. He and the other members of his family are my clients. The other thing that bewilders me is the beneficiary in the Will you hold. Under the circumstances, I feel I'm not betraying a confidence. I suppose it's common knowledge that Mr. Pilling and Stephen Pilling did, to put it mildly, not get on. However, I made no mention of the matter at that last meeting. Mr.

Pilling was rather ill at the time and he was under a lot of pressure. I would however be betraying a confidence if I explained further. Is there anything else, Inspector? I really do have a lot to do.'

'No that's all for the time being. But I would appreciate a copy of the Will as soon as possible. One of my people will come for it today.'

'I will see what can be arranged. Goodbye.' The line went dead.

If Inspector Fox could have seen Brockley's face as he put the phone down it would have been like looking into a patch of foul weather. Brockley pressed a button on his desk and a young woman entered.

'Yes Mr. Brockley!'

'Do me a copy of that immediately and place it in an envelope then seal it and bring it to me. Thank you Miss Copley, that will be all!'

Miss Copley left the office and as she passed Sandra's desk she leaned over and whispered, 'Broccoli's got the hump on.'

Sandra said, 'What's new?'

Inspector Fox called Detective Sergeant Heaves and Detective Constable Thorpe into his office.

'I want you round at Pilling's solicitors Wendy. I want a copy of the Will they're holding. Don't come back without one! Right off you go.'

'Right Sir.'

When Thorpe left, the Inspector turned to Heaves. 'How did it go with the Pilling's yesterday?'

'Blood from a stone Sir. I spoke to all three of them. It was hard graft!'

'Go on.'

'I got nothing worthwhile from the youngest, and not much from the daughter, other than, she'd enough on her mind without me adding to it. She had no idea who could have killed her father. Her words were, "I know he was a hard man to understand, and he was abrasive at times, but that's no reason to kill him. He was dying anyway. So why murder him?" I left it at that because she was getting badly wound up.

'The eldest, Stephen, he was something else. Wendy rang and told me about the Will and when I asked if he knew about it, he just sneered and said, "Nonsense, impossible. Why would my father change his Will or leave anything to me at all. We hated the sight of each other!"

'I told him I'd no idea but there was definitely another Will and he was the sole beneficiary. He didn't believe me. Neither did the other two.

Andrew, the younger brother, burst out laughing and said, "Did you write it yourself? You're pretty good at signatures aren't you?"

'He told his brother to shut his big mouth or he might just mention what his brother's pretty good at! Andrew went pale. If looks could kill. I thought there was going to be trouble but he sat back down. The elder brother, Stephen, was on the phone to his solicitors as soon as his brother shut up! They confirmed it, which was pretty obvious from his reaction.'

'Well Adam. The one dated two months ago gives equal shares to the three of 'em.' Inspector Fox waved the folded papers. 'And this gives it all to Stephen, that's motive enough some would say! But his father would be dead in less than a month and he knew it, so why kill him? It would be absolutely stupid and completely illogical. I don't go with it. There's something else, something we don't know about.'

'It could have been euthanasia Sir; one of the family might have helped him on his way? I know it's a bit way-out Sir, and to shoot him seems stupid, but there's plenty of it about.'

Fox didn't even consider Adam's theory. 'It could have been the tree fairies Adam and there aren't many of them about! He was shot twice Adam, that's not mercy killing or euthanasia. That's murder! No, nothing about this killing is right, nothing!' Chief Inspector Fox shut his eyes and relaxed for a moment. Adam decided he would be a little more careful before he made any suggestions in future.

'We need to find out what the problem was between the father and the eldest son, Adam. I know there was something, and something pretty bad, that was perfectly obvious from what the solicitor said on the phone. We'll find out what it was from the daughter. She's probably the best bet. Go and see her at her home, not at the office. I'll leave that with you. Oh, before you go! I've had a thought about the robbery in Franklin Road. There could have been two taxis. One real, one not. Four women all made up to look the same. That way all the witnesses would have seen a taxi with two blondes getting out! Two go into the chemist shop! Two go into the bank... I think, Adam.' The Chief Inspector closed his eyes again. 'I think the two who went into the chemist to do the robbery finished the job. Then at a prearranged time, it wouldn't take long to get the drugs and what money there was in the till. Then say in four, maybe five minutes, the two women leave the bank, get back in the taxi and the two women from the chemist shop follow suit at exactly the same time. It fits perfectly with what the witnesses have said, especially the taxi driver. I can think of no other way it could be done. Can you?'

Adam didn't answer straight away; his last offer had gone down like a lead and concrete cocktail, but even when he did it was obvious to Adam that it wasn't what Fox wanted to hear.

'I don't think that's possible Sir! The witnesses would have seen two taxis!'

'Not if the fake one drove a bit further along the road as the genuine one arrived, just far enough to be out of sight of the bank.'

'I still don't see it Sir. I think the taxi driver's in on it and there were four of them in the taxi. And I think there was somebody waiting in the chemist shop to give them the all clear. Nobody can remember the exact time the taxi arrived. I think they waited in the taxi, got a signal of some sort from whoever was in the chemist then two of the women got out and went into the bank. Then the other two got out and went to do the job! That's how I see it Sir!'

'Ok, that's another possibility; I'll give it some thought.' Fox studied Adam for a minute as though he was considering Adam's suggestion. Then said, 'Right, we'll go over it together again later. One thing we must do is to find out how much of the road is visible from the window of the bank and the window of the chemist shop. That should settle it! But we'll skip all that for now; you go and have a word with the daughter. I'm going to have another look at Hagg Wood Cottage and then I'm going down to Cawfield's. I want to check the view from the window of the bank. Call me at about four.'

'Right Sir.'

Adam left the office and Chief Inspector Fox followed him out into the hive to get a driver. Adam knew he'd done the right thing by suggesting a different scenario for the robbery.

Adam knocked on the door of number fifteen Holly Berry Avenue. It was a quite large detached house. 'These people aren't short of a few quid,' he said to himself as he looked round the garden and at the big detached double garage. He'd always wanted a place with a double garage. He turned again to the door. The door was opened by a tall, fair-haired man who was smartly dressed. Adam reckoned he was in his fifties.

'Yes,' was all he said.

'I'm Detective Sergeant Heaves. I would like to speak to Mrs. Porter.'

'What about?'

'Do you mind if I come in? I don't want to talk about it out here Sir.' Adam didn't like the man or his attitude.

'If you must? Wait there, I'll go and have a word with her.'

Adam stepped inside and waited in the hallway. The man returned and motioned him to come through. Adam followed him into the sitting room. He was very impressed. Adam thought compared to his flat, this room had been furnished by the goddess of good taste.

Mrs. Porter was standing in front of a big window that overlooked the back garden. She turned when Adam entered the room.

'You'll have to forgive Nat's manners, he's very protective, Sergeant.'

'That's ok Mrs. Porter,' Adam smiled. 'We get used to it!'

'Would you like a drink? I'm having a whisky!'

Adam hadn't noticed the tumbler she was holding between both hands as if to hide it.

'No, I'm fine thanks, a coffee would be good. But I don't want to take up too much of your time.'

'Don't worry Sergeant, I'm fine now. I'm beginning to accept my father's death. Perhaps it was better the way he died. At least it must have been quick!' She turned away momentarily. 'Nat, will do you a coffee?'

She called her husband and asked him to make them all a coffee. He merely nodded and went out again. He was not a happy hippo. Adam had seen his type before and wasn't bothered in the least – he was doing his job and he would do it as thoroughly as he could regardless of the atmosphere in the house.

'What is it you want? Have you found father's murderer?'

'No, we haven't. But we will. No, what I want to ask you about concerns your brother Stephen. I know there was bad feeling between him and your father. He said yesterday that his father hated him, do you know why?'

'Yes I do, but I'd rather you asked Stephen about it. It was nearly three years ago. He was proud of what he did. Andrew was involved in it, not in the ruthless way Stephen was or the underhand way he went about it, but he was definitely involved later. Father didn't know Andrew was helping Stephen; well as far as I know he didn't. I'd rather you got the details from one of them.'

Mrs. Porter sat on the arm of one of the easy-chairs and sat her glass on her lap. Her coffee remained untouched on a small table next to the chair. She seemed to Adam to be preoccupied.

'If this is a criminal matter, Mrs. Porter, you should tell me everything you can. It's not a good idea to withhold information from the police, especially when it's a case of murder. I don't want to have to take you or your brothers in for questioning!'

Mrs. Porter slowly shook her head, but before she could answer Mr. Porter snapped, 'Leave My wife out of this. It's not a criminal matter; it has nothing to do with the police. It was a business matter, for God's sake! My wife wasn't involved. Perhaps if Jerry had held more shares in the firm she could have done something but she didn't and that's the end of it! Now if you don't mind, I'd like you to go. I think my wife's had enough for today.'

Mr. Porter showed Adam to the door and Adam followed him. He was reluctant to go but he could see Mrs. Porter wasn't in any mood for talking.

He rang Chief Inspector Fox from the car. 'No joy Sir, she won't give us anything. She told me to ask Stephen or the other brother about it. The husband saw me off. But before he did he said it had nothing to do with the police. He said it was something that happened within the firm. He didn't say what! But he did say if his wife had had enough shares at the time she might have been able to do something about it. He didn't say what she could have done! She wasn't involved. Sounds like some sort of takeover to me Sir.' Inspector Fox agreed.

'Do you want me to go and have a word with the brothers, Sir?'

'Yes, sort them out Adam. This is a murder enquiry, not a parking offence!' Adam's phone went dead.

He drove round to Pilling's office and both brothers were there. He ignored the secretary when she said they were in a meeting and a lot too busy to see anyone this afternoon, perhaps at eleven tomorrow. She looked up at him unsmiling as she closed the diary. He wasn't smiling when he repeated Foxy's words. Then said, 'I will see them now!' She picked up a blue coloured phone and spoke to Stephen. He didn't hear the reply but she asked him to go through. She pointed to the door on the right. He thanked her as a black phone started to ring.

He opened the door and went in and he could see he wasn't welcome; Stephen was red in the face and it took him a minute to regain his composure. Adam could feel the tension in the room. As soon as Adam accepted the chair he'd been offered, Stephen sent two men out, saying, 'We can go over this later. I'll buzz you when we've finished.'

'Now, what's this all about? Jerry's been on the phone and she's been having a go at me because of you. She said you were asking about my father and I. Well? What about us?' demanded Stephen. 'Can't you see I'm up to my eyes in it!?'

Adam didn't like him or his attitude; manners cost nothing, but he controlled his anger and said, 'Before we go into that I noticed a red coupé in one of the directors parking places. Is it yours?'

'Yes, it is, why?'

'A red car was seen at your father's house the night before the murder. Were you there?'

'Yes I was, I made no secret of the fact. My father was murdered the following morning. I was here, with two other members of the board. So you can eliminate me from your enquiries. I think that's the term you use!'

'My Chief Inspector does the eliminating Sir, not me. The other thing we want to know about is the problem between you and your father. You said yesterday that he hated you, and you couldn't understand why the new Will is in your favour.'

'Perhaps hate was too strong a word, but then again perhaps not. I suppose he did hate me for what I and some others did, but if we hadn't got rid of him when we did there wouldn't have been any need for a board of directors. There wouldn't have been a business at all, Sergeant Heaves! He was the Chairman. He was also the Chief Executive and a major shareholder. But he was losing his marbles, or deliberately trying to destroy his own business and do you want to know how?'

Adam wanted to grab him by his lapels, pull him the rest of the way over the desk, and smack him one right between the eyes. He didn't like people to stick their face in his, but instead he said calmly, 'If it will help with our enquiries Mr. Pilling, yes I do?'

Pilling sat back rather quickly. Perhaps he'd seen something in Adam's eyes.

'You've seen my father's house, so you will have seen the clocks. If not I'll…'

'I have seen the house Mr. Pilling.' It was obvious by the look on Stephen Pilling's face that he wasn't used to being interrupted. He was drumming his fingers on the desk.

'He bought most of those with company funds.' The drumming ceased. 'He said they were an investment for the future. He said he was concerned about the business. He was buying them in case there was a fall in world markets. What markets and which world, he didn't bother to mention. We do not deal in goods as such Sergeant; we deal with the people who deal in goods. The dealers or ghosts we represent trade mainly with the Chinese, and China if you read the papers is a bottomless well, and not only for dirt-cheap labour! If they don't have the necessary resources

375

themselves, they will get them from wherever they can and, no questions asked! That is the main reason why Andrew and I, in his words, "Knifed him in the back". Is there anything else you need to know Sergeant?' He spoke as if he'd memorized every word he said. Pilling glanced at his watch. It didn't impress Adam. He could sit here all day if necessary.'

'You can tell me why you went round there the night before he died.'

Stephen Pilling sighed. 'He asked me to go round; he invited me; he said there was a prowler in the grounds. I stood outside his study window in those lupins like an imbecile because he said he wanted to make sure it was me. He questioned me through the window for at least five minutes and then he went to the door and let me in. He asked me to come to his study and put an envelope in his wall safe for him. He said he couldn't turn the key. He didn't use those words! He was obviously in pain but he wouldn't have let me help him and I didn't offer to! And besides, all his medications were at Geraldine's, where he should have damn well been, Sergeant. He was only allowed to leave the hospital if he put himself in her and the nurses' care! God knows how he got there? I put the envelope in his safe, locked it and gave him the key. I asked him why he'd dusted the room. He told me to mind my own business and to get out of his house! I got out all right! I was fuming. I tried to get hold of Jerry to find out what the hell she was thinking of to let him out of her sight, but there was no answer. That's it Sergeant Heaves, that's the last time I saw him alive. Now we must be allowed to get back to our meeting or I may have to start selling the damned clocks!'

'We'll need you to come down to the station tomorrow morning to make a formal statement Mr. Pilling and we'll need samples of your fingerprints. And yours Sir.'

'We have no problem with that, do we Andy?'

'Not at all, Steve.'

'It will have to be before nine, Sergeant, if the law permits? We're away from noon tomorrow for a week.'

'And if we need to contact either of you?'

'Geraldine, she'll be here, she knows where we're going.'

Adam closed his notebook and stood up. 'Thank you for your cooperation, I'll see you both tomorrow morning, goodbye.' The brothers didn't bother to acknowledge the Sergeant's barbed goodbye. Stephen was already on the phone; the other one was going through a file on the desk. Adam was glad to be out of there. The elder brother couldn't finish a sentence without hanging a sneer on the end of it.

He rang Chief Inspector Fox as soon as he left the building and gave him a brief rundown. Inspector Fox told Adam he was on his way back from Hagg Wood Cottage and he'd see him either back at the station or in the morning first thing. He also told him that it was probable that there were two taxis because nobody could get to the window on the front wall of the bank nearest the chemist's because there was a desk in front of it. He'd leaned over to try and see out but it was impossible. The window was too high and the desk too deep. There was at least a ten foot blind spot from the bank window to the street. Any customers waiting in the bank wouldn't look out of that window. Chief Inspector Fox also said he didn't think Pilling's death was murder, but if it was then the victim was party to it! Adam thought his boss was being a bit dramatic if not mad, but he didn't say so. He would be happy to wait for the morning meeting.

Adam was at the nick by eight-thirty, he couldn't wait to shoot down his boss's theory. He'd considered what the Chief Inspector had told him and Adam thought it was impossible. Adam couldn't get it out of his head that there were two shots fired. He would face the Inspector with this fact as soon as possible. But the Inspector wasn't there; he'd left a message saying he'd gone out with Harry and he would contact Adam later in the day. He also told him to go over all the details of the death – everything!

Harry had picked the Inspector up at eight-thirty-five. Foxy was waiting on the station steps talking to Percy Green, the Senior Traffic Inspector. He saw Harry and got in the back of the car. Isobel had dropped him off on her way to Walford.

'I want you to pick up a friend of mine on the way Harry. He's coming over to the cottage with us.' Chief Inspector Fox tapped his nose when Harry asked him why. 'You'll see when we get there. His shop's at the far end of Albert Street, you'll have to follow the one way system, steady as you go!'

'Which shop is it Sir? There are dozens down that end.'

'It's the junk shop next door to the pet shop. Not the big one on the right.'

'I know it Sir, it's the antique shop.'

'Aren't they all?'

Harry grinned, indicated and pulled into the central lane slotting nicely into the stream of traffic flowing past the church.

'That clown's on his mobile. The chap there, in the white shirt. The red escort behind the silver Mondeo. Are we invisible Harry? Pull him over and give him a scare! Don't be too long though I told Jim we'd be there before half-nine.'

Harry switched the siren on for a couple of seconds. The car pulled over. Harry got out and had a few strong words with the driver. The driver (a man in his early thirties) nodded then shook his head then nodded again. Harry tapped on the car roof and told him to be on his way.

'He'll think twice about using it in future,' grinned Harry with a twinkle in his eye as he pulled back into the traffic. 'I told him it was his last and only warning and his name and number will be on the computer Sir.'

'He's lucky, we're in a hurry the moron.'

Harry nodded. In less than fifteen minutes Jim was in the car and they were on their way to Hagg Wood Cottage. They were there less than half-an-hour when Inspector Fox rang Adam.

Adam arrived at the cottage in less than twenty minutes. He went straight through to the study. Chief Inspector Fox, Harry and a scruffy-looking chap were there. They were grouped round the front of the long-case clock standing on the left of the window. On the front of the clock a small panel, just below the face but fixed in the body, was wedged open with a pencil. There was an identical panel that was closed in the clock, standing on the right-hand side of the window.

'Sam, this is Detective Sergeant Heaves. Adam, this is Samuel Makepeace, master clockmaker. Adam Sam.'

Inspector Fox introduced them to each other. They shook hands. Then Sam took a step backwards and turned again to look at the clock.

'Clever, skilful even. They look to the layman to be a pair. The inlay and the burr maple veneers he's used to camouflage the joints is perfect, but when one stands back to get the whole picture, the symmetry, one can see that the carcasses on both clocks are out of balance! The craftsman who constructed such magnificent clocks would never have made them so. Do you see what I mean? It's the length you see, it's all wrong.'

The man swept his hair back, took off his glasses and rubbed his eyes. 'I must say Peter, if Pilling did this to these exceedingly beautiful and valuable pieces to incriminate his eldest son, well he must have truly hated his lad, he really must! He used to buy from me you know. Terrible sod to deal with. He always wanted things at trade prices you know. I used to tell him there was no such thing, there was only the market price, and that was my price.'

378

'Well, he did hate him Sam, there's no doubt about that. The son's said so himself. But we'll never know for how long. We can only assume it's from when he got him kicked off the board of his own business.' The Inspector raised both eyebrows.

'Sounds like the eldest son was the prime mover, Adam?'

'Yes Sir, definitely. Andrew's wary of Stephen. It's obvious, Stephen's got some sort of hold over him, and I'm sure there were some dodgy share dealings done by the eldest to get rid of his father, and it's obvious the father found out?'

Adam took out his notebook and flicked through the last two pages. 'Yes it's here Sir. Andrew said something about Stephen being good at signatures! But he soon closed his mouth when Stephen referred to something in Andrews's past. It's like Mrs. Malcolm said, they're a bad bunch, and the only one worth bothering with is the daughter!'

Adam glanced round for a second expecting to see the weapon but he couldn't see it. 'Where is the gun, Sir? I still can't believe he shot himself. How could he get rid of the gun?'

Chief Inspector Fox smiled at Sam and said, 'Show him how Jack got rid of the gun for him Sam,' smiled Foxy.

'In there mi-lad. It's in there!' Sam pointed at the clock! 'Remember the Jack-in-the box Adam. Remember how it shot out of the box then went slowly back in! That's how he got rid of the gun; it's fixed in there behind that small panel I've wedged open with my pencil. I didn't think of it then. I only realized later.'

The Inspector stared at the clock. 'When we came back here after speaking to Mrs. Malcolm that morning and hearing the background of the victim and how much he hated his sons, I immediately suspected one of them, which is exactly what Pilling intended and when the weapon didn't turn up, I was sure it was one of the sons. But if one of them killed him, why didn't anything fit? They're not simpletons. They could have covered their tracks a lot better than was done here. No, nothing in this room was right Adam, especially with the body draped across the damned desk and a bullet embedded in the top directly under him! Then I looked at the window and that skeleton clock over there. What nonsense was that? Pilling, as ill as he was wouldn't have stayed sitting at his desk while a person forced and then climbed through the window! The lock on the safe with the bolt bent in the wrong direction; two shots fired! Then the will left in the safe pointing the finger straight at Stephen Pilling.

'There are three main motives for murder Adam as you well know.' Adam nodded and Sam joined in. 'Love, power and money.'

'Yes Sam, those are they. He has power; he doesn't know the meaning of the word love, which leaves money. One of the best motives there is for murder! But Stephen (if his office address is anything to go by) has plenty of money, and he's made it clear he wants nothing from his father, which shows how much he hated him. No nothing was anything like right. I decided there were only two possibilities: somehow he either killed himself to make it look like murder, or he got someone to do it for him with the intention of incriminating one of the sons.

'Why leave the crowbar outside the window and not the gun? Why not take the crowbar, the duster and the gun and ditch them somewhere? That fact alone negated the idea that someone else helped him or none of them would have been found. There's no way he could have got Stephen's fingerprints on to the gun or the crowbar. I came to the conclusion the reason the crowbar and duster were outside the window was because he put them there before he killed himself. Once dead, the gun would have been in his hand or on the floor near the desk. He unlocked the safe and then battered it with the crowbar; it doesn't weigh much. He tried to make it look as if it had been forced. He didn't have the strength to pry it open, that's why the latch was bent outwards. Then he dusted the room. He wanted us to think the murderer had done it but missed the fingerprints – one on the door handle of the bookcase, and the safe and the door handle. Those prints will without a shadow of doubt, be Stephen Pilling's.'

'Why two shots though Sir?'

'That was the clincher, Adam. The bullet in the top of the desk but only one entry wound in the body! That's because he didn't line up the target exactly right. He set the clock to fire at say ten o'clock and sat at his desk pretending to write a letter. The gun did its job, but the first bullet only grazed his neck. He had to try again. That's why the drips of blood over by the clock are circular and not elongated. They dropped to the floor from the gash in the side of his neck. You wouldn't know about them Adam, I didn't find out about them myself till after you'd gone. The second time the gun fired it killed him. He fell forwards and his body covered the hole left by the first bullet. Sam's shown me the work in there. He's set it so the barrel comes out nearly six inches, fires a round and goes back in. It's a clever piece of work.' Inspector Fox shook his head.

'Mad Sir, not clever. I don't mean the mechanism, I mean him.'

380

'I think he was Adam. So, each time the gun fired it wound itself back into the panel there. Exactly like the jack-in-the-box did at Mrs. Malcolm's. That's about it Adam.' The Inspector shook his head at the sadness of it all. 'You can speak to Mrs. Porter about her father's death tomorrow; I know you'll handle it with care. Then you can give a statement to the local papers, but don't forget to mention Sam. We have him to thank for the final touches. Now Sam, know anything about four blondes in two taxis?'

'No, not recently Peter, more's the pity!'

Richard Lee Wilson 2004.

Trip of a Lifetime

'How much did you get for the earrings Joan?' asked Harry from across the room. His strong shoulder muscles rippled as he almost threw the weights above his head for the tenth time in as many seconds.

Joan's lovely blue eyes sparkled wickedly as she tossed her long blonde hair out of her face. 'Eight-hundred pounds. He said the emeralds were a bit small but they had the finest depth of colour he'd seen in years.'

'No problems with your disguise then? You looked the part when you left here?'

'No, none at all. He called me sir or Mr Jones all the time I was in there!'

'Brilliant, we'll have the day off and do another couple of the silly old sods tomorrow! I saw a row of old fogies' bungalows yesterday when I was coming back from the gym.'

'Easy pickings then Harry, Pet?'

'Yep, like taking sweets from a baby!'

'I know what we'll do, we'll go to that theme park place, that new one in Blackpond. It's called Babylon I think?'

'Yes it is and they say it's brilliant. Lots of new rides and one of them is the highest and the fastest in Europe.'

'You won't be getting me on any rides like that; you know they make me sick.'

'You soppy wimp! Look at you, you aren't thirty yet and you're as strong as a horse. Why should things like that bother you?'

'They don't bother me; they make me sick that's all. You saw what happened to me when I went on the Waltzer; I made myself look a right nerd. No thanks, I want to enjoy myself while I'm young. That's what life's for, Pet, to enjoy. There'll be plenty of other stuff to go on and plenty of time to sit about when we're old and grey! There's the river, that's supposed to be terrific so we'll have a go at that.'

'Whatever!'

Joan picked up a magazine and settled on the settee. She liked the big rides but Harry would never go on them. She got a face on and flicked through the pages of the magazine without even looking at them. Harry ignored her and continued to pump weights.

The weather put paid to their visit to Babylon Theme Park, it absolutely poured down, so they decided to work on their next job. Joan worked on her computer forging the necessary forms while Harry worked on their fake identity cards; they never used the same identities twice. This time he was Mr Senior from the Council; she was Mrs Prior Maintenance Director in estates and properties. They'd checked carefully that both people worked for their respective departments so there would be no problems. They would do the business if it stopped raining, preferably after lunch. Everything was ready by two o'clock and it had stopped raining.

They left the house in a Ford Escort van; they'd fix stickers on it when they were clear of the town centre. Harry drove while Joan set the phones up. He pulled into a lay-by on the A111 where the traffic was somewhat sporadic. Quickly and carefully, Harry fixed the stickers to the sides of the van and when he was satisfied that they looked authentic enough to do their work, he drove back towards town. In ten minutes, having picked the bungalow out with the scruffiest garden, he went and knocked on the door while Joan stayed in the car. Harry's theory about picking the most untidy garden was that the occupants were likely to be infirm or at least not good on their feet.

Harry walked up the path and knocked on the door. There was no answer so he knocked again.

The woman next door came out. 'She won't hear you, she's half deaf. What do you want?'

Harry started his spiel. 'I'm Mr Senior. I represent the Council and I'm here to do a refurbishment assessment on these properties. New kitchens and so on.' He offered the woman his identification.

'Let me have a look at that,' demanded the frail old woman. Harry passed his card to her.

'This could be a fake you know, there's a lot of thieves going round. They say they're from the Council or the Gas Board and they're not!'

'That's why we have that Madam, and you can see that's not a fake. But if you want to do a check on me ring the Council. The number is in the book; in fact I have it here!'

The number wasn't in the book. A very similar number was in the book and if the woman became even more suspicious, Harry would offer to dial it for her and let the woman speak to his manager.

'Do you want to give her a ring? I have my mobile here.'

'I'll get the book, you wait there!' Harry waited and thought it was all going perfectly but the old woman had locked her door.

Harry waited until he heard the key turn and the door opened. The woman brought out the phone book. Harry offered to take the weight of it while the woman turned the pages so she sat the book on his hands.

'Is that it there? I haven't brought my glasses.'

'Go and get them Madam, there's no hurry. You know what they say about Council workers. Steady day, steady income!'

The old woman laughed and so did Harry. It was going like clockwork.

'Can you make it out Madam?' charmed Harry, smiling and pretending to read the number out. 'Here's my phone, I'll read it out to you and you can talk to my boss.'

Harry didn't wait for her consent before he pretended to read out the number as the old woman pressed the buttons. Joan waited a minute then answered the phone.

'Hello, Angela speaking. How may I help you?' replied Joan, who had a repertoire of a dozen voices.

'My name's Mrs Crosby and I want to speak to whoever's in charge.'

'Which department Mrs Crosby?'

'I don't know which department. There's a chap here who wants to inspect Mrs Wilkinson's bungalow.'

'You want Mrs Prior in Estates, if you hold the line I'll put you through.'

Joan covered the phone. 'Hello, Estates and Management Mrs Prior speaking. How can I help you?'

'There's a man here who says he wants to look at Mrs Wilkinson's bungalow so the Council can do some refurbishment. I want to know if you know anything about it.'

'Yes I do, all those properties are due for refurbishment. Is the man's name Mr Senior?'

'Yes, it says so on his card.'

'There should be a security number printed in the top left-hand corner of the card. Could you read it out please?' Mrs Crosby squinted as she tried to focus on the numbers.

'I'll have to get my glasses.'

'They're in your apron pocket Madam,' Harry pointed to it and tried not to burst out laughing at the old lady who Harry thought was a silly old sod.

'Four, four, six, seven, two, one, seven.'

'The number is correct,' lied Joan smoothly. 'But there should be a letter after the number; can you tell me what it is please?'

'It's the letter B!' replied the frail old lady.

'That's perfect Mrs Crosby; he is who he says he is. I hope that clears any doubt in your mind and thank you for calling. I only wish all our tenants were as careful as you. Goodbye.'

Joan had hysterics as she threw the phone in her handbag. 'Silly old bitch!' she said to herself still laughing.

Mrs Crosby, who was completely taken in by the pair of con artists, opened her neighbour's door and they both went in.

Mrs Crosby shouted out who they were then turned to Harry and said, 'She won't hear me till we're stood on top of her, she never does. Why she won't wear her deaf aid is beyond me! She'll be in here.'

Harry smiled and nodded and followed Mrs Crosby into the tiny sitting room. He noticed a door off to the left that he thought might be the bedroom, he also thought that if there was anything to be had from here it would be in there.

They heard someone call from the door. 'Hello, Mr Senior are you in there?'

'Yes, we're through here Mrs Cobcroft.'

'Hello there, I'm Mr Senior's colleague.'

Joan offered her hand to Mrs Crosby then turned and said hello to a very old lady sitting staring at the television. The very old lady in the chair didn't acknowledge the gesture.

'I'll have to tap her on the shoulder, she's as deaf as a post and you might give her a nasty shock.'

'Ethel,' shouted Mrs Crosby. 'These people are from the Council, they've come to see if your house needs looking at. They're from the Council!'

Ethel turned her almost skeletal face and looked at Mrs Crosby then shaking her head she pointed a bony finger at her ear.

'Well turn your deaf aid on for goodness sake or I'll finish up with a sore throat again.' Mrs Crosby mimed somebody turning a control knob clockwise.

Ethel nodded and fished about in her thick woollen cardigan. 'I was just having a minute Doris,' wheezed the blue-lipped old woman. 'I haven't been feeling too well lately, I've got a bit of a cold so I thought a nap might do me good!'

'Well I hope it has done Ethel.'

'Who are these two? What do they want? If it's insurance I don't want any! I'm fed up with 'em calling here all the time.'

'It's all right Ethel, they're from the Council. They've come to see what needs repairing round your house.'

'There's nothing wrong with it. Nothing's broken that I know of.'

Harry stepped in. 'It's not for things that are broken, Madam; it's for things that need bringing up to date. Some of the kitchen fittings and other things need renewing; we do it every so often. It's as I told your next-door neighbour, all the bungalows along here are to be renovated. That's why we need to do an inventory in each bungalow.'

'I see,' said the old woman and promptly went back to sleep.

'She'll be dead to the world for the next half-hour; I'll go and put the kettle on. I'll give you both a shout when it's ready.'

'Do you want to start in there Mrs Cobcroft while I do in here and the kitchen?'

Joan nodded and opened her briefcase. She took out an impressive-looking form attached to a clipboard and disappeared into the bedroom. She went through the cupboards like a whirlwind. Harry made pretence at measuring cracks in the walls and gaps between the doors and their jambs in case the neighbour came back in. Joan found money stashed away in every tin, every box and every vase. The best haul by far was what was hidden under the mattress. They could count it later. The neighbour called to tell them their tea was made. Harry called back saying they'd finished in here and that they were on their way. His last act was to gently remove the very old lady's diamond necklace, matching bracelet and matching earrings. He knew his precious stones and these were worth a small fortune. Before they left the pair did Mrs Crosby's bungalow.

Harry said with his usual charm, 'We might as well do yours while were at it.' But they didn't get much.

'We can have a month off after that little lot Joan,' said Harry sipping at his champagne. They'd done extremely well.

'We'll go on holiday to the South of France and when we come back we can start again. I've had a brilliant idea how to make even more killings. We can open an old fogies' home and then we can rob them, left, right and centre. What do you think to that for a cracking idea?'

'Terrific, nothing to stop us. Cheers Harry.'

'Cheers, Pet. Here's to us and a long, long life of luxury.' The evil pair downed their champagne and refilled their glasses. 'Let's go to

Babylon; the sun's boiling hot and it's lovely out. Makes you feel good to be young and rich! Cheers come on then.'

'I'm with you chuck!'

They finished their drinks and left their stunning apartment. They should have read the local paper before they left; had they done, they would have found out that the deaf old lady had died of a heart attack when she found out that she'd been robbed of her life savings. Her son told reporters about the theft of his mother's jewellery and how much it had meant to her. My father got it for her on their first wedding anniversary; I hope the scum that did this burn in hell. The neighbour who'd let them into the bungalow was under sedation in the local hospital. The death of her friend and the responsibility she felt for being the cause of it had been too much for her.

The wind flowed over the windscreen of the Alpha and through Joan's hair making it swirl and dance like copper-coloured waves of silk. Harry's didn't; he wore his hounds-tooth flat cap and his shot-silk cravat loosely fastened at the neck. He liked to look the part. Joan was wearing her sexy-bitch outfit, as Harry called it. The short, skin tight leather skirt rode well-above her knees. Her matching black top showed off her figure and pierced bellybutton to perfection. They arrived at Babylon just after one-thirty.

'Do you fancy something to eat before we go in?'

'Such as?'

'You can have a lobster salad and I'll have a veal schnitzel!'

'Sounds good to me, Chuck. Come on.'

The pair ate a hearty lunch which they washed down with more champagne. This evil pair loved the good life no matter how they financed it!

'Let's go on the ghost train first Joan, then we can go on the river. I've heard it's scary!'

Reluctantly, she agreed to go on and it was scary, very scary. The nasty pair was glad when they crashed through the last door into daylight.

'Wow, brilliant!'

'I wasn't keen Harry;' Joan looked sick. 'I didn't like the spiders or the skeletons with all them strands of flesh hanging from their bones. They looked like them old fogies we scammed.'

'The corpses put you through it didn't they? Must have scared the life out of you. I thought you were going to crush my fingers to pulp, you squeezed them so tight.'

'No, they were rubbish. They reminded me of what we do as well!'

'Don't tell me you've suddenly got a conscience?'

'Get real Harry! Me, a conscience?' she sneered. 'Come on; let's see if the boats are worth bothering with.'

'Here you are sir and you Darling, get your tickets here!'

'Watch who you're calling darling, mate.'

'Figure of speech, Lad, figure of speech. Nothing personal but she is a lovely young lady.' Harry glared at him.

'Well, are you going on the river?'

'Yes we are,' snapped Harry.

Joan winked at the attendant and he winked back.

'Five pounds a boat, no more than four in a boat!' bellowed the man.

'Do you have to shout your bleeding head off? We're right in front of you.' The red-faced man in the overcoat ignored him.

'Two in one boat?' snapped Harry.

'There you are, take any boat you like, they're all the same.' The man said as he tore the tickets.

Harry took the stubs and said, 'Bit hot for a thick overcoat Mate!'

'It's not that warm here, Lad.'

Harry shrugged his shoulders and thought if the halfwit wants to stew, let him.

The nasty pair went to the moored rowing boats and picked a red one with blue oars.

'What's the map for Harry?' asked Joan who was beginning to get uncomfortably hot.

Harry looked at the map. 'I don't know, he gave them to the other punters.' Harry opened the small map. 'It looks like you can choose which branch of the river to follow. There are two. There are no rapids if you take the left fork but you don't see as much if you go that way.'

'What's there to see?'

'I don't know. Dinosaurs and stuff. It's supposed to be like Jurassic Park.'

'What's down the other way?'

'Futuristic themes it says here, whatever they are. Which do you fancy?'

'Neither, I'm boiling. No wonder that guy had a red face. You pick one Harry!' whinged Joan.

'Don't throw your toys out of your pram; I've heard it's fantastic.'

Joan looked sulky. 'Help me into the thing before I frigging melt.'

The evil pair climbed in and Joan tried to pull her skirt down a bit. She'd seen the red-faced man looking at her and it had, for some reason, made her feel uncomfortable.

'Come on Harry, get the thing going.' Harry pushed the boat out.

The red faced man in the blood red overcoat kept his eyes on them. Joan turned away hoping he'd melt. The current was stronger than Harry thought it would be and the long slim rowing boat was picking up speed at a tremendous rate.

'Slow the thing down Harry; I don't want it to go as fast as this.'

'I wish I could, Pet. It's the current. It's pulling us!'

'Well stick the damned oars in and hold it back.' Joan was beginning to panic and her face was a red as a beetroot.

'What do you think I'm doing? I'm not Mogul the frigging mighty. Shut your mouth and let me concentrate on what I'm doing.'

'Watch what you're doing, you nearly had us on that big rock!'

They must have heard her shout a mile away. Harry jumped a mile and tried to ignore her he was doing his best to keep the boat from crashing into every obstacle in its path.

'This is awful,' moaned Joan. 'You never said it was as bad as this. This is dangerous Harry. I don't like it. The boat could tip over! We could drown!'

'Will you shut your face and give me a hand, I'm trying to get over towards the left fork; that's supposed to be the calmer one.'

'Don't you shout at me,' she shouted to the back of Harry's head. 'Tell me what you want me to do?'

'I want you to tell me when we start going over to the left. I can't keep looking over my bleeding shoulder all the time.'

Joan did her best to steer Harry over towards the left bank but it was useless. She kept shouting left but the boat went right.

'I said left.'

Harry pulled hard but the thing went right.

She pulled at his shoulder. 'I said left. TURN LEFT CAN'T YOU!'

'NO I FREEKING CAN'T. SO SHUT IT!'

The current got stronger. Harry, mad as hell and pumping sweat, fought with the oars. The boat was caught in mid-stream. No matter how he tried, he could do nothing about it.

'The current's got us!'

Joan was getting well scared but she tried hard not to let Harry see. 'What's that, smart arse? You said there were only two choices!'

Joan tried to sound casual and sarcastic but because of the tremor in her voice it didn't come out right.

'What's what?'

'That,' Joan's finger stabbed in the direction of a third choice. 'There's another branch there.'

Harry turned and looked over his shoulder.

Joan was pointing at another body of water. 'It's not on the map.'

Harry twisted further.

'Now look, we've lost one of the oars.'

Harry went over sideways when the oar spun out of the rowlock and banged his head against the side of the boat. The current wrenched the other from his grasp when he scrambled to make a grab at the first.

'Get them,' yelled Harry rubbing his head.

'I can't reach. Don't push me you idiot. I can't reach them!' screamed Joan. 'You nearly pushed me in, and the water's filthy.' She was seething.

'Jesus Christ,' blasphemed Harry as he watched the oars get swept out of reach.

Harry wanted to throw her in and make her swim for it. He took a few deep breaths, wiped the sweat off his face and said, 'Calm down, Pet. It's no use screaming at one another. We can't do a bleeding thing about it.'

'I will Harry, but keep still will you. I don't want to fall in there.' Joan held tight to the sides of the boat.

'That sign,' said Joan turning to look again. 'It said the River Six.'

'What sign?'

'That sign over there by that tree. That weeping willow tree.'

Harry looked but he couldn't make it out.

Joan pointed. 'I've never heard of the River Six, have you Harry?'

'No, Pet I haven't. At least the current's slowed down.'

The flow of the river had slowed down, and noticeably so. The surface of the water was smooth with barely a ripple. Their trip seemed to last forever.

'I'm going to complain when we get off this river,' she moaned.

'You're not the only one Joan. This bloody river's lethal and God knows how long it will take to get to the end of it.'

'There should be a cover over these boats to shield us from the sun. I'm going to tell them about that, and I'm having our money back. There's nothing to see down here. It's a bloody con!'

'Well we should know all about that, Pet!' Harry laughed. On and on they went. Slowly but surely drifting along with the current.

'We're there,' shouted Joan. 'I can see a landing stage.'

Harry turned round on his seat and stayed facing the prow of the boat. 'Brilliant, I can't wait to get out of this thing.'

'I bet they'll want money for the oars, Harry.'

'I hope they ask for it. They'll get it rolled up and stuck right up their………'

Joan screamed and went pale.

'What the hell's wrong with you? You nearly had us over.'

Harry grabbed hold of the boat.

'I've just seen that old deaf woman and her neighbour. They were over there. There, where the ripples are. They were smiling. They were pointing at the boat. Ugh, I've gone icy cold!'

Her lips trembled as her voice faltered. 'I, I, saw her.' She couldn't stop shivering.

'There's nobody there! That's water, Pet. Oh hell, do you know what you're saying? It's sunstroke. Quick, Love, splash water on your face. Come on. Hell fire! I'm going to go mental when we get off here. Come on, Pet splash some on or you'll finish up in hospital!'

Harry cupped his hands and splashed water over Joan's forehead and dabbed at her temples. 'Is that better Joan? You look as rough as a bear's bum.'

'No, I'm not all right! I'm icy cold and I'm sweltering. We've been on here forever.'

'No we haven't and I'm stewing as well but it won't be for much longer, we're nearly there. Any minute now. Are you all right? You look shattered, Pet.'

Harry wondered what the hell was happening to her as the boat bumped gently into the gaudy red-painted landing stage.

The same chap who had given them their tickets and the map tied the boat to a mooring. Harry leaped out of the boat as if it was on fire, or at least he thought he did. It was certainly hot enough.

'Right you, I want to see your boss and I want to see him now!'

'I wouldn't be too keen if I was you Harry.'

Harry turned round and helped Joan onto the landing-stage. Sweat was pouring down her face. Harry's face was the same and he was exhausted.

'I said I want to see your boss Mate and I mean now!' But there was no authority in his voice whatsoever. His throat was so dry his voice was no more than a crackling whisper.

Joan pushed past them both and hurried towards the red-painted building. Or at least she tried to. 'Is your boss in there?' she croaked.

'Yes he is, but are you sure you want to see him?'

'Of course I want to see him. This lot's a stinking con!'

The red-faced man smiled. 'There's lots of it about, old Dear.' He smiled again.

'Don't, old Dear me; you nearly had us killed out there! Useless thing of a boat and no cover to protect us from the heat. We want our money back and the address of your head office. I'm going to sue you lot!' Her hands shook and she couldn't make them stop.

'As you wish. If you'll follow me Joan, and you, Harry.' It didn't click that he'd addressed them by name. 'I'll tell the boss what you said. Wasn't it, "The river of Babylon is nothing but a con"?'

The man in the red uniform pushed open the massive red door and called, 'Are you busy Sir? I've a couple of eighty-year-old pensioners out here who want to make a complaint!'

A tremendous blast of searing heat poured out of the building as a dreadful echoing voice said, 'Do come in! No need to wipe your feet.'

Richard Lee Wilson 13 4 04

The Diary of Elspeth De Morance

I'd never seen anything like that sort of stuff in my life before. The things they got up to in the name of witchcraft are beyond belief. I don't know where to start. I suppose first I should say where and how we found the diary. If it can be called a diary? It said on the front it was a diary. Some diary!

Me and Joe worked for a builder. We didn't know he was dodgy. About three months ago we went to the yard early Monday morning as usual and the creep had done a runner on the Saturday. After telling each other what we'd do to him if we ever met up, we thought we might as well have a go on our own doing general repairs and renovations. Not massive jobs just the usual small stuff. We weren't ready to go too big.

We put a couple of stickers on my van saying, 'No job too small'. Joe put one in the back window of his car. After a few weeks we started doing ok. We'd got over two thousand pounds in the kitty and we were well on our way to getting the five thousand we needed for another second hand van. When we started we got bits of work from the lads in the pub and from friends and relatives. Then they got us work and on it went. It sort of snowballed from then on.

One night I got a phone call from a bloke offering us work on an old lodge house. I never thought to ask him where he got my mobile number from; the number's not on the side of the van. There was a fair amount of re-plastering, paint and paper stripping and doing a bit of second fixing; new architraves, spindles and mouldings. There was a lot to do. It was our biggest job yet. He sent us the details and a set of keys. When we'd a minute we went to have a look at it, and it wasn't that bad.

The lodge was set back a little just off the B631 to Carthedge. It was in its own bit of garden which was surrounded by a seven foot high stone wall. There was a door on the right set into the garden wall. That door was the only way onto the property. Or so we thought at the time.

It was a weird shaped house. There was an extension on the left hand side at the back and one on the right hand side at the front but it was all built with the same sort of rustic-red brick. It had a really steep roof and a very tall chimney. It stood at the bottom of a tarmac drive leading to a big old Manor house about three hundred yards away. We'd done all the estimates over the phone and to be fair to him, he'd described the state of the lodge spot on. We gave him a quote and he accepted it. So we ordered the stuff we needed.

We'd only been up to the manor house once and that was when we went to tell him we were starting the work on the following Monday. He'd sent me the keys and I'd returned them in the post. We asked him for the keys back. He looked us up and down then gave us the key for the back door muttering in his gravelly voice that if we needed to, we could open the front door from inside but to make sure we locked it securely before we left, and not to forget the top and bottom bolts. He said he would prefer us to use the back door. The bloke was about five feet ten, wiry, and must have been in his seventies, He had a good head of grey hair, his eyes were a funny pale blue colour and he'd a scar down his left cheek. And by the way he looked us up and down he must have thought we were school kids. We assured him we wouldn't forget the bolts if we used the front door and came away. We'd already ordered the boards and the finish for the front room to be delivered in the afternoon; there was plenty to be getting on with.

We got there on the Monday at eight o'clock, had a coffee and started ripping some rotten board off the fireplace wall in the front room when Joe, who was messing about suddenly disappeared through the wall on the left of the chimney breast. He'd been doing his Stan Laurel impersonation and he'd leaned one handed against the wall and twiddled his imaginary tie. I heard a loud creak then a cracking sound and his arm went through then as he tried to grab me and I tried to grab him, but missed by a mile, the rest of him went through. I couldn't stop myself. I just burst out laughing. A massive cloud of dust wafted out as the plaster on the other side collapsed.

After a bit more foul language and a lot of clattering and banging he staggered out. His face was covered in muck. He was coughing and mouthing off at the same time. His cig was crushed and it had burnt his lip. His face, and he wasn't laughing, was as black as his grandma's kettle. I told him in between creasing myself that what he'd just done was funnier than anything Laurel and Hardy had ever done. He told me it wasn't. He told me the laths and stoothings were rotten and full of woodworm. He told me a few more things which I can't repeat. I told him it was his own fault and he shouldn't have been messing about. And if the uprights were rotten we'd have to go and see the old bloke and get him down here to see for himself. We aren't rip-off merchants, but we don't work for nothing. He ignored me and limped off outside with my hand brush.

I opened all the windows to get some air into the place. Then popped my head through the hole to see what was in there. I could hardly see a thing! It was pitch black. I went to get a torch out of the van. I found the diary with some more dusty books on a shelf at the top of a flight of stairs in the small walled up room. There was a bookmark slotted in it and the book was wrapped in a purple cloth. It was weird. All the other things were covered in dust but this one looked as if it had been used recently! We didn't go down the stairs because of the smell, and we shouldn't have touched the bloody diary, one because some of the drawings in it were sickening, we're both broad-minded but they were, and two because the day after we'd looked at it all the bother started! We haven't opened the bloody thing since. We opened it later, but not to look at! We didn't know it then, but Brian at the Bridge Inn had a good look at it when we left it with him to look after.

We'd finished most of the prep jobs by six o'clock and decided we'd do a mix first thing in the morning. We locked up and left. Because he'd got over it we had a good laugh about him going through the wall. We called in at the Bridge Inn on our way back. We had a couple of beers and went home. I'd pick him up on the corner at seven. That was fine by him. I'd left the diary with the weird signs and sicko drawings in it on the mantelpiece hidden amongst the tools and plaster dust. I didn't want to bring it with me and Joe didn't. He said if his girlfriend saw it she'd rip his head off.

The old bloke rang me at eleven o'clock to tell me we hadn't locked up and we hadn't turned the lights out. I was just going to bed. I told him we had locked up and we hadn't even turned the lights on because there was no need. He wasn't having any of it. 'We would have to come back and deal with it. He couldn't go down there at this time of night it would be too much for him!' That's what he said. I couldn't think why it should be but I didn't argue with him. I asked him how he knew the lights were on. He said he could see them blazing away when he went to close the curtains at his bedroom window. I said we'd come back and see to it. I rang Joe. He wasn't impressed!

The lights were on; even the ones upstairs and we hadn't even been upstairs. Both outer doors were wide open and an open bag of finish had been tipped out and kicked all over the place. Another had been ripped open and emptied. Plaster was everywhere. I said oh dear. Joe said dash it! Or something that might have been a little bit stronger. We checked the windows and turned the mains off. None of the windows were broken and the fasteners were ok, we locked up. We'd leave the mess till morning. I said bloody hooligans! Joe said it was druggies! I never even thought about the locks. I should have, because they couldn't be opened with any old key, or one of them magical bent pins; they were five lever dead-bolts! And anybody who had the gear and the skill to open that sort of lock wouldn't be bothering to waste their time on a place like this! It was long past midnight when we got back home. I couldn't remember seeing any footprints in the plaster dust. But by the time I'd thought of it, I was half asleep.

The next morning we got to the lodge at half past seven. We used the open bags first and cracked on till one o'clock. We got the ceiling done and two of the walls, they looked good. I'd forgotten about the footprints but when I remembered and asked Joe about them. He said he couldn't remember if there'd been any footprints or not and anyway it was too late now, our footprints were everywhere.

We went to the café in the village for our dinner, we were starving. It was good grub, all homemade, and it didn't cost an arm and a leg. A fairly long arm but not a leg. We got back at ten past two and the front door was open.

'I locked that and bolted it! Somebody's taking the mickey!'

'I saw you lock it Al!'

'Get me the wheel brace; it's under your seat.'

Joe grinned and went to fetch it.

'If there's anybody in there they're going to get this wrapped round their head, come on. Did you lock the van Joe?'

'Yes.' He replied under his breath and laughed. Joe's a nutter sometimes.

We went in as quiet as we could. There was nobody downstairs. There was no stair carpet and the steps creaked like hell as we tried to quietly creep our way up. There were only two bedrooms and they were built into the roof and there wasn't anybody in either. There was a skylight window out of reach up on the left in the smallest bedroom, but that was full of cobwebs and hadn't been opened for years.

'It must be the old man. He must have come down here and didn't bother locking up when he went.'

'But you put the bolts on! That's weird. Can the old bloke reach the top bolt?'

'He's as tall as you Joe. You can reach it easy!'

'Yes but is he strong enough?'

'How the hell should I know? It's not difficult to slide back.'

'Not for us, but it could be for him Al.'

'We'll go up there tonight and find out. Let's crack on or we'll be still here in a bloody month!' We went downstairs.

'Do a mix and I'll slap it on.'

'Not with that you won't Al.'

'Why what's wrong with it?'

'The handles been broken off and your boards split down the middle!'

'Not my float!'

'Both that and your board are useless. You can't skim with that! And you can't lift it off that! And somebody's nicked the shovel! What's happening? I think we should go up there now and get to know what's going on. Do you think somebody's got a grudge against him? It could be that.'

'No Joe, get real. An old bloke like him. Who'd want to sabotage this place, it's not his?'

'I didn't know. I thought it was his place. I thought it was part of the manor.'

'No Joe, have you forgotten? He told us it belongs to his brother!'

'Well let's go and see his bloody brother then. Somebody might have a grudge against him!'

'I doubt it. Well maybe, who knows? But surely if anybody had a grudge they'd just lob a few bricks through the windows. They wouldn't bother with our stuff. We can replace them for a tenner! Anyway I've another in the van. Probably got two or three thrown in there. And we've a spare shovel.'

'I think we ought to go up there and have a chat with him. They might do a lot worse next time. And we don't want to do the job and find it wrecked'

'It won't matter to us Joe will it? He's given us half up front remember. He won't want to lose that! But if you want we'll go and see what he says. Come on we'll go up in the van.'

An immaculately dressed bloke of about forty answered the door. He asked us inside after we'd told him who we were and what we wanted. He said we should tell him because his grandfather was resting and he didn't want to disturb him. His grandfather had made him aware of his plans for the restoration of the lodge. We told him everything what had happened and asked if we could talk to his great-uncle. He laughed and said that would be difficult unless we knew of a very good medium. I'm afraid he's been dead for fifteen years he laughed. I told him his grandfather said the lodge belonged to him. He told us that it had belonged to him, past-tense but now it was part of the estate.

He had no explanation for the incidents. He had no explanation for the walled up room or the diary, and he didn't ask for any information from us about any of it! I thought that was a bit weird, and I knew he was lying. It was his eyes that did it. A soon as I mentioned the diary, it sounds stupid but it felt just for a split second like I was looking at somebody else. He seemed to sort of widen and brighten his eyes as though he was glad to see me, unlike most liars who try to blank their eyes. He must have noticed my reaction because he repeated what he'd said. He wasn't going to tell us anything so I suggested we change the locks. He agreed to cover the cost but he'd need a key! Front or back door, it didn't matter which.

'Is that ok with you Joe?'

'Yep, it's fine by me. What I don't fancy doing, is finishing the job and some josser wrecking it.'

'I understand your concern but if someone else has a key and the locks are changed it will be of no use to them, there should be no more hiccups. Now if that's all? I have an important phone call to make.'

'Yes that's it we'll get back to it.' We left him to it.

'That bloke was lying. Did you see that look he gave me when I mentioned the diary?'

'No.'

'He's a lying bugger. We need to get that diary away from here.'

'What for?'

'Trust me Joe; I've got a feeling about this!'

'No don't say that. Not a bloody feeling. Last feeling you had cost us wodge of cash if you remember?'

'That was just a bit of bad luck.'

'No it wasn't it was a pile of bad luck.'

'I'm sure about this. We don't have to take it home; we can leave it at the pub with Brian, he'll have somewhere to put it. I sure can't take it home. If my mother saw it she'd go mental. And you can't, I reckon Bri's our best bet. Agreed.'

'We should leave it where it is or burn the bloody thing. Why do you want to keep it?'

'Nobody lives at the lodge. They'll just throw it out with the other stuff in there. We can stick it on E By Gum Bay. It'll fetch a bomb. People collect that erotic stuff. You've seen them on the Antiques Road Show haven't you? All that, what the butler saw stuff. They go mad for old gear like that. That diary must be two hundred years old!'

'I don't think they'll show that muck on the telly mate! Anyway it's about witchcraft isn't it?'

'I don't know, I thought it was devil worshippers who used that design!'

'What's that star shaped thing in a circle on the front.'

'Pentacle you berk.'

'Anyway whatever it is, they'd get a lot more viewers on that Antiques Road Show if they did show it on the telly.'

'I think you're mental if you nick it.'

'I'm not bloody nicking it. The things stuck on a shelf with a load more rubbish in a walled up room. Who knows the thing's there? They probably dumped it there because they didn't want it.'

'Take it then!'

We got the spare gear and started on the last wall. I got the diary and put it under my seat in the van.

'That bloke didn't ask about the room. I thought that was weird. He didn't tell us to leave it or what. We should have waited for the old bloke.'

'We can sort it out with him tomorrow Al, there's no bust a gut rush. We'll be here for a few days. There's still plenty to do.'

'True enough.' We got stuck in.

We made a coffee at five o'clock, I was pumping sweat.

'She's called Elspeth De Morance!'

'Who is?'

'The woman who had the diary, her name's on the front. It's embossed like the rest.'

'I didn't notice her name; I was busy if you remember.'

'Yes I remember.' He grinned and so did I.

'She must have had it made for her. Must have cost a bomb a diary like that.'

'Probably did. Maybe she lived here?'

'This place isn't old enough is it?'

'I don't know, but that house up there is!'

'Yes she could have lived there, that house is definitely old enough.'

We finished our coffee break. I went into the kitchen and swilled out the pots.

'Is it back on our heads time, or do you want to knock off.' I shouted through but he didn't answer. I left the pots on the sink and went back through.

He wasn't there. I called out again and he shouted.

'I'm down here and it's minging!'

'Have you got both torches?'

'Yes, I'm looking for a light switch!'

'Any joy?'

'No, come down I'll shine a light on the steps. Is that alright Al?'

'Yes.'

'Hell fire it is minging. What's in there?'

'I don't know. I haven't been in.'

'Here take this and have look.' Joe gave me a torch.

'I'll look for a light switch.'

I went through a doorway into the other part of the cellar.

'Joe come through here. I've found something. Some curtains and an altar. There's a cross and candles as well!'

'Can't find a switch Al. Wow, it is an altar. I thought you were having me on. But hang on a minute, how come it's not filthy in here? Look, the slab's been cleaned. And them black candles and the candlesticks, and the floor's been washed. Them sofas are more like beds. Somebody's using this place; I'm getting out of here. The stench is bad enough, and I don't want to find out where it's coming from or what it is! No thanks. Come on Al, something not good's going on here! Where are you now?'

'I'm through here. I'm wondering where these other steps go. They're very narrow.'

'I don't give a sod. I'm out of here!'

'Hang on a minute Joe. Come over here; this must be another way out as well! Look at the bottom of the wall.'

'Where?'

'There. No not there, down there. It poured down last night didn't it?'

'Yes.'

'See that trickle of water. It's coming under the wall but only under that bit. It must be a way in.'

'Bloody hell Alan what are you trying to do?'

'I'm trying to open it, what does it look like.'

'That's a bloody stone wall!'

'Is it? Laugh if you want mate but it just moved. Bring your torch and shine it on that crack. There's another there. And there's one that joins them together. I'm telling you Joe, that's a doorway. And this could be the way the nutters are getting in. If you help me to push it, we might get it open. Is the crowbar in the van?'

'You've lost it you, and yes it should be in the van, we haven't used it for months.'

'I'll go and get it and I'll see if we've any spare batteries while I'm there.'

'I'll come with you, just in case it is a door and some bugger comes through it! Where's these other stairs you were on about?'

'Through there in the corner across from the Altar. It's full of spiders' webs. Why, are you off to have a look?'

'No I'm not.'

'Still frightened of spiders then?'

'Sod off.'

We had some batteries and we had the crowbar. And we had some fresh air.

'I think we're crazy coming back down here. It stinks to high heaven! Hey you don't think there's a dead body hidden down here, do you? They sacrifice people you know!'

'Do they hell. What planet are you on? They play sex games with young virgins. It's all to do with sex. They're all dirty old men! Don't you watch telly?'

'No but I've read Dennis Wheatley.'

'That's fiction, you know, like not for real.'

'And there's me thinking it's for real!'

'Sarcasm Joe is the lowest form of whit.'

'All right wise guy, what do you want me to do?'

'Not bad if that was supposed to be Bugs Bunny.'

'Get wired!'

'Ok I will but first we're going to have one quick try at getting it open and if we can't, we'll jam it under there with the crowbar.'

'It might open the other way!'

'It's ok Joe, I've thought of that. When we go back up, we'll shut that door at the top of the steps and screw a couple of three by twos across it. No probs!'

'We haven't changed the locks Al!'

'I've thought of that as well Joe. We lock and bolt the front door ok? Then after we've locked the back door I'm going to pop a couple of fifteen millimetre staples inside the lock. If anybody tries to open it the staples will jam the levers, ok?'

'Yes, sounds good to me.'

'Now can we have a quick go at it? I want to be away before bloody midnight!'

We tried but we couldn't budge it more than a couple of millimetres. We went upstairs, secured the doors and left. We called at the pub and left the diary with Brian. We told him what it was. He didn't seem bothered. He said he'd wrap it and stick it in his safe just in case. He said he didn't want his daughter Karla to find it. We left him one in the pump.

We got a good strong seven-lever mortise lock the following morning and fitted it as soon as we got to the job. It took us twenty minutes to get the staples out of the lock. We went in and had a quick look round; everything looked exactly as we left it. We didn't look in the cellars, we should have done! Instead we went up to the big house and asked to see the old bloke. A woman answered the door. We explained what we'd come for. She said Mr Lambert wasn't in. I told her we hadn't come to see Mr Lambert, we'd come to see Mr Frankler, the elderly gentleman who'd first contacted us. She said the only Mr Frankler she knew died years ago. I grinned and said. We spoke to him only the other day. He looked pretty much alive then! She shook her head and said come back when Mr Lambert's in, he's Mr Frankler's grandson. Perhaps he will be able to help you. I asked her when she expected him back, she said between five thirty and six. I said we'd call when we left the job. She said that would be the best thing to do and closed the door.

We heard somebody shout. 'Where is he?' We didn't hear anything else. We got back in the van. We didn't go straight away. Joe said hang on and lit a cig.

'How much have we in this job, Al?'

'Roughly seven hundred quid. Why?'

'Because I reckon we should leave it before we lose out. This bloke who's supposed to be dead has only paid us half. Who's going to pay the rest of it? He can't pay it if he's dead!'

'Well not if he's dead Joe, that's bloody obvious. That's if he his dead. He wasn't when we spoke to him on Monday. I don't get it.'

I opened my window. 'I wonder Al, if they're trying to get out of it?'

'Out of what?'

'Having the job done!'

'It's going to cost 'em if they do!'

'What will we have if we walk off the job and call it a day?'

'We'll lose what he owes us, about fifteen hundred. And remember Joe, we've turned other work down to do this little lot!'

Joe looked tee'd of. I said we should call back and sort it out!

'Ok, if that's what you want.'

We went down to the lodge to sort out our gear just in case the stuffy hit the fan!

We found the old bloke when we went down the cellar for the crowbar. He was lying on the floor by the doorway in the wall and the door was open! He wasn't dead but he looked as if he wasn't far off! I told Joe to call an ambulance. The old bloke wouldn't let him. He wouldn't let us call the police either. We thought he'd been hit on the head. He said he cut his head when he tripped over the crowbar! We argued with him long enough to get him to go and get it seen to but he wouldn't hear of it. He was perfectly alright. He asked for a drink of water. Joe went to get it while I helped the old bloke upstairs.

He told me he wasn't an old bloke! He told me he was retired. He said he was an ex SAS officer and he was perfectly able to get upstairs without my help or anyone else's. I apologised for calling him an old bloke but I said I call my father old bloke sometimes! No disrespect intended. He sat on a bag of plaster and sipped at the water. Joe asked him if he wanted a cup of tea. The old bloke said he didn't drink tea. I didn't know how to broach the subject of us being told he was dead! In fact I didn't really know how to ask him about anything. The cellar, the altar, the vandalism. I hadn't a clue where to start. While I was wondering where to start Joe jumped in with both feet.

'That woman told us you were dead! And we would have to talk to your grandson about the problems we're having!'

The old bloke looked at us as if we were dip heads. 'Do I look dead? And I certainly don't have a grandson; and I don't have a wife. If you have been told this by those up at the house, forget it. I'll deal with them. They like to think they are protecting me. There have been death threats. To say from whom would be conjecture, I have numerous enemies. As if I can't look after myself. They wouldn't have known who you were! I'll talk to them.' He sniffed and smiled a grim little smile.

'And what did you mean about vandalism? I have no idea who that could be unless it's some young hooligans from the village. They've done nothing serious I hope?'

'No just a couple of bags of finish and some tools. It's no big deal.'

'Good, then how soon will you be finished?'

'We need to know what's going on first, don't we Joe?'

'Yes we do. And about that set up in the cellar. What's all that about?'

The old man dabbed his forehead. 'Don't concern yourselves with that, I have an arrangement with some rather odd people in the village. They like to think they're witches or devil worshippers, or both! In actual fact they could be both! Idiots with strange perversions if you ask me.' He smiled again. 'They want to buy this place. They claim a famous witch once lived here. That maybe true, but I very much doubt it. I want rid of the place and the sooner the better. Oh, and while I remember, did you change the locks?'

'Only the back door, the front one didn't need changing, I'd forgotten about the two deadbolts.'

'Fine. Do you have a key for me? No doubt my so called grandson will ask for one, but I would prefer he didn't get one.'

'He's asked for one already.'

'Has he?'

'Yes. When we called at the house to see you. Here's yours. If he asks again I'll say there isn't a spare'

'Those special branch people don't miss a trick.' He smiled a wry smile. 'Right that's fine. I'll be off the way I came.'

The old bloke got up and went down the cellar. We followed. We wanted to see how the door worked.

'Damn and blast, my flashlight's useless. The bulb most likely.' He gave it a shake. 'Do you have one I might borrow?' I gave him mine.

Joe used his to light the way. The door was fully open and Joe was right, it did open outward. It was a solid job but it was made of stones about fifty mil thick fixed to vertical and horizontal iron rods; it certainly did the job. Joe shone his torch down the passage it was covered in filth and cobwebs and this is where the stink came from.

'There we are, my bolthole, not a very nice smell, is it? Used to be a sewer before the house was modernised. I think I'm becoming inured to the stench of it.'

'I'm not. Where does it lead?' Joe had his hand over his mouth.

'Up to the house. Comes out below the old kitchens.' We followed him.

'Originally this was a passageway connecting the manor house and the lodge, but that was in the late seventeenth century. The conversion was completed in the late nineteenth century. That was long after Jules de Morance had died.'

'Morance! That's the name on the book!'

'Which book?'

'The Satanist's book.'

'Indeed, pure coincidence I'm sure. There were lots of Morance's in those days. Normans I'm sure. Probably came over here after William the Conqueror had paved the way. It was bought by Sir William Longthorne in eighteen seventy-nine and his family lived here until the first war. My uncle bought the place in nineteen twenty. I believe it had been on the market for quite a while. Quite dilapidated. He left it to my brother and me. After my death it will go to my niece. Both my brother and I wished it.'

He shone the torch up the passageway. 'Here we are. You can see here where the fork in the passage was bricked up. I'm told that way leads to where the Morance's cashed their ill-gotten gains. Hardly believable, it leads out to the old pump-house under the lake!'

We walked a bit further.

'I'm going up here; you're more than welcome to come up.' He gestured to a stone staircase.

'Ta but we have to crack on. You're sure you're okay.'

'I'm fine; I've taken a lot more than this in my time young man. Just one more minute of your time. I don't want you make any mention of this passage or the cellars to anyone, and I do mean anyone. It's for your own safety!'

I looked at Joe, he looked at me and we said we wouldn't say a word about it.

'Good, I am very sorry but I can only tell you this much. Certain things are moving at a pace I didn't expect. They are in hand. Have no concern about that! The break in the wall upstairs must be closed immediately. No one must know you are aware of the cellars and what's down there. That is also for your own safety.'

'Ok, we'll do it straight away. We'll need the torch to get back. Mines gone dim.'

'Of course. But do remember what I said!'

'We will, definitely.'

He went up the steps. We set off back down the passage.

'I don't know how we do it Joe but we could find trouble in paradise.'

'Yes well according to my Grandma that's where it all started.'

'She comes out with some stuff. She creases me your Gran does.'

405

'We ought to knock a hole in that wall and find their stash.'

'Get real man. He said it went under a lake. I aren't going under there mate, no chance. We finish this lot as fast as we can and get away from here. I believed every word the old bloke said. There's something not right and I don't bloody know what it is. So we get done and away.'

'Ok, you're the boss.'

'No I'm not, I'm the eldest.'

'By a bloody week mate, that's all!'

'Why, what do you want to do?'

'Same as you.'

'Well then let's do it. Three more days. Four days max! Yes?'

'Yes all done by Saturday. We hope.'

'We'll do the hole first.'

'We'll frame it out Al. We've got some four by two's and some spare boards in the van. Put a hundred on the bill. He'll pay it, he looks loaded.'

'Ok Joe, I'm right for that.'

'My eyes are running with the stench.'

We got the hole filled and plastered before we left at half-seven.

On the way home we called for a beer. We got chatting about some work with a middle aged couple at the bar. He was a weird bloke. He had dyed blond hair. He wore a cravat and one of them long leather coats which go half way down your leg muscle. And she looked like an advert for Kalvin Kline! They wanted an extension building on the side of their garage. We said we'd come and have a look at the job if they wanted and they said that would be fine. They asked us what we were doing now and could we start immediately if our estimate was acceptable. I told them where we were working and couldn't come till next week because we hadn't finished the job we were on. They asked how long it would take and. I told them we should be finished by Saturday; Monday at the latest. And if everything worked out ok, we could have a look at their job on Tuesday. They said that was fine. We gave them a time. They said fine and we left it at that.

They turned round to talk to Brian and we came away. I didn't think anymore about it. What I hadn't noticed but Joe had, was all the time they were talking to us, Brian was watching them, and he'd given Joe the signal. Joe didn't say anything till we got outside.

'He wants us to call back.'

'What for?'

'I don't know he gave me the nod that's all.'

'Shit I hope he hasn't opened that diary or whatever the bloody thing is. He'll think we're bloody pervs!'

'Will he hell, Brian's not bothered about stuff like that, he used to have strippers on. Are we calling in later then?'

'Yep we can bring the girls if they fancy it.'

'What, about nine.'

'Yes Joe that should give the girls time to get sorted.'

'I meant nine tonight, not tomorrow night!'

'Good one. I'll call you later to see if it's on.'

'Ok, see you then.'

It was sorted. The girls didn't want to go so me and Joe went.

We got in the pub at ten, it was busy. Brian told us as soon as he'd a minute he'd come over. We played pool till eleven. When he finally came over he told us about the couple who we'd been talking to. He said they'd been asking questions. Too many for his liking. They'd wanted to know where we were working. I told Brian he'd already asked us and I'd told him. Probably wanting to make sure we're good. He told us he asked who for. He'd told them he'd no idea. He'd recognised the guy but the guy hadn't recognised him. He said he'd never known me as Brian. It was always Boggo then. Brian didn't tell us why. But he told us the guy was a bit of a lad then. Into drugs and burglary and all sorts of dodgy stuff. He said we wouldn't think so to look at him now. Got on about the blokes coat costing him a month's wages.

Then he went on about the woman who was with him. Said she wasn't his wife. He said she used to tart down John's Gate till the residents sorted it out. Coppers wouldn't do anything. They said it would put it underground and lead to more serious crimes. Then he laughed and said the real reason they wouldn't do anything about it was because half the coppers used the services they offered. Well that's the story that went round.

Then he finished by saying. 'All I wanted to say was watch him and watch out. He's a bad man and a hard man. So get some money up front! Or better still steer clear altogether. And get rid of that book! I've had a look at it and it's nasty! Now I'll go and sort that lot out over there. I don't want any trouble in here.' We thanked him and said don't worry; we'd knock the extension on the head. We'd tell him it was too big a job for us. He said 'good idea'. Then he went to sort a bunch of students out. I went home Joe stopped on for another. The bad man came to see us next morning.

We decided to put the other doorframe in, that way we wouldn't have to wait for the finish to dry out before we started hammering. We'd just finished that, the banister rail and spindles and we were making a start on the last of the work in the kitchen. We'd about five metres of fifteen mil piping to chase in; plaster over and we'd finished in there. Just the tiles to gob on and we'd done. Joe was using the angle grinder to notch out but he hadn't wet down. Brick dust was flying everywhere, He had his mask on but the dork hadn't opened any windows. I couldn't see a thing.

I dashed in opened all the windows and was about to sort him when somebody shouted. 'I hope you two are doing a great job for me!'

It wasn't the old bloke it was the bloke from the pub who'd asked us to do some work for him.

'Don't look so surprised, I'm buying the property friend. Thought I'd check. We don't want any rig ups do we?'

'Neither do we,' I answered.

The other bloke with him was as big as a house and his face looked as if it had had a few good thumpings.

'These are the lads Michael who are going to do the garage. What do you think to the standard of their work?'

'Let's wait and see Mr Horner. We can't see much now. The plastering doesn't look too dull'

'True, Michael, that's very true. Oh and while it's fresh in my mind I think you have something that belongs to me!' Then he turned to his mate and sneered.

'You think so too don't you Michael?'

'I'm positive Mr Horner.'

I looked at Joe he looked at me. I said. 'I can't think what. We'd never seen you before last night.'

'It was here lad, in this house. Michael knows it was here and now it isn't! Is it Michael?'

'No Mr Horner, I've searched every room. Even the secret room.' He laughed. 'It's not in here, it's not in there. Looks like the book ain't anywhere.' He laughed again. 'Somebody must have taken it. Do you think the Frenchies have found it Mr Horner?'

'No I don't think so. They couldn't find the Scarlet Pimpernel could they Michael? And these are the only persons who have been here so they must have taken it. Does that make good sense Michael?'

'Yes it does. It can't disappear on its own Mr Horner.'

'I am not being unreasonable am I Michael?'

'Not from where I'm standing Mr Horner. I'd say you were being very reasonable indeed.'

'If you tell us what it is we're supposed to have taken Mr Horner, we might be able to help!'

He gave me a right evil look. These two were frightening.

'I'd call it an illustrated biology book. A very old illustrated biology book. I think that describes it perfectly. Don't you Michael?'

'Very droll Mr Horner. But an illustrated biology book it is.'

'It belonged to a Miss Elspeth De Morance long deceased spinster of this parish. And according to some rather old documents in my possession a former tenant of this property. Those are the facts Michael are they not?'

'Correct in every detail Mr Horner.'

He turned to Joe and accused him of taking it. Said Joe he had the appearance of a petty criminal. When I saw Joe's face I thought he was going to start something but instead he told the bloke somebody had broken in and thrown plaster all over the place. It had to be them vandals that stole his book! Then he turned the grinder on to start the second cut.

The bloke wearing the cravat gave a little nod and the big sod went and grabbed Joe by the shoulder, spun him round, wrenched the grinder out of his hands, yanked the cable from the socket and threw my grinder out of the door. 'Bad idea lad. Very bad idea. Bad manners especially when Mr Horner's talking.' He gave Joe a right smack. Well hard enough to send him banging hard into the edge of the outside door. I thought he was going to go backwards down the back steps but he grabbed the door handle and sort of swung back in. I glanced down at a piece of four by two leaning against the wall. I backed towards it and slowly reached out for it. I didn't take my eyes off the bloke wearing the cravat and he wasn't looking at me he was smiling at the big sod who was dusting off his hands.

'Touch that sonny and Michael will remove your arms and batter you unconscious with their bloodied ends! Now you wipe the blood off your face and show Michael where the book is. I do hope you can!'

Joe watched the big sod leave the kitchen. I watched the bloke with the tie move his left hand to his coat pocket. I was sure he was going to pull a gun. I didn't know what the hell to do. Then the old bloke walked in and said hello. I felt like I was going to throw up. I don't know how I didn't.

'Hello there, are you making sure they're doing a good job of it Mr Horner.'

As he turned the bloke with the cravat changed completely. He was all smiles. The old bloke stuck his hand out. Horner shook hands and said 'he certainly was'.

'I don't want to knock a nail into the wall and find myself up to the knees in plaster.'

The old bloke laughed. 'I think you'll find their work well above average. Doing a good job lads, indeed you are. I have a few bits and pieces up at the house that need attention. Perhaps you would call up when you're finished here?'

'Yes no trouble.'

'Now Mr Horner there are one or two details concerning the leasehold which need to be ironed out, if you can spare an hour?'

'No problem at all Mr Frankler. Perhaps while we are on with it you could show me the deeds. You did say there was a wine cellar of sorts?'

'Yes, I believe so although I must say neither cellars nor wines have ever taken my interest. Goodness knows how one gets into it.'

'Perhaps the entrance is from the outside?'

'Perhaps so, shall we?'

'Yes, Michael would you bring the car round to the side? I'll have a chat with you two later.'

He wasn't smiling when he said that to us. But the old bloke didn't see his face, he had gone outside.

Then he came back in. 'Give me a tin of paint and a brush. Now! Then get finished in here as quick as you can. Don't be here in an hour's time. Understand!' Then he stuck his hand to his ear making a phone shape.

We nodded our heads like imbeciles.

'Thank you'. He called as he left. 'I'll let you have them back later today.'

We were out of there in three quarters of an hour. Everything. Tools, useable wood, and two unopened bags of plaster. We didn't finish in the kitchen. We called at the Bridge on the way back, left the van in his garage and got Brian to let us go into the back room.

We had a pint and Brian asked what was going on. We said we were sorry but we couldn't say much. I fell like an idiot. I'd got really scared back there. I'm sure the Horner bloke had a gun. Bloody animals. I can't say how Joe felt but he downed his pint in one! I wasn't far behind.

'All I ask Brian is that you don't mention a thing about that book we left here, not one word to anybody or we're in it. Deep in it. It's that mate of yours. He's a bloody thug. His clown gave Joe a right wallop. And that psycho told him to! Look at his mouth.'

'Hell fire, who's the clown then Alan?'

'Don't know. He's called Michael and he's as big as a bloody house. He must have been a boxer because his face and his nose have taken some grief, that's for sure.'

'Big Mick, is he out and about then? Hell fire. He's another you want to stay away from. He got seven years for giving a chap a good kicking. He nearly killed him. He lost a lung and an eye. Big Mick must be out on parole. That's a laugh! Parole for thugs like him.' Brian shook his head and looked disgusted. Then he asked if we wanted another. He said he'd have one with us?

'You look as if you need one!' Brian went and got us another.

'Can we leave the van here? We don't want the scummies to find out where we live.'

'Yes sure, it's no hassle. Where is it now?'

'It's in your garage. We brought it in off the road. We've shut the garage doors and we've shut the big gates!'

'It will be ok in there.'

'The bloke we're doing the work for is ringing me later. We might be able to tell you something then, but don't hold your breath Brian.'

'Don't worry Al, I won't.'

My phone went. It made me jump. It's the old bloke. I mummed.

He said we hadn't to go back to the house under any circumstances; the so called Satanists would be there over the weekend. We had to burn the book! He knew we had it! Pointless denying the fact. It had served its purpose. I said it was too valuable to burn. He said it hadn't any value whatsoever. He said it was only a copy. He said the department had it made six months ago. It was bait. The real diary was elsewhere. He didn't say where it was. He said we had to burn it. He said he was sure we wouldn't want to put ourselves in grave danger. He said Horner isn't the only member of the sect. There are twelve more and we don't yet know who four of them are. We do know that they are no less dangerous than the rest of them. By Monday if we are successful we will know who they are. So two things. Don't go near the house and do burn that book! I asked who the 'we' were and the bloody phone went dead! The call ended just like that. He was no old bloke! That's for sure! Then I had a thought but no I told myself, he can't be.

411

I told Joe and Brian everything he'd said. Joe said he didn't need telling to stay away from that place. There was no way he was going near. He splurted a bit because his mouth was sore. And he said he didn't care what happened to the diary. He didn't want the bloody thing in the first place. He said it was me who wanted it! We burned it bit by bit in Brian's skip.

We went to the coast that night, all four of us. We borrowed my Dad's car and my brother's tent. Joe and Mandy had one of their own. We didn't come back till late on Tuesday. My dad was a bit miffed because I'd promised we'd be back Monday. He made us pay for the hire car he had to get. Joanne wasn't well pleased. Can't win them all is your motto Alan. I got a call from the old bloke the day after. He said the miscreants were all in custody. Serious charges would be made. If Joe and I would like to call round that afternoon at the lodge he would explain everything. Not wise to say too much on a land line! That's what he said. I'd no idea what religion a miscreant was but Joe and me went over there just the same.

We couldn't believe the mess in the lodge. The hole we'd repaired was kicked in. Three of the windows were boarded up. The new banister and half the spindles were smashed. What a mess.

'You have the job if you want it.'

The old bloke smiled. 'I'm afraid they didn't want to go quietly.'

He smiled again and sat on a kitchen chair.

'It was the book that gave me the idea. I am by the way Commander Briggs of Special Branch. Of course I retired some time ago.'

I said I don't think so. He ignored me.

'Mr Lambert who I believe you met up at the house was approached by the Chief Constable who requested what he called urgent outside help. The chapel in the cellar he had heard was used supposedly for devil worship. Nothing illegal in that. But what actually went on down there most certainly was.

Horner and most of his chums are well known to the local police and the police are well known to Horner and most of his associates. They asked our people to come in because they knew nothing about us. Strangers on the manor as it were! The Assistant Chief Constable is a good friend of mine. It was in fact Lawrence who approached me He knew they were using these cellars; all quite legal, because at that time Horner leased the property. We had no idea it was his intention to own it. He wanted, it transpired somewhere out of the city. But Lawrence had no idea why. He did know Horner, and he knew there was a lot of money about and that it was going in Horner's direction. He was also made aware that some of the dealers had suddenly disappeared from the streets, and a number of prostitutes were missing! Not the older end, mostly teenagers who were registered users. We now have video evidence which explains why.

It was all quite simple really. Horner got his heavies onto the streets and after a few of the dealers and pimps were hospitalised he took over. Now that he had control he added. That's the main reason he wanted to buy this place. Away from prying eyes. The chapel down below and the fake Satanist regalia is in actual fact a studio! He makes pornographic films down there. He exports the stuff to Holland and blackmails the clients who visit his nightclubs. They're brought here; need I say more. We found three cartons of a well-known date-rape drug in his Cross street warehouse. Each carton contained ten boxes. Each box contained sixty tablets. You can do the arithmetic!"

'Why did you have us doing the work if you knew what he was doing down there?'

'We didn't have anything concrete. We had to have solid evidence! These renovations were our cover. You did the repairs, and during the night our chaps installed the cameras and sound equipment.'

'So your lot were the vandals?'

'Not vandals Joe. They had to lay cables under the floorboards in here. The boards are old and dry. The plaster dust covered the more obvious splintered boards. I'm afraid we couldn't risk you two finding the cables! Silly devils left the lights on.'

I looked at Joe He looked at me. We both shook our heads.

'What had that old diary to do with all this? And how did Horner get to know about it? And why did he want the bloody thing? I'd like to know that wouldn't you Joe?'

'I'd like to know why I feel like a first rate pillock!'

'Join the club.'

'We involved you two because we found out from various people that you two were reliable. You would do the work in the time agreed and the work would done. We couldn't risk our chaps fitting surveillance equipment and you two disturbing it. That is why you were selected. Others were checked but rejected. You can take your selection as a complement!'

I sniffed, Joe sniffed but we felt a bit better.

'What about the dairy?'

'As evil as it is, the diary in some quarters is priceless. We had use of it through one of our chaps from a certain museum. I'm not allowed to tell

413

you which museum because once the diary was resealed, it remained in the museum. Of course it wasn't quite as simple as that, but that is all I can say on that matter. We had a similar one made. Obviously we didn't replicate it exactly. That would have been more than lunacy. The copying took quite some time.' He looked at his watch.

'We then arranged for one of our chaps to deliberately incur a rather large gambling debt at the Purple Gardens; one of Horner's infamous gambling clubs. He of course couldn't honour such a debt. He told Horner about the diary. Its contents and its value. If Horner wiped out his debt and gave him ten thousand pounds, he would give him the whereabouts of the diary. Horner said there are no pockets in a shroud! And that's what he would be wearing in ten seconds if he tried being a smart arse. He also told Horner that the old recluse, who owned the diary, had no idea of its immense value! Of course I am the old recluse.'

I said I don't think so. You'd think I hadn't said a word!

'He went for it! After all the preparation I can tell you we were to say the least, delighted when the ploy worked! The imbecile paid me four thousand pounds for it and used it as a stage prop during the goings on downstairs. A very dangerous thing to do. Very dangerous indeed.'

I had to ask why.

He looked at his watch. 'I must be brief.' He looked at his watch again. 'Elspeth De Morance was a witch. In fact she was rather more than a witch. She was also a medium of the worst sort. Not only did she talk with the dead, she was able with the help of the diary to, well shall we say bring them from the other side in material form.'

'What bring the dead back to life! You're having us on! He's pulling our strings Joe!'

'I assure you both I am not! However whether you choose to believe me or not, those are the facts. The Servant Bishops who were asked to unseal the thing certainly believe it because they wouldn't let it out of their sight until it was resealed. Now I must be off. Give me a quote for this lot. Don't go over the top mind. And sorry about the deception concerning the locks.'

He smiled. 'Goodbye and thank you both for your splendid help.'

'Cheers.'

'Bye.'

'You haven't told us how they got in.'

'Who?'

'Horner and his bunch.' '

Through the front door and down the stairs! Where else?'

He laughed and went.

'He enjoys it doesn't he! And they couldn't because it's bolted.'

He must have heard me because I shouted my head off! He didn't answer.

'There's three weeks' work here Joe for reliable workers.'

'Easy three weeks. Come and look at the front door.'

'Why, there's nothing wrong with it.'

'You mean it's not damaged Al!'

'I didn't say it was did I? Just come and look at it. The whole thing opens. The frame and everything. Come and have a look. That's why the old bloke said don't forget the bolts! Watch.'

Joe turned the key, turned then pulled the handle and the frame was fastened to the door. Then as if to make us look even more stupid one of the bloody wall panels slid open leaving a doorway into another corner of the walled up room!

'That's them narrow stairs. Devious sod that Lambert, Briggs Frankler, or whatever his real name is. But not sneaky enough. We'll never see him again I'll tell you that. And I'll tell you something else Joe this is going to cost them a lot more than a bloody second hand van!'

'That's fine by me Al! But I don't get you! Why won't we see him again?'

'Didn't you notice his scar had shrunk?'

'What scar?'

'The scar on his face.'

'Hell you're right! He didn't have much of a scar just now.'

'Absolutely right pal. I reckon he left it off deliberately as a warning maybe. And offered us the work as a sweetener. Same as that nonsense about the diary.'

'What are you on about Alan? Come on I want to call for one on the way home.'

'So do I but work it out. Better still, where's the splintered floorboards? I can't see any. I know his chaps as he calls them could have been back here and took all their gear out. But there'd have to be patched up holes for lenses. Fixings repairs where speakers have been.'

'They'll be downstairs in the cellar.'

'Well go and have a look Joe. I'll give you a hundred quid for every one you find! And why leave a book here that's priceless.'

'Calm down, how should I know?'

'There's loads of stuff all wrong. Come and have a look. Go and look at the spindles. They've been kicked out to make it look like there's been a right ding dong here. I'd like to see the bloke who could knock somebody through oak spindles from a less than a metre away.'

'Big Mick could have.'

'No he couldn't. Even if he swung one at you from two steps up he couldn't. You'd either go over the banister rail or backwards down the stairs. But I'll tell you this Joe. He could have laid you out but he didn't. This big hard man who's supposed to have hospitalised people gave you a bit of a thick lip. If he'd have wanted to he could have hit us with each other. No it's all crap. They're after the real book, all the bloody lot of 'em. Made us look like idiots! Well we'll see.'

'Do you know what the clincher was?'

'God can't we go for a pint.'

'Yes we can if you want Joe. If you want to leave it alone. But he dropped a real nallack when he said Lawrence was a big pal of his. You know the Assistant Chief Constable.'

'That Lawrence.'

'Well he's not called Lawrence, he's my ex wife's uncle and he's called Lawson. Rodger bloody Lawson. They must think because we do a bit of building work we're as thick as the bloody planks we stand on! Whether you're with me or not I'm off up there tonight!'

'Where?'

'The manor mate, the manor. The diary's up there and I bet it is priceless. And the real old bloke's up there. And that lot will have him. It'll be dark enough at eight. I'm going to ring Rodger at half past seven. He really is a good friend of mine, and I'm going to tell him Mr Frankler is being kidnapped at eight o'clock tonight and see what bloody well happens!'

'This isn't one of them feelings is it? Say it isn't one of them Al.'

'It isn't one of them Al!'

'Say it isn't one of them Joe!'

'It isn't one of them Joe. Satisfied?'

'I'll have to be won't I? Now we can go for a pint.'

'Yes!'

So we did. Joe had three I had two. I was driving. We were creeping across the lawn at five to eight and the grass was wet through.

The cops came as we got behind a tree. The drive with all the blue and red flashing lights looked like a mixture of Brands Hatch and a rave. I could hardly focus. It was like a bloody disco. There must have been thirty cops. They didn't bother knocking or anything. They just battered the door open. Then some of them raced inside. The others spread themselves out round the house. Big Mick smashed his way out through a window and four coppers were on him in no time. Then they were off him in no time. Then he laid one out. Then they were on him. Then one of the heavy mob prodded him in his chest with what looked like a long stick and Big Mick shot backwards into a flowerbed and laid there moaning and groaning. Me and Joe got smart arse and he'll have a real scar now. Horner came out in handcuffs. He looked as if he'd been kicked from the attic to the cellar. He was covered in blood. Then three more were dragged out. The old bloke was okay. He'd refused point blank to tell them where the diary was. The scum were waiting for his granddaughter to come back from holiday. They'd told the old bloke they'd kill her if he didn't tell them where it was. He'd laughed at them. The old bloke was Maurice De Morance and he looked old, in fact he looked extremely old. I told Joe to guess what the old bloke's granddaughter was called.

He looked worried and said, 'I hope to God she's called Alice?'